THE EXECUTIONER'S RIGHT

THE EXECUTIONER'S SONG BOOK 1

D.K. HOLMBERG

CHAPTER ONE

The house reeked of money. It was more than just the ornate sculptures that littered the entryway of the home, reflecting off the gleaming marble, and set into the alcoves. There was something about the air itself that stunk, a musty odor of age. Finn grinned to himself.

"Stop smirking and get to work," Oscar said.

"You realize that we could take pretty much anything here and sell it for a profit," Finn said, stopping before a small sculpture set into one of the alcoves on the wall. It looked to be modeled after one of the gods, though not one that he celebrated. Maybe Fell, as he appreciated wealth. "I should just grab—"

"You don't grab anything. That's not the job. The Client only wanted a specific item. Now get looking."

Finn looked at the old thief and ran his hand through his shaggy brown hair. "Is this what it was like when you did jobs with my father?"

"When I did a job with your father, he didn't talk so much," Oscar said.

Oscar darted inside the room. Finn wasn't going to be much help here. He didn't even know the target. Oscar had agreed for him to come along on the job, mostly so that he had some experience. Oscar had always been the one advocating for Finn to progress with the crew.

Through the closed door, Finn could make out the din of the Gallows Festival. They were far enough off the procession that they didn't have to fear the Blood Court would make an appearance, but near enough that they had to dress in their finery, rather than the typical thieves' darks.

"Is this what all rich people's homes look like?" he muttered, shifting his attention back to the inside, shaking his head. "Can you imagine what it must be like having this kind of money?"

Oscar worked along the shelves, going quickly. The man known as the Hand had a practiced approach and had no difficulty searching. "Every day."

He stood up on his toes, picked a lock for a glass case, then grabbed what looked to be a bowl set apart from everything else on a high shelf, holding it up, and then stuffed it into a pocket.

"Are you kidding me? That's what we were after?" Finn asked.

"We do the job we were hired to do," Oscar said.

"I get that, but—"

Two sharp whistles rang out.

Oscar darted to the window, pulling the curtain back. Finn stepped up behind him, looking over his shoulder.

"What do you see?"

"Not a damn thing with you breathing over my shoulder," Oscar said.

"That was Rock."

"It was. Now back away."

Rock was their scout today, keeping watch for anything unusual. Like Archers patrolling along the street that might indicate they'd been spotted.

"What if someone is home?" Finn asked quietly, looking toward the main hall. Shadows seemed to move, though Finn wondered if that was just his imagination.

"You *were* watching, weren't you?" Oscar asked, and Finn nodded. "And you said it yourself. No one is going to be here during the festival."

Another whistle. Two sharp sounds.

Finn hurried out of the room, down the hall, and stopped at the windows alongside the door. He peered out along the street.

They were in one of the nicest parts of the city. Not only were there shops found here that weren't found in other places in the city—jewelers and seamstresses and artists, among others—but Heshian Palace, the king's residence when he came to the city and supposed home to the crown jewels, was visible just in the distance.

"See anything?" Oscar asked, standing on the opposite side of the door, looking out of another window.

"No Archers, if that's what I'm supposed to be looking for," Finn said. The city guards would be just as busy as anyone on a day like this. "Maybe Rock was just… Damn," he said. He pointed to the far end of the street.

An Archer dressed in the distinctive maroon and black colors of their office marched along the street. He rested his hand on a short sword strapped to his waist, and the shield on his back gave him an air of authority.

"That's a palace Archer," Oscar whispered.

"They shouldn't be here," Finn said, recognizing the stripe on the man's shoulders. A second stripe would indicate command within the palace; a third would mean command of the city. Even a single striped Archer could be deadly.

"It's because we're close to the palace," Oscar said.

"Aren't they supposed to guard the crown jewels?"

Oscar shot him a look filled with annoyance. "Don't go getting ideas in your head."

"What ideas are those?"

He shook his head slightly, turning back to the window. "The same kind of ideas your father liked to go on about."

Finn laughed. He and his father shared many traits. The same average build, though Finn liked to think he was more muscular than his father ever had been. Definitely more than Oscar. A good height, even if it wasn't nearly as tall as the Hand.

"I didn't know that he thought to go after the jewels," Finn said.

His father and Oscar had pulled jobs for a few years before he'd ended up pinched and imprisoned. Oscar never liked to talk about what kind of jobs they had taken and certainly didn't like to talk about what had happened to his father. No thief wanted to contemplate the possible consequences of the job.

"Not like that. Just looking for the big score. Never content with what was dealt before them."

"Aren't you the Hand? Shouldn't you be the one in charge of what's dealt before you?"

Oscar waited until the Archers slipped along the road, disappearing. "You've got to be content with what you have, Finn. Otherwise you're always going to be looking for a more dangerous job."

A shuffling sound behind him caught Finn's attention.

He spun, looking into the darkened house, frowning.

"Are you sure this place was empty?" Finn asked.

"You watched it the same as me. We saw them head out to the festival."

Finn had, and he and Rock scouted for the better part of two days, a long time for a job as simple as taking a single bowl. He thought they had seen everybody from the household leaving, everyone dressed as formally as possible for the festival.

The shuffling sound came again.

He swung back around, looking toward the window. The palace Archer lingered out in the street, not moving away.

"We can't go that way," Finn said.

"Then we take the back way," Oscar said, motioning for him.

They hurried along the hall, and as they passed through it, Finn grabbed a small, silver statue and stuffed it into his pocket. Near the back of the house, Oscar paused, raising his hand, and tipped his head to the side.

If there was somebody in the house, they'd been too loud.

"Through here," Oscar whispered.

They ducked through a doorway into an enormous kitchen. It looked like it could serve an entire tavern, and yet it was empty. The smell of the recent breakfast lingered, that of sausage and eggs and fresh breads. It was enough to make Finn's mouth water, and his stomach rumbled.

"If we get trapped here…"

"We're not going to end up trapped here." Oscar reached a door at the back of the kitchen. He paused, pulling it open just a crack, and then leaned out. "Come on."

They stepped out into an alley. Even the alley in this part of the city spoke of wealth. It shouldn't be so clean. It needed to stink like a proper alley did. Oscar motioned for them to head to the right, away from the streets that Rock guarded and where the Archer patrolled.

"I know a shortcut through the alleys," Finn suggested.

"No shortcuts," he said. "We finished the job. Now we have to regroup. You know the time we're meeting." He waited for Finn to nod. "All you've got to do is…"

They had reached the end of the alley, and Oscar blocked Finn from going any further.

Another Archer.

"They shouldn't be patrolling here so heavily," he muttered.

"Maybe the merchants pay them?"

Oscar shook his head softly. "I don't know. Something's not right." He looked over his shoulder. "Take the alley to the end, and if it's open, get moving."

"What about you?"

"I'm going to try something different."

"I'm not going to leave you to get pinched here, Oscar."

Oscar frowned at him. "Whoever said I was going to get pinched? This isn't like what happened to your father, Finn."

Oscar gave him a shove, and Finn went stumbling down the alley. When he was about halfway down the alley, he looked back to see Oscar bending down, seemingly fidgeting with his boots.

A shadow moved along the street. One of the Archers.

Oscar continued working on his boots.

Finn hurried along the alley, passing the doorway to the home they had come through, and he hesitated for a moment. If he darted through there, he could end up back on the other side…

The door started to come open.

Finn raced down the alley.

When he reached the other end of the alley, he paused, pressing his back up against the wall. Maybe he'd been wrong about dressing up for this job. It might've been easier to be in his darks. At least then he could sneak through the alleys like a proper thief.

He didn't see any movement.

He didn't see Rock, either.

He was supposed to be standing guard, but maybe he'd

gone off when he realized that Finn and Oscar had slipped away. It was harder to keep watch in the middle of the day. Especially for somebody like Rock. With his size, just standing around was noticeable.

Finn didn't see anything.

He started out of the alley.

Finn hazarded a glance back, looking along the street where they'd been. The cobbled road was clean, and all of the homes along here were well maintained. They were nice. Almost too nice.

He headed away. Now that he was out in the open, he needed to keep moving.

He tried to look casual and look as if he belonged, but he feared his discomfort drew attention.

As he neared the end of the street, a voice shouted after him. "You. Hold!"

He looked back and saw the Archer who had been patrolling the street coming toward him.

Where was Rock? What about Oscar?

He had a few choices here. He could run, which meant the Archer would chase him, or he could wait.

Only he couldn't.

He'd taken the stupid silver sculpture out of the home. Had he not, then he could have waited. The Archer wouldn't have had anything on him.

Finn spun and ran.

He darted along the street, reaching another alley, and slipped along it. He had scouted through here with Oscar, and he knew these alleys. If he remembered it right, this alley would veer off soon.

He turned, following the alley.

The sound of boots on stones thundered behind him.

Finn raced forward, taking a hard right as he rounded deeper into the alleyway. The network of alleys wound throughout the city, and regardless of Oscar's hesitation with using them, they *did* shave time off travels. Heading in this way, he thought that he could tell where he needed to go and anticipated that there would be another side street, but he didn't come across it.

The alley ended.

Shit.

He turned back.

Rather than taking a right, what he'd needed was to turn left. Now he remembered.

Would there be time?

The thundering of Archer's boots on the stones didn't sound quite as loud now, but he didn't know if he could backtrack and get where he needed to go.

Racing the way he'd come, he caught a shadow of movement from the other alley as he raced through the small intersection, following the narrow path and then out into the street.

He could hear the Archer behind him.

Finn didn't slow. He might be the newest in the crew, but he was also the fastest. Now was the time to use that to his advantage.

He had to be careful. Now wasn't the time to head straight back to the Wenderwolf. The tavern had enough attention from city Archers. They didn't need him to bring the palace Archers into the mix. And it wasn't even the right time to meet.

Find the festival. Blend in. That would be how he'd keep out of the reach of the Archer.

The sounds in the distance loomed nearer.

Finn could hear the festivities and raced toward them.

When he reached the first of the streets where the Blood Court would parade down, he slowed, winding into the crowd. He risked a look back and saw the Archer still heading in his direction. Each turn he made seemed followed by the Archer.

It was the clothing he wore.

While it might fit in within the city center where they'd intended the job, it didn't fit quite so much out here near the Teller Gate, where everyone squeezed out to watch the execution. He should have headed toward the palace. At least there he would have been better able to blend in with others.

What he needed was to get farther into the crowd.

Finn passed a cluster of young women, flashing a smile at them. One of them, a curvy redhead, smiled back. He offered a rueful shrug and hurried along the street. When he reached the vendors, he veered in front of them. They bought him a little time. A younger woman at a pastry stand watched him a moment before glancing behind Finn.

He turned to see the Archer still chasing.

Damn it.

Maybe he could hide. All he needed was a way to sneak through here and avoid attention. There had to be someplace where he could blend in. The crowd was thick enough to mask his presence.

Shouts rang out from hawkers selling their wares. The smell of baked breads, sweet treats, even roasted meats all came to him. He glanced over his shoulder to see the Archer behind him, weaving through the crowd. They separated around the Archer, giving him space.

"Traitors," he muttered. This was *his* section of the city. *Shouldn't they protect me?*

He ducked behind one of the carts.

Then he waited. Staying there might be risky, but what he needed was for the Archer to get ahead of him. Let the Archer lose him in the crowd. When he did, Finn could disappear. Then he could head back to the tavern where he hoped Oscar had already returned and figure out what happened to Rock.

The sound of boots along the stones came louder. Finn fixated on that sound, focusing on it over the roar of the crowd, the hawkers calling out their wares, and even that of a steady chanting.

The chanting was new.

The procession of the Blood Court.

If he wanted to lose the Archer, he'd better do it soon.

Or I could wait.

If he waited, the Blood Court would pass by, and he could get caught up in the crowd.

That might be the best option for him.

Finn maneuvered behind the cart. People passed by him, but he bent over, trying to look as if he were fixing his boots. Oscar had one good idea on him. He couldn't linger there that long or he'd start to draw the wrong sort of attention—that of the hawkers.

Out of the corner of his eye, he caught the Archer moving slowly through the crowd. At least he was shorter. This man seemed to be standing on his toes, bouncing so that he could peer over the crowd.

The chanting got louder.

The crowd around him pressed toward him.

He wasn't going to be able to stay where he was for much longer.

The crowd didn't give him a choice. It was either stand or get trampled.

Finn stood.

The Archer was barely a dozen paces in front of him. Close enough that were he to turn, he'd be able to reach Finn quickly. The advantage Finn had was that the Blood Court and with the condemned were making their way along the street, and the crowd pressed forward so they'd be better able to see the procession.

Slowly, the Archer moved away, heading toward the gate. The crowd separated to let him pass, though not nearly as much as before the sound of the procession started coming through the streets.

Finn smiled to himself. He'd gotten away.

So long as he didn't run into the same Archer, he wouldn't have to worry about getting questioned. Seeing as how he rarely spent any time in that part of the city, and never in the palace where the Archer would be stationed, he didn't have to worry about that.

He turned his attention to the Blood Court.

All of the condemned were known as Poor Bastards, and this one had to be about the same age as Oscar. He had a lean, almost haggard appearance, and followed the executioner with a halting gait. He kept his gaze fixed straight ahead, a haunted expression to his dark eyes.

Finn knew the man.

Knew might be a bit strong. He'd seen him. Heard of him. Dalton Pegg, a man he knew to be an incredibly skilled thief from the city's Unlear section. Finn hadn't known he'd been caught. He really was a Poor Bastard.

The priest trailing after him continued his steady chanting from the Book of Heleth.

The sound of it was much more musical than the song he'd used to draw the Archer's attention, though as it droned toward him, Finn didn't feel the urgency within it he knew he was supposed to.

The Blood Court moved past.

The crowd veered after, peeling off and heading alongside.

A tomato came hurtling out of the crowd and struck Pegg in the chest. A chunk of it broke off and struck the executioner, staining his gray jacket and leaving a trail of juice dripping down toward his heavy boots.

Were that Finn, he would have reacted more than the executioner did. He marched forward, his eyes straight ahead, a look of concentration on his face that was not all that different from the one he saw on Pegg's face.

Finn had met the executioner once. He'd been caught and accused of stealing meat from a pig butcher. He'd claimed innocence—though he was not—but the executioner hadn't been swayed. The flogging had been terrifyingly painful—he still had the two scars on his back to remind him—but nothing like what Pegg was about to endure.

The priests passed.

Finn fell into the crowd.

A boy in front of him slipped his hand inside the satchel of the man next to him and fished out a few coins before moving on, sliding along the crowd. He grabbed another few coins from a woman clutching a bag, and when he accidentally bumped into another person, he reached into their pocket to pilfer still more.

One of the vendors caught sight of the boy and started toward him.

Finn grabbed him, shaking his head, and pointed at the vendor. "You don't want to end up like Pegg, now do you?" he asked, before pushing him off and into the crowd.

The boy's eyes widened, and he darted off, dropping the coins.

Finn scooped them quickly off the ground, stuffing them into his pocket.

When they reached the Teller Gate, Finn followed the crowd out.

In much of Verendal, buildings sprawled beyond the gate and past the wall, with the neighboring forest just visible. There were no buildings near the Teller Gate. Finn suspected the executioner had something to do with that —he'd seen him making preparations near the Raven Stone a few times—but there were still more shacks built closer to the stone than he would have thought would be comfortable.

The crowd slowed as the procession neared the Raven Stone, and the executioner forced Pegg to climb the stone.

Finn didn't even know what kind of punishment Pegg had been given. Probably hanging, befitting a dishonorable like Pegg. The viscount and his lackeys wouldn't offer a thief—even one of renown like Pegg—the honor of a quick death by sword.

The day had grown late, and he knew he should return to the tavern. He'd been gone long enough, and by now, he suspected Oscar and Rock would have returned. If he didn't get back, the King would be annoyed at his delay, but then Finn hoped Oscar would regale him with the story about how he'd helped him escape. Maybe then Finn would be given the opportunity to be more involved with the next job. That was all he really wanted, anyway.

A murmuring overtook the crowd, and Finn looked over. In the distance, atop the raised stone platform the people of the city called the Raven Stone, the executioner had brought Pegg. A rope hung around his neck, and the chanting from the priests began to build.

Finn didn't want to watch, but at the same time, he didn't know if he could even look away. There was something strangely compelling about the whole ordeal.

Pegg began to argue.

It was the first time that he'd seen any sort of emotion out of Pegg, and as he watched, he couldn't help but want to be closer to see what he might do.

The crowd around him didn't let him get away. If he

made a wrong move, messed up on a job—worse than had happened today—something like this might be *his* fate. Take the wrong job, upset the wrong wealthy merchant, and it would be the noose and not a flogging.

All for what? Taking a little from someone who had more?

The executioner probably enjoyed it, though from a distance, Finn couldn't tell.

One of the priests came closer, ceremonially raising his hand, and Pegg leaned back before spitting in his face.

A gasp fell across the crowd.

The executioner started forward, wrapped the noose around his neck, and pushed away the small stool as he sent Pegg spiraling from the gallows, hanging. He kicked for a moment. The crowd remained silent, only speaking again when he went still.

Finn couldn't take his eyes off of him, though disgust filled him. What had Pegg done that had warranted such a fate? The King probably knew, given the connections he had, though he might not tell Finn. He'd have to ask Oscar and hope that Oscar had heard something enough that he might find the answers.

Tearing his gaze away, he headed back toward the gate. A chance glimpse of an Archer sent his heart hammering, though he didn't think it was the same Archer as before. He squeezed the silver sculpture in his pocket, the coins he'd taken from the pickpocket, and kept his head low to avoid attention.

When he reached the gate, he paused before heading in. A woman stood at the gallows, looking up at Pegg. She wiped her eyes, and one of the priests came over as if to console her.

He tried to think of someone who felt that way about him. His sister wouldn't feel that way, and his mother was too sick to care. That left only his crew.

Would they feel that way about me were that my fate?

A flash of maroon caught his attention before he could think too deeply on that—another Archer—and Finn darted back through the gate and into the city. It was time for him to disappear.

CHAPTER TWO

F inn always found it strange that the city would hold a festival when someone was sentenced to die, but it did have its advantages. He sneaked away, knowing he'd have to get to the others soon enough, but it wasn't the meeting time yet.

The streets in the Brinder section were narrower than those where he and Oscar had wandered earlier in the day, with buildings and run-down shops lining them, and tall homes scrunched together on others. Not only were they narrower, but they stank in ways that part of the city didn't. There was the stench of the pigs corralled near the slaughterhouse, a foul odor that permeated everything in this part of the city. It mingled with that of refuse and waste, both human and other. No chain gangs were assigned to this part of the city to keep it clean like there were in other sections.

It was home. Or had been before he'd lost his father,

and his mother had sunk into illness. Finn had given up thinking that his father would ever be released, which meant he had to provide for his mother. Someone did.

As he'd been leaving the execution site, he'd considered heading toward the tavern with the others, but the King had specified a specific time to meet—four bells—and it would be too early. A better use of his time was to stop at his home and drop off some of the coin the boy had snatched then dropped. Knowing his sister, Lena wouldn't even want the money, as if she were too good for it. She hadn't been too good for it when it had come from their father.

The homes out there were small and crammed together. There weren't the same alleys as there were in other parts of the city, and when there were, they were even narrower than those higher up in the city. He stepped over a puddle of water—or piss; he couldn't tell with the angle of the sun reflecting off the surface—and nearly slipped in something else.

What he wouldn't give to get out of there. It was the reason he preferred to sleep at the tavern as much as possible these days.

Three small children ran along the street, chasing each other. Their clothing was tattered, and all had wild hair. One of them carried a rope, chasing the others. Their high-pitched voices carried, and in the distance, someone shouted at them, but the boys ignored it.

Finn nodded to a pair of men about his age. Bruisers, given their size and the leathers they wore, and he would have expected them to have been more discreet about the role they played, but one of them even carried his club in hand, leaving it dangling at his side.

Ducking to the side of the road, he let them pass. It was better to stay out of the way of bruisers. Who knew who they worked for? Anger the wrong boss and there could be repercussions—the kind Finn tried to avoid. He needed to stay in good with the King; he worked with one of the best crews in the city and didn't want to mess that up.

When the bruisers were past, Finn hurried onward. Though this wasn't the nicest section of the city—or even close to it—it was uncommon for there to be bruisers. There must be a crew working here.

Turning the corner, he practically ran into Helda. She was a year or so younger than him and friends with his sister. She had a pretty face and rich brown eyes he could imagine swallowing him when she looked at him.

Helda and Lena had been friends for as long as Finn could remember, though Helda had the advantage that her father was a baker and had more connections than Finn and Lena's parents had. Besides that, she was pretty and nice and didn't really belong in Brinder.

Before becoming the thief, his father had been honorable like Helda's father. As an assistant to a cartwright, there had always been the possibility that he would learn the trade himself, even if he was not formally apprenticed. When Finn's mother got sick, his father had needed money that working as a cartwright's assistant wouldn't provide.

"Finn? I heard you got yourself a crew. What are you doing working outside your section?"

"I'm not working. Just coming to see my mother."

She tugged on her drab green dress. When she saw him looking at the flash of cleavage, she flushed briefly. "I figured you'd be outside the Teller Gate, watching."

"Most people enjoy the festivals, Helda. I could go with you sometime."

"My father doesn't like me going out there. He says it's too dangerous."

Finn started to smile before realizing that she didn't. "You could stay inside the wall and enjoy the festivities. You don't have to go out and watch it."

"I couldn't imagine watching," she said with a shiver.

"Watching is bad enough. I can't imagine pushing a man to his death."

Helda offered a hint of a smile. "That's because you wanted to be a surgeon."

"That was a long time ago," he said.

"Not that long." She frowned at him. "You can't run with a crew your whole life, Finn. I bet you could still find a guild to take you in."

"The guilds don't pay as well as the crew."

"That's all that matters to you?"

"Shouldn't it?"

Helda looked as if she wanted to say something but bit it back. "Good day, Finn."

He nodded as he watched her go, wishing he knew a way to better talk to her. He could try another time. Right now, he needed to keep going before it got too late.

When he reached the door to his old home, he paused.

The paint had long since faded. In this section of the city, paint didn't last long on many of the doors. It was almost as if something about the city repelled it, turning everything into streaks of faded color, giving it a sad and dreary appearance. At least the door remained solid. Finn had spent everything he'd collected since their father had disappeared to ensure the door and the home were as protected as he could make them. Seeing the bruisers out on the street, he knew that was the right thing for him to have done.

Fishing a key from the band he had tied around his neck, he unlocked the door and hurriedly stepped inside before closing and locking it behind him again. A dim lantern glowed in the small entrance, but there wasn't much light otherwise.

The home smelled musty.

Hadn't my sister been here recently?

Finn didn't spend that much time here any longer. Most of the time, he caught a rest in one of the rooms in the tavern, but on the occasion when he *did* return, he didn't usually find it like this.

"Mother?" he called out, heading along the hall, before stopping at her room. Finn tested the door, and it swung open with a creak.

His mother rested on the bed, snoring softly.

She was thin, possibly even thinner than she had been when he'd last seen her. Color had drained from her face, and she breathed irregularly.

As much as he'd wanted to, there wasn't anything he

could do for her. Before his father had gotten pinched, Finn had entertained approaching one of the guilds to learn healing to help her. But that was long ago, and he was a different person now.

She rolled over at the sound, and he tensed. He didn't want to wake her. She needed her rest, and he didn't know if she'd been sleeping that well lately.

He pulled a fistful of coins from his pocket and stacked them on the table next to her bed, where she'd find them when she awoke. It was where he left them each time he came to visit. Finn didn't know how she spent them, or whether she was the one to do so, but the coins always disappeared, so he made a point of bringing more each time he came. This time, he left the sculpture he'd taken as well. He couldn't move that without Oscar realizing what he'd done, so it was better to just leave it here for now.

Back in the entryway, he started to head back out before hesitating. There wasn't any real urgency to leaving. His mother rested, and he didn't have to get to the tavern until later. He could take a few moments and truly make sure his mother had what she needed. Lena should be taking care of her, but what if she used the coin on herself?

The thought of that made him smile.

Not Lena.

She might live in this bleak part of the city, but there had always been something so dignified about his sister. It was almost as if she were there because she chose to be, not because she had no other choice.

The small kitchen was a mess.

The lantern there had been dimmed to barely more than a glowing ember, and he brightened it, pushing back the darkness. The musty odor that he'd noticed seemed to come from there. Dishes were piled in the washbasin, some with food still caked on them. A loaf of bread rested on one of the counters, barely touched. He squeezed it, finding the bread too hard. He pulled open the cupboards. Potatoes and some carrots but no other food.

What was my sister doing?

This wasn't like her.

Not only wasn't it like her to have so little food around, but it wasn't like her to leave the dishes a mess in this way.

If there had been trouble, Helda would have said something to him.

Finn pulled the dishes from the basin and stacked them on the counter. He carried the basin out the back of the house to the small pump shared by everyone along the street and worked at the smooth wooden handle until water poured out of the spigot, filling the basin. When he was done, he carried it back into the house.

This wasn't how he envisioned spending his afternoon, but it had to be done.

Tossing some wood into the oven, he used a flint to get the wood lit and glowing, coaxing the fire until it burned brightly. When it did, he placed the basin of water on the stovetop to heat it.

"I didn't expect to see you here. Nor did I expect to find you cleaning the dishes."

Finn turned to see his sister standing in the doorway.

Her blue eyes were drawn and weary. She tucked her auburn hair behind her ears.

"It looked as if it needed to be done," he said.

He picked up the bar of soap from the counter and set it into the basin, stirring it around until suds formed.

"I was going to get to it."

"I'm sure you were." Finn set the soap down, dropping it onto the counter before turning to his sister. "Where have you been, anyway?"

She shot him a stern look. "You've been gone for the last week, and you come in and ask where *I've* been?"

Had it been a week?

He was usually better about stopping by, but perhaps he'd been distracted with the job. "Shouldn't I?"

"What are you doing here?"

"I left some money for supplies."

His sister pulled a faded leather sack off her shoulder and set it on the small table near the back wall. "You don't have to leave any money for us. I'd rather not take your tainted coin, anyway."

"Come on, Lena. It's not tainted."

"I'm taking care of Mother. We don't need you putting us at risk."

"I'm not putting you at risk."

She started to pull a few items from the sack and set them on the table. Most were food. One was a small vial with a dark powder inside. "You are if we come to depend on you and your contribution to the family." Lena pushed past him and headed to the cabinet where he'd found the potatoes and carrots. She set some of the food inside and closed it before turning to him. "You haven't said why you came by today."

"You haven't said where you've been."

Not that Finn expected her to share too much with him. With everything he did trying to serve the crew, he hadn't been around. He didn't know what his sister was doing. Much like she didn't really know what he had been doing, which he preferred.

Lena let out a heavy sigh, her shoulders slumping. "I was working."

He started to laugh, but the irritated gleam in his sister's eyes cut him off. "Where?"

"Master Jorven took me in."

"Jorven? But he's the—"

"Butcher. I know what he is. And it took some convincing on my part to even get the job."

"You can't even stand…" Finn shook his head, deciding against saying what had first come to mind. Besides, she had a job, and he knew jobs anywhere could be hard to come by, even in Brinder. He just hadn't expected she'd need to work with the butcher. "What did you have to do for him?"

She pulled a chair out and sank down into it. Finn realized just how tired she was.

It reminded him of how tired their mother had looked in the year after their father had been put away. She'd taken on any and all work she could to keep food on the table, but even that hadn't been enough. That was why Finn had started taking jobs. Small ones at first, but more and more had been necessary for him to get the coin needed to provide for his family, especially as the jobs his mother was able to do began to diminish as she started to grow increasingly tired. It wasn't until later that they realized just how sick she'd gotten.

"Why don't you just take the coin I've brought? It's more than enough to keep you fed."

"I'm sure it is. What happens when the Archers come and demand to know where we've gotten it? What happens when the coins you bring to us are marked in some way they can trace them back to what you've done?"

"That's not how it works."

She sighed again, shaking her head. "I don't know how it works anymore. All I know is that you're not here." She rested her elbow on the table, and he thought she might fall asleep. "You could have taken that apprenticeship offered to you. Mother had it all lined up."

"I'm sure I could manage to learn what I need to be a knacker without an apprenticeship."

"You wouldn't have the guild support if you did."

Finn hated the guilds. They were nearly as bad as the high-class merchants who sought to buy favor throughout the city, only they did it more discreetly. Control one means of progress toward an honorable profession—even those as questionably honorable as the knackers that cleaned out the strays in the city—and they thought they should control everything.

"You can still spend the money I've brought," he said. She shook her head. "Why not? At least tell me that."

Lena opened her eyes, and for a moment, a bright clarity shone within them. The fatigue that he'd seen from the moment she'd come into the house was gone, and now she looked at him with an expression of irritation.

"I've kept the money."

"Really? I thought you were so concerned about how you could spend it and whether the Archers could track it. Which they can't, by the way. If you'd have paid any attention to Father, you'd have known they don't have any way of tracking the coin we bring in."

"I paid attention to Father. You should have too. Had he not done what he'd been doing, we wouldn't be in this situation. Mother wouldn't be the way she is. You wouldn't have to join your gang or whatever you call it and risk your future. We could be a family." She said the last softly, lowering her gaze.

"I'm making my future, not risking it."

"There's no way to honor by stealing, Finn."

He chuckled. "You chastise me about honor, but you're hoarding all the coin I bring in? Had you told me, I would have placed the coin in your room. That way, it'd be easier for you to pile wherever you keep your hoard." He pulled the basin off the stove and began to stack the dishes into it. The water was hot—almost too hot. He'd left it sitting on the stove for longer than he'd intended. "You're like a dragon sitting over your precious gold, keeping it from others all while telling them the evils of greed."

"Stop."

She barely had any energy in her voice.

"If you need more, you can have it." He pulled the rest of the coins from his pocket as irritation flashed within him. What did these coins matter when it was a relatively simple thing for him to get more? Find a crowd, work his way through them, and take a few coins here and there. It was never that much, certainly not as much as he wished that he could get at one time, but a few coins spent just fine, regardless of what his sister might claim.

Finn slammed the coins on the counter. Lena didn't flinch.

"How much more do you need to make your pile high enough? Would you like to sleep on it, or is there something more you want to hoard it for?"

"It's for Mother," she whispered. "I'm saving it to pay for a physician."

The words hung in the air.

Finn's stomach sank.

I'm an ass.

Here he'd taunted her, and it wasn't about her at all. Of course it wouldn't be. Not Lena. She always cared. Sometimes too much. It was why he couldn't believe she'd work for a butcher.

"Why wouldn't you just say that?" he asked, looking at his hands.

"I didn't think I needed to."

She dropped down to her knees and started to sweep the coins that he'd slammed onto the counter into a pile.

Finn joined her trying to help, but she only swatted his hands away.

"Let me help," he said.

"You've done enough."

"Listen. I'm sorry. I didn't know you were saving for a physician."

Lena sat back and rested her hands on her lap, twisting the fabric. "The apothecary can't do much. Oh, they try. They've offered a few different compounds the last times, but nothing has made a difference." She looked up at him. "I know you wanted to work with them—"

"I never wanted that."

Lena held his gaze. "I know you, Finn Jagger, even if you want to pretend I don't. I know what you *really* wanted were you to have the choice."

He swallowed, looking to where he'd slammed the coins down. Were he to have the choice. Finn wouldn't be a thief; that much was true. He'd want to be honorable, but he didn't know how he would have gone about it. There had never been a choice.

"You could try a different apothecary," Finn said.

"I have. They're all the same."

Guild, she didn't add. Which meant their training would be similar.

"How much do you need for a physician?"

Finn couldn't imagine how much it would cost but suspected it would be pricey. Not only were there few physicians within the city, but they would often require a certain amount before they'd even start attempting to heal.

"More than my dragon's hoard," she said, getting to her feet. She made her way to the door and paused. "I don't like what you're doing, but I'm not throwing away the coins you're bringing to us, either, if that's what you think. What kind of a fool do you take me for?"

She looked at him a moment longer before heading out of the kitchen, leaving Finn staring after her.

He was the fool, not her. The fool who thought she was too good for his ill-gained money. His sister deserved better from him. Gods—his *mother* deserved better from him.

There might be something that he could do. The King didn't always pay that well, especially not at his position, but if Finn could take the right job, he might be able to help his mother. And Lena. She didn't need to work at the butcher. That wasn't the kind of job for someone like her. It might be honorable, but what was honor when it paid shit? His sister deserved better for everything she did. And Finn was going to get it for her.

Getting to his feet, he started scrubbing the dishes in the basin. Earn enough—or steal enough—to help their mother. That would help Lena. His family.

Which was what he had to do. He owed her more than a few coins and clean dishes.

CHAPTER THREE

The Wenderwolf tavern was situated at the edge of the Olin section of the city, far enough away from the stench in the outer sections that those who frequented it could almost imagine they were part of a different class, never mind what they had to trudge through to reach the tavern or the kind of people who frequented it. None of that mattered. All that did was the perception, along with the belief those who came had of themselves.

The Wenderwolf had a charm of sorts, though mostly that came from the people who were there. His sister wouldn't understand that. They might not be honorable in the way she preferred, but he'd found a different sort of honor.

Taking a seat in a corner booth near the door, he looked across the table at Oscar, putting thoughts of the conversation he'd had with Lena out of his mind for now.

The older man leaned back in his seat, sipping at his ale, barely looking up through half-open eyes.

"You got away," Oscar said.

"No thanks to you."

"Not all of us need to go storming through the streets. Not that you would know anything about subtlety. I thought I'd been teaching you better than that."

"You have."

"Hmm." Oscar took a long drink before setting the mug back down again. "How far did the Archer chase you through the city?"

"I lost him in the alley."

"Liar."

"Fine. I lost him near the Blood Court. What's the difference?"

"The difference is between you almost getting caught and you getting away cleanly. How sure are you that he didn't get a good look at you?"

"I can run pretty fast when I need to."

"You ran?"

Finn looked up as the tavern's proprietor, Annie, sauntered over, showing the kind of cleavage he would have preferred to have seen from Helda—though with Helda, there was the promise of something more. That made it intriguing. Annie was older and with streaks of gray in her chestnut hair, and had a slip of ribbon tying her hair back while trying to look like a younger woman.

"To save his ass," Oscar muttered.

Annie grinned and reached over to pinch Oscar's

cheek. "Not quite as fine as young Finn's ass over here, but yours will do."

"You're old enough to be my mother," Finn said.

She grinned. "That don't mean I don't have my charms." She leaned forward, and her grin widened. "Besides, it doesn't seem to me you mind all that much. You look just as much as the older boys."

The door to the tavern came open, and Rock strode in. He was a good head taller than Finn, all muscle, and had his dark gray cloak slung over his shoulders, probably to cover the pair of knives he kept on him. Not that he needed anything other than his fists. He slipped into the seat across from Finn and grunted.

"What are you all going on about?"

"Annie was telling me about how her girls don't like you much," Finn said.

"That's not what they were telling me last night," Rock said, grinning at Finn.

"Which ones?" Annie asked as she sat upright.

"I don't keep track of names."

"Because you can't think fast enough to make them up," Finn said, laughing. "Gods, Rock, if you're going to pick on Annie like that, you've got to pay attention to her girls."

"Can't all be like you," he said, laughing mostly to himself.

Annie leaned back, looking over at Oscar. "What were you doing that drew the notice of the Archers? I thought you were one of the most skilled thieves in Verendal."

"Might be *the* most skilled now that Pegg caught the rope," Finn said.

"Pegg?" Oscar asked.

Finn nodded. "That's who they held the festival for today. Saw him when I wandered out past the Teller Gate."

"I saw him too," Rock said. "Had to keep an eye on Shuffles."

Finn made a fist, and Rock laughed again.

"You went all the way to the Stone?" Oscar asked.

There was a hint of something more in the question. Irritation? Disappointment?

"The crowd pushed, and I wanted to see what Pegg might do. Hanged him."

"Figures," Annie muttered. "Can't even give a man with a reputation like that a clean death."

"No death is clean," Rock said.

"Some are better than others," Annie said. "I'd rather have the sword to my neck than the rope. At least with the sword, you don't have time to think about your dying." She ran a finger along her neck. "Take it clean if you're going to take it at all."

"No one's taking your head, Annie," a deep voice said.

Finn looked up to see the King standing behind her. He rested one hand on her back and leaned in, breathing in her ear as he whispered something softly to her that made her smile.

"Can't be so sure of that, Leon. Word gets out about the kind of business you have here, and you never know what the court decides."

The King shook his head as he took a seat, forcing

Finn to move along the bench. Though even older than Oscar and with flowing silver hair, there remained something robust about him—and intimidating. He wasn't as muscular as Rock, but he wasn't as whip-thin as Oscar, either. "The court isn't going to shut your business down. It would take too much work. Besides, most of them up there"—he made a motion with his head as if to indicate the center of the city—"or over in the churches spend more than their share of time in places like this tavern."

"Not quite like this." Annie tugged on her blouse, shifting it to make her cleavage even more pronounced. "Were we to get men like that down here, we wouldn't run into trouble like we do."

"What kind of trouble?" Oscar asked. The question seemed directed at Annie, but he looked at the King when he said it.

"The kind of trouble the crew don't need to worry about. I take care of everything so the rest of you don't have to," the King said. He turned to Annie. "How about you fetch some ales for the table?"

"Why don't you go off and fetch them yourself?"

"Annie…"

"Leon…"

She was the only person Finn had ever heard call the King by his first name. Within the crew, most of them had their nicknames. Since he'd joined, he'd been given the name Shuffles by the King. Finn wanted something stronger. Rock or the Hand or the King all had stronger connotations. Then there was Wolf. He didn't even need a nickname as it was his surname. He wanted something that meant he had skill, but a man didn't get to choose his nickname.

"Give us a moment. I need to talk to my boys."

"Boys? The Hand here is almost as old as you, and young Finn is damn near twenty. The way he leers at my girls tells me he's far more man than boy. And look at Rock. That's a man if I ever saw one." She winked and leaned toward Rock, resting a hand on his arm.

The King shot her a look dripping with annoyance, but it was a measure of the relationship he shared with Annie that he didn't force her to leave. She was the only one Finn had seen who managed to push the King that way—and who the King didn't push back against.

"I'll see what I can get for these *boys*. You'll have to fend for yourself, Leon." She pulled herself from behind the table at the booth and patted Oscar on the cheek, holding her gaze on the King while she did it.

Oscar breathed out with a hint of amusement, though it didn't show on his face. Finn had been around him enough to recognize the sound, though. Usually, it came at his expense. It was better that it come at the King's.

Annie sauntered off toward the kitchen, leaving them alone. The King watched her go for a moment before turning his attention back to Finn and Oscar.

"What happened today?" There was a tension in his voice that hadn't been there even when talking to Annie. "Tell me you got it."

"I got it," Oscar said.

"Rock informs me there was an Archer?"

Finn looked over to Rock. Other than Oscar, Finn was closest to Rock. When had he talked to the King?

"There's always an Archer, King. You know that. It's not like we were out past the damned curfew, so they wouldn't have any reason to pinch us," Oscar said, leaning back and taking a drink from his mug of ale.

"The curfew is a problem." He pulled a sheet of paper from his pocket and unfolded it, setting it on the table. Finn realized it was a notice of curfew. It was unusual for the Archers to enforce anything like that. "Can't say I care much for this."

Oscar looked over the top of the mug, glancing briefly at Finn, the corners of his eyes narrowing as if warning him. "We did what we always do. That's why we have scouts."

"Don't usually need them," the King said.

"Not usually, but this time we did. On a day like today, it was a damn good thing, too. If those Archers keep up the curfew, then we'll need them even more." Oscar took another drink, setting it down on the table. "Did you know it was Pegg?"

The King's face darkened for a moment, but then a shadow appeared over the table as Annie returned with mugs of ale, setting one down in front of each of them. When she got to Oscar, she noted his mug and how he kept his hands wrapped around it and shrugged, pulling the last one back for herself.

"We need some time to talk," the King said.

"You can talk around me like you always do. You don't always get to hear who the Poor Bastard is before they get dragged along the Blood Court with these sorts of things. Heard about Pegg, though."

It was always *Poor Bastard*, and never *poor bastard*. A title. The church had a different title for them—the Repentant—though Finn doubted many of them were too repentant by the time they were dragged to the gallows. Seeing Pegg today, he felt sure he wasn't.

"Something like Pegg is why we don't want the attention of the Archers," the King said.

"Not palace Archers, anyway," Oscar said.

The King set his mug down and stared at Oscar. "Palace Archers?"

"We passed one. Single stripe. Far too curious to be a city Archer."

"I can handle city Archers," the King said confidently. "You just have to pay them better than the crown, and they'll do whatever you need. Palace Archers are a different breed. Wolves compared to dogs."

"More like wolves compared to pups," Annie said. She rested her hands on the table and leaned forward. "It was a palace Archer that caught Pegg. Way I heard it, he took a job up *there* that got him squeezed. Stupid to think you could break into... What is it?" She looked over at the King.

"Nothing."

"I see that look in your eyes, Leon Konig. Don't think I don't recognize it."

"I said it was nothing."

She glared at him before shaking her head. "Anyway, you don't want to hear what this old working girl has to say. The *King* sure don't." She said his nickname with a sneer that made it sound almost like a swear. "Not like I hear all the gossip that comes through here. Not at all. Certainly don't hear more than the *King*. I didn't hear anything about Dalton Pegg thinking he'd break into the palace on a job and get squeezed by the Archers. I'll tell you what kind of fool does that." She shot the King a look. "Someone after more than coin. You go there, you take what the gods give you. Even Pegg had limits."

"Who would want him to break into the palace?" Oscar asked.

"If you take something like the crown jewels there..." Rock started.

Finn shared a look with Rock.

Other than Oscar, he was the only one who knew of Finn's mother.

That kind of money would more than pay for his mother getting the help she needed. They could get her a physician. Not just an apothecary. They could get her *real* help.

"You can't move something like that," Oscar said. "They're too distinctive. You might have the wealth, but what's wealth if you can't unload it?"

Leave it to Oscar to be practical about things like that.

"There'd be a way to break it down. You get jewels like that, I'm sure you can find a buyer. You just have to go to the right person." Finn looked over at the King. "Right? I'm sure you've got someone who could break down the jewels. Gold is gold. The gods know you could melt that down, mold it into something else. The jewels probably pop right off, and you can—"

"Pop off?" Oscar asked. "What sort of trinkets do you think the crown keeps here?"

"I don't know. No one does." Finn took a drink of ale and leaned back, welcoming the warmth as it rolled down his throat. It left him with a pleasant sensation in his belly. Better than most anything. "I'd like to have a look, though."

"I'll look with you," Rock said, grinning.

"You wouldn't. If a man like Dalton Pegg can't get into the palace and get away, there ain't anyone who can do it."

"Right. The Hand couldn't manage to break in?" Finn looked from the King to Annie before grinning at Oscar. "You don't want to take the credit that you're due."

"I take everything I'm due. I also know my limits. Just like I know a job like that not only can't be done, but Pegg must've been a fool to take it on. Like I said. No way to move it. Who wants to risk trying to sell it and drawing the attention of the Archers?"

"Unless he had a buyer," the King added softly.

"Could be," Oscar said, scratching his jawline. "I've heard the Mistress has been active."

The King shook his head as his brow darkened. "Don't talk about her. You never know when one of her people are listening. Besides," he said, his expression shifting, now smiling again, "we both know a job is only as good as a buyer. A job like that would require that someone have a way of moving it before you decide to take it. It's too dangerous otherwise."

"Some claim the hegen pushed him to take the job," Annie said.

The King almost spit out his drink while laughing. "The hegen? No magic is worth dying for. This was about coin, plain and simple."

"Maybe it was *good* magic," Rock said in between drinks. "You know, like the kind the Alainsith have in the forest outside the city."

"There's a difference between dangerous and good," the King said. "And the hegen can't give any man enough magic to make it worthwhile taking the kind of job Pegg did. Maybe the others"—Finn noticed he didn't want to mention the Alainsith; some feared speaking of them would draw their attention, though it had been several centuries since they'd attacked—"might have that power, but we haven't seen sign of them in ages."

"Other than the forest," Rock said. When the King shot him a look, Rock shrugged. "I spent some time outside the walls. I know what's out there."

"Nothing is outside the walls but the hegen section and trees. At least nothing we have to worry about. Stay in the city and get paid. You do the wrong job, you risk attention. That's why you have to do it smart. Keep it clean." He glanced at Oscar. "Which Pegg didn't do."

"Pegg wouldn't have gone into anything without knowing the risks," Oscar said. "I knew him a little. We pulled a few jobs together when I was younger."

"That must have been quite some time ago," Annie said. "You still look beautiful, though." She traced a finger along the scar under his chin, a glimmer of a smile hanging on her lips. "The girls like the scar on you, anyway."

Oscar snorted. "I'm sure."

"What was he like?" Finn asked.

Finn had recognized Pegg, but anyone who spent any time in the city's outer sections would have recognized him. The more challenging jobs all went to him and his crew, mostly because he was the most skilled. The most exacting. Taking jobs like that put his people into danger, but from the way Finn had heard it told, none of the jobs that he took ever felt as if they were heading into all that much danger, mostly because of the level of preparation that Pegg put into each job.

It was why him getting pinched came as such a surprise. As far as Finn had heard, Pegg had never been caught. Those who got caught in the outer sections of the city got noticed. The crews they worked with got noticed.

"A thief, Shuffles. No different than the Hand," the King said.

As much as he disliked the nickname, he tried to embrace it, at least as much as someone could embrace a name like that. Better that he not argue about it, especially not with the King.

Annie tipped back her drink again before setting it on the table. "I'll let you boys talk. I've got others in the tavern who need my attention. Most of them are far nicer to me than Leon these days, anyway."

She got up, collecting the mug from where she sat, looking to Oscar who nodded, and headed toward the kitchen.

"Let's see it," the King said when she'd been gone for a while.

Oscar leaned off to the side and moved his pouch out so that he could flip it open. When he reached inside, he set a bundle of burlap onto the table.

The King looked around the inside of the tavern. It was empty other than a small booth in the far corner. No one from there would even be able to see them from where they were.

He started to unwrap the burlap around it.

"You sure that's safe here?" Oscar asked. "You know where I went for that."

"I'm well aware of where you had to go to retrieve this. That's why I want to see it. Got to see if it's what we were hired to get."

Finn and Rock leaned forward. When the King had it unwrapped, he regarded the small bowl with writing all around the perimeter they'd taken. The bowl wasn't even painted all that well, just swirls of pale red and some deeper maroon toward the bottom of the bowl.

Annie came from a nearby table and looked down. "I thought you didn't want me talking about the hegen. Now you've got one of their bowls?"

The King looked up at her. "It's not hegen."

She shrugged. "Could've fooled me."

She strode away, and Finn turned his attention to the bowl.

"With everything in that place, I still can't believe that's what we went for." Finn shared a look with Rock. "I bet had the Archer known what we were after, he wouldn't have cared. What does that Client want with that?"

These days, it was always about the Client.

The King had the contacts, and in this case, the contact provided the job. Sort of how Pegg would have needed to have someone lined up to move jewels from the palace.

"That's not on me to know. Or care," the King said. He held the bowl up toward the lantern resting on the table, turning it from one side to the other. The light didn't reflect off of it.

Junk.

That was what it was. Not something valuable, though even junk could get them paid with the right buyer. This time, the buyer had made it known what they wanted, so they'd taken the job. It wasn't even supposed to draw attention. Even if the bowl *was* hegen, it didn't matter so long as they got paid.

The King reached into his pocket and pulled out a stack of coins, setting them on the table in front of each of them. An equal cut this time. That wasn't always the case.

Five silvers to take the bowl. Five silvers would get his mother closer to paying for a physician. He still didn't know how much they'd need, but that *had* to be getting close.

"Now to talk business." He glanced beyond them, toward Annie. "Not something I wanted to bring up today. Especially today. But we got a job offer from the Client. It's not going to be easy. A job like this is going to take the whole crew, but the payout will be worth ten times what I just gave you."

"Ten times?" Finn reached toward his pocket but noticed Oscar didn't.

Rock did the same as Finn, looking across the table and grinning at him.

"What's the job?" Oscar asked softly.

"It'll be a difficult job. The kind of thing that I normally turn down, but the Client is insistent on this one. The timing could be better, but I figure with our crew, we shouldn't have too much trouble. Besides, I got some inside information that should make it easier."

"What's the job?" Oscar asked again.

The King looked over at him. "The viscount's manor."

Oscar simply stared.

Finn realized Oscar had suspected something like that. It was the pay.

The job they'd done earlier paid decently. Typical these days for the kind of thing the King asked them to do. Some of the jobs were easier than others, but all of them had a bit of danger—mostly exposing them to the Archers. They were the kind of jobs he wouldn't get were it not for the King. Finn didn't have those connections. He had to rely on pickpocketing and smaller jobs. Things that could go wrong. Draw in the Archers.

"Pegg—"

The King shook his head. "It's not the same job as Pegg. He tried the damn palace. This is just the viscount." He looked over his shoulder. "Despite what Annie might be trying to fill our heads with, this is just about the coin."

Oscar leaned back, frowning as he stared at the table. "Job like that is too dangerous for us."

"Client will hire another crew. Not just for this job but others. I can push for more pay. He's already paying plenty—more than five times what this job paid. With what happened to Pegg, I should be able to convince him we need to double it…"

Oscar squeezed his eyes shut, and Finn could practically see him working through what to say. When he opened his eyes, he looked over at Finn for a moment before taking a short breath.

"Get him to double it. Triple if you can. And find out what we're taking."

"We'll know what we're taking by the time we do the job," the King said. "I'll have plans of the home to follow, and we go after the item only. Nothing else. We'll have Shuffles here keeping watch, and Rock will help. The rest of us go in, finish the job, and be on with it."

He said it with confidence that Finn didn't necessarily share, but who was he to argue with the King? He had the reputation he did for a reason. If the King said they could do the job, then they could.

As Finn looked over to Oscar, he could tell the Hand was troubled as well, but rather than arguing, he nodded.

"When are we doing it?"

"He wanted it done soon."

"When?" Oscar pushed.

The King started to smile. "Tomorrow." He looked from Oscar to Finn. "So we've got to be ready."

CHAPTER FOUR

Finn sipped his ale, looking over at Oscar. He'd been silent since the King got up and went over to chat with Annie. The tavern had gotten busier since he'd shown up but was still quieter than it would be later in the evening when a crowd filled it.

"What do you think, Shuffles?" Rock asked, leaning across the table.

"About the job?"

"Damn right about the job."

Finn studied Oscar before turning his attention back to Rock. "It's dangerous. Breaking into some high-class merchant is one thing, but this is the viscount."

Rock leaned closer. "Your mother…"

Finn nodded. "That was my first thought."

Oscar glanced toward Finn.

"Think about what this can do for her. For all of us.

Damn, but we do this and then don't have to do any jobs for a while."

That wasn't the way the King ran his crew, but the idea of having a score like that…

Oscar got up without saying a word and slipped out of the tavern.

"What's up his ass?" Rock asked.

"I don't know. I'm going to see. Catch up with you later?"

Rock shrugged. "I'll be here. Might have a few more of these." He lifted his empty mug and waved it at a cute brunette waitress making her way past.

Finn chuckled and followed Oscar out of the tavern.

Oscar had moved away down the street, and Finn had to hurry to catch up to him. The shops lining the roadway were all shuttered for the night, a few with lanterns glowing, though not brightly enough that he could make out details within them. He pulled his cloak around his shoulders more tightly, clutching it against the breeze carrying the stink of this section down the street.

He crept quietly, following the shadowed form in the distance.

Why would Oscar sneak off like that?

The Hand didn't usually disappear at night, but something had been off. Finn needed to know why. A few of the shops along this street were completely closed off. His gaze drifted to the locks, assessing which of them would be easier to break into. He could pick many of them, but the barred windows suggested he wouldn't get far from there.

He was troubled as he trailed after Oscar.

Break into the viscount's manor?

Probably not a good idea with Pegg having been pinched.

Oscar was a good thief. Pegg had been a great thief.

As Finn followed, he still didn't know where Oscar was going. Maybe just out for a night stroll. It could be the King had given him another assignment. If that were the case, Finn might be able to help. Not that Oscar would allow it. If he wanted Finn's help, he would have told him.

Each step Oscar took, Finn mirrored.

At first, it was easy. Plenty of people wandered the streets of the Olin section. Not as dangerous as some of the outer sections, and not as uptight as the central sections, as the taverns here had a more ribald feel. Music drifted into the streets as he'd walked, the darkness giving the sound an undercurrent of excitement. Maybe that was only because he knew it well enough, he didn't fear coming through there.

The shadowed form of Oscar turned and headed toward the center of the city, taking one of the side streets that would wind around and past the Vinlen River, along the Pelthan Chapel. By the time he reached the winding street with the palace in the distance, Finn knew exactly where they were going. He hurried toward Oscar, holding his cloak tightly.

"About time you slunk up here," Oscar said softly as he joined him. "You've been making too much noise back there. You have to work on steadying your breathing."

"My breathing was steady enough." He was getting tired of everyone scolding him today.

"Maybe it was your feet, then. Shuffles."

Finn glared at him. "The King send you up here?" Finn pitched the words softly, keeping his voice low. You never knew who was listening.

"Scouting."

"You're not scouting. If you were, you'd be at the viscount's manor."

"Fine. I wanted to see what Pegg tried. Damn fool if he thought to break into the palace. Nothing worth that risk."

"Not even the jewels?" Finn asked.

"Jewels for your life?"

"Then maybe he *did* owe the hegen something."

"That's not how they work," Oscar said. "They don't want their pound of flesh so easy."

When Oscar moved on, Finn stayed with him. As the street wound ever closer to the palace in the distance, it widened, though didn't *feel* as if it widened. The maze of the streets felt more like it closed in around him, though that was probably nothing more than his imagination.

At one point, Oscar paused and studied something along the street, though Finn couldn't tell what it was he looked at. He stared at a building on the far side of the street. No lights were lit, and shadows around the sign made it difficult for him to make anything out.

The breeze he'd felt throughout the walk picked up, blowing out of the south, carrying the stink of air from farther out in the city toward them. He wrinkled his nose against the stench.

"You could've brought us through a different section. You know, one that wouldn't attract so much attention. Or carry the slaughterhouse to us." Finn leaned against the building, watching Oscar as he crouched down. This time he actually seemed to be adjusting his boots. No one else was out on the street this late.

Oscar straightened and turned to him. "I could've. I didn't. You didn't have to come with me if you were going to complain so much."

"You slunk off so quickly, I had to make sure nothing was wrong."

Oscar looked over, arching a brow. "You could go back and drink with Rock. I know how the two of you are."

"What's that supposed to mean?"

Oscar shook his head. "Not saying it's a bad thing. It's like your father and me when we were your age. Well, after your father got into this line of work. You're young. You *should* have fun. And you don't need to be here."

"Neither do you."

"It's got to be done."

"So we don't end up like Pegg."

Oscar shook his head slightly. "Pegg had probably been pinched a few times before. You don't get the noose for one offense."

"Even if caught *there*?"

Oscar paused before shaking his head. "Even there. They've got to save that for the really nasty crimes." Oscar looked up into the darkness. "This was more for me and less for him."

In the darkness, the rigid set to his jaw wasn't quite as

evident, though his scar seemed to catch the light and make it gleam.

"If you're going out to do this, then I'm going with you," Finn said.

Oscar grunted but said nothing more. Finn figured that was agreement.

They continued along the street toward the palace. Every so often, the street would turn so the palace would be visible, but then it would turn again and disappear. They got closer to the palace, but the maze of streets made it difficult to head straight toward it.

"What's got you bothered? Don't tell me you aren't troubled. I know you well enough, Oscar."

The Hand paused and motioned for Finn to follow him into the shadows of the street near an alley. Finn glanced at it, thinking how he could follow this alley, though it wouldn't be as easy. He *thought* he knew where this one connected, but he might be wrong. Better check if they were going to take this job. Oscar might not like alleys, but Finn recognized their value. The wrong turn and you could get caught—the way Finn had almost gotten himself caught.

"It's this business with the Client. I've been trying to figure out who we're working for."

"You have? If the King finds out—"

"He's just going to have to deal with it. I'm not taking jobs like this until I know who we're dealing with. Neither should you."

"That's what got you troubled?"

Oscar grunted. "It's these jobs. You don't notice

anything about them?"

"How am I supposed to notice? I'm a scout, remember?"

"That means you watch."

"I have been."

"Then what have you seen?"

"Well, today, we went up to the—"

"Don't say it. Not here."

Finn looked around. He didn't see anyone, but maybe Oscar was right. They should be more careful about speaking up even in places like this. Probably especially places like this.

"Whatever. We were there. Took… whatever that was. Then brought it to the King. No different than many of our recent jobs."

Oscar looked past him and along the street. "That's my concern."

"What is?"

"What we took today," Oscar said softly. "I'm worried about the King. Something is off lately. Something's pressuring him. I haven't figured out what it is, but he's taking jobs that don't make the most sense for the crew."

They made their way along the street, and the palace loomed into view. The street straightened, now heading directly toward the palace, widening as it did.

The palace itself was enormous. A separate wall surrounded it, high enough Finn couldn't make out the gardens rumored to be on the other side. *Rumored* only because he didn't know if there really was a garden there. Turrets rose from the center of the palace as little more than shadowed forms against the darkness, making it difficult for him to make anything else out. A lantern flickered high in the palace, the only light visible from where they stood.

"See that?" Oscar asked, taking a place along the edge of the street and looking toward the palace.

"I see it."

"Not the palace. The wall. That's the first step. He would've had to get past the wall. Once over, then the next challenge begins, but that couldn't have been easy."

Two Archers patrolled the high stone wall. Finn couldn't imagine there'd be that much room along the wall for them to patrol, but they seemed to have no difficulty marching. Moonlight gleamed off the metal helms and chainmail, and their boots thudded dully as they moved beyond them.

"Why do you think he did it?"

Oscar breathed out slowly. "Don't really know. Too dangerous. A damn sight too dangerous."

They stood there for a while before making their way from the palace. They stayed on the same street, but it veered down a gentle hillside, past a few massive shops, before another stone wall appeared, though smaller than the one surrounding the palace. It was still in one of the city's nicer sections, though at the western edge of the city where it practically abutted the forest.

Finn could almost imagine the forest just beyond the wall surrounding the city, a place no one ever visited. The Alainsith had some strange influence over the forest that kept anyone from venturing too far. Some thought the forest barrier shifted over time, though Finn thought that nothing but rumor, the same kind of rumors he often heard spread about the hegen.

The viscount's manor wasn't nearly as large as the hillside palace, though several stories high, with lanterns shining in the windows lining the street, but it was nonetheless impressive. Protected by palace Archers, the manor home would be almost as impenetrable.

"Two," Oscar whispered.

"We can time it so we don't have to deal with the Archers," Finn said.

Oscar frowned. "It's not going to be easy. I see two now, but..." He leaned forward, his eyes narrowing. "I think I'm going to have to come by in the daylight to see if there's more I can't see."

"You'll have to dress better than you did today if you're going to do that."

Oscar shot him a look.

"I was just trying to be helpful."

"If you think you've got some way of getting in there and finding out more than I can, be my guest."

"You wouldn't trust what I told you, anyway."

Oscar shrugged. "Your father taught you to count well enough."

A moment of silence passed between them. "What do we have once we get past the walls?" If they were scouting, they might as well do it right. Talking it through with Oscar made him feel better about the plan.

"Once through there, we have to get into the manor itself. The King is saying the direct approach is best, but

I'm not as certain. It all depends on what we're going after."

"I'll check with Rock. The King might have said something to him."

Oscar nodded slowly while Finn watched the wall, noting the regular procession of Archers across the walkway. They came often enough he didn't think they'd be able to sneak past them all that easily. It would take impossibly consistent timing, and he didn't know if he'd be able to do that.

That had to be what Oscar wanted to know. How often the Archers came by. Whether there was a break they could take advantage of to slip through. Perhaps even if there might be a weakness somewhere else along the wall they could use.

"It's not going to be easy," Finn said softly.

"It's not."

"Easier than what Pegg tried, I guess."

"Pegg took on more than he should," Oscar said with more force than Finn thought necessary. *What sort of rivalry had existed between the two men?* "Damn fool always thought he could outsmart everyone and get into things most know better than to do."

"Did you keep in contact with him?"

"Not much lately. Ever since…" Oscar clenched his jaw a moment. "I suppose it doesn't matter." Oscar shook his head and turned away from the palace as if he'd seen everything that he'd needed. "Got what I needed here."

He started off, and Finn followed, but a sign along the street caught his attention. He recognized the symbol for the physician, nothing else. With the light on inside, he thought he could go and investigate. With the job they were about to pull, it had to be a sign. The gods *wanted* them to pull this job.

"Oscar?"

The Hand slowed and turned toward him, frowning. "What is it?"

"Do you think it can be done?"

"The job?"

Finn nodded before looking along the street and toward the manor house in the distance. "The job. Getting over the wall. Breaking into… *there*. Do you think it can be done?"

Finn studied the manor home, but he wasn't able to see anything from there. The wall made it difficult to make out anything beyond. Even if they got beyond the wall, they still ran the danger of what was on the other side. They didn't know. Sure, Finn suspected the King had sources that would tell him what they might find. Possibly even Archers who'd once served there. That wasn't the same as having been there themselves. Knowing the layout. And having a definite plan of approach.

That was how jobs went well. Oscar had taught him that, but so had his father. As much as Lena didn't want to talk about their father, he *had* been skilled. The jobs he'd taken had provided for them. His sister had known that as well as Finn did, regardless of whether she wanted to acknowledge that anymore.

"Almost any job can be done. Just have to have the

right approach. We've got the right crew. Everyone knows their job. Skilled. That's what matters on a job like this."

"Like Pegg."

"Don't go there, Finn. We don't know what Pegg did when it came to his job. For all we know, he thought he could break in alone."

"What are you going to tell the King?"

That was really why Oscar had come out here.

Finn might serve as scout on the job, but Oscar was the real scout. If he said no, Finn figured the King would agree.

Not doing the job meant the Client would find a new crew. It meant the jobs they'd been taking—all of them paying much more than they were accustomed to earning with their jobs—would disappear. Another crew would benefit.

His gaze drifted down the street and toward the light in the shop in the distance.

"I told you we can do it. It's just going to take planning. This isn't the kind of job you rush into. You do it right, get the information you need, and make sure that you cover all the possibilities. The King ought to know that, regardless of what his Client wants from us." Oscar motioned for him. "Come on. Let's get moving. Maybe you and Rock can find some trouble before the night falls."

Finn headed toward an alley, laughing softly. "Let's catch up later. Either tonight or in the morning."

"Don't be up too late with Rock. Neither of you, but I know you'll at least listen to me. Can't have you miss when the King wants us to meet."

Finn nodded, though he didn't know if Oscar could see it against the darkness. "I'll be there."

Finn wandered through a few alleys before emerging onto a street that would bring him back to the Wender-wolf—or back to the physician he'd seen. He was still on the palace side of the river, and with the curfew, needed to be careful, but there was no sign of Archers.

As Finn made his way along the street, he caught sight of a shadowed figure. When he got close enough, he realized it was the King. He was talking to another man, a heavyset person with a dark cloak hanging over his shoulders.

Could this be the Client?

Finn snuck closer, staying in the darkness of the shadows, trying to move the way Oscar had taught him, and snuck into the entrance of an alley to watch. The King leaned forward and passed something to the man, who quickly stuffed it into his pocket. The King whispered something Finn couldn't hear before striding off down the road. Finn lingered in the alley, and as the man turned the opposite direction, Finn caught sight of him. He had a ruddy face and prominent jowls but was dressed in an elegant jacket beneath his cloak. Somebody of wealth. Maybe it really *was* the Client.

When the man disappeared, Finn should have headed toward the Wenderwolf, but something pulled him in the other direction and toward the physician's shop with a light in the door. Finn slowed, studying the symbol above the door. A thick-walled square set on one point, a curved staff angled through it. The mark of the physician. It had to be chance that he'd come across a physician while scouting with Oscar.

Finn lingered at the door for too long.

A shadowed form moved behind the window before peering out, and the door came open.

Pale white light streamed out from within. A man younger than what Finn would have expected stood in the doorway, a book clutched in one arm.

"Is someone there?"

Finn debated slipping off into the darkness. It wouldn't be difficult for him to hide. He didn't need to say anything. He could claim he was passing by…

The physician started to pull the door closed.

"Master…" Finn started, realizing he didn't even know the physician's name.

That alone would make his presence stand out. Most who came to the physician would know his name, so his *not* knowing would draw attention to the fact that he didn't really belong here.

"Master Porgen," the physician said, holding the door open. He looked into the dark, cupping a hand over his eyes as he stared. "Come toward me."

Finn approached. Now that he was here, there wasn't much of a point in hiding.

"What are you doing here? You don't look like you need my services."

His tone had shifted, gotten brusquer. The physician stared at Finn in a way that left him feeling as if he were examined—and discarded.

It was nearly enough to convince him to turn away.

Nearly.

"It's not for me. My mother. She's been ill for quite some time, and I wanted to know if you—"

"You have to pay up front. My fee for consultations is three branna."

Finn's breath caught, and he didn't know how to react.

Three?

One branna was more than he had. The silver in his pocket was a start, and if he added it to the collection he'd made over the years—all of which it seemed his sister hadn't spent—it might get him close.

Were there really people who paid that much?

"I can see from your face that's more than what you can afford."

"It's more than I have on me," he said hurriedly. "I have the rest. She's been sick for the last year and now barely awakens. She eats, but only when fed. She sleeps most of the time, and there has been—"

The physician ignored him. "That's only for the consultation. If someone has been ill for a while as you say your mother has been, there are often tests required. Occasionally, it will necessitate a person travel to Brandelton, where additional testing can be done. Then there are the other physician fees, and travel costs, and... you can imagine it gets quite expensive."

And *he* was the thief?

"If you don't want to help, you could just say it."

"Did I say I wouldn't help? I wanted you to have an honest understanding of the costs involved. All told, it will likely run closer to five branna."

That much money was more than what Finn would be able to make—honestly or otherwise—in years.

Hadn't Lena looked into what a physician would cost?

She couldn't think they would be able to help their mother with a cost like that. Even with him taking on ever more dangerous jobs—and breaking into the viscount's manor was a dangerous job—it would take a long time to make that much money.

"If that is all, I will say goodnight."

He started to close the door, and Finn stepped toward him.

What am I doing?

He couldn't assault a physician. He *needed* him.

"I can pay. Just come with me, and I'm sure you can do something to help her. It's not far, only in the Olin section—"

The physician's expression clouded. "You're better off asking a surgeon for help." He said it with disdain.

"The surgeon we've contacted couldn't help. Said to get a physician. He even recommended you."

The physician sniffed. "Indeed? What *surgeon* would make such a recommendation?"

Finn didn't know enough about the surgeon his sister had used, only that he'd cost more than she'd been able to afford at the time. Probably more than she'd be able to afford even now. And probably only a fraction of what this physician would cost.

"I can show you to her," he tried again.

"A surgeon, an apothecary, or the gods know, even a hegen would be more what you can afford."

Surgeons and apothecaries cost about the same—more than Finn had. The hegen exacted a different cost for their magic, but still would be more than what he wanted to spend. Some claimed the hegen made people steal for them, others claimed they took a part of their soul, and others made even more outlandish claims about the hegen witches and their magic. Finn had avoided them his entire life and had no idea how much of it was true.

"I'm not asking the hegen to help my mother," Finn said.

Could the physician really have suggested that?

"I know what your kind believe. You might even find some value in it."

"My kind?" He took a step closer. Now he grew irritated, and he had to suppress that.

If he *could* find the necessary funds, he didn't want to put the physician off from helping.

No. What Finn needed was to keep the possibility open to him and his mother.

If the job went well, he'd be close to having the necessary consultation fee. Once he had that, he could figure out if there was something more his mother might need. If that involved heading to Brandelton, then that was what he'd do.

"I mean no disrespect." The physician glanced past Finn before turning to look at him. "I'm sorry that I'm not able to help."

Stepping through the threshold, he started to close the door.

"If I bring you the consultation fee?" The fee would

probably be the same with any physician he found, but that didn't make it right.

"If you bring that, then I will see what I can do. Only then. Good evening."

He closed the door, and Finn stood in front of it. His hand went into his pocket, fingering the coins he had. Not enough. Not nearly enough.

He could get close, though.

It would take work. It would take risking himself. Doing jobs that concerned even Oscar.

He'd have to risk it.

The sound of heavy boots thudded along the street.

Finn looked up to see an Archer marching down the street.

Gods!

He hurried toward the alley and slipped along them until he didn't think the Archer followed him. He thought about the job. The money he needed. The look on the physician's face when he'd mentioned the Olin section. What would he say if he knew the *real* section?

None of that mattered. Not until he could get the coin.

When a bell on the Elia Tower tolled for midnight, Finn jumped.

He'd lost track of time.

He was going to meet Rock, but he also needed to rest. And to be ready for the job.

CHAPTER FIVE

Finn listened for anything that might be off. It was something Oscar had been working with him on trying to master. The key was noticing the change in the sounds around him, that of the city itself, along with the wind and, according to Oscar, even the energy in the air.

He noticed nothing.

Oscar glanced in his direction. He marched along the street with his usual quiet gait, saying nothing. In the distance, Finn saw Rock, though the massive man couldn't do much to hide. They hadn't stayed up too late the night before, though Rock had pushed Finn to have *just one more* mug of ale, the way he always managed to.

"I warned Rock his shadow is big enough to get us caught." He needed to say something to break the silence. "At least we've got Red and Scruff and Jiggers running off any archers who might come through."

They were all low level cutpurses looking for promotion into a crew. A job like this wouldn't pay well for them, but they'd get credit with the King.

"Not now," Oscar said. "You're making too much noise."

Finn felt as if he had to talk. His nerves made it difficult for him to keep quiet. Not like Oscar. It didn't seem to Finn that the Hand worried at all about heading out on a job that might end with them getting captured by Archers.

"I'm doing my best to be quiet," Finn said.

"You're not. If you were doing your best, then you would've been quiet. Stop chattering so much. You're acting like you've never pulled a job."

Finn followed him along the street, keeping up with Oscar as much as he could. He stopped talking as they went, trying not to irritate Oscar. They veered along the main streets through the city. Were it up to him, he would have had them taking the alleys. There were plenty of ways they could have gone through the alleys that wouldn't risk them drawing the attention of the Archers, but he knew Oscar wouldn't do it.

The street widened in front of him just as a bell tolled nearby.

Finn counted how many times the bell rang. This was the Shisen Bell, one near the center of the city, and it rang more softly than some of the others. Four tolls.

Late.

Late enough after the new curfew that there wasn't anyone else out in the streets. Late enough that were the Archers to see them, they'd know something wasn't quite right.

Finn found himself looking all around as he walked, worried about what he might find. There hadn't been any sign of Archers, but that was part of the reason they'd split up as they made their way there. They *should* have come from different directions, but the King didn't want to hear his suggestions. He'd listened to Wolf and Oscar. That was it. Even then, Finn thought the King had already made up his mind about how he planned to take the job. He didn't need their input.

"We're getting close," Finn said, once again breaking the silence of the night.

"I know we're getting close."

"That alley there connects to one of the others on the far side," he said, motioning. "I still think we'd be better off by using the alleys than the streets."

"Archers watch the alleys, too," Oscar said softly. "Harder to escape down an alley when you're pinched by an Archer there."

They might watch the alleys, but they didn't watch them quite as closely as they watched places like this. The homes along this stretch of the street were well maintained. Nothing like in his section, or even in the Olin section. Most were freshly painted, and none of them had cracked and damaged shutters or doors. Most had smooth glass windows, though a few had stained glass on the upper levels. Many homes even had small spaces behind the home, a luxury anywhere within the cramped city. The farther they went along the street, the larger the homes became.

Oscar paused and looked around.

Finn tried to listen, focusing on what the Hand might have heard, but there wasn't anything. Just Oscar acting as jumpy as the rest of them.

Finn shifted his pack. He'd be working as a scout, but on this job, that involved him getting over the wall, heading toward the manor, and watching from there. If something went wrong, he'd even have to be ready for the possibility that he'd have to go into the manor. The pack carried rope, powders he could mix into an explosive, and a drawing the King had given each of them of the manor house layout which Finn had memorized. Not that Finn expected to need to use it. If the Hand failed, none of them were getting out of this.

"Keep moving," Oscar whispered.

"I'm coming."

The street ended near the circular road leading around the walled manor house.

The King and Wolf stood near a large home at the end of the street, talking softly. Rock was on the other side of the street. Watching.

"He's got to be careful. I told him he'll look suspicious," Finn said.

Rock hurried across the street and lowered himself into the shadows beneath the wall around the mansion.

Finn always gave the big man credit. For a large guy, he moved fairly quickly. When he ducked down, he did manage to hide in the shadows enough that Finn couldn't see him as anything more than a blur of darkness. The darks helped. Finn's weren't quite as nice as what Oscar wore and didn't fit him as well as they could have, but then, they'd been his father's.

The Archers along the wall made another pass.

They either didn't see the King and Wolf, or they passed by without paying much attention to them. When Finn and Oscar came closer, he realized it had to be the former. The angle of where they stood protected them, blocking them from the patrols seeing them.

"You two ready?" the King asked.

Finn nodded quickly. Oscar didn't respond nearly as fast.

"We get to the other side of the wall, there's supposed to be a row of hedges. We regroup there," Wolf said. His black beard matched his darks. Even his normally gray eyes looked black against the night. Of all of them, he would blend in the best. A real wolf. Finn didn't know how old Wolf was, but he was clever, with something in those flat gray eyes that spoke of cruelty. All crews needed a man like Wolf.

Oscar regarded Finn for a moment, his hand twitching the way it did when he considered things. He didn't say anything, but Finn could tell something bothered him.

"We get to the hedges, and we regroup," the King said. "From there, the Hand and Wolf go in like we planned."

They shared a look and nodded.

They had the most challenging jobs.

Not that either of them would have it any other way.

Oscar was the thief. Slippery. Quick. Elusive. One of the most skilled and renowned in the city for good reason.

Wolf was deadly. The sword strapped to his waist was

more than just decoration. Still, it was his mind that made him almost more important to the crew than the King. The planner. Cunning. Conniving. Between him and the King's connections, they were a powerful combination.

Finn looked up at the wall.

Oscar's preparations had revealed a pattern to the patrols. That was what they had to follow now. By paying attention to the patrol and knowing when they would pass by, they had a sense of the time between each patrol.

"Now," Wolf said.

They hurried across the street to where Rock waited.

Wolf was the first over. Rock linked his fingers together, providing a boost, and Wolf went up to the top of the wall, quickly disappearing to the other side.

Oscar went next. His gaze lingered on Finn for a moment, holding him with his dark gaze, and then he shook his head and jumped off Rock's outstretched hands.

"Your turn, Shuffles."

Finn took a deep breath. He nodded and jumped up so that he planted his boot into Rock's hands. Finn wasn't nearly as tall as Oscar and not as heavy as he suspected Wolf was. Still, Rock flung him far higher than he expected.

The suddenness of it jarred him.

He went soaring for what seemed an eternity.

Then he landed on the top of the wall. The sounds of movement near him drew his attention. He rolled forward, toward the other side of the wall.

Hands grabbed at him.

Finn struggled but heard Wolf's harsh whisper, "Stop thrashing!"

They lowered him to the ground, and Wolf gave him a shove. He started forward, reaching the row of hedges much like they'd promised.

Oscar was already there, crouching and looking all around him. His eyes darted around, as if he were expecting to see something jump out at him.

The King rolled over the wall and landed gracefully next to Wolf.

Finn wondered how Wolf looked landing. Not nearly as skilled as even the King, and he was the oldest of them. Oscar had probably bounded off the wall and into the hedges, moving so quickly that it would be like he was never there.

The other two joined them, crouching. They waited as a pair of Archers patrolled along the wall before disappearing in the distance. While they were near, Finn held his breath. Everything seemed more momentous from this side of the wall.

This was the viscount's manor. As the king's appointed hand in the city, he ruled in his absence. Attacking the viscount's home was no different from attacking the king. If they were caught…

"That's about how it needed to go," the King said. "Wolf figures we've got about an hour before we run the risk of morning activity catching us, so let's get moving. You all know your responsibility."

Everyone nodded, including Finn.

His role was to stay outside and watch.

Scouting, the kind of scouting that involved a greater danger than he'd taken on before.

They crept along the hedges, following a path Wolf seemed to know, before pausing when the hedges ended and open lawn stretched in front of them.

Finn waited.

"You stay here until we get in," Wolf said, looking at Finn and Rock. "Keep your eyes open."

Oscar and Wolf slipped off, quickly disappearing into the darkness. The King eyed him another moment before he moved off. Finn crouched down, looking all around the yard.

The lawn was incredible, though that wasn't surprising, given someone of the viscount's stature. Not only were the hedges completely groomed, but the small trees that grew in clumps seemed to have also been sculpted.

The air had a pleasant fragrance to it. He could smell the flowers that had to be growing nearby, the grass under his feet, even that of the earth. All of it was far more pleasant than the scents he'd gotten used to in the outer sections. No wonder the viscount rarely left his grounds. The only time he was rumored to do so was on the rare times when the king came to visit.

That hadn't occurred in several years. With Verendal on the edge of the kingdom and so close to the forest and the people of Alainsith beyond, Finn doubted he had much reason to make his way here. The Alainsith had warred with the kingdom years ago, but there had been peace for as long as Finn could remember. They were said to have magic, but no one actually knew whether that was true seeing as how no one actually saw the Alainsith any longer—other than the king, and he wasn't saying anything.

Peering around the hedges, Finn searched for what would suggest they had to move. He hadn't seen anything. Archers patrolled the walls, and he didn't have any idea if they patrolled the grounds as well. Were he the one in charge of the security here, he would have suggested it. It didn't take much to get over the wall and reach the grounds.

A shadow moved toward him from near the wall.

Finn stared. It was too small to be an Archer.

And too fast.

A dog.

Shit.

It began to bark.

Finn looked around him. If the dog continued to bark, it'd draw attention to him.

He should've figured there would be something else out there in the yard, patrolling. It didn't have to be an Archer. An Archer might even have been better. At least there he wouldn't have to worry about it racing toward him the way this dog did, howling…

Finn lowered his shoulders and braced for the dog to come crashing into him.

It jumped.

Someone moved toward him.

Rock grabbed the dog around its legs and spun it, slamming it to the ground. The dog whimpered. Rock clamped his hand around the dog's jaw, holding it in place for a moment.

"Just relax," he whispered.

"What are you doing here?" Finn asked.

"Heard the noise. Wolf told me that if I heard anything, I was supposed to find a way in."

"You heard it from out there?"

How loud had the damn dog been?

"Lucky I did," Rock said.

"How are we supposed to incapacitate a dog?" Finn asked.

Rock looked down at the dog. "I've got a pretty good idea."

"The plan was to get in and out without anyone knowing we were here. You kill the dog, and they're going to know we were here."

"Fine. Not killing the dog."

It still whimpered, and considering the way it had been howling only a moment before, the whimper seemed like a good change, though it was still too noisy.

This was what he was supposed to scout for.

Finn should have anticipated a dog.

Gods—Oscar should have anticipated one. What were we thinking?

Rock pressed his hand more tightly around the dog's snout. Thankfully, it didn't struggle. Finn didn't know what he'd do if the dog struggled against Rock.

Another shadow moved across the grounds. This one was back the way they'd come, closer to the wall.

An Archer.

Likely they'd heard the commotion and had come to investigate.

"We've got to move," Finn said.

Rock grunted softly. He leaned close to the dog. "Sorry about this." He slammed its head on the ground, harder than Finn thought necessary but hopefully only knocking the dog out.

The dog twitched but didn't move. It didn't howl anymore, either.

Rock nudged him. "Get moving."

"I think you killed it."

"Nah. Just stunned. We'll share a drink about him later."

Finn crept forward, moving closer to the hedge. From there, he could peer out and found an Archer making his way toward them.

He was a shorter man, though solid. Sort of like Rock in that way. A sword strapped at his side suggested he wasn't concerned about the dog howling. Yet.

The moment he came across the dog, he was going to raise the alarm.

Finn spun, raced over to the dog, and dragged him back toward the hedge, hiding him beneath it.

Rock looked over and opened his mouth as if he were going to say something, but Finn silenced him by raising a finger to his lips.

The Archer moved past.

They stayed where they were until Finn was sure he was gone.

"You should get back to the other side of the wall. The

King wanted you to watch to make sure nothing happened on that side. I don't want him pissed that you came over."

"I didn't want anything to happen to you. That's why I came."

Finn thought he would have managed something as simple as a dog, but Rock had moved *fast*. He didn't know if he would have been able to grab the dog the same way, and he doubted he would have the stomach to slam it to the ground that way. Stealing was one thing. Hurting someone—or in this case, something—was another problem.

"Stay here. I'm going to get closer."

"Don't do anything I wouldn't do," Rock said.

"Is there anything you wouldn't do?"

"Probably not." Rock grinned.

Finn snuck forward.

The Archer had disappeared, but that didn't mean he was gone. Finn didn't know if the Archer would return— or if there would be others.

For now, the garden was empty.

He hurried along, looking for another place to hide and watch.

Finn looked up the viscount's manor. It was a massive two-story stone building, probably two hundred feet long, with enormous glass windows facing the gardens. No lights were on in the home, and there was no sign that anything was amiss. He didn't even see a door ajar or anything to suggest that the crew was just inside.

Creeping forward, he paused by a small tree.

From there, he looked around, searching for any movement.

A soft whistle behind him caught his attention, and he spun.

Rock looked toward him, watching.

He grinned again.

Whistling like that was only bound to get them pinched. Worse, if any of them inside heard the whistling, they might think they'd been detected and come back out. Finn waved his hands at him, but Rock only grinned wider.

Finn moved away.

Another low row of hedges ran along a small path in front of the manor. The house was enormous, and the path up to the front entrance widened. Finn stayed close to the hedges, keeping as low as possible. The darks should mask him.

A light in the house came on.

One of the upper windows, but that was unexpected, especially at this time of the night. There shouldn't be anyone up yet.

Had the howling dog alerted someone?

He whistled softly, with a slight rise at the end. Once. Twice. A third time.

A warning.

Looking behind him, he found Rock frowning.

Finn motioned toward the light in the window. Rock stared at him, mouth open, as if he couldn't imagine what Finn was trying to get at.

Whistling again, he tried to alert them inside.

Someone should be inside and ready for the alert.

He expected a door to open. A window. Something.

There was nothing.

Finn whistled again.

Still nothing.

The light moved inside.

Now he saw it in a nearby window.

How much time did we have before the lantern shifted even more?

Looking back at Rock, the large man still hadn't moved. It was almost as if he didn't see the trouble with the lantern shifting locations within the house at this hour. Finn would have to get to the others and hope Rock didn't run into trouble.

Finn headed toward the house.

When he reached the door, he tested the lock and found it open. Pushing the door open, he whistled three times.

Everything seemed to stop. The energy in the air faded. A stillness hung over everything. He lingered there a moment, holding on to the door, waiting for someone to appear.

Finn whistled again.

The lantern would be moving. In his mind, he could envision it shifting from one room to the next, heading toward stairs—and then down.

They'd get caught.

Getting caught there at the viscount's manor would mean certain punishment. Probably a flogging. Maybe exile. It was doubtful it would be anything less than that.

A dark form moved toward the door.

Finn froze.

"Get moving, Shuffles," the King hissed as he hurried past him.

"Where's the Hand? Wolf?"

"Get moving! Need to get out of here."

The King raced past, clutching something in hand.

Finn couldn't tell what he had, only that he held it up against his body. The King ran straight across the yard. Thankfully, Rock was there.

He whistled again.

The others had to be warned. They didn't deserve to get caught there.

Suddenly, Wolf burst past him.

That left only Oscar.

Finn should go. Do the smart thing as the King said. Stay with the crew and pass his testing. He'd be in then.

Where was Oscar?

He waited for another moment. Two. Still no Oscar.

Finn ran inside.

The home was dark. It made navigating difficult. He couldn't see anything, though the smell of cut flowers seemed to lead him. A thick rug running the length of the hall provided cushion under his feet. Portraits hung on the wall, though Finn couldn't make anything out in the darkness.

Finn remembered the map the King had given them. He'd studied it, even though he hadn't anticipated coming into the home. There wouldn't have been any reason for him to have come into the home—he was the scout only. He *did* have to know which rooms to watch, though.

Racing along the hall, he glanced into each of the rooms.

One was an enormous sitting room. A table. A pair of chairs. A hearth. Shelves shadowed against the night.

The next looked to be similar.

How many sitting rooms did the viscount need?

By the time he reached the third room, his heart racing, he worried that he'd been here too long already. The person with the lantern would have to be coming down the stairs by now. He could imagine them finding their way toward him. He'd whistled for the crew, after all. That would draw attention.

The next room was smaller.

A body lay unmoving on the ground.

Dressed in darks.

Oscar?

He ran into the room and rolled him over.

He moaned softly.

At least he lived.

What had happened there?

Finn pulled on him. "You've got to get up!"

Oscar didn't move. Only moaned.

"Come on, dammit!"

He stirred.

The sound of footsteps came along the hall near him. Muted.

The carpet helped with that.

Finn looked around. They'd either have to find a place

to hide or find another way to escape. Within this room, he wasn't sure where they could go to hide. It was a plain room. A small table with three chairs surrounding it. A checkered game board rested on the table. A wall with a painting hung behind him. That was it.

The footsteps sounded closer.

Finn looked back. A faint light surrounded the door.

Gods!

Wolf and the King should have dragged him out with them—unless they hadn't known Oscar had been out. Someone else might be in the home.

He looked over to the window.

That might be his only bet.

He dragged Oscar toward the window. The Hand was heavier than he looked. With his lithe frame, Finn wouldn't have expected him to be this heavy.

When he reached the window, he pushed to open it.

The light seemed closer.

That can't be good.

The footsteps that he'd heard had fallen silent as well.

He shoved on the window. It squealed.

Everything within him tensed.

Finn acted as quickly as he could. He forced the window up a little higher, then grabbed for Oscar, dragging him toward the window. When he got him resting on the bottom part of the frame, he moaned again.

"You could help, you shit," he wheezed, heaving against him. He continued to push on Oscar, throwing his shoulder into his backside to shove him up and over the window.

Finally, he started to slide out the window.

It wasn't a long drop, but long enough. Maybe it would wake him up, even. When he'd been watching outside, he had seen a row of hedges along the manor, so hopefully Oscar would end up in the hedges. The King might even see him, if Finn were lucky, though he probably had bolted from the yard, not wanting to get pinched.

Finn would have to be the one to drag him out.

He threw his leg toward the window, starting the climb, when the door flung open and bright light glowed from the other side.

Everything within him went still.

Panic set in.

Finn ducked under the window but saw Oscar lying there. He still hadn't moved.

Were Finn to jump, he'd end up next to Oscar, but they'd still have to escape the yard.

There wouldn't be time for that.

Oscar had prior convictions. His punishment would be harsh. Flogging and exile, most likely.

Finn had only been sentenced to a chain gang once and had been flogged with two blows one other time, though it had been excruciating.

But he didn't have Oscar's past.

The solution was simple. *Protect the crew.* He had to take the blame.

Finn pulled his leg back in the window and turned.

The viscount stood before him.

Finn had seen him during festivals and recognized him immediately. His gray hair was neatly groomed despite the late hour, and with his maroon robe, it gave off the impression that he'd been waiting for them. Anger contorted his thin face.

"Take him," the viscount said.

Finn's shoulders sagged. There was no getting out of this.

With that, two Archers rushed into the room.

When they grabbed him, Finn barely had a chance to react. He looked behind him, down toward the hedge, and thought Oscar had gotten away, but couldn't be sure.

They pinned his arms to his sides and marched him away.

CHAPTER SIX

A rat scurried across the floor before disappearing into the shadows. Finn thought he'd seen the rat earlier but didn't know if it was the same one or different. No one other than the rat had been in to see him since he'd first been brought to the prison. The Archers had dragged him in—he hadn't fought, knowing it would have been worse if he had—and then left him.

The room was barely a few paces in either direction. Small enough that he couldn't even stretch out to lie down, not that he wanted to do that. He didn't have any idea what he'd lie in were he to do so. Better to stand.

Finn tried to cover his nose to ignore the stench, but it seemed to infiltrate everything around him. It was foul. Rot. Piss. Shit. The stench of death. Even cut flowers from the viscount's garden wouldn't be enough to cover that stink.

This wasn't where he'd expected to be brought.

When he'd been sentenced to the chain gang, they'd thrown him into the Volthan prison. The cells were small, but they were mostly clean. The guards in the prison weren't bad men, either. Most lived in the Olin section, and he'd even seen a few of them in the Wenderwolf. Finn didn't have any idea which prison they'd brought him to, and so far, he hadn't seen any sign of the guards who ran it.

At least he'd have a story for the crew when he got out. He and Rock could drink about it when he saw him next.

He didn't know how he might be sentenced. He had some history, though not as much as anyone else on the crew. Maybe it was best he'd been grabbed. Better than Oscar, anyway.

Hopefully, the Hand had gotten away. Finn hadn't seen any sign of anyone else when he'd been dragged through the streets, so he didn't know if they'd found him. He'd tried to stay in front of the window long enough that they wouldn't see Oscar on the ground outside the window, but if he were hurt badly enough, it might not have mattered.

Something had gone sideways with the job. Like the one they'd pulled when Finn had *almost* gotten pinched. And like Pegg.

Bad luck, or was it something more?

Finn looked around the inside of the cell again. Walls of stone on all sides surrounded him. Iron bars blocked him from escaping. There was no window. The only light came from a lantern along the end of the hall, though he couldn't see it.

He stayed near the back of the cell, his arms wrapped around himself while he tried to think through what he'd experienced. They'd started the job around four bells. If it hadn't taken longer than an hour, that meant it was barely five bells now. It would take several hours for the rest of the city to come around, and then the magister would summon him to sentence him.

Still hours before he was given his fate. Longer after that to know when he could get out.

It might be a few days there.

The rat scurried outside of his cell, pausing and peering into the cell at him. Finn held his hand out, wiggling a finger at the rat before it scurried off. He grunted to himself.

Crouching along the wall, he tucked his heels back, resting as carefully as he could so that he stayed off the floor. Finn closed his eyes, drifting.

He was tired. Having been up for most of the night, all he wanted was the opportunity to sleep, but he didn't know if he'd be able to sleep in this place or in this position. The only thing that he could do was try to let his mind wander.

And it did.

His mind went back to a different time, back when his father had still been with them, working as a cartwright, when they'd been a family, before his mother had gotten sick. It seemed as if it were so long ago, though it really wasn't. Dreams came to him, drifting through his mind before fading again, until one stuck with him longer than the others.

A tall, thin man leaned toward his father. They spoke quietly, and from where Finn stood on the street, he wasn't able to make out much of their conversation, though the smile on his father's face told him all he needed. This was someone he knew—and knew well. Not that Finn needed that smile to recognize Oscar. His father's oldest friend had been around the house a few times, though not as often of late, ever since Finn's mother started getting sick.

The two men started off through the street, and they moved quickly. Oscar had a way of moving that struck Finn as more graceful than his father. They headed out of this section, over a narrow bridge, and toward the center of the city.

At one point, the city opened up briefly. There weren't many places from within the city where the palace could be seen. Not like it could from outside of the city. The narrow buildings on either side of the street blocked it from sight, but there in the small square on the far side of the river, Finn saw the majestic palace towering high into the sky. It had to be nearly six hundred feet long, and much taller than even the nearby Elia Tower—and that was supposed to strain toward the god of the sky.

A patchwork of steep roofs surrounded the castle where it rose on the hillside, hundreds of houses and shops crowding around the palace, though never able to get much closer than where they were. A wide street surrounded the palace, one Finn rarely had the opportunity to visit. His parents preferred that he stay away from the palace, a warning to avoid his betters. Spires from the main churches twisted into the sky, one for each of the gods celebrated within Verendal. In addition to the Elia Tower, there was that of the Loren—an enormous structure with three separate spires that framed a central tower. He could almost imagine the bells tolling within those spires, a steady ringing during the Festival of Summer. As the god of harvest, Loren had an honored place within the city. Not far from that was the tower for Ihalth, one that wasn't nearly as majestic as some, a stout circular structure without any obvious windows, and whose bells rang with an almost angry tone.

His father and Oscar moved away from the square, heading along the street. He fingered a piece of paper in hand, though it looked small, almost like a card. They passed shops with hawkers outside, calling out to the crowd mingling along the street. An armored Archer patrolled, and his father and Oscar veered away from him before entering a nearby building, leaving Finn's father on the far side of the street, watching.

He noticed the slight tension in his father's face and in the way he stood. He barely nodded to the people passing, ignoring them as they moved along the street, staring instead at the building Oscar had entered. Every so often, he fingered the paper he held.

The crowd jostled him, sending him staggering forward.

The movement put him out into the open, and with as alert as his father was, he glanced over, his eyes widening slightly when he saw Finn before shaking his head.

A warning.

Somebody else bumped into him.

Finn turned, and he looked up at a palace Archer. The Archer shoved him off to the side.

He watched as the Archer approached his father. His father whistled once, then a second time. Finally, his father turned away, heading down the street, moving as if he had always been heading in that direction.

After watching for a while, the crowd swallowing his father once more, he turned back. When he got to the bridge's far side, he turned toward home, and someone grabbed him on the shoulder.

He spun to see his father watching him. The tension Finn had seen from a distance had faded, and the twinkle in his blue eyes when he looked at Finn had returned. He flashed a wide grin.

"What were you doing over there?" his father asked. "It's not always safe to head beyond the river."

"What were you and Oscar doing over there?"

"We were just looking for some supplies." His father looked all around him, his gaze darting from side to side before settling again on Finn. "If you see me with Oscar, I don't want you to follow me. You understand?"

His father started away, and Finn hurried up to him. "Why was there a palace Archer out there?"

"I don't think there was," his father said.

Finn tapped his shoulder. "I saw him. Well, I bumped into him." His father's frowned slightly, and Finn shook his head. "Not on purpose. It was after you saw me. I knew you wanted me to head back."

"He was probably out shopping, much like Oscar and I

were." His father glanced behind him, looking along the street. "If there was a palace Archer, you need to stay clear of them. The palace Archers can be the worst."

He reached his hand into his pocket, fingering something. Probably the paper Finn had seen. Did it have his father's list?

A thudding came from somewhere near him, and Finn jerked awake.

That had been the last time he'd seen his father as a free man. The last time he'd spoken to him without someone else around. Why have that dream now?

The thudding came from down the hall.

He turned toward the sound, trying to understand why he would hear it so loudly now.

Finn got to his feet. His knees ached from how he'd been crouching, but he still hadn't touched the ground. And he wouldn't.

Could I have rested long enough that the magister would have come?

The thudding moved past him.

At first, he thought it was one of the guards, but that wasn't what he saw.

Dressed in dark clothing—though not darks like he still wore—the man who passed down the hall had a dangerous step. He stared straight ahead, marching quickly. Two other guards followed.

They stopped not far from him.

Finn didn't move.

A rat raced into his cell before disappearing into the darkness away from him, as if leaving Finn to his fate.

Every so often, he would hear the scurrying sounds of a rat moving throughout the prison, but rarely did they come close enough for him to see.

Within the small cell, any step toward the front would bring him close to the guards. At least standing where he was, he remained out of reach. A door opened with a squeal of metal on metal. Someone shouted though it was quickly muted.

The guards started back along the hall, passing his cell and dragging a thin, bearded man with them. His face was gaunt, and his eyes had a hollow expression in them. The first man he'd seen followed. When he passed Finn's cell, he glanced in his direction briefly. A darkness passed over the man's face as he looked at Finn, but then he continued down the hall and away.

Finn waited until he was gone to make his way to the front of his cell. He grabbed the bars. Something was unsettling about that man.

"Don't let the Lion catch you looking in his direction."

Finn noticed a face poking from between the bars across from him. The cells were staggered so that he couldn't look directly across and see one on the other side. It wasn't until he came to the front of the cell that he could see anything. The man looking at him had a wider face, chubby cheeks, and his forehead was creased and smeared with dirt.

"Who?"

The man grunted. "The Lion, that's who." He nodded toward the end of the hall. A door closed loudly. "Trust me. You don't want the Lion to catch you looking in his direction when he roars."

"Who is he?"

The man across from him started to laugh, a wild sound that was more a cackle than anything else. "You don't know the Lion?"

"No."

"You will. If you're down here, then you will."

"Where is here?"

The man shoved his face into the bars of the cell, squishing his face up so that he could look through the cell and look over at Finn. "You're in Declan Prison." He laughed again, this time even more crazed-sounding than before.

Finn took a step back. He knew the prison. Anyone who operated within Verendal knew the prison. Only the worst of the worst were kept there.

Finn hadn't done anything to deserve that.

Other than breaking into the viscount's residence.

"Just be ready when the iron masters come through again. They don't pay them well, so they like to take it out on us here. Not that the Lion cares all that much. So long as we're pretty when they bring us out, none of that matters."

He laughed again, his wild and crazed cackle unsettling Finn.

He backed up to the far wall so that he wouldn't see the other man.

If he was in Declan, then he might be there for a while.

Even his father hadn't been brought to Declan Prison.

He leaned against the wall, time stretching out.

How was it that time seemed to pass so slowly when I wanted it to pass quickly, but the reverse was never true?

Sounds in the prison drew his attention, startling him. Every so often, the man across from him tried to engage him in conversation, and when Finn considered answering him, his wild laughter punctuated each question, changing Finn's mind.

After a while, he lost track of time.

The door at the end of the prison opened at one point, and a pair of guards came down the hall. Iron masters. That was what the crazed man had called them. They stopped in front of his door, heavy keys jingling, and they pulled the door open, shoving a tray in and spilling some of the broth they brought him onto the floor.

The door closed quickly, and the keys jangled again as they locked him back into place.

Did they really need two guards to bring food to me?

Perhaps in Declan they did.

In all of the other places Finn had been, admittedly only two, a single guard had been responsible for the prisoners. Of course, the prisoners were typically like him. Petty criminals, nothing more.

Not in Declan.

The prisoners in Declan were dangerous. Depraved. Murderers. Rapists. The kind of criminals that faced much more severe punishment.

Is that what I face?

As the time stretched on, he found himself dozing, drifting off while leaning against the back of the cell, still not bothering to sit, not wanting to touch the ground. The stench still bothered him, though he noticed it less than he had before.

Finn worried about what that meant for him.

The door opened again at the far end of the row of cells, and he stirred to further alertness and looked down the length of the hall. He expected another pair of iron masters, but what he saw was the dark and the stern face of the Lion.

Finn stiffened, leaning back against the wall.

The man they had dragged out of there before had not returned.

When the Lion stopped in front of Finn's cell, he nodded to the two guards. "Bring him to the chapel."

Across from him, the crazed man started to laugh.

The guards pulled the door open and stepped into the cell.

Finn was too startled to do anything.

When they grabbed him, they dragged him forward. Out in the hall, the crazed man pressed his hand through the bars of the cell.

"Be careful what you pray for in the chapel," he said, cackling again.

One of the guards swatted at the crazed man's arm, and there was a sickening *crack*.

The crazed man continued to cackle, though a shriek of pain mixed with it.

"Stop crying," one of the other guards said, looking at the man with his face through the bars. "You just got a few weeks of reprieve."

The Lion moved down the hall, ahead of them.

The guards dragged Finn, and he wondered where they were taking him, but if it was to a chapel, they would be disappointed to learn that he wasn't much for prayer.

If it got him out of the cell for a little while, then perhaps pretending to pray would be worthwhile. He didn't fight as they dragged him along the hallway, upstairs, and down another hall. Finally, they stopped in front of an open door.

Inside, a single chair occupied the center of the room.

This is the chapel? Which god do they celebrate here?

In Declan, Finn didn't know if there was a specific god they would celebrate. Perhaps all of them. Maybe the chair was there so that if he had a particular god he followed, he would be able to pray to any of them—or all of them.

The iron masters dragged him to the chair, setting him down, and then one of them grabbed for leather straps and began to bind his arms and legs to the chair.

"What are those for?"

One of the guards struck him across the face, a blow that stung. Finn winced, trying to reach up to his face, but the bindings prevented him from doing anything.

The guards pinned his arms down more forcefully.

When they were done, they stepped away.

"That will be all," the deep voice of the Lion said from the other side of the room.

The guards nodded, heading out.

Finn looked around. The room was larger than his cell by quite a bit. A stained glass window with a picture depicting the god Heleth looking down on him, her golden hair letting in a faint amount of moonlight.

Could it still be the same night as when I'd been brought here?

The Lion stood with his back to Finn, looking down at a table. Finn could make out nothing on the table, but he heard the sound of metal shuffled across a wooden surface. The rest of the room appeared empty. The stone walls were smooth, with thick mortar lines, a curved ceiling overhead creating shadows high above him. He caught a glimpse of symbols on the ceiling but nothing else.

Finally, the Lion turned back toward him.

"Do you know why you're here?" The Lion watched him, an unreadable expression on his bearded face. His dark eyes seemed to swallow Finn, shadows seeming to hang within his eyes as well.

"I really don't."

Anything he said was considered an admission of guilt. That was one thing Oscar had drilled into his head. *Don't acknowledge what you did or where you were.* The Archers would serve as witness, but there was only so much they could have seen.

As far as the Archers knew, the only thing Finn had done was break into the viscount's manor. Anything else they would have on him would have to come from him. It would have to come from an admission of guilt.

Finn refused to admit anything. He'd protect the crew.

The Lion watched him. "You broke into the viscount's home."

"The door was open. I didn't break into anything."

The Lion tipped his head slightly to the side. "That's the angle you want to take?"

"That's the truth," he said.

"Who else was with you?"

That was what this was about. They needed to know the crew.

He had no idea if the King had been successful in grabbing what they'd been hired to take. If he had, then it would make the questioning mean more. They would want to know where to go to find whatever they had taken. Thankfully, at least in this case, Finn had no idea what they'd taken.

"There was no one else with me."

"How could there be no one else with you if the door was open?"

"The viscount must not have locked his door."

The Lion watched him. "Others were observed in the yard. Others were observed in the home. You will tell me their names."

"There was no one else with me."

"This will go much better for you if you acknowledge who you were with."

Finn started to laugh, but the hard look on the Lion's face made the laughter die in his throat. "What will go better?"

The Lion stared at him. "I would encourage you to think about your actions. Think about what you want out of your remaining time. Think about the way the gods will look upon you."

He watched Finn for a moment before leaving him.

When the door closed behind the Lion, Finn sat strapped in the chair, looking at the table that the Lion had blocked with his body. He caught a glimpse of metal implements lying on the table, one with what looked like a razor, several metal spikes, and a strange circular item that he couldn't quite place.

The metal items he'd heard scraping on the table made more sense.

Torture tools.

CHAPTER SEVEN

F inn screamed.

He couldn't help it. The pain in his legs was excruciating. He could do nothing more than focus on the pain, trying to ignore the way the Lion tightened the screws into his shins. Each time he twisted, more pain shot up and down his legs, to the point where he wanted to cry out the answers the Lion wanted from him.

That, of course, was the entire point.

Tears streamed down his face, and with his hands bound by the leather straps, Finn couldn't even wipe them away. It amazed him that he could still have such tears with as much as he'd cried throughout the torment and with as little as he had eaten over the last few days.

The Lion straightened and stood across from Finn. "There were others seen with you. We should go back to the beginning. You entered the viscount's garden with several others. I need their names."

Finn swallowed, forcing down the bile threatening to rise up within his stomach. He needed to be strong. "I was alone. I've told you this. It was just me—"

The Lion *tsked*. "A shame that you persist with this line of argument. We have already established that others were observed within the garden along with the home. All I'm asking is for you to confirm what we already know. You won't be violating any honor among your friends in doing so."

The pain surged again.

It was the second day in a row for the Lion to use the screws on his shins.

The first day had been agony, and when he had returned to his cell, the crazed man across from him—now in a sling for a broken arm—had cackled, laughing at the way Finn had limped back. When they had come for him again in the morning—at least, Finn thought that it was the morning given the bright sunlight streaming through the window high overhead, the only sun he had seen in days—the man had laughed again, crying out for him to enjoy the chapel.

He looked up, staring at the curved ceiling overhead, the symbols marked on it. Prayers came to his lips unbidden. It had been a long time since Finn had gone to one of the churches, and even longer since he had believed. Still, there was some comfort in offering those prayers regardless of knowing how little they would do for him.

"Why choose to suffer for them? Do you think they would do it on your behalf?"

Finn shook his head. "I was the only one there."

He would get out of this. He would survive.

"I'm afraid I still don't believe you."

The Lion twisted the screws on Finn's shins again, pain shooting along his legs.

The longer the Lion tormented him, the more Finn wondered how long he would be able to withstand it. He had limits. Everyone had limits. He suspected even the King had limits.

The pain shooting through him began to ease.

The Lion turned back to his table.

The first day Finn had been there, the Lion had worked his way through various implements, describing them in detail to him. Finn had shuddered at the idea of any of them being used upon him, though so far, the Lion had only used the leg screws.

They were painful enough.

Anything else he might use on him would probably be even more painful.

"Perhaps we will transition to water today. Very few need that progression, but you are particularly stubborn."

The Lion flashed a sad smile at him.

He headed out of the room, leaving Finn to sit alone, tears still streaming down his face.

He tested the leather straps on his arms and legs, pulling upon them, but he couldn't get free. They held him too tightly.

The Lion wasn't gone long before he returned again. This time, he carried a pitcher with him. He set it on the table near the torture tools, and he turned back to face Finn. "Most who experience water don't care for it. It can be unsettling. I will ask you again and give you the opportunity to tell me the truth, but if you fail to do so, you will leave me little choice."

"Little choice in what?"

Finn barely got the words out before the Lion stood in front of him again.

"Who else was with you?"

"I told you. I was alone."

Finn grew weary of repeating the same thing over and again.

He was of half a mind to make someone up, but he suspected they would use that to go on a search through the city, and wondered if the torment he might face would be worse if they determined that he misled them.

It was better for him to say nothing. Better to claim that he was alone.

Protect the crew.

"You were not alone."

The Lion headed over to the table, picked up the pitcher, and carried it over to Finn. He grabbed a handful of Finn's hair, pulling forcefully, the pain not nearly as much as what he'd experienced already, and jerked Finn's head back.

He tipped the pitcher over Finn's mouth, pouring warm water in. It ran down his mouth, into his nose, and he coughed, but the Lion continued to pour it slowly over him.

Finn tried to swallow, but he couldn't keep up with the force of the water pouring into his mouth and down his nose. He started coughing, but the Lion continued pouring water steadily.

His lungs started to burn. Excruciating agony filled him.

With each passing moment, he felt his vision starting to cloud, his mind starting to slow, the panic rising in his chest.

He was drowning.

Everything burned.

Just as Finn thought he wasn't going to be able to tolerate anything more, he stopped, releasing Finn's hair and stepping back.

"Most unpleasant, isn't it? I must say that it's not my preferred method of obtaining information, mostly because so very few can tolerate it well enough for me to trust the information I'm given. Those who do…"

"I… was… alone."

He barely got it out between coughs.

His body throbbed, but not nearly as much as the terror that filled him. He would die here.

All he had to do was tell this man what he wanted to know.

Doing so would be a betrayal, though.

Oscar wouldn't have done that. His father wouldn't have done that.

Finn couldn't betray the crew.

The Lion pulled Finn's head back again. He poured water in once more.

Finn had already been coughing when he started, and he wasn't able to react in time, barely able to swallow before water started to pour down his throat and into his lungs. He coughed again, but the water continued to pour into him.

He was drowning.

Panic set in, sending his heart racing. He thrashed, kicking at the bindings around his ankles. His wrists. He jerked, trying to toss his head, but the Lion held firmly to his hair, keeping Finn from moving.

The Lion released his hair and stepped back. "When you're ready to answer, this will be done."

He vomited, only water coming out, and vomited some more until nothing else came from his stomach. The only thing he was left with were his dark thoughts.

That, and the knowledge that the only reason Oscar remained free was because his father didn't betray his friend.

He was terrified. Everything inside of him screamed out, demanding that he tell the Lion whatever he wanted, if only it would get him free.

But if he did, others would suffer.

His friends. Rock. Oscar. The King. Even Wolf.

I will not betray my crew.

Finn coughed, clearing the rest of the water from his lungs.

"I was alone."

"Then we will continue."

Finn rested on the floor of the cell. He could barely move. His shins hurt from where the screws had worked into them, blood pouring down his legs.

He couldn't get up.

He had tried, but he could no longer bear weight on his legs. It had taken the iron masters to drag him back to the cell.

So far, he had held out, saying nothing more about who else had been with him, though Finn started to question whether he would be able to withstand the questioning from the Lion much longer.

Eventually, he feared he would break.

If that happened, who would I give up?

A rat crawled forward, beady eyes looking up at him.

"You can come in," Finn whispered. His voice was hoarse, and he didn't dare say anything too loud. "What are you watching for?"

The rat turned its head, watching him.

"It's all right," Finn said. A chunk of gray fur on the rat's back looked as if it had been pinched off. "What happened to you, Pinch?"

The rat tipped his head forward before scurrying toward him.

It stopped several feet away, looking up.

At least he had a friend in here, even if it were a rat.

"Tears and fears give the gods good cheer! Your weeping fills their hearts with glee. They know your thoughts, your prayers for naught! All waiting for your bended knee."

The crazed man cackled after his song, and Finn

leaned forward, spitting. "Shut up," he said. Pinch raced off as Finn yelled, disappearing into the darkness. A part of Finn regretted yelling and scaring it off.

The man laughed again. "You've gone to the chapel three days in a row. Have your prayers been answered?"

Finn ignored him.

It only seemed to make the man happier. He started to laugh again, banging on the bars of his cell with his uninjured arm.

Finn leaned back against the wall.

How much longer was I going to be able to hold out?

It might not even matter. For all he knew, they had grabbed Oscar.

If they had, then what sort of information had he given up? Would he have revealed anything about what they had done?

Not Oscar. He wouldn't have said anything. He would keep the faith; he would protect the crew. He would say nothing to harm the King.

Finn had to do the same.

He sat in place, pain coursing through him. Every so often, he drifted off to sleep.

After a while, the sound of boots thudded along the stone, stirring him back awake. He had been dreaming, and when he came awake, he couldn't remember all the details of the dream, only that his father had been there.

Was this what it was like for him?

He had been imprisoned for a long time. Years. Finn and his family hadn't been allowed to even see him. He had no idea when his father would be allowed to leave, if at all.

He couldn't imagine his father being tormented like this for years.

He wouldn't survive torment like this for much longer.

He suspected the Lion knew that. It was why he continued to push, tormenting him to get answers. The water hadn't worked, which suggested that he would try something else next.

Would I be able to withstand the next torment? What about the one after that?

Finn had seen the torture tools lined up, and they had been described to him in such detail that he didn't think he could tolerate most of them.

What he'd seen already had been more than what he could tolerate.

"Tears and fears give the gods good cheer! Your weeping fills their hearts with glee. They know your thoughts, your prayers for naught! All waiting for your bended knee," the man said again, laughing as he did.

Finn could only stare.

There wasn't anything more he could do. Nothing more that he could say. The only thing that he could do was to pray that eventually the Lion would grow tired.

It was possible that he never grew tired.

Pinch came crawling forward again, crouching just out of reach.

Finn waved his hand at him, and the rat just watched.

At least he had a friend here.

His crew would find a way to break him out. They would have to.

But no one had rescued my father.

He looked up as the thudding came closer, and a pair of iron masters approached his cell. It couldn't be time for his torment again. He hadn't been there long enough. Typically, the Lion gave him time in between his torments. Time enough to recover, however briefly. Time enough for his mind to begin to wonder what else he might do to him, what worse way he might abuse him.

In some ways, that was worse than anything else.

Finn's mind created plenty of different ways that he could be tormented. All of them worse than the last.

The iron masters stopped in front of his cell, pulling the keys out, jingling them as they unlocked his cell door. They headed in, making their way over to Finn and jerking him to his feet.

"Back to the chapel so soon? Someone really needs to find his faith," the crazed man cried out.

"Quiet, Hector."

The other man cackled again.

They dragged Finn forward. He tried to bear weight on his legs, attempting to walk. It was easier for him to walk than to have them drag him, but he couldn't.

"You don't need to bring me there," Finn said.

Hector cackled. "Now he doesn't want the protection of the gods. Oh, how they will make you suffer!"

One of the iron masters banged on the bars.

Finn jerked his head from side to side, trying to get his arms free. Even if he were to do that, the pain in his legs made it so that he wouldn't be able to go very far.

Hopes of freedom were empty hopes.

They dragged Finn forward. When they reached the door leading up, he heard Hector crying out again.

"Repent! Repent! Lest the gods find—"

Finn never heard what would happen if he didn't repent. The iron masters dragged him up the stairs. When they pulled him past the landing with the chapel, he looked down it, confusion filling him. He looked over to one of the iron masters. He had close-cropped hair, a soft chin, and a scar underneath one ear that reminded him somewhat of Oscar.

"Where are you bringing me?"

"Your trial."

"My trial?" Finn could barely comprehend what they were telling him. His mind struggled to work through everything, though most of that came from just how much he hurt.

They dragged him up another flight of stairs, and Finn stared.

Light poured in from windows along the hallway. It was almost overwhelming after having been down in the dark for as long as he had been. He blinked for a few moments, trying to get his eyes to adjust, but they wouldn't. He couldn't.

The iron masters dragged him along the hallway, taking a left down another hall and then dragging him out into the street.

The sudden change was all too jarring for him. The air smelled cleaner than it had in days. Finn breathed it in, trying to clear his nostrils of the filth that he had inhaled in the time that he'd been in the Declan prison. The iron masters didn't allow him to take the time he wanted, dragging him along with them, forcing him forward.

Finn didn't care.

If he was heading to his trial, then he would finally know his fate.

They dragged him quickly through the streets, and in the distance, he caught sight of the City Hall. *Had they really brought me so far into the city?* They must have, though Finn had a hard time concentrating. Pain, fatigue, and dehydration from everything he'd experienced made it difficult.

As they made their way through the street, several children started to trail after him. They were young, about the same age as he had been when he had followed his father and Oscar, but they made no effort to hide. No attempt to play the game the way that Finn had played with his father. Instead, they taunted him, calling out, yelling toward him.

Finn didn't react.

There was no way for him to react.

At one point, one of the iron masters waved at the boys, trying to send them on their way, but the boys only laughed and continued to follow, though at a little bit greater distance than they had before.

By the time they reached the City Hall, there were a half dozen boys following them.

"What happens here?" Finn mumbled.

"You find out your fate," one of the iron masters said.

He looked around him. This was a part of the city he didn't know well. There were merchants, shops, and homes, but none of them were familiar to him. None of them were places where he or the crew had spent much time. The buildings looked maintained, not like in Brinder or Olin. They were plain, single- or two-story, and had painted wood around a stone frame.

They headed up the steps to the City Hall.

Finn felt a growing trepidation.

As he climbed, a shrill whistle behind him caught his attention.

Three short bursts.

That meant his crew.

They were coming for him. They hadn't abandoned him.

He stiffened, and he tried to look behind him, but the iron masters jerked on him, dragging him away, keeping him from looking backward. They dragged him into the building.

Finn tried to look around, but they stepped too quickly, and he was too tired.

They reached a door along the hallway and pushed it open. A chair inside reminded him of the one in the chapel, and when they set him down, strapping him into the chair, Finn moaned softly, though there was no sign of the Lion, and no sign of any other tormentor, for that matter.

They left him alone for a little while.

He was strapped in place, but as Finn looked around, he saw no sign of any torture tools.

He looked up, staring at the ceiling, and saw nothing similar to what he experienced in the chapel.

Maybe this wasn't a chapel.

A prayer still came to him, the words forming, long ago memorized.

He licked his lips. His mouth was dry.

The door opened, and he looked up, expecting one of the guards.

An Archer entered. They were dressed in maroon and black, the colors striped along the jacket and pants, but there was something strange about it.

"Shuffles," a familiar voice said.

Finn blinked, trying to clear his vision. That sounded like the King, but that couldn't be it. Only, as he looked at the Archer, he realized that it *was* the King.

"How are you here?" he asked.

Hope started to rise in his chest. Maybe he could get out of this somehow. The King was here, and he had connections. Bribed Archers. That had to be how he'd gotten in. The King would have to help Finn find a way free.

"Don't mind that." The King looked around him. "You hurt bad?"

Finn tried to force a smile. "They can't hurt me."

"That's our Shuffles." He came closer. "What have you told them?"

Finn blinked again. "What have I told who?"

"The guards." The King stared at him for a moment. "I don't know how much time I have. I just need to know what you've told them."

Finn shook his head. "Nothing. I told them that I was alone."

The King stared at him for a long moment. "That's it?"

"That's all. I didn't say anything about the crew. I don't know why the job went sideways like the one before it almost did." He'd thought about it when he'd first been imprisoned, but the pain following his torment made it hard for him to think about much else lately. The King had come here for a reason. "Why are you worried?"

"Rock was almost pinched on another job. Escaped, but now we got the damn Archers looking for him."

"Not Rock," Finn muttered. He didn't want his friend to suffer the way he had. "I didn't tell them anything."

"You sure?" the King asked. "Damn, Shuffles, but it looks like they've been torturing you. Any man would slip with that."

Finn tried to lick his lips, but his mouth was too dry. "No slip. I said I was the only one." He looked around the room. "The Lion tortured me, but I didn't break."

He'd nearly broken, though. He'd fought as much as he could, resisting the pain. The agony of the torture. The way the Lion had twisted the screws into his shins to the point where he couldn't even walk. All for the crew. For *his* crew.

"The Lion? You were at Declan."

"You didn't know?"

The King shook his head. "We couldn't find where they brought you. I used my resources to find you but couldn't uncover what they had done with you. Didn't think they would have brought you to Declan."

Finn nodded, pulling on the leather straps on his arms. They hurt.

At least the crew had been looking for him. While sitting in his cell, he had begun to think that they had decided to leave him.

"Listen—I don't know what happened to Oscar, but—"

The King's mouth tightened when Finn used Oscar's name. "The Hand got out. Says he was hit by someone in the home. That fucking job. Still don't know how the Hand got out."

"I pushed him out the window. That's when they got me. Had I followed him out, they would have caught one of us." Or both. Finn didn't know.

"Why'd you do it? Hand said you sacrificed yourself for him."

"I don't have the same priors he does."

"You think you're going to get an easier sentence than the Hand?" The King turned away briefly. "Not where we were." He said it quietly and under his breath.

"Can you let me out of here? I don't know what they're going to do to me, but since they think it was only me, it can't be good. It'd be better if I—"

"Stay to find out the sentence. Then we'll get you out," the King said.

Finn pulled on the leathers. "You could spring me. They wouldn't know it was you."

"We've got to know what they intend. You understand, Shuffles. Can't let it get back to the crew."

The glimmer of hope he had allowed himself to feel started to fade. He swallowed back the lump that rose in his chest.

Finn understood. That was the reason his father

remained imprisoned. His crew hadn't sprung him, either. Not that he expected the King to spring him. All he wanted was for him to release the leathers. Finn would make his way out on his own. With his legs hurting the way they did, he might not make it that far. He'd try, though.

"Do you know what they're thinking for punishment?"

"Don't have much of an idea. Declan, though…"

Finn noticed the steady sound of boots outside the door.

"I've got to go. Keep your mouth shut about the crew. We'll come for you soon," the King asked.

Finn nodded.

With that, the King slipped out into the hall. Murmured voices drifted through the door, though Finn wasn't able to make anything out. When they fell silent, the door opened, and the two iron masters entered. They loosened the straps from his arms and legs and lifted him.

"Where now?"

"Sentencing," one said.

They dragged Finn down the hall, stopping when they reached a pair of double doors. MAY THE GODS GRANT THE WISDOM OF THEIR JUSTICE was scrawled along the upper edge of the doors. Carvings of the seven gods were worked into the wood. Finn barely had time to look at them and think of a prayer, not that he expected any prayer he might come up with to be answered.

One of the iron masters pulled the door open. They didn't give him the chance to register anything on the other side, though the long table at one end of the room caught his attention. Six people sat at the table, though there should be seven—with the magister in the middle. Finn had seen him before but never quite like this, and not with jurors on either side of him. The magister was appointed by the king, an expert in the law, but the jurors were elected by the sections, supposedly to represent the city. Though there were now more than six sections in the city, the number of jurors had not changed. Finn doubted any of them represented his section.

One of the jurors looked familiar, and it took a moment before Finn realized why. He'd seen the man. Not only that, but he'd seen him talking to the King. He was the heavyset man Finn had spotted in the night before they had taken the job.

Could he be the Client?

If it was, that would explain why the King wasn't concerned about Finn.

A solitary chair sat opposite the table. The iron masters dragged him to the chair and left him. At least they didn't strap him down the way they had before.

He was free. As free as he could be in this place.

If his legs worked, he might even consider running.

The magister looked up from a stack of papers on the table before him. Short dark hair grayed around his temples, and his pudgy face made Finn think he never got up from the table. Thick glasses were tilted on his nose, and pale blue eyes looked down on Finn. Full lips pressed in a tight frown.

Finn quickly looked at the other jurors, surprised to find two women. Both were older—both with dark graying hair. One had severe features, including a sharp nose and thin lips. She eyed him with suspicion the moment he sat. There would be no sympathy from her. The other had a round face, rosy cheeks as if she'd just come in out of the cold, and dabbed at her nose with a cloth. The men were dressed formally, all in dark colors. One had glasses like the magister, though not quite as thick. All appeared older.

The door opened behind him, and the magister looked up. "You're late."

The last juror swept into the room dressed differently from the others. He had a crimson cloak he pulled off, revealing a matching jacket and pants. Blond hair hung down to his shoulders, and he had bright blue eyes. He was nothing like the other jurors and could be no more than a decade older than Finn.

"I was waylaid. You could have started without me," the man said, taking his place in the empty chair next to the magister.

"We couldn't, and you know it, Bellut."

"I'm here now. You can begin." He looked up and over to Finn, his eyes locking onto him. "Have you started with the allegations?"

"The allegations against this one are straightforward."

Finn looked over, realizing the Lion was there. He hadn't seen him before as he'd been standing in the shadows, but he stepped forward and toward the jurors.

"Finn Jagger. Professional thief. Known accomplice of the man known as the Hand."

Finn swallowed. They knew more about him than he'd realized.

"Was found on the night of Janral the fourth, breaking into the royal home of the viscount. Apprehended at the scene."

"With little fight, I must add."

Finn looked over to the other person. An older man stood behind a post, making it difficult for him to make him out. His voice was firm. Almost hard.

The magister nodded, as if this man's comment mattered. Finn hoped that his not fighting would make a difference.

"Yes. Little fight," the Lion said. "During interrogation, he claims to have been working alone, though with his known associates, this seems unlikely. I suspect that in time, I will obtain more information about the nature of these associates, which we can then use to understand the purpose of the attempt on the viscount."

"There was no attempt on the viscount," the other person said.

He stepped forward, and Finn recognized him. The executioner.

He was taller than Finn would've expected and solid, still muscular despite his graying hair at the wrinkles around his eyes. There was a hardness to him.

"As you are well aware, I am traditionally tasked with obtaining confessions," the executioner said, pressing his hands to his sides. His gray jacket and pants looked fancier than anything Finn had ever worn.

"For which you have done well on behalf of the city," the magister said. "We only thought—"

"I'm quite aware of what you thought," the executioner said without looking at the other jurors. "For this confession, I would prefer to be the one to procure the information the jury needs."

The Lion looked over. "I am more than capable. When the court sent me—"

"I request one day with the prisoner," the executioner said.

The magister sat up and offered the executioner a placating smile. "I'm afraid we don't have the time you request, Master Meyer. As King Porman will be visiting soon, the viscount would prefer to have this whole ordeal resolved as soon as possible."

Two thoughts came to Finn. One—*the king was coming to Verendal?* That would explain the curfew, at least. The second—that they wanted to resolve this quickly. That could work in his favor. If the executioner questioned him, he suspected he'd break even faster. So far, he hadn't. Maybe this would serve as his lucky break.

"He claims he worked alone," the Lion said. "As that's unlikely, given the circumstances of the attack, I think—"

"If he's working alone, then he should be sentenced alone," Bellut said. "For such a crime, I would think banishment appropriate."

Finn's heart sank. Exile. That meant leaving the city. Everything and everyone he knew. Starting over.

"We need more time to know who else was involved," the Lion said. "We discovered a silver statue in his known residence that had been stolen from a local merchant. More time would allow me to identify what else they have taken. If there are other crimes…"

The statue.

Finn had forgotten about that. Now it would help convict him.

Stupid. Oscar would never have made that mistake.

"I agree with Gerdan," the executioner said, nodding to the Lion. "I will uncover the truth behind this before sentencing."

The magister leaned forward. "The viscount is most determined to see this resolved." He looked at the other jurors. "Given the known crimes and his history, there is but one sentence the viscount would support given the king's pending visit. The law supports it."

Finn had the sense that the jury would do whatever the magister requested. He served the king directly. His stomach sank. He had a sense the magister would *not* let him off lightly—if at all.

"That's not typically—" the executioner started.

The magister raised his hand. "You are a servant of the crown, Master Meyer."

"As are you," the executioner said softly.

"Indeed. We have had far too many attacks like this of late. *Far* too many," the magister added. "The viscount— and the crown—are determined to make examples out of each one until they cease. How do we know he's not working on behalf of the Alainsith? It is therefore my recommendation that Finn Jagger be sentenced to death by hanging."

The words hung in the air a moment. Long enough for them to register with Finn.

"Any opposed?"

Finn prayed someone would oppose. Bellut. The juror the King had been speaking to who might be the Client. Other jurors. The gods knew even the executioner.

None did.

"It is so sentenced," the magister intoned. "In three days, Finn Jagger will die by hanging for the crimes of thievery, breaking into the royal residence, and assaulting the viscount."

Finn felt everything begin to swim around him. His head felt heavy and light at the same time. He barely registered the iron masters grabbing him and dragging him from the room, and barely saw the executioner looking at him, a strange hardness mixed with some other emotion —disappointment?—in his eyes.

All Finn could think of was that he would die.

CHAPTER EIGHT

Finn barely registered anything on the way back to Declan Prison. The streets seemed a blur of people, a mass of activity, but nothing he could keep his mind on. He kept thinking back to the way the magister had rushed through his judgment. They hadn't even allowed him to say anything on his behalf.

The stench in the streets alerted him when they reached Declan.

Finn shook himself from his stupor. He had no choice but to do so.

They were going to hang him.

Three days. The crew wouldn't have time to break him free. It was too complicated of a job in too short of a time.

Unless *he* could find some way to escape.

The pain in his legs meant it would be difficult now, but he couldn't let that stop him. If he did nothing, if he let the iron masters bring him back into the prison, he *would* die.

The prison loomed into view.

A large building of black stone, it occupied one entire block of the city, with the shops across from it seemingly abandoned. *Who would want to shop across from Declan?* The slaughterhouse was nearby, which seemed fitting. The stench from the blood and the death drifted along the streets, though that wasn't the only stench in this section of the city.

Some of it came from him. From the fear leaving him struggling to walk.

He looked up at the iron masters.

They walked him steadily back toward the prison. They weren't even holding on to him that firmly, not the way they had been before.

His legs didn't hurt the way they had before, either.

Finn tested putting weight on them.

He could run, but only if he could figure out *where* to run.

All he needed was to get a little way from the prison. Then he could blend into the streets. It would be difficult in the prison clothing, but he would have to discard it and find something else. He was a thief, after all, and he could do that.

Then where?

Not to the Wenderwolf. That would come later. When the hunt for him died down. The Lion had proven they knew who he associated with, which would put the crew in danger if he went back to them. That meant he would have to stay somewhere else. Maybe even outside the city.

Finn thought he could make it to the forest surrounding the city. From there…

He'd have to go east. The road between Verendal and the next city over, Holaf, was difficult. The king claimed his peace extended throughout these lands, but his peace didn't mean robbers and worse weren't out on the roads, waiting for the first chance to steal. Traveling alone would make him an easy target.

The forest itself wasn't an option. The Alainsith magic meant he couldn't go very far into the trees, but that also meant others couldn't venture in after him.

Maybe I could…

Finn shook.

The crew would protect him the way he'd protected those in it.

He just had to get free.

They neared the prison.

If he was going to do something, it would have to be soon.

He pulled on the nearest iron master. With a sharp jerk, he freed one arm.

The iron master whipped his hand toward him. Finn reacted and dropped to the ground. His leg screamed at him.

He had no choice but to ignore it. Doing anything else was certain death.

The other iron master still held tightly to him.

Finn jerked, trying to get it free, but the guard gripped

him too tightly. Finn jerked again, straining to get his arm free, but he couldn't.

Gods! Help me.

He offered a quick prayer to Volan, begging the thief god for help, not expecting an answer. Finn should have prayed more often.

The iron master reached for his other arm and stumbled.

That was Finn's chance.

He pulled again, yanking his arm as hard as he could.

It came free. He staggered forward.

He could run.

His legs screamed with each step, but he hurried as quickly as he could, trying to get as far along the street as possible. He raced toward the slaughterhouse. It would be a good place to lose the guards. From there, he could hide.

Who would look through the slaughterhouse for me?

Footsteps thudded behind him.

Finn didn't dare look back.

He ran. Each step was an effort. He could feel them gaining on him, and he prayed again to Volan, begging the god for help. If any god were willing to help him, it would be Volan, the patron god of thieves—

This time, Finn stumbled.

His toe caught an irregular cobblestone, and he went flying forward.

He braced himself, holding his hands out in front of him, catching himself and trying to push off and get to his feet.

Finn rolled over.

One of the iron masters flew past him.

He started getting to his feet when the other iron master grabbed him.

He struggled.

There was no point in holding back now. The alternative meant death.

He jerked on the iron master, twisting to try to get free, and found a small bit of space. Kicking, Finn sent the iron master back. He'd been tortured and starved, but panic gave him strength.

He staggered to his feet. Then stumbled forward again.

The pain from the leg screws into his shins made it so that he could barely stand. Running had put too much stress on them.

Fight through it.

He had no choice.

He thought of his crew. His sister. His mother. Even his father.

Finn willed himself forward.

He reached a corner.

Just a little farther. He could almost imagine what it would take for him to round the corner, get beyond the iron masters. Find a crowd and slink into it, never mind that he wore the distinct prison browns.

Finn looked along the street. The iron masters were behind him. He could *feel* them.

Rows of shops greeted him, but there wasn't anyone heading toward the shops. He'd have to break into one of the buildings for him to escape, and even then, he might not be able to get away.

An alley.

He knew these streets. The alleys that ran through them. He knew how to hide.

Finn ran forward…

…and was slammed to the ground from behind.

He looked up.

An Archer stood across from him, his bearded face unreadable. He held one hand on the hilt of his sword, his gaze flicking from Finn to the two iron masters racing to catch up to him.

"Looks like you lost a little rabbit," the Archer said when the iron masters caught up to him.

"We would've caught him. No place for him to go hopping off to and hide. Bastard kicked me!" The iron master grunted as he said it, his breath coming in a soft wheeze.

The Archer brought his boot back, and Finn started to scramble away. He didn't want to get kicked. The Archer looked solid. Strong enough that were he to kick him, Finn was sure that he'd feel it for a few days.

The thought almost made him laugh.

Why would it matter if I felt it for a few days?

At this point, that was all he had left.

He'd rather it not be spent hurting, though.

"No," the other iron master said. "Poor Bastard just got sentenced. Only has a few days."

The Archer lowered his foot. "What's the sentence?"

"Rope. Don't give thieves like him an honorable death."

"I could do it here if you'd like," the Archer said.

"Maybe we put him down like we should be putting down those Alainsith dogs gathering in the forest."

The gleam in his eyes made a different sort of sense. Finn had known men like him before, men who reveled in death and had no qualms killing another. There were plenty of men like that in the work he did, though he made a point of steering clear of as many of them as he could.

"Got to wait for the Gallows Festival," the iron master said. He grabbed Finn, lifting him from the ground and jerking him to follow. They headed along the street. "Don't you get any ideas about running again. They might want you pretty, but I can find ways to hurt you they won't see."

The other guard joined and pinned Finn's arms against his sides, making it so that he couldn't do anything other than follow where they led him.

They reached the prison. The stench wasn't quite as bad on the upper levels as it was on the lower levels, but still awful. He tried not to breathe, and when that didn't work, he tried to breathe through his mouth, but it seemed almost as if he tasted the foulness in the air. That might even be worse.

The guards dragged him back down the stairs. They paused on the landing below, and there was a moment where he thought they might bring him to the chapel, but they descended farther. His heart skipped forward as the darkness swallowed him.

This would be his fate.

This would be all he would know in the remaining days he had.

They reached the doors to his cell. Hector had his face pressed up against the bars of his cell, looking out. A wild expression filled his eyes, and he grinned at Finn.

"Back so soon! The gods didn't free you, which means they have more in store for you. I can only imagine how they'll have you dancing soon—"

"Quiet, Hector," one of the iron masters said.

The other prisoner laughed again and backed into the cell, his cackle wild and crazed and filling the cell.

The iron masters shoved Finn forward into his cell, and he staggered, trying to catch himself, but he couldn't. He fell to the ground.

It didn't matter how foul the ground was. It didn't matter how disgusting the prison was. None of it mattered. Not anymore. All that mattered was that he would spend his remaining days there.

Then he would die.

The iron masters pulled the door closed and locked it. The sound of their boots along the stone thundered through him, a taunt at his captivity. He was trapped.

Finn curled his knees up to his chest.

What else could I do?

He rocked in place, reliving the memory of what had happened to him in the sentencing. The executioner hadn't wanted him to be sentenced yet. Maybe he could beg him to release him, override the sentencing. He had to have some pull with the magister.

It wouldn't work on the Lion. Finn didn't have the

impression the Lion would do anything other than try to torment him to get whatever information he thought he might be able to obtain from Finn.

Pinch crawled forward from the shadows at the edge of his cell, looking out at him.

"I'm glad you're here," he whispered. At least he had one friend here.

He held out his hand, and the rat looked at him for a moment before inching toward him.

"You can come here," he whispered.

The rat crept toward him again. When Finn reached out to try to touch Pinch's head, the rat sunk sharp teeth into his finger.

He jerked his hand back, biting back a cry, and the rat scurried away.

Even his little friend betrayed him.

"The long walk there with nothing to gain. The sigh of children and the cries of lost love. The Poor Bastard counts down all that remains. The gods listen to prayers but ignore from above!" Hector cackled as he finished his singsong poem.

"Shut it," another voice said, this one from farther down the hall.

"The great Charon deigns to speak!" Hector said.

"Is it true?" the other voice along the hall asked. "*Are you a Poor Bastard?*"

When Finn didn't answer, Hector laughed again.

"He don't have to speak for us to know. The gods know! I can feel their excitement grow!"

"Shut it, you crazed fuck!" Charon said. Hector fell

silent for a moment. "What was your crime?"

Finn didn't want to talk. He wanted to sit where he was. Say nothing. Wait for the day when his time would come. When it did, he'd have to decide how he wanted to go out. Would he go willingly, repentant for what he'd done, or would he go out fighting the way that Dalton Pegg had gone out?

Most repented.

Finn hadn't watched too many Gallows Festivals. That time was usually a good time for his kind to be doing other work. Those he'd seen mostly involved men—and a few women—who'd begged the priests for forgiveness. Finn hadn't been a religious person, but he didn't know how he would react when his time came.

"You don't have to talk, but the shit across from you is going to keep ranting if you don't."

Finn shook his head, not opening his eyes. "Breaking into the viscount's home."

Hector laughed again, this time wilder than before.

Charon whistled. "The viscount? That's a daring job."

"It didn't work."

"Didn't work, he says! The gods watched and decided you were wanting. They saw and chose—"

"Shut it!" Charon shouted.

Hector fell silent.

Finn rested his head against the back of the cell, his eyes closed.

"Mine wasn't quite as dumb. Got caught on the northern side of the city. Said I was disturbing the Alainsith marker, as if I could do anything that would move something touched by their magic."

Finn looked up briefly. "What were you doing?"

"Supposed to meet someone. Then I'd take a trip." He shrugged. "They didn't show. I got shoved in here." He laughed bitterly. "To hear them tell it, I'm responsible for upsetting the damn peace with them. I got no magic and no reason to care about the Alainsith."

Finn said nothing, and Charon didn't speak for a while. Every so often, Hector cried out, but none of it was intelligible.

"You really a Poor Bastard?" Charon asked.

Finn inhaled deeply and immediately wished he hadn't. "Yes."

"How they going to do it?"

"Rope."

"When?" Charon asked.

"Three days."

Hector cackled again. "Three days to find the gods. Three days to find your faith. Three days—"

"Shut it!" Charon shouted.

Finn tried to rest but couldn't.

They came for him sooner than he expected. Finn drifted. Dreams of his father had come to him. Even with everything he knew his father had done, he hadn't been sentenced as Finn had, though his father had never broken into royal land.

The pair of iron masters who came for him were different from the ones he'd run from. If Finn thought that might make them more sympathetic, he was wrong. They grabbed him with a firm grip and dragged him to his feet, not even giving him much of a chance to wake up.

"Get moving," they said.

"The Bastard begins his march to the grave! Time to beg and not be brave!" Hector cackled and banged on the bars of his cell.

The iron master on Finn's left only shook his head. "You really are a crazy fuck," he muttered.

They pulled Finn out of the hall, with Hector still cackling. When Finn reached the end of the hall, Charon shouted again. "Shut up!"

It only made Hector laugh even more.

Up the stairs.

They stopped at the next level.

The chapel.

They were going to torment me again? I couldn't have that much time remaining, and this would be how I'd spend it?

They brought him past the room with the chapel.

Finn sighed as they passed and one of the iron masters chuckled. "No more of that," he said. "The gods know you've got to be intact for the procession. Can't have the people think we mistreat our Poor Bastards."

The other guards laughed with him.

They stopped at another stair before guiding Finn up and to another hall. This one was shorter than the last. Four wooden doors with an iron frame around them lined the hall. They brought him to the first and opened it.

"Here's your last room," the first one said.

Finn headed into the cell.

It was larger than the other. The floor looked almost… clean. A narrow cot on one wall had a thin mattress. A basin with a pitcher of water rested on the ground near it.

"Think about what you want for your last meal. Make it worthwhile."

They stepped out of the room, pulling the door closed behind them. Finn stood in the center of the room, looking around. It was probably ten paces in either direction. A narrow window along the top of one wall let in sunlight—actual sunlight.

This was the kind of place the crew could rescue him from.

They would come for him. They had to.

The sound of the iron masters' voices drifted out from the small opening in the door. "Got another thief to hang. Wonder if he'll cry all the way to the Stone like ol' Lether did."

"That Poor Bastard just shaking the whole time. Talking about his little daughter. Like that would change his fate."

Finn had heard the name Lether before. A thief who'd hung a few years back. Other crews used his name as a warning for making a mistake. Not the King, though.

"Think this one will cry?"

"Never know. The way he ran…"

Finn couldn't hear much else and didn't care to listen.

"Wonder who they'll get to replace the Lion," the iron master said.

Finn perked up and headed to the door, stepping up on his toes to listen. The Lion would be replaced? The idea that the Lion would be the one to hang him didn't sit well with him, but what did it really matter who did the deed? Finn could spit in his face, at least. Get one last kick at him for all that he'd done to him.

"Probably someone appointed by the crown again. The headsman didn't care for the last one."

"Got to find his own, then."

"No one wants that job. Gods. You think *we* get pissed on."

The other man grunted. "He was really a poor shit. Gutted and dropped into the river like that?"

"Not so much lion as a cub, was he?"

They both laughed, their voices growing more distant.

The Lion was gone?

It was hard to know how to feel. The Lion had tormented him, hurting him to the point where Finn could scarcely tolerate it any longer, driving him into helplessness and despair. Now he was gone. Maybe that meant no more torture.

Finn looked at the window before climbing onto the cot and trying to peer out of it. He could *just* get the top of his head up to the window, but not much beyond that. From the cot, he could see a little out of the window—a tower. *Which church tower was that?* In this section, it would be the Giver's Tower. Bells at two and eight, a reminder to give freely to the church. It was meant for the gods, but they didn't need the coin the way the church claimed they did. They had to build their towers somehow.

Getting back down, he sat on the edge of the cot.

There wouldn't be much time remaining for him. A day or two.

This wasn't how he imagined his last days, though he hadn't given any thought to his last days. It was easier not to think like that.

A soft knock came at the door, and Finn looked up. When the door opened, a brown-cloaked priest stood across from him, the Book of Heleth clutched in hand.

Iron masters stood outside the door, watching Finn.

What did they think I'd do there? There wasn't anything he *could* do. They'd proven he couldn't run.

"I'm here to ask if you have anything to confess." The priest had a soft voice that went with his delicate features. He looked young, at least younger than Finn. Though he stood stiffly in the doorway, it seemed he shifted from foot to foot nervously.

They sent a new priest to me, not even someone with experience?

Not that it mattered.

"What's there to confess?" he asked.

"You would want to go to meet the gods with a joyous heart. The way to joy is acknowledging your sins and repenting. Heleth the Mother will welcome you back and guide you as you learn to walk with the other gods."

Finn resisted the urge to smile. It wouldn't do for him to argue with a priest in the little time he had left, though the idea that he would care whether he had the opportunity to walk with the gods left something to be desired.

"I don't have anything I can confess," he said.

"Then you've found the gods?"

Finn turned away, looking up at the window. "The gods don't care if I find them. The only thing they care about is punishing me."

"I serve the gods. As should you. I can help you find your first step with Heleth the Mother. From there, I am certain you would be able to find the next steps on your own. By the time you reach that fateful day, you would be well along the path to returning to the gods' embrace."

"Don't bother," he said.

Behind him, the iron masters glared at him.

What did it matter, anyway? He was going to die. Executed for the crime of breaking into the viscount's home. Finn didn't deny that he had done the crime, but could it really be so terrible as to warrant execution?

"I will visit with you again. Perhaps in the morning you will find repentance."

"I doubt it," Finn said.

The priest turned, nodding to the iron masters, and stepped out of the room.

They closed the door behind him and sealed it shut.

If there was a chance he'd find the embrace of the Mother, maybe he *should* take it. He shouldn't risk the possibility he would die missing the opportunity to accept the gods. Finn stepped up on his toes, looking out the small window of the door, but the priest had already disappeared.

The hall was empty.

Finn took a seat on the cot, looking up at the window. He stared, watching the sky, thinking about when he used to look up at the sun as a younger boy, watching it with his father and sister, happier times.

The day passed slowly, but it passed.

The crew didn't come for him.

It was too much to expect.

At one point, he heard a scurrying sound and looked to see if Pinch might have come back, but there was no sign of him.

He would never have a chance to say goodbye to his mother and sister.

He would never have a chance to say goodbye to Oscar and Rock.

He would die alone.

Maybe he had always been alone, anyway.

Finn had felt separated since losing his father, and only when Oscar had brought him into the crew had Finn begun to feel as if he had a purpose. He had begun to belong.

By the time moonlight began to stream into the room, Finn still sat unmoving. At one point, the iron masters had returned, asking what he might want for a last meal. Finn had tried to think about what he might want, thinking he should come up with something exotic, but the only thing he really wanted was the stew his mother had once made. It had been years since she'd made it, a long time since she had been well enough to do so.

When a soft stirring came at the door, Finn barely registered it. He looked over.

"Finn," a hushed voice whispered. "It's Oscar."

Finn stood on his toes, looking out of the door.

Oscar stood on the other side, wearing priest's robes. His eyes were drawn, shadows formed within them. There was something haunted about the expression that he looked out at Finn with. Hope surged in Finn, for only a moment.

"How did you know?"

"I've been watching," Oscar whispered. "Waiting for the right time."

"Are you here to break me out? What about Rock?"

Oscar shook his head. "Rock is fine. I can't get you out. I tried, but I can't." He was quiet a moment. "I needed to see you. When they announced the festival for the following day, I questioned the King. He didn't think it was going to be you, but..."

Finn turned away. "You should get out of here before you're caught. You're a known associate of mine. They made a point of saying that at my sentencing."

"I'm not worried about that."

"You should be. You're the reason... It doesn't matter." He wasn't about to make Oscar feel bad for what happened to him.

"I haven't had the chance to thank you for what you did. You shouldn't have come after me. All this for a damn ceramic bowl. Too many of our jobs have been stupid like that these days."

Another bowl?

That's what we'd gone into the viscount's home for?

"Someone had to," Finn said. He leaned on the door, resting his head. "Drink with Rock when it's over. He's going to be…" Finn realized he didn't know how Rock would be. Angry, probably. "Just do that."

"I will," Oscar whispered.

Finn swallowed. "Does… Does my sister know?"

"I don't think so."

"Tell her that…" Finn didn't know what to have Oscar tell his sister. Lena rarely went to the Gallows Festival. "Tell her I was banished from the city. It will be easier for her. And for my mother. Can you do that for me, Oscar? Let her believe that as long as possible."

It probably wouldn't work forever. Lena would eventually hear rumors.

There was a moment of silence. "I can do that."

"Thank you for taking me in after what happened to my father."

There was another moment of silence. "I'm sorry," Oscar said. Somewhere along the hall, the thudding sound of boots along the stone rang out. "I can't stay here. I'll be there with you when they take you along the Blood Court."

"Don't," Finn said. "None of you should come. You can't get caught."

"You need to see someone who cares."

The sound of boots continued toward him. Oscar went silent, and Finn stood up on his toes, looking out through the small window, but the Hand was gone.

When the iron master reached him, the door opened,

and he brought in a tray of food. His last meal. He set it on the ground. The iron master looked at him, an amused expression on his face. "You could have asked for anything, and this is what you request?"

"It's comfortable," Finn said.

The iron master met his eyes, then nodded. "Enjoy." He turned away, stepping out of the door. "Poor Bastard," he muttered.

The door closed behind him, the sound of the key in the lock sealing him inside.

Finn looked down at the tray. The stew looked nothing like what his mother had made, but it smelled better than what he'd eaten in the last few days.

He lifted it, carrying it over to the cot, and took a seat. As he started eating, he closed his eyes, trying to think back to happier times, trying to think back to when he had been younger, before he had lost his way, dragged into a life that his mother never wanted for him. Even his father hadn't really wanted this life for him. It was the reason Oscar had resisted bringing him along, but Finn had been persistent.

Oscar might blame himself, but really it was Finn's fault.

How could it be anything else?

At one point, he thought he saw a pair of eyes and thought of Pinch.

Finn looked away. He had already betrayed Finn. Finn wasn't about to offer him any of his food in the time he had remaining.

The crew wasn't coming for him. No one was.

He was alone.

And he would die.

When he finished the stew, he leaned back against the cell wall and looked up at the window, staring at the night sky, the faint moonlight streaming in, and he wept.

CHAPTER NINE

The jingle of keys at the door jostled Finn awake. He stirred from where he sat upright on the cot, glancing up at the window, realizing that sunlight now drifted in, shining a shaft of light on the opposite wall.

It was morning.

Morning meant his execution.

Finn looked over. He didn't have the energy to even look up. Not that it would matter. When they came for him, they would take him away, and he would have no choice but to go with them.

The door came open, and a person he hadn't expected to see entered. Finn recognized the executioner from his sentencing. He had a wrinkled face, broad shoulders, and strong hands, and he was dressed in gray leathers.

"This is how it starts?"

"I am here to prepare for your sentencing," the executioner said. He had a deep, almost gravelly voice. He entered the room, closing the door, but didn't bother to lock it again.

Not that it mattered much when it came to the executioner. Finn doubted he would be able to escape. Though he hadn't seen any iron masters, doubtlessly they were out there.

The executioner strode across the room, and he motioned for Finn to sit up.

Begrudgingly, he agreed, sliding to the edge of the cot. If the executioner wanted him to stand, he would have to force him up. Finn wasn't going to do all of it for him.

The executioner traced a finger around his shoulders, working up to his neck and then around. Finn shuddered at the touch; understanding filled him. The executioner wanted to know what length of rope he needed.

The reality of what he faced sank in even more than it had before. His heart started to hammer, and sweat beaded on his brow.

The executioner stepped back from him and crossed his arms over his chest. "Why did you do it?"

"Does it matter?"

"It matters."

Finn sighed. He looked down, staring at his hands. They trembled slightly, and he forced them against his thighs to keep them from shaking. He might die today—well, he *would* die today; there was no *might* about it—but that didn't mean he had to go out shaking and scared. He would have to find strength within him.

"It doesn't matter to you or the others."

"Did Gerdan ask why you did it?"

"He didn't care about why. He wanted to know who else was involved."

"That is our responsibility."

"He didn't *care* why."

The executioner grunted. There was something that reminded Finn of Oscar in the way that he did. "You didn't reveal your crew."

"I was alone," Finn said.

The executioner grunted again. "Alone, but the grounds of the garden showed at least two other sets of prints. Possibly three." He tipped his head to the side, shrugging. "I was curious, so I went to take a look for myself. Sometimes, the captain of the Archers gets a little complacent and overlooks simple details. You had a crew with you. Given what they claim about you, and that you are a known associate of the Hand, I suspect you're in his crew."

"I'm not in his crew," Finn said softly. Not anymore.

"I imagine you were trying to make a name for yourself. Perhaps the Hand forced you to do this so that you could become a full member of the crew."

"I wasn't forced by the Hand to do anything," Finn said.

And he'd already been a part of the crew. Oscar had brought him in, which was the reason Finn had gone after him. He owed him for more than he'd ever admitted to Oscar.

"You did it voluntarily, then." The executioner stopped at the door, resting his hand on it.

"You wouldn't understand."

"I might. And you might find it valuable to share." The

executioner shook his head. "The priest will visit with you soon. You will be given the opportunity to confess one more time. Most men find it comforts them to confess in their final moments. I encourage you to find whatever peace you need and make amends with whatever god you celebrate."

The executioner stepped out of the door, closing and locking it behind him.

Finn sat on the edge of the cot. His heart still hammered, and he wiped the sweat away from his forehead.

It seemed as if time quickened, moving much more rapidly now than it had before. The door opened up again, and the priest was there, the same man Finn had sent away before.

He looked at Finn with a mixture of sorrow and a little bit of pity. He studied him for a moment. "It is time," he said.

Finn took a deep breath and got to his feet.

He was going to be strong for himself. Not for any other reason than that, only so that he wouldn't leave this world in a way that would dishonor him or his family. He had spent too much of his life as a dishonorable, and he had no interest in leaving it that way.

The priest looked over. "Have you decided whether you would be willing to accept Heleth the Mother as she would guide you along the road to redemption?"

"I didn't do anything."

"If that is the way you see it, then you may leave the world, still searching for redemption. Know that the

Mother would offer you her embrace up until the moment of your death. I will be with you each step of the way. Praying."

The priest stepped off to the side, and one of the iron masters entered, handing a bundle of cloth to Finn. He looked down at it for a moment, confusion in his eyes, until he realized the purpose behind it.

The Sinner's Cloth.

The iron master nodded to him, and Finn unfolded it. They were gray, much like the executioner's leathers, and as he slipped them on, they were more loose-fitting than he had expected.

This would be the last clothing he ever wore.

When he was dressed, the priest nodded to the iron master, and they guided him from the cell.

The first step was the hardest.

Every step after that meant he was closer to his death.

In his mind, Finn knew what he would find on the outside of the prison. The festival would be in full swing. People would be collecting near the gate, wanting to get close enough to watch the actual execution. Some would remain as close as possible, usually hegen who wanted to get near enough to the body they could take parts from it for their magic, but not so near that they drew the Archers' attention. At this point, he didn't know if it mattered if they took a part of his soul. That would be gone soon enough anyway.

When they stepped outside of the prison, a chill to the air sent goosebumps along his skin. He cupped his hand over his eyes, the bright sun shining down offering no real warmth. Even if it did, Finn didn't know if he would feel it. He felt numb, as if he were in some sort of magically induced trance, almost as if one of the hegen already had a hold of him.

The iron masters guided him forward to the street outside of the prison where the executioner waited. His gray leather seemed to gleam in the sunlight, giving him a pale glow. The priest started reading from the Book of Heleth, the words blending into the noise all around him.

Even in this part of the city, vendors had set up makeshift stands, and a crowd had begun to form. He smelled sausages, cabbage, bread, even sweet treats, all of which seemed out of place so close to the Declan Prison. None of them had been there when he had attempted his escape, but now the crowds and the shops were busy.

Had they been here when he had broken free from the iron masters, Finn might have escaped.

The executioner studied him. "Finn Jagger. I, Master Henry Meyer, first inquisitor of Verendal, serving at the behest of King Porman Arcald the Righteous, am present to escort you for final sentencing. Have you anything to say before we begin?"

Finn could only shake his head.

"You will be offered one more opportunity to bare your soul before the gods."

A bell tolled nearby, soft and carrying across the city. Others began to join in.

Finn had never paid attention to the sound of the bells during the Gallows Festival before. They filled the city with their song, a mournful sound that rang out all around him. The priest muttering his prayer added to it, combining with the sound of the bells and creating a sense of sadness for him.

This would be how he left the world.

The executioner guided him forward. They hadn't gone very far when three others joined. One was the magister, and he was dressed in his red-and-black finery, holding on to his staff of office, his peaked hat covering his hair. He nodded solemnly to the executioner before moving forward. Two other jurists joined him, one the heavyset older woman and one of the other men. Finn didn't know either of their names. It seemed a shame he would die not knowing the names of those who had sentenced him to death.

When they reached the end of the street, two more jurors joined the procession. The Blood Court continued to progress, growing with each additional juror. Finn regarded the one he'd seen with the King, wondering for a moment if he might be the Client, before shoving the thought away. There would be no salvation from this. Not from the King, anyone he bribed, or the mysterious Client.

The priest murmured a steady prayer behind him. He had reached the part of the Book of Heleth Finn actually remembered. It was a section his mother had favored, and Finn found himself speaking the words along with the priest. The executioner must've heard, as his back straightened.

"The Mother leads us all on our first step, and she welcomes us back with her embrace for the last. The warmth of her touch guides us through the cold of death and leads us to our meeting with the Others."

The priest nodded encouragingly to Finn.

Finn licked his lips, knowing that he needed to continue.

Speaking the words *did* help. It surprised him that it would. He had thought he would not find comfort in the gods in his remaining time, but somehow, there was some reassurance in saying those words. He could almost feel the warmth of the Mother, as if she truly were walking with him.

"The Mother protects those who remain behind. She comforts them, the rain her tears shed on their behalf. The sun and the warmth of her embrace. The fresh blades of grass each spring, her way of reminding those who still live that life persists."

Finn's voice caught at the last.

They turned a corner.

Teller Gate was visible.

Had we really gone so far?

Finn didn't think that he'd been walking that long, but everything had become something of a blur. He no longer paid attention as he had when he'd first come out of the prison, not aware of the crowd lining the street, paying no mind to the vendors, the people shopping as if this truly were a festival rather than a celebration of his death. He had even ignored the occasional vegetable thrown in his direction.

The only things he paid attention to were the pealing

of the bells and the priest speaking the words of the Book of Heleth.

When they reached the gate, a chill washed over Finn's skin. The sun had risen in the sky, and bright shafts of sunlight streamed down but provided him no warmth. The crowd followed, almost a physical presence pushing upon him, guiding him beyond the gate. Finn moved forward with the crowd. He had no choice. He trailed behind the executioner, the jurors and the magister leading the procession, the priest bringing up the rear.

The Blood Court.

A strange thought occurred to him. Were he a more prominent prisoner, the viscount would have been part of the procession. Finn thought that having the viscount a part of it might have been fitting, especially as the viscount was the reason he'd been sentenced to death. He had seen him in his home but had not seen any sign of him since then. The only connection to the crown that he had seen had been the magister and the jurors.

The Raven Stone loomed in the distance, the gallows on top of it a dark shadow.

That would be his final destination.

He made out a blur behind the Stone, the hegen section and the forest beyond, but his heart hammered too fast to focus on either.

The priest's voice rose. He had to do so to be heard above the sound of the crowd behind them. Every so often, there was a shout, someone swearing at him, someone else calling out, and even that of laughter.

It was the laughter that he found the hardest.

At one point, Finn swore that he saw Oscar looking at him from a place within the crowd, but when he turned to try to see him, the Hand was gone.

He had been wrong.

Having Oscar watching him during this final walk might have been better.

As it was, Finn found it harder to take each step.

His legs felt heavy. His heart pounded wildly. His breathing came in short bursts.

Only the words of the Book of Heleth helped.

Maybe he was more religious than he had realized.

Or maybe it was just a matter of him wanting to go to his final meeting with the gods prepared. He didn't want to go having not made any amends.

He found himself chanting along with the priest. The words came easily now.

When they reached the Raven Stone, the jurors parted off to either side, taking up a position in front of it. The magister stood at the center of the raised platform, looking up at the gallows. Bellut stood next to him. Finn hadn't realized before, but he wore a similar maroon-and-black cloak as the magister, though the hat on his head wasn't quite as tall. The crown's symbols were marked on either shoulder, one for the throne and one marking him as serving under the king himself.

Had they waited even a few more days, King Porman would have been there. Finn might have been able to make his plea to the king, a cry for clemency, though he doubted that would have been heard. Even if it had been heard, the fact that Finn had broken into the viscount's home would have been reason enough for the king to have sentenced him no differently than he already had.

The executioner guided Finn up the stairs.

The priest stayed with them, still speaking the words of Heleth behind him, though Finn no longer spoke them along with him.

He had seen several executions during his time in Verendal. They were common enough, though not something that he particularly enjoyed watching. The Raven Stone took up space just outside the city gate, and though he had gone outside of the city with his father many times over the years, Finn had never approached the stone before.

There was something surreal about climbing it.

The steps leading up to it were solidly made, and he realized that a symbol etched on each stone represented one of the gods, as if he were climbing toward them with each step he took toward the Raven Stone. Once he reached the top of the stairs, the platform was made of heavy stones, darkly stained.

Blood, he realized with a hint of revulsion.

Why should I be repulsed by that?

Soon, once the hegen claimed their prizes for their magic, his blood would join the others.

The executioner turned Finn so that he could look out on the crowd. Thousands of people crowded around the Raven Stone, watching.

The priest stood at his side.

"Have you decided to repent?"

Finn found himself looking down at the magister. Anger filled him.

It was unexpected.

"No."

"All you must do is find a way to welcome the Mother into your heart. She will embrace you. You can accept her forgiveness. She will guide you the remainder of your way to the rest of the gods."

Finn turned to the priest. "What, do the gods care when my mother suffers? The gods don't care that my family has been broken. Why should I embrace them when they have never embraced me?"

"If you accept the Mother—"

"The Mother hasn't embraced my family. If she had, my mother would not have been sick. My father wouldn't have been lost. My sister not forced to..." Finn couldn't even get it out. "I might have been able to be something honorable." He said the last softly. Finn looked away and found the executioner watching him. "What? If you're going to wrap the rope around my neck, then do it."

Where were these words coming from?

It surprised Finn that he would react in such a way. He thought that he would have been more accepting of his fate at this point, but how could he accept what they were doing to him? How could he accept what the magister and the jurors, most of them nameless to him, had chosen for him?

He was a criminal. There was no denying that. Only, who had he hurt?

No one. That wasn't the kind of crime Finn ever

participated in. Stealing from those who had more than he had was no crime to the gods. It certainly was no crime that warranted execution.

Only because he had broken into land owned by the king.

He glared out at the magister, at the jurors. "I don't deserve this."

"You have been sentenced for your crimes, Finn Jagger," the magister said.

The other jurors stared at him, and Finn liked to believe that he saw a flicker of a question in their eyes, though he doubted that was real. The only one that stared at him with any sort of empathy was Bellut.

The magister was to blame. All because he wanted to move this along more rapidly. All because the king traveled toward Verendal. All because they wanted to prove the viscount had been working to diminish crime at the edge of the kingdom. All because they feared the Alainsith beyond the forest.

Executing Finn did nothing to make the city safer.

"Do you have any last words?" the magister asked.

"Is this really necessary?" one of the jurors demanded. Not the one Finn had seen with the King, though. "Get on with it, executioner. Do your job."

The executioner came forward. He rested one hand on Finn's shoulder. "Custom demands that the condemned be offered the chance to speak. Would you violate custom?"

"There is far too much that must be done before the king's arrival. Get on with it."

Finn could scarcely believe it.

His execution was an inconvenience to the jurors.

The executioner stared at the magister and the jurors. Finally, he pulled Finn back, toward the gallows. He dragged something down from overhead.

The rope.

He fit it around Finn's head, sliding it down to his neck and adjusting it.

The rope felt rough, scratching at his skin, irritating his throat.

Why should I be thinking of that?

Nearby, the priest continued to pray for him. The words seemed a blur. The crowd out in front of him was a blur. The only ones Finn could make out at all were the jurors and the magister standing not far from him.

The executioner studied him. "Is what you said true?"

"I told you, I was alone."

The executioner regarded him. "Choose your next words carefully. Is what you said about your family true?"

Finn looked over. The executioner's deep brown eyes seemed to hold him in place and compelled him, almost as if he were looking into the eyes of one of the gods.

"Yes."

"Your mother is sick?"

What did it matter if I shared the truth now?

"Yes. She's been sick for a while. We need money to help her, though everything goes to the apothecary. I wanted enough to pay for a physician."

A darkness clouded the executioner's face for a moment before fading. "Why did you not share this before?"

Finn frowned at him. He looked past the executioner toward the jurors. "Would it have mattered?"

"Perhaps not with them."

"Then it wouldn't have mattered."

"More than you might know."

A murmuring began to build in the crowd, and behind the executioner, Finn heard the magister cry out.

"What is taking so long?"

The executioner ignored them, focusing on Finn.

"What would you have done?"

"What?"

"Had you not needed to steal. What would you have done that was honorable?"

Finn looked at the executioner. It was a question he'd never been asked, and with everything that he'd gone through, it was a question he had never even really considered.

What would *I have done?*

"I don't know. My father was dishonorable." Though that had not always been the case. His father could have been honorable. Assisting the cartwright certainly had been.

"Just because your father was dishonorable doesn't mean you must be," the executioner said.

"Apparently, I'm going to die dishonorable as well."

"What would you have done?"

Finn hadn't thought about it in a long time. "A surgeon or apothecary, I suppose. If the guilds would've had me."

"Why?"

"Does it matter?"

"Why?" the executioner demanded.

"My mother has been sick a long time," Finn said. "I've seen how hard it has been to get her any sort of help. My father… well, my father did what he could to help my mother, but there was only so much that can be done for her."

"If you were given a second chance, that is what you would choose?"

What was this line of questioning?

"If I were given a second chance, I would want to do whatever it took to help my mother. I don't regret doing that."

A hint of a smile curved the executioner's mouth. He regarded Finn for a long moment before nodding.

The executioner stepped away, leaving the rope around Finn's neck.

This was it.

Soon, the executioner would demand that Finn climb the small stairs. He would tighten the rope. He would kick the stairs out, and Finn would hang until his breath escaped him. Either that or his neck snapped.

His body would be left hanging. The hegen would sneak in in the dark, claiming his hands, his feet, his eyes and ears and nose, probably even his manhood, all for their magic. The ravens would swoop down, picking at his flesh, tearing away what remained after the hegen had taken their cut.

And he would be forgotten.

The crew would move on. Someone else would be

brought in to take his place. The King would take on different jobs, hopefully something less dangerous.

Only his sister and his mother would remember him.

Hopefully, Oscar had done what he'd promised and told Lena that Finn had been exiled. It was easier that way.

Unless she came out for the execution.

He blinked, realizing that tears filled his eyes, but he couldn't clear them. He couldn't move. His body didn't seem to react to him the way he needed it to, and as he looked out over the crowd, they were nothing but unfamiliar faces. All of them looked up at him with anger and disdain.

Impatient shouts rang out.

It was only then that Finn realized the executioner wasn't near him. He stood at the Raven Stone's edge, speaking to the magister, along with the jurors.

Something strange was happening.

"You cannot," the magister said. His voice carried above the din of the crowd.

"There is tradition, and I invoke it. Seeing as how the king will be visiting in several days, you can bring it up to him if you are so inclined."

One of the jurors regarded the executioner. "You know what the crown requires of us. All we need to do is summon the viscount—"

"The viscount can't override this," the magister said, his lips pressed together in a sour frown. "This is spelled out within the law. The only one who may override it is King Porman himself."

The executioner stood looking down at the others. Tension filled Finn's body.

Finally, the magister shook his head. He climbed the stairs to the top of the Raven Stone before taking up a place next to the executioner. He leaned close and spoke to him, his voice loud enough that Finn could hear. "I don't know what you're playing at, Henry, but this is a dangerous gambit."

"It's not a gambit. I am simply invoking my right."

"If the king intervenes—"

"If the king intervenes, then the sentence can be carried out at that time."

The magister studied the executioner for a moment before nodding. He raised his hands, and gradually, the noise in the crowd began to die out. The magister spoke, his words carrying far more than Finn would've expected, projecting out over the crowd.

"The gods have intervened." A murmuring came over the crowd. "And Master Meyer has invoked the Executioner's Right."

The executioner turned away as the murmuring in the crowd intensified.

He stepped up to Finn, resting a hand on the noose around his neck. "Pray the king doesn't intervene," he said.

"What is this?"

"You have been granted a reprieve and a chance to serve."

"Serve who?"

The executioner held his gaze. "Me."

CHAPTER TEN

The flowers in the small lawn seemed out of place. Purple petals surrounded a bright yellow center, connected by a long stem. They were beautiful. Finn leaned toward the raised flower bed, breathing in the fragrance of the flowers.

"Come along."

He looked up. The executioner guided him through the yard and toward the door of the tidy house near the edge of the Reval section. Situated as it was near the river, the house sat almost on the border of the citizen sections, though it straddled some of the outer sections of the city.

He still didn't know what to make of what had happened. The executioner had invoked his right, which meant Finn got a reprieve, but a reprieve for what?

The executioner hadn't explained during the walk through the city. He'd taken side streets, trying to avoid the crowd as it dissipated, saying nothing to Finn. At one point while they'd been walking, Finn thought he saw Oscar, but he couldn't be certain. There had been so many people out during the day that it could have been anyone, not necessarily the Hand. Still—the person's face had appeared several times, enough that Finn began to question if that *wasn't* the Hand after all.

He looked along the yard. It would be easy enough to sneak through there undetected. Not during the day. Too much sunlight streamed down, filling the small garden with light. At night, though, it would be an easy job. Slip past the gate—Finn didn't even think it'd been locked— and along the path through the garden toward the small home.

Wearing darks at night would be easy enough...

He shook away those thoughts.

The executioner led him into the home.

It was larger than Finn would have expected. Richly stained wood lined the floor, the walls, even the beams overhead. The scent of flowers filled the inside of the home, much like those out in the garden. A stair led up to the upper level of the house. Though it was a larger house than he was accustomed to, he didn't see anything worth taking in there.

The executioner motioned to a door along a narrow hall. "You can use that room."

Finn blinked. "For what?"

"For your belongings. To sleep. That's what."

Finn still didn't understand all of what was happening around him. Some of that came from how tired he felt. The long days had gotten to him; the time in the prison passed quickly, though not with much sleep. Finn needed more rest than he'd gotten.

"Why?"

The executioner grunted. "You're going to serve. That's why you're here."

"You said that before. You mentioned a second chance."

"That's right. This is it. You're to be my apprentice." The executioner turned away. "When Gerdan died, it opened a position."

"And Gerdan was—"

"My assistant. Assigned to me." He looked over. "You likely knew him as the Lion." He pushed open the door to the room. "There's not much here. A bed, but that's what you get when you're working with me. It's been a while since I had anyone stay with me, anyway."

Finn looked into the room. A narrow bed ran along the length of the wall. A wardrobe took up space on the opposite wall. There was a desk with a lantern atop it. That was it.

"This is for me?"

"For now." The executioner turned toward him. "Let's go through a few details before we begin. I have rounds I need to make today, which now means you're going to make them with me. When you get useful, then you'll divide up the work with me. First off, this may be your room, but this is my home. Treat it as such. Second, you're here because I invoked my right. The king visits in a few days, and from the way the magister looked disappointed, I figure he'll push the viscount, who will petition the king to enforce the magister's sentencing. The Executioner's Right is an old tradition, though, so while I don't *think* King Porman will overrule my claim, you need to be prepared."

Everything came at Finn too fast. The executioner seemed almost dismissive of the viscount. "Prepared for what?"

"For the king to decide to carry out your sentence. Right now, you've received a reprieve. I figure you've got a few days to prove you deserve it. After that, you have to prove you can stay; otherwise, the brief reprieve disappears."

"How long?" Finn asked. He still didn't know what would be involved, serving as the executioner's assistant, but that would be a question for later.

"For the king?"

Finn shook his head. "For the other. How long to prove I can stay?"

"That's only partly up to me. The court also has a say. Just do what you're asked, work hard. And study. You might be able to earn your second chance."

"What will that entail?"

"You'll train to replace me." The executioner pulled the door to the room closed and motioned for Finn to follow him. "Gerdan had been assigned by the court. Not my choice, but he was competent enough. A little overeager in some aspects and ignored others, but he would have been fine if he would have listened. Seeing as he ended up at the bottom of the river, the position opened up."

"What happened to him?" Finn asked.

The Lion had been killed, and Finn didn't feel much pity for the man—he *had* been a bastard to him, after all, and his death had saved Finn—but he was curious.

"Killed while investigating a crime. You don't have to worry," the executioner said, as if Finn were worried about the same thing happening to him. "I've asked the Archers to step up patrols. Between that and the curfew, we should find answers soon enough."

Finn knew exactly how well the curfew worked when it came to crime, and the Archers weren't much more of a challenge.

He *was* curious about the Lion, though.

There wasn't the chance to push the issue anymore. They stepped back out of the house and into the walled garden. Finn still felt like he was having a hard time keeping up with what the executioner told him.

"Now you'll fill his position. If you do well, you'll get paid well. I'll see what I can do for your mother in the meantime." He stopped at the gate leading outside the garden and back onto the street, looking at Finn. "That is, if you weren't lying about that."

Finn shook his head. "I wasn't."

"No. I didn't think so. You had a look about you of a man who truly wanted to help his family."

They started along the street.

Finn still wore the gray Sinner's Cloth given to him by the guards when he'd marched along the street. It was loose-fitting and itchy. The executioner remained dressed in his dark gray leathers, though he didn't seem uncomfortable in them. He moved quickly, marching along the street at a brisk pace, and Finn was forced to keep up.

The executioner intended for him to replace him.

Finn didn't know how he felt about that.

That wasn't quite right. He knew *exactly* how he felt about that. It wasn't something he wanted. But it *was* an opportunity to live.

He wasn't hanging from the gallows right now, so that much was a better state than the alternative. He could wait until the king granted him the clemency, and then…

Maybe he couldn't wait.

"Part of your training will involve learning the various sentences. Seeing as how you've seen one firsthand, you know what a hanging involves. There's the sword, fire, water, the wheel, drawing, and probably a few more the jury might come up with if they decide to get cute. The king doesn't care for *how* the sentence is carried out, mind you. It's all about enforcing his law. The viscount and magister, along with the jurors, ensure that's done."

Finn could only nod.

If the king decided to carry out his sentence, to override the executioner, then he wouldn't have the opportunity to run.

Maybe his best bet would be to escape now. He could find a time to sneak away from the executioner and disappear. Finn thought he could get out of the city and find a way to disappear. They'd go looking for him, and if they caught him, the fate would be the same as it would have been were he to stay.

Only, did he *have* to run?

He could stay.

It would be a gamble. Finn didn't know if the king would choose to carry out his sentencing, but if he did, then Finn would hang. If he didn't, he still had to prove himself. He would have to serve the executioner. He would have to do what the man said.

How hard would that be, really?

He tortured and killed. That was how hard it would be.

Finn followed the executioner as he made his way over a bridge and into the Thaner, one of the merchants' sections.

"There are other aspects of the job you'll need to learn as well. Questioning. Investigation. Stitching—pretty much surgery. Care of the various prisons."

As the executioner continued to go on, Finn only partially listened.

He had time to decide what he'd do. He didn't have to choose now. Gods, he might not even be able to choose now. It would take time for him to develop a plan, and he didn't have to rush anything yet.

The executioner didn't look back at him, almost as if he weren't concerned about what Finn might do.

The executioner slowed near a store on the edge of the merchants' section. Finn didn't recognize the sign. It wasn't one where he ever visited.

"Wait here," he said.

"You don't want me to come in with you?"

The executioner regarded him for a moment. "Some of these shop owners can be touchy when it comes to who visits their shop, especially in my line of work. I find it's best not to push them when they aren't comfortable. Wait here. When we've worked together for a while, you'll come to know them and they'll come to know you. Then you will be permitted. For now..."

The executioner headed into the shop.

This would be the time when Finn could run.

Only, as he looked around the street, he didn't feel as if he could run. Where would he go? The crew would take him in, but that put friends in danger. One thing the King had preached was to protect the crew.

Running to them now wouldn't protect them. Not Oscar. Not Rock. Not any of them.

What about his sister?

She might not even know anything about what he'd been through. Short of someone learning his name—and during the Gallows Festival, there weren't that many who actually knew the condemned's name—they wouldn't have any reason to question anything about him.

Oscar had promised to go to Lena and convince her that Finn left the city.

That might be best, to leave the lie as it was. Anything else...

He thought about his father and what his father had wanted for him. He had wanted Finn to have a better life than he had. He'd wanted Lena to have a better life as well. So far, neither of them had. Finn had fallen into the same things that his father had done, and Lena was forced to work, taking on jobs that she would rather not have done. All because he'd been pinched doing a job to help their mother.

Then the same had happened to Finn.

Would the cycle repeat itself with Lena?

Finn had been so caught up in what he'd gone through that he hadn't even considered what Lena might do when the money Finn could bring in stopped coming.

She didn't need to get into the same work Finn had done. She'd been exposed to it enough because of their father, and then because of Finn, but she didn't need—or deserve—to get caught up with it as well.

He looked over to the shop.

As the apprentice, he'd be offered pay. The executioner hadn't spoken about how much the position offered, but there would be some pay to it. Then there was what he'd said about how he might help his mother. Finn didn't know what sort of connections the executioner had or whether he could even do anything, but didn't he need to wait and see if there might actually be something he could do for her?

Finn closed his eyes.

Now might be the time for him to make a run, but it also *wasn't* the time for him to make a run. The crew couldn't protect him. Not from this. Finn had to protect the crew from him.

The door opened, and the executioner strode out. He carried a sack in one hand and eyed Finn strangely. "You're still here."

"You told me to wait for you here."

"I did. Didn't know if you would use the opportunity to run."

"I doubt I'd get very far if I did run."

The executioner shook his head. "Probably not. The Archers at the gate have your description. They'd make sure you were brought back to Declan, were you to run."

The executioner started off, and Finn hesitated a moment before racing after him. "How would they know I'm not on a mission on your behalf?"

"Because I hadn't told them that you were."

"Did you expect me to run?"

The executioner paused and turned to him. "I expected you to consider it. Have you?"

Finn stared at him, uncertain of how to answer. "Yes."

"Good. Shows fight. You won't be able to do this job without a little fight."

"Your job is tormenting and killing people. What's that got to do with fighting?"

The executioner grunted. "That's a part of it. No use denying it. Not the main part. Were it all the job involved, I might have retired years ago. Only so much torture and killing a man can do, even when it's in service of the king. That's not why you'll need to have a little fight. You'll see soon enough. Executioner and apprentice isn't an easy job. If it were, I'd have a line of applicants looking for work. Seeing as how I don't…"

The executioner headed along the street, shifting his sack into his other arm as he carried it with him.

"Come along. If you don't run today, you're already further along than I would have expected you to be."

The day consisted of errands. Nothing more than that. Finn didn't know why, but he'd expected there to be something more glamorous to the executioner's job. Part of him had figured that the executioner would spend most of his time planning the executions, perhaps coming up with a new way to torment the prisoners or any number of other horrible things. Instead, it seemed he spent most of his time collecting supplies.

His feet hurt. His legs still hurt from the screws, making him limp. When they'd given him the Sinner's Cloth that morning—*Could it have been only this morning?*—it had included slippers. He felt every cobble through them, irritating his feet, rubbing up against them in an awful way. It was probably still better than the alternative.

Not probably.

By evening, when they'd stopped in the sixth shop—all in different parts of the city—Finn finally spoke up. "Is this all you do?"

"Not usually. When Gerdan lived, he did most of the supply runs. You stick this out long enough, and it will be a part of your responsibility. Considering your background, I suspect you've been paying attention and could find your way back to most of these shops?"

Finn hesitated before nodding.

"Thought as much. That'll be good. If I don't have to walk you around the city a dozen times to get your bearings, you're going to be much more useful to me."

"That's all I'm going to do?"

"That's what you'll be doing to begin with. Learn the basics. Supplies needed. Where to obtain them. The contacts needed for those supplies. The people to reach out to when you can't find what you need. You get that down, then you're on your way."

"To being an executioner?"

He nodded. "It's a start. Didn't say it was the *only* part. Just a start. The rest will come in time. You'll have to work at it."

"At gathering supplies." Finn shook his head. "I think I can manage."

"We'll have to see. You do this, then you get brought into the other aspects of the job."

"Like torture."

"Like knowing the city."

"I know the city."

"You know your part of the city. You know your crews and how to avoid conflict between them. That will be useful. It's politics, no different than you'll encounter in the rest of the city. Only, the kind of politics that you'll deal with in the rest of the city has to do with the king and those who serve him directly. Make a mistake, and you'll lose your job—or worse."

Finn hadn't considered the challenges the executioner lived under, though the Lion *had* been killed.

"What now?" Finn asked.

The executioner looked off into the distance. Finn couldn't tell what he stared at. More buildings? Another place he had to go for his errands? Whatever it was seemed to draw his attention.

"Now you can rest. You've had a long day. Longer than me, I suppose. Can you find your way back to the house?"

Finn nodded. It would be easy enough for him to return to the house. Situated as it was along the river, Finn only had to backtrack through the city until he reached the river, then he could follow that until he came to the house.

"Good. Get some rest. Tomorrow, we start early."

He started away, heading out along the street.

"What am I supposed to call you?" Finn asked.

The executioner didn't turn. "Master Meyer."

Morning came as sunlight streamed in through the window. The window was small, though larger than he'd had in the prison, and without any curtains, it woke him before he was ready to get up. Finn supposed that was the point of it. Wake him and be ready for the day. That was what Master Meyer wanted.

Sitting on the edge of the bed, Finn looked around the room, his gaze lingering on the desk. When he'd come back the night before—ignoring the urge to run and try to disappear into the city—he'd found that he was every bit as tired as Master Meyer had expected him to be. He'd fallen asleep quickly, having not changed out of his clothes, lying on the bed in the dress of the condemned.

What am I doing here?

Those thoughts kept coming back to him. He didn't know what he was doing. Only that he hadn't run. Yet. It had to be *yet*, didn't it?

The sound of footsteps came from outside the room. Meyer was already up.

Finn imagined that he'd looked in on him whenever he'd come back for the day, likely staring at Finn with a smug expression.

Not smug. I doubt he does smug.

That wasn't the sense he had from Master Meyer. Finn didn't yet know why he'd let Finn come with him to stay, but there had to be a reason. Perhaps it was only to thumb his nose at the magister. He *did* have the sense the executioner hadn't cared for the sentencing, though not because of anything that Finn had done. It was more about him not caring for it for another reason.

Getting to his feet, he grabbed his slippers from the door and headed out of the room. He needed shoes if he were going to keep traveling through the city with Master Meyer. Other clothes, too.

"You're up. Good."

Meyer leaned out into the hallway and glanced in his direction.

How had he known?

"I'm sorry if I overslept. I didn't mean—"

"Give me a hand in here."

Finn nodded. It began again. Errands. Whatever task Meyer wanted of him. That was his life now.

But it is life.

Meyer stood in front of a hot stove, the smell of grease and eggs sizzling in the pan almost too much for Finn to bear. His mouth watered at the scent.

It had been a while since he'd eaten well. Longer than his imprisonment.

"What can I do?"

"Can you cook?"

"I have some experience," he said. "When my mother started getting sick, my sister and I—"

"If you can cook, then you get to take over. I've been doing this long enough. Not my favorite task."

Meyer grabbed a steaming mug and headed away from the stove, taking a seat at the table. Finn hurried over and grabbed the spatula to work at the eggs. Meyer had used a large pan, and six eggs congealed together in the bottom of the pan. Finn started to separate them, working the spatula between the eggs.

"We're going to begin some of the basics of your instruction today," Meyer said as Finn worked.

"I thought the basics were yesterday."

"Yesterday was part of determining whether you were going to run. As you didn't, I figure that today, we can begin with your instruction. I have only a few days to determine whether you'll be useful enough for me to make my case to the king."

Finn tensed. He hadn't known that yesterday was a test. "What do I have to know to be useful?"

"In the time we have before the king arrives? Not much. You'll need to prove that you can follow the tasks set before you. Other than that, you need to prove that you're open to change. Not sure we can accomplish all of that in the time we have, but we'll try."

The eggs were getting done at different times. One of

them had burned, and Finn scraped at it, trying to get it off the pan.

What had Meyer done with them?

"The next few days will be long. For both of us. With Gerdan's loss, my responsibilities have increased, especially with all the activity in the city. Until—and if—you become useful, we're both going to have little sleep. Get used to it."

Finn pulled the best of the eggs from the pan and slipped them onto a plate, bringing it over to Meyer. The executioner stared at the plate for a moment before looking up at Finn.

"You cook?"

"As I was saying, my sister and I had to learn after my mother got sick."

Finn looked around the kitchen. It was small but cozy. Dishes stacked near a basin reminded him of the way Lena had left a mess in the kitchen. The executioner likely had easy access to water—gods, he might even have a well of his own in his home—but it didn't look as if he took care of it any better than Finn's sister.

"Do you have a wife?"

The executioner looked up briefly in between bites of food. "I did."

Finn decided not to push on that. *Did.* That could mean many things in Verendal.

Looking around the kitchen with a different eye, he noticed there were a few decorations. Enough that he suspected Meyer's wife had once placed them.

"Eat. Then we get started."

Finn scooped the remaining eggs onto his plate and took a seat at the table. The executioner sat silently while Finn ate. His were burned, though he didn't complain. At least he had the chance to eat something.

When he was done, Meyer got to his feet and motioned for Finn to follow. Finn set his plate in the basin and followed Meyer. They went down the hall toward the back of the house. Meyer paused at one door along the hall a moment, stepping inside briefly before emerging with a longsword. The leather-wrapped hilt looked well-worn, and the scabbard plain, but Finn recognized the blade.

"Is that—"

"Justice," the executioner said.

The sword of justice, or Justice, as it seemed the executioner called it, was the means to an honorable death. Not many in the city were offered it these days. Most were sentenced to hang—or worse. Finn hadn't seen some of the worse punishments the magister and jurors assigned and should be thankful he'd only been sentenced to the rope rather than anything more.

"Do you have an execution this morning?" Back-to-back seemed rushed, even with the way things were going these days, when there had been more executions than usual. Finn didn't know if he could stomach assisting with an execution so soon—if at all.

"No. You're going to learn the basics."

"Of using the sword?"

Meyer grunted. "Of cleaning the sword. You have to

know how to keep the steel clean before you learn to use it."

They headed out into the garden. The sun had just started to clear the neighboring buildings, filling the yard with a bright light. Little warmth came from the sunlight, though enough he didn't feel cold out there as he would have in the shade.

Meyer took a seat on a small wooden bench along the wall. Finn waited across from him, watching as he rested the scabbard of the sword on the ground in front of him and then unsheathed it.

He rested the sword across his lap. The grip was long enough for two hands, and a silver circle adorned the pommel. The blade was different from most Finn had seen. Not that thieves generally carried swords, but he'd seen enough to recognize how it was different. Long—nearly up to Finn's waist, were it to rest on the end—the sword was squared off so that it lacked a point like so many other swords had. It seemed Justice didn't need to stab someone if it could shear off their head.

Meyer pulled a stack of rags and a bottle out from a satchel resting on the ground. "Like all things in your life, you have to maintain it if you expect it to last. A blade can rust if not cared for. Even one like Justice."

He ran one of the rags along the gleaming surface.

"The blade should be oiled weekly. It's probably more than necessary, but if you remember to do it weekly, then you've done it often enough. You'll find the oil inside. I assume you remember the room?" He looked up briefly, long enough to see Finn nod. "When it's out, additional supplies can be purchased at Tahn's general store. I prefer his personal blend. More clove oil, I suspect. The scabbard should be oiled once a month. A different oil. Don't mix them up. I'm partial to lemon oil, though it can be difficult to acquire in some months."

Meyer dabbed a little oil from the bottle and worked it along the length of the blade. When he was satisfied, he used a clean rag and wiped the excess off.

"Why do you do it?" Finn asked.

"Care for the blade?"

That wasn't what Finn *really* wanted to know, but it was a reasonable question. He had many other questions he wanted answers to, but this would be easiest.

"I've told you. For it to last, it must be maintained. The blade is old. It's been with the executioners in this city for several hundred years, so treat it that way." He looked up, holding Finn's gaze. "It's more than that, though. I've been given a heavy burden. It's one I don't enter into lightly. The gods chose me to wield the sword of justice, so I must do so wisely. A clean blow to send those so sentenced to the afterlife."

Finn found it strange that Meyer would be so seemingly religious. How could he hold on to his faith with the horror he had to inflict?

Perhaps it was nothing more than an act.

If so, it seemed strange to Finn that he would keep it up for him.

"Do you think you can manage?" Master Meyer asked.

Finn nodded.

"Good. This will be part of your responsibilities. Once

a week. When you prove you can maintain the blade, we'll begin to teach you to use it."

"Isn't it just swinging it?"

Meyer looked up, intensity in his gaze. "Have you not been listening?"

"I've listened—"

"The gods chose me. Now us. We must honor them by cutting cleanly. Not hacking. We aren't butchers. We're better than that."

He turned his attention back to the sword, steadily running the rag along the surface of it.

Finn could only stand and stare.

Better than a butcher? What would Lena say to that?

At least the butcher provided food for others to eat. To Finn, that was more honorable than this. There was a time when he wouldn't have thought that way, but now he began to wonder if he'd ever be honorable again.

CHAPTER ELEVEN

The days leading up to the king's visit left Finn feeling more anxious than he would have expected. He hadn't anticipated that he'd feel a growing sense of unease about his fate the longer he spent with Master Meyer, but that was exactly what he felt.

He'd debated going to the crew but held off. For now. He didn't know what would happen if he were to slip off, and it seemed better to bide his time.

He *would* go back to them, though.

The second day with Meyer involved various types of knots. The executioner had given him a length of rope and demonstrated tying them. There were different kinds of nooses, something Finn had never known.

"Tie it like this," he said, looping it around and slipping the end up and through, "and the knot pulls tight more slowly. It suffocates the condemned." He untied it and then looped it again. "Like this, and the neck snaps as long as you drop from the right height. A quick death. There are others, but these are how you should start."

Finn took the rope and practiced much of the day, tying and untying, working until his fingers felt as if they were bleeding, though they didn't. He still felt as if there would be a way to run, but he hadn't taken it yet.

The third day, they traveled along the massive wall surrounding the city, near enough that Finn could see the Archers manning it every couple dozen paces, and he wondered if he might be able to slip past. There were several gates through the wall, so more than one way in and out of the city. He wouldn't *have* to head past the Raven Stone on the way out, though it might be the easiest. Finn didn't know if the Raven Stone were watched as closely as the other gates.

Every time he thought about running, he would look over to Master Meyer, and he'd realize that he couldn't. The executioner had given him a warning about what would happen were he to run, and he believed the Archers would be watching for him. That was probably the reason the executioner hadn't given him anything different to wear than the grays he was supposed to have been executed in. It would make it easier on the Archers to search for someone wearing grays like that. He doubted he'd be able to easily slip through the gate.

Not that he couldn't find a way to steal something different. Finn had been observing the shops near the executioner's home to see what he might be able to find and whether there would be anyplace he could use to uncover anything useful for him to escape. One place might have been useful, though it was too close to Master Meyer's home. Close enough that Finn didn't want to risk it. Yet.

"Where are we going today?" Finn asked. He'd gotten used to the patrols. Most of them involved the executioner leading him around the city.

"I think it's time to bring you into the prison visits."

"You do?"

Meyer looked back at him. "Seeing as how you haven't run, I think it's time to give you a chance to determine whether you might be useful. There won't be anything too exotic today, but perhaps you'll find something intriguing about it."

"Is this what your last apprentice did?" Finn hadn't heard Meyer talk about the Lion that much.

"Assistant. He was not truly my apprentice. He was a journeyman before he came to me."

Finn wasn't sure what that meant, but Meyer didn't seem eager to explain. "You've looked into what happened to him?"

"Yes, but I have done this long enough to know when a truth does not want to come out. That happens often enough these days. Now with the king's visit, I doubt I'll find anything."

"Why would you say that?"

Meyer glanced over to him. "He was investigating your case; it's entirely possible one of your friends murdered him."

That didn't sound like his crew. They were thieves, not killers. Besides, why murder the Lion and not rescue Finn?

"Doesn't that seem like an answer that wants to come out?"

"His death offered you this opportunity, so perhaps you're better off if it does not."

As they headed toward a familiar prison in the distance, Finn pushed away the thought of Oscar visiting him in prison.

He couldn't have killed the Lion, could he?

This was a section of the city Finn knew all too well. "The debtor's prison?"

"You don't think this will be interesting?"

"I just don't think the people you have captive here are all that worthy of captivity."

"Many of them owe a significant debt."

"I'm sure the gods are so disappointed in them," Finn muttered as he shook his head. "You don't seem to care that there are those who have much and don't care about those who have nothing."

"I care. I also understand my role."

Was that what Finn would have to do as well? He didn't know if he'd be able to have the same view as Master Meyer.

"How do you do it?"

"I serve the crown."

Finn shook his head. "Not that. How do you do things when you disagree with them?" When Master Meyer didn't answer and continued heading toward the debtor's prison, he decided to push. "I had a feeling that you weren't pleased with my punishment."

"I don't serve in that capacity."

"You intervened," Finn said.

The executioner's back stiffened. "I did what the gods would have wanted me to do."

"Because you think I can serve the gods."

"All men can serve the gods."

"I didn't deserve the sentencing they handed down. You didn't think so either."

Master Meyer didn't say anything.

They reached the walkway leading into the prison. Meyer unlocked it with a key from a massive keyring. Finn could imagine Master Meyer as having access to the different prisons all throughout the city—and perhaps he did. To do the job he had, he'd have to be able to get into the prisons, torment the prisoners, and then…

"What do you have to do here?" Finn asked softly.

Meyer looked over at him. "Not all here are as innocent as you'd like to believe."

"I didn't say that."

"And not all here are for the crime of owing the wealthy."

He didn't give Finn the chance to ask more about what he meant.

They stepped into the prison.

Finn had been in Volthan Prison, in addition to Declan. He'd laughed and gossiped and basically waited for his sentencing, knowing that it would be unpleasant but that there wouldn't be anything more that he'd need to worry about. Declan was hard—harder than he ever would have expected before he'd been sentenced. He couldn't imagine what it would be like, were he to be there for weeks. Months. Even years. Volthan had been almost a community of thieves.

The debtor's prison felt like neither.

Finn hadn't realized how many windows lined the walls. From outside, it was difficult to tell, but inside, sunlight streamed down through those windows, illuminating not only the hallway but the walls themselves.

Lanterns that lined the walls weren't really necessary. They gave off a bright and almost cheery light, adding to the shafts of sunlight streaming along the walls.

That wasn't even the part of it that surprised him the most.

The smell was different.

In Volthan, the prison had a stench, though it was one of the mass of men. The stench of sweat permeated the prison, the unwashed prisoners giving it an odor. It still was nothing like what he'd known in Declan.

In hindsight, Declan was the scent of death.

He hadn't known the death would be his, or that it would be a slow death, only that it would be death. Some of it might have come from those prisoners punished and sentenced to death like him. He imagined the fear lending a particular odor to the prison. Other aspects of the stench seemed like that of rot. A stink that Finn hadn't been able to pinpoint, nor had he really wanted to. All he'd wanted was to ignore it.

The debtor's prison just didn't stink.

"What is it?" Master Meyer asked.

"Nothing."

"Each prison is different."

"I know."

"Do you?"

Finn nodded.

"How many different prisons have you been a part of?"

"Volthan and Declan."

"Volthan can be unpleasant. I suspect you were assigned to a chain?"

Finn nodded, wondering if Meyer remembered being the one to sentence him to that fate. Probably not. He must sentence hundreds each year. Hard to remember one more boy.

"Not a bad punishment, though I doubt it changes many men's minds. It's not something those who are sentenced to it fear."

Finn could only shrug. The executioner was right. Most on the chain gang he served under hadn't reformed. Finn knew many of them had immediately returned to their crews, though it wasn't as if they had many options when they were let out. Most who'd been caught had done what they thought they had to to get by. Finn knew that he had.

The executioner turned along the hall, taking a side corridor.

"Do you have to let anyone know that you're here?"

"Do you think I should?"

"I don't really know. Do they care that you're here alone?"

Meyer turned to him. "As master executioner in the city, I'm in charge of all the prisons. One aspect of my job is that I'm responsible for all sentencing. That can be big and small. Most know only about the big."

"The Gallows Festivals."

The executioner's face soured at the term. "If you must call it that."

"What would you rather me call it?"

"A sentencing. That is what you must begin to refer to it as. Each prisoner is given a sentencing. Yours was the rope. I can't change that—"

"Only, you did."

"Yes. Well, in your case I did, but that is the exception. I invoked my right."

"Why?"

It was the question Finn had been wondering about ever since he'd been saved from death. Why him? Why would the executioner have been willing to protect him? Finn didn't feel as if he deserved that saving. Though he didn't think he deserved the punishment they'd given him.

"It doesn't matter." The executioner continued on through the hall. "You'll find that some of the prisoners require additional questioning. Most can be questioned by inquisitors, though some must be questioned by those with more experience. And authority."

"You mean there are those who must be tortured."

"Interrogated. I would rather question and release than put the city at risk by releasing someone who might commit another crime against the crown."

They stopped at a cell. Meyer pulled his keys out and slipped one into the lock of the cell.

"You don't need any guards with you?"

"Do you think we need them here?"

Finn looked along the hall. This hall was as well-lit as the other parts of the prison. No sunlight came through there, though there were still lanterns lining the hall, giving off much more pleasant light than he had seen at any time in Declan. There wasn't the sound of anyone calling out. No shouts like there had been in Declan. Not even the ongoing gossiping that he'd heard in Volthan.

"I guess not."

Meyer jingled the keys again and pulled the door open.

Finn looked past him. The man inside the cell was dark-haired and had a massive belly. He looked over at the executioner with annoyance.

"You here to release me?"

"Not release. You are Jon Habrans?"

"You know I am, or you wouldn't have asked. Who are you two?"

"I am Master Meyer." Jon immediately tensed. He recognized the name of the executioner. Before his sentencing, Finn didn't think that he would have recognized him. Would it have mattered had he heard the executioner's name? "I am here to ask you a few questions."

"I told the Archers the truth. You can just go to them. You don't have to do anything to me."

"My notes from the Archers are incomplete. I would

like to ask a few clarifying questions." He motioned for Jon to take a seat. Finn hadn't noticed that Jon had a small cot, much like the one that he'd been given in Declan after he'd been condemned. Jon took a seat. He was a large man, and the mattress bowed slightly under his weight. "You stand accused of stealing twenty fils from Mistress Krell. Is that true?"

Finn looked over at Meyer. *That was what this was about? Twenty fils?* Finn could steal twenty fils in a single swipe if he targeted the right person. *How could they be concerned about such a small sum?*

"I told them that I'd pay it back. You understand that I can pay that back, Master Meyer. You don't need to—"

"The crown demands that I obtain the answers. Do you deny that you took twenty fils?"

Jon hesitated, but only a moment. Finally, he shook his head. "I don't deny it."

Finn could have practically seen his mind working as he'd tried to decide how he would answer. On the one hand, admitting to stealing meant a certain punishment. Depending on the amount, and any history of the same, the punishment could be severe. On the other hand, admitting anything to the executioner seemed like a bad idea.

"Would you confess the reason behind your violating the trust of Mistress Krell?"

Jon licked his lips and ran meaty hands through thinning hair. A bead of sweat had already started to form on his brow, and he wiped it away. "I... I suppose I don't have a good reason, Master Meyer. She'd forgotten about the difference, or so I'd thought."

"When she called it to your attention…"

"I should have paid her what she was owed." He bent his head forward.

It was a good act. Finn had seen better.

Meyer nodded slowly, as if he bought what Jon was selling. Knowing when someone lied was something his time working with Oscar had given him. Maybe despite all the time that Master Meyer spent around criminals, he still didn't have that ability.

"I will pass on what I've uncovered to the magister. When he suggests his sentencing, pray that he's merciful."

Jon bobbed his head low.

Was that a smirk on his face?

It was enough for Finn to almost laugh. Almost. Were he to do so, he thought he would disrupt the sanctity of this visit.

"I've been praying the entire time I've been here, Master Meyer. The gods have to listen to me eventually."

Meyer motioned for Finn to move, and they left the cell, locking it behind them. The door was different from the cells within Declan. Solid wood with iron running along its length for reinforcement; Finn doubted even that much was needed in the debtor's prison. There probably weren't all that many attempting to break out of it.

"Come along. We have a few more to visit before we pass on the information to the magister."

"You actually do?"

Meyer frowned at him. "It is my responsibility to

acquire as much information about the innocence or guilt of those imprisoned within the king's prisons. As lead inquisitor, I am ultimately responsible for ensuring the appropriate questioning of those within our control."

He made his way down the hall, and Finn hurried to keep up. "Did you believe him?"

Meyer held his gaze a moment. "Did you?"

Finn shook his head. "I've seen better acting in street theater. He wanted you to think he was contrite, but I didn't have the feeling from him that he was."

"You would trust your feeling?"

Finn shrugged. "I trust that I've seen men like him before. Not that he's lying about all that much money, but—"

"The twenty fils was more than Mistress Krell made in two months' time doing honest work. What do you think of how much he took from her now?" Finn said nothing. "What if I told you it was more than she made in a year's work?"

"I'd think that she needed a better job," Finn muttered.

The executioner stared at him. "That may be, but it doesn't change that he took what amounted to a fortune to her. The actual value matters little, neither to me nor in the eyes of the law. What matters is the one he wronged."

"And you coming here did what?"

"It gave him a chance to be honest with his intentions. That he did not…"

"You knew?"

Master Meyer frowned. "I have been at my job for the better part of three decades. In that time, I've interviewed hundreds of condemned, thousands of common criminals like Jon Habrans. I have come to know the difference between a man who feels remorse and one who does not. You will learn to identify the same. Knowing a con and knowing the emotion behind it are different." Meyer regarded Finn a moment. "It's likely that he feels the way you do—that he only took a small amount of coin, so there was no harm in it. Ask Mistress Krell about the harm she sustained. I'm sure she will tell a different story."

Finn shouldn't be surprised that Meyer had known the act, though he was surprised by the passion in the way he spoke. He cared about his job.

He might have been assigned to work with him, but there wasn't any way that he'd ever be able to care for what he would have to do the way Master Meyer did. If he couldn't, did that mean Meyer would recognize it? Would he report that to the king when he visited?

Finn would have to be a much better actor to convince him if he wanted to live. Either that or make a run for it. Before he did, he wanted to visit his sister and mother, maybe even tell them why he had to leave so they understood.

Meyer waited for him at the end of the hall, watching him. Finn couldn't shake the feeling that Meyer knew his thoughts.

The streets were quiet. Finn glanced around him, feeling self-conscious, not only in how he was dressed but also worried that Meyer had followed him. After visiting another prison—this one Gayel's Prison for women—Finn had wanted to be out in the open. Maybe it was nothing more than thinking about the way that his father must feel trapped the way he was, or maybe it was the anger he saw in everyone's eyes within the prison, as if he were the one responsible for what had happened to them, despite how Meyer was the one who kept them imprisoned, not him.

A steady wind blew, carrying a cold chill to it. The Sinner's Cloth wasn't warm enough for the weather. He supposed that he could ask Meyer for warmer clothing, a cloak or something like it, but he also supposed this was all part of a test.

Returning to the crew pulled on him, but he couldn't do that. Yet.

First, prove he could stay with Meyer. That meant convincing him—and King Porman.

He *could* visit his home and check on his mother. Meyer would understand.

When he reached his family home, he raised his hand as if to knock before shaking his head and muttering to himself about how stupid he'd been.

The air inside the home had a medicinal odor to it that covered something else. Something worse. The time in the prisons had been just as bad, though in a different way. What he smelled now was foul and unpleasant.

What had Lena been offering our mother these days?

Finn headed toward the small room at the back of the home and pressed the door open, looking inside.

His mother lay atop the sheets, a thin gown all that

covered her. Her pale skin seemed to glisten with a faint sheen of sweat, though the air in the home was cool. A mug rested on the table next to her, along with a tray of half-eaten food. Most of it looked like scraps. Nothing more than that.

When was the last time that she'd eaten anything of substance?

Finn pulled a chair over to sit next to her. Though she rested comfortably, a faint tremor persisted in her hands. She gripped the sheets on either side of her, fists balled up, and the fabric squeezed into them.

He touched her arm softly. It was damp and warm. The moment that he touched her, he felt the tension within her arms.

"Easy, Mother," he whispered.

She could feed herself, or had been able to, though she hadn't spoken in months. She hadn't walked in years.

Turning to the tray next to her, he lifted the mug and sniffed it. The liquid was a greenish-brown and had a strange spicy aroma to it. The temptation to sip it to see what his sister had been giving his mother came to him.

"I wouldn't do that," Lena said.

Finn looked over. "You're here."

"I'm here. Where did you think I'd be?"

Finn turned back to his mother. "I didn't know. It was late enough that I thought you'd be here, but since you got your job…"

"Yes. My job." She grabbed a chair from near the wall and dragged it over to sit next to him. "What are you doing here?"

"I wanted to see how you were doing. How she was doing."

"The same as she's been the last month. Worse than she'd been the month before. She's getting worse, Finn."

"I know. I wish there was something we could do. I know Father wanted to help her."

Lena's brow darkened. "He tried, but he couldn't help her, could he?"

"You know he did everything that he could."

"The same way that you did everything you could."

Finn breathed out. He had no idea if Lena knew what had happened to him, but with her accusation, he didn't think so. She didn't even seem to notice how he was dressed. "I'm going to find a way to help," he said to her.

She looked tired, and she frowned at him before shaking her head.

"Did you bring more coin?"

Finn looked over. "I didn't think you cared for my way of acquiring it."

"I don't. You're going to end up just like Father." Finn tensed, waiting for her to mention the Gallows Festival. "If she ever does come around, it's going to kill her."

Finn thought they were probably beyond that now. As he looked at his mother, he couldn't imagine what a physician would be able to offer to her, if anything. She didn't come around, she didn't eat anything more than what Lena poured into her throat, and she continued to grow weaker. Eventually, she would waste away.

"I don't have anything more."

"You don't? I thought…" She let out a long sigh. "I guess it doesn't matter."

Finn looked down at the mug. "What is this?"

"I tried something different."

"A different apothecary?"

She looked up, defiance in her eyes. "No."

"Not an apothecary?" He brought the mug up to his nose. The strange smell lingered in his nostrils. If it wasn't an apothecary, there was only one place where she'd get something like this. "Lena! You know how Mother felt about the hegen. The gods only know what they put into their magic—and what it will take from her."

Lena glared at him before it softened. "I know how she told us she felt, but I also know that she would have wanted to live were she given a chance. And it's not her who pays the price."

Finn shot her a look before holding the mug up to his nostrils. The hegen used their strange kind of magic, though most claimed it was barely effective. Finn didn't know if it would even do anything. At this point, it was possible that anything that she might give their mother wouldn't change anything for her, anyway.

"What is it?"

"You're not mad?"

Finn sighed. "I don't know that I get to be mad about this. You're the one who's been sitting with her most days." He should have been there for her. For them both. "What is it?"

Lena took the mug from him and started to swirl it around. "It's an elixir they gave me. I had to describe her symptoms to the hegen healer, and then they made a specific compound."

"What was the price?" When it came to the hegen, there was always a price. Most of the time, it was money. There were times when they required something more. That was what Finn feared.

"Three fils. That's it."

Finn thought about visiting the prison with Master Meyer and the man who'd stolen twenty fils. That had been a lot of money for the woman he'd stolen it from. Twenty would be a prize to Lena as well. But that wasn't the *only* fee the hegen would require.

"I didn't know what else to do," Lena said. "She keeps getting worse. I've tried to be patient. I know that's what you would want—"

"I want her to get better too."

"Would you have done it?"

Finn closed his eyes. It had been so long since he'd had his mother with him that he didn't know. Everything that he'd done, the entire course of his life, had been tied into the illness that consumed her. It had changed everything for him. First with the way that his father had gone away from the honorable work he had done as an assistant to one of the local cartwrights, and then leading Finn to follow him, to beg Oscar to work with him. To teach him. The Hand hadn't needed *that* much coaxing.

"I did what I had to do to help her, so I suppose it only makes sense that you've done the same."

Lena watched him. "I won't go back if you don't want me to."

There was something more in the question, and Finn could practically hear how she wanted to know if he would draw more money soon. Had the job gone the way that he'd hoped, it wouldn't be an issue. He would have had a significant haul. Enough coin that they could go and see if a physician—not the bastard who'd chased Finn away, but a better and smarter one—would be able to do anything for her.

Only, there wasn't anything that Finn could tell his sister. What she wanted wasn't anything he could offer. She wanted hope.

"If it's working, you should keep doing it," he said.

"I don't know if it's working or not." She continued to swirl the mug. "She told me to come back if it didn't make it better. She thought she might have something more she could offer us."

"At what cost?"

"I don't know. She didn't say."

Finn turned to his sister, taking the mug from her and setting it down on the table. He wanted to dump it out. If it came from a hegen, he wanted to discard it and keep his mother from drinking their magic in, but something stopped him. Maybe it was the look in his sister's eyes. Maybe it was the fact that he didn't have anything more that he could offer.

"Promise me that you'll be careful. Don't commit to something you can't do."

"What about you?" When he didn't answer, she shook her head, though he still didn't see any recognition in her eyes about the Sinner's Cloth he wore. "I don't know everything that you're doing, Finn, but I know it's not always safe. You could end up just like Father—or worse. I… I can't lose you, too."

Finn swallowed back the lump in his throat.

He'd almost died. Had he been hanged without a chance to tell her what happened, he had no idea what would have happened to her. Oscar might have helped Lena and Finn's mother, but there was only so much the Hand could do.

"Listen, Lena. I'm working on something different. I can't explain it to you just yet"—there was no point in explaining it until he knew whether the king would uphold the Executioner's Right—"but I might have something more I can offer Mother. Just don't get locked into the hegen before I get a chance to help. Can you promise that to me?"

Lena looked at their mother. Tears welled up in her eyes. "I'm tired, Finn."

Finn took her hand and squeezed. "I know you are. I promise I'm going to do all that I can to help you and Mother. You just have to give me a little bit more time."

Lena nodded absently, staring at their mother. "I'll do what I can."

"That's not what I'm asking."

"I know, but I don't know when you're going to return —or if you will. You disappear, and I have to do everything that I can to help Mother while you're gone. When she starts to get worse…"

If she got worse, Lena would do whatever she needed.

Including going to the hegen again.

How much of herself would she sell?

He sighed. The crew couldn't help him now.

There would be no running from this.

Not from his mother. Not from his sister. And not from his fate.

He could only hope the king would give him a chance.

CHAPTER TWELVE

The chapel felt different from this vantage.

Finn remembered the times he'd been there all too well. Sunlight streamed in from a stained-glass window overhead, giving swirls of color across the walls. The markings on the ceiling were difficult for him to read in the bright light, the colors blurring the shapes so that he couldn't see anything about them.

The man sitting in the chair wasn't strapped in it the way Finn had been. It surprised Finn. The man had to outweigh him by ten stone, and his size reminded Finn of Rock. Muscular like him, too.

Master Meyer stood across from the prisoner, seemingly unconcerned by the lack of restraints on the man. His technique was different from that of the Lion.

Not entirely, though.

Meyer had gone through the tools resting on the table the same way the Lion had done with Finn, describing them in incredible detail. Finn found himself looking down at the table, studying the tools and trying to keep the disgust pushed to the back of his mind.

He had to tolerate this now.

Not that he had to be the one to carry out anything. That would be on Meyer. Finn only had to be there, to learn, to observe.

"You will find that you want to answer my questions," Master Meyer said. "To do otherwise will incur my irritation. Trust me when I tell you that you do not want my irritation."

The man looked over at Meyer, then his gaze drifted past him, locking eyes with Finn.

He knew many other crews, but this wasn't someone he recognized. Lind Rassum, a criminal of questionable past. Meyer hadn't given Finn much more about him than his name. Finn suspected that was part of a test.

Given his size, Lind was probably a bruiser, though Finn would have said the same about Rock, and he served mostly as a scout. The prisoner had a wide nose that looked as if it had recently been broken and a yellow bruise on one cheek that looked to be healing.

"I've told you the truth." For a large man, he had a surprisingly soft voice.

Not like Rock. His was loud. Brash. One that had always made Finn laugh.

"You've said the same to each inquisitor. You would continue to deny me the truth? The gods watch as you speak, Lind, so find the truth within you to appease them."

"I've told you the truth. The damn Archers are rounding up everyone who has even the smell of…"

"Of what?" Meyer remained a pace away from him. No closer. His voice was low, dangerous.

Had Meyer been the one to question him, Finn didn't know if he would have been able to hold out. There had been something about the Lion that he'd *wanted* to ignore. With Meyer, he had a different sense. He wanted to tell him anything. Whatever he wanted to hear. Whatever it would take to keep him from turning back to the tools.

"Nothing. It don't matter. If you're here, they've already made up their mind."

"Who has made up their mind?"

Lind looked at Meyer defiantly. "The jurors. Magister. Gods, probably even you. Do what you need to do. Get your kicks. You can't hurt me. I done what I had to."

Meyer sighed. "I assure you I can most definitely hurt you."

He turned toward Finn and stopped at the table with the torture tools. When he'd described them, it had seemed as much for Finn's benefit as for Lind's. Meyer began to move them around, shifting some of the tools along the top of the table, sliding the boots over so they would be visible. Finn hadn't known about the boot before Meyer had started describing it. The tool was different from what the Lion had used. Made of a dark iron, it latched on to the prisoner's foot. From there…

Finn didn't want to think of what the blades buried in the bottom of the boot would do when the knob holding them twisted.

"What do you think?" Meyer whispered.

Finn looked up. He wasn't accustomed to Meyer asking him questions like that.

"I don't think he's guilty of anything."

He kept his voice low and hoped it didn't carry. Even if it did, it wouldn't help Lind at all. It wasn't like Finn had the authority to release him.

"Why not?"

Finn looked past Meyer and focused on Lind. He sat in the chair, his shoulders sagging, not fighting or trying to do anything—despite the lack of straps around his ankles and wrists the way Finn had when he'd been brought to the chapel.

His head leaned forward, and he looked at the ground. His breathing had quickened when Meyer came over, suggesting to Finn that he was scared.

"A feeling, I guess."

"The same feeling you had with Jon Habrans?"

"I felt he *was* guilty," Finn said.

"Exactly. That same feeling?"

Finn kept his gaze on Lind. "That was different. With Jon, I could tell he was lying."

"You can't tell that with Rassum?"

Finn shook his head slightly. "It's not the same. I think he's telling you the truth."

"As he knows it."

Finn frowned and looked up at Meyer. "Isn't that the case with all men?"

"It is."

"You don't think he's telling you the truth?"

"I think he's telling me *his* truth. That's not the same as my truth. Or yours."

"I don't understand."

"What he's shared with us is the truth as he knows and believes it to be." He looked down, moving one of the tools—a long, pointed rod—off to the side, where it struck another tool and created a loud clang. Lind's breathing quickened again. "That doesn't mean his truth is the truth I seek. That doesn't mean his truth is the truth of the king. All it means is that it's the way he sees the world."

"If you say so."

"What were you accused of doing?"

"Breaking into the viscount's home."

"Did you do it?"

Finn frowned. Was this another test? It was a strange one, if so. "You know I did."

"Did you think what you did was wrong?"

"What?"

"Did you think what you did was wrong?"

"I know I wasn't supposed to be there, if that's what you're getting at."

"That's not the same. Did you think it was wrong?"

"According to the laws of the city, yes."

"Under what laws wouldn't it have been wrong?"

Meyer watched him, and Finn couldn't tell what he was trying to get at. He still suspected this was some sort of test, though if that were the case, then it was a strange kind of test.

"I don't know."

"Did you think it was wrong?" Meyer asked again.

"No," Finn said finally.

"Why not? You broke into the viscount's home to take something that did not belong to you. How would that not have been wrong?"

Finn shook his head. "It doesn't matter."

"I think it does. It gets to the heart of why I invoked my right."

"Because I wasn't doing it for myself."

Meyer held Finn's gaze then turned back to Lind. "Do you have anything more you'd like to say?"

"I've said what I can say. It's enough."

"You were beginning to tell me about something else. I would like to know why you feel you were unfairly targeted."

"You don't care. You've already made up your mind. I can see that on your face."

"Can you?" Meyer started toward him and held one of the long, slender rods. The end was pointed and Finn wondered what Meyer might do with it.

"You're the same as the others who come here. Threatening and trying to prove that you're stronger than me. It don't matter. You'll do what you want regardless."

"Why do you feel you've been unfairly targeted?"

"Because I have. Blame me for going to the hegen all you want, but that's not a crime."

Finn looked over to Meyer before turning his attention back to Lind. *That* was why he was here? He hadn't been able to uncover the reason before, but if that were the case, then having Lind in the Declan Prison was far more than what he deserved.

What would happen if Lena were caught going to the hegen?

"It wasn't going to the hegen that brought you here. It was what you did on their behalf."

Finn watched Lind, and couldn't tell if he still hid anything from them. Normally, he was good at reading others. Looking at Lind, he didn't have a sense from him about whether or not he had done anything on behalf of the hegen, though when Meyer mentioned it, Finn saw a darkness behind his eyes.

"I didn't do anything," he said.

This time, his already soft voice was even fainter. Finn watched him, trying to gauge whether Lind told the truth or not.

His posture had shifted. He sat upright more than he had before, and there was the way he glanced up briefly, as if to see if Meyer watched him.

He wasn't telling the truth.

At least about that.

Surprisingly—or not, considering what he'd seen from Meyer—the executioner knew he wasn't telling him the truth.

"What did you do for the hegen?" Meyer asked.

"Like I said—"

"Nothing. I understand you don't want to be implicated in something that will cause you more trouble. Unfortunately, I'm going to have to keep asking these questions until I get a satisfactory answer. As it doesn't appear that you want to help provide an answer that will placate me, we will have to continue this discussion."

Meyer brought the slender rod toward Lind.

Finn wasn't sure what Lind might do. The iron masters hadn't bound him in any way, so he was just sitting there in the chair, free to get up and move. That he hadn't seemed surprising to Finn.

Perhaps it shouldn't be.

What would Lind do to the executioner?

That he faced the executioner would be enough to intimidate anyone. Finn had been intimidated by the Lion, and that was without knowing that he'd served the executioner. He'd been his tormenter.

That would be the same thing Lind felt. Only it might be even worse.

"If you would care to share with me what the hegen assigned for you, I might be able to assist you in a reprieve. As you've refused, there isn't much I can do."

"I… They wanted me to find something for them!" Lind's voice went up, though Finn couldn't see what Meyer did. The executioner stood in front of him, arms raised, the slender rod held up, as if he were stabbing it down toward his thigh—or his groin.

"What did they ask you to find?"

Lind hesitated, then started to whimper softly. "Nothing. Just a trinket. It shouldn't even matter—"

"It matters where you were."

"It don't matter. I didn't take anything!"

"That's not what the report says."

"The report is wrong! I didn't take anything. You've got to believe me!"

He whimpered a bit more, and then Meyer stepped back toward Finn, still holding the rod. Lind continued to whimper, an awful sound that filled the inside of the chapel.

Meyer set the rod back down on the table.

"Why did you stop?" Finn asked.

"Because he told me what I needed to know."

"That's it? You just wanted to know whether he took something?"

"He was seen in the home of Ophel Grunson. According to the report Master Grunson gave, he was missing a gold necklace, two silver earrings, and a ceramic bowl."

Finn looked over to Lind. "He said he didn't take anything, though."

"And I believe him."

"You do?"

"Do you?"

Finn watched as Lind continued to whimper. That wasn't the sound of a hardened thief. He might look like Rock, but that was where the similarities ended. He had done what he had for a different reason.

The hegen.

"Why did he go to the hegen?"

Meyer shook his head. "Does it matter? Most of what you believe about the hegen is rumor. Nothing more than that."

"They don't have magic?"

"They have that, at least of a sort, but they don't steal souls or eat the remains they gather."

"I never said they did."

Meyer grunted. "You don't have to. I know what most

think about the hegen. If you want to know the truth of their magic, go and ask."

Finn looked over to Lind. "Then if he went to the hegen and they sent him after something, aren't they responsible?"

"Was your employer responsible?"

Finn said nothing.

"A man is responsible for his own actions. The gods know this. Lind Rassum made a choice, and he will be punished for that choice."

Meyer headed out of the room, and Finn followed.

Once in the hall, the iron masters stepped past and went into the room. Finn could still hear Lind whimpering.

"He doesn't deserve the torment."

Meyer cocked a brow at him. "Deserve?"

"Until you've seen someone you care about suffer, or you have to make a choice between starving or stealing, or…" As soon as he said it, he wondered if maybe Meyer *had* that experience. "I'm sorry, Master Meyer. I misspoke."

"If there's one lesson you must learn now, it's that you must follow the law, and in doing so, you follow the gods. In all things."

What he'd seen in the room, though, made Finn question whether that was something that he'd be able to do.

"How do you stomach what you have to do?" Finn asked as they reached the main entrance to Declan. They had come to question a few prisoners, though Meyer had only had Finn in on Lind's interrogation. Finn suspected there was a reason behind it. Perhaps a message to him, though he might be overthinking it.

"You learn what must be done."

"That's not an answer."

Meyer turned to him, arms crossed over his chest. "I would ask you the same thing. How did you stomach what you did? Violating another? Acting in opposition to the will of the gods. How could you stomach such crimes?"

"The gods wouldn't want me to suffer."

That was a better answer than the alternative he had— that the gods didn't care.

"The gods ask many things of us. Some must suffer so that we might become what we are meant to be. Others accept their fate and know the purpose the gods have in store for us. Still others wander their entire lives, never satisfied, never knowing who—and what—they were to have been." Meyer studied him. "What will you be, Finn Jagger?"

Finn didn't have an answer. Even worse was the way Meyer watched him, leaving Finn wondering if perhaps that was a mistake.

Out in the street, he expected Meyer to head toward the Brinder section to investigate, but he went a different way. Toward the wall. When they reached the wall, Meyer headed through the gate and out toward the section surrounding Verendal.

The hegen section.

The hegen were a people who lived outside of the city, though Finn had never known why. Maybe it was because they preferred it or because they weren't welcomed within the city walls. They were widely known to have access to magic, though Finn didn't know if everyone could use magic or if only some of the hegen were witches. It was a place that he had always avoided going, though that was partly because he feared what the hegen would ask of him and what he might be willing to give.

Meyer remained quiet as they walked.

The homes were small, huts really. Many of them were painted brightly, as if to draw attention to the hegen, though not all were. The streets leading into the section were little wider than paths, though people still crowded along them.

As they neared the outskirts of the hegen section, Meyer started to slow. "You'll need to let me do the questioning," he said.

Finn nodded.

This part of the city didn't scare him so much as make him nervous. It was in the kind of people he knew to be there, but it was more than that. It was the use of magic. Living near it and being confronted by it were different.

The streets running through the hegen section were different from those in the city. Within the city, the streets twisted and turned, creating a maze that protected the palace, but outside of the city, the narrow street that ran through was something else. He and Meyer had a hard time walking side by side, so Finn was forced to keep behind him, pacing as quickly as he could as they made their way through the narrow street.

The street itself twisted, but more often, it was as if a home had simply sprung up, forcing him to veer off and take a different turn. He quickly lost track of where they were.

"How do you navigate through here?" he whispered.

"You get used to it. They have their own sort of organization."

"How often do you come out here?"

"As often as is needed."

Meyer left it at that. There were others in the street, enough that Finn found himself looking all around him, staring at the people who were there. Most were dressed in colorful clothing. Scraps of mismatching fabrics. His drab clothing felt out of place comparatively.

The children he saw all had dark hair and dark eyes. Some were dirty, with smudges of dirt or soot on faces and arms, but not as many as he had imagined. The adults were dressed in bright colors, some almost a patchwork as if repairing damage to their clothing.

"What are you looking for out here?" Finn asked, following Meyer through the hegen neighborhood. Everything seemed disorganized, and though there were only a few dozen people out, he couldn't shake how it felt as if the streets were filled.

"I investigate everything."

It dawned on him what he meant. They were coming to investigate why the hegen would have asked Lind to do what he had.

"Even out here?"

"This is still the domain of the king. I will investigate all that is necessary for me to better understand what his people have done."

They weaved through the street. Meyer paused at a storefront, looking in the window, frowning for a moment, before moving on. He did that several times before they stopped again. The streets emptied out the farther they went, with fewer and fewer people out as they wandered.

"What are you looking for?"

"I'm looking for signs of the hegen," he said.

"All of this is hegen."

"It is, but I'm looking for something in particular. With the Alainsith gathering and the king planning to meet, all of this is unusual."

Finn waited for him to expand on that, but Meyer didn't say anything more.

When he stopped at a door, he knocked.

It was a tidy building. The door was brightly painted red, so different than the other colors nearby. Finn stared at the door as Meyer knocked, his heart starting to race.

He had never been out in this section of the city.

He'd lived in the city for the entirety of his life, and he knew the hegen had been there for much of that. Still, coming into this section was only for fools or those who were desperate.

Like Lena had been.

Finn shook those thoughts away.

There was no answer at the door.

"It doesn't look as if they're home."

Meyer rested his hand on the door, holding it there for a moment. "She's home," he said softly. "She has chosen not to answer."

"Who?"

"Esmerelda."

"Who is she?"

"One of the hegen with power." Meyer knocked again.

Finn could only stare.

This was the home of a hegen witch?

A part of him wanted to know what she would look like, but another part, a part that was the practical one, knew that he needed to avoid their attention. It was the part that remembered the stories he'd been told as a child. The hegen always exacted a price.

It wasn't always the price someone would want to pay, but it was a price.

"How do you know her?" Finn asked when the door still didn't open.

"I have served many years," he said.

He knocked again, lingering for a moment before shaking his head. He nodded to Finn.

They wandered through the hegen community a while longer. They took strange, twisting turns to the point where Finn got lost. That was a rare enough thing for him. He usually knew exactly where he was, and in this case, he found that he couldn't keep track of where Meyer guided him. Many of the homes looked the same as the hegen home had looked. Every so often, he caught a glimpse of an older hegen, not just the children they had encountered for the most part, but then they disappeared.

"Where is everyone?"

"They have chosen to make themselves absent," Meyer said. He let out a frustrated sigh. "It seems that we won't find anything today."

"Why not?"

"Because the hegen have chosen not to share."

They wound through the streets until they reached the edge of the hegen section, the Raven Stone looming in the distance. Forest pressed upon the city on the far side, though as far as Finn knew, few ever dared to venture into the western edge. It put them too close to the Alainsith lands—and their magical influence. No one wanted to get any closer to that than necessary. Having the hegen along the edge of the city was considered bad enough.

Meyer guided them back toward the city, and when they neared the gate, Finn looked back toward the hegen section.

Lights shone brightly, and he saw movement in the streets.

"We could go back," he said.

"It would change nothing," Meyer said. "Until they choose otherwise, we will not find what we need."

"And what is that?"

"A reason why the hegen have called in so many favors recently."

The road led through the main part of the city, winding past wealthy merchants. The streets were cleaner, the air having a different scent, and there was a vibrancy within this part of the city. In the distance, the pure, sweet sounds of a bell tolling rang out. The Church of Fell, Finn suspected, celebrating a god Finn had never fully understood, though it was one of the few religious places he'd ever set foot in. That was only because entering Fell was considered something of an honor, and when his father had brought him and Lena to the church, they'd gone willingly—despite neither of them having gone to church that often.

"Where are we heading now?"

He appreciated that Meyer didn't mind the questions. The King had tolerated them within the crew—up to the point where someone questioned his approach to a job. Oscar could get away with it, but Finn and Rock would have to mutter about things over ale after they learned details.

What he wouldn't give to sit and have a drink with Rock again. That would at least feel normal. Not like any of this.

"Another task for the day."

"It's getting late."

"Do you think the time of day matters?"

Finn looked around him. The sun had started to set, so he knew it was late enough that most of the shops would be closing. Once it got dark, there weren't many others who came out into the streets in these sections. It had made it easier to take jobs there.

"The last few days, you've ended before it was too dark." Other days, he'd returned home, dismissing Finn. Because he hadn't known whether he wanted to run or not, Finn hadn't lingered around the house, wandering until it was late enough and only then heading back.

"Today is different."

"What else do you have to do? Is there a prison in this part of the city?" Finn smiled as he said it. All of the prisons were in the city's outer areas, many of them near the walls. All of them were in less desirable parts of the city, though he had wondered if that was because of the prison or if the prison was placed there for that purpose.

"Yes, but that isn't where we're heading."

Finn frowned. "Where is the prison in this part of the city?"

"I need silence to collect my thoughts."

Finn didn't push.

Instead, he looked around the streets. It was strange to him to come through this part of the city without planning a job. He knew where he was—the Perend section was one of the wealthier merchant sections, and the shops there all catered to those with significant wealth. There were jewelers there that had pieces worth more than most would make in a year. Some that were worth more than most would make in their lives. Artists occupied one end of the section, and he'd heard rumors that some of the art would sell for even more than the most valuable jewels. Finn couldn't imagine paying something like that for a painting, but men with money could be fools.

What they didn't find there were butchers. Bakers. Taverns.

None of the kind of places where *he* would have liked to spend his time.

What did he need to collect his thoughts for?

Were they heading to a particularly difficult interrogation?

That seemed unlikely. The executioner didn't fear the interrogations he did. He'd only observed a few, but it didn't seem as if Meyer relished them or that he was particularly troubled by them. They were simply a part of the job. He questioned, and men answered. Or they didn't, and he continued to question.

The bells stopped tolling. Finn hadn't paid attention to how many bells there'd been, but from the angle of the sun, he thought he knew.

Then the street turned.

In the distance, he saw the palace rising high in front of them.

It was magnificent. Sunlight trailed along the spires, giving it something of a gleaming appearance, making it seemed as if the gods blessed the palace. More guards were atop the wall than Finn was accustomed to seeing, and he realized where they headed—and why.

The king had come to the city.

That was why Master Meyer had to collect his thoughts.

He was heading to the palace on behalf of Finn.

Meyer never slowed as they approached as Finn wanted to, though this was Finn's fate rather than

Meyer's, so perhaps it wasn't quite as intimidating to him. Not the way it was for Finn.

"You didn't tell me we were meeting with the king today," Finn said as they neared the palace. With each step, the trepidation within him continued to grow. He shouldn't be surprised that they were coming to the palace, either. Finn had known the expectation. It hadn't changed in the time that he'd been working with Meyer. He'd known that he would be brought there and that he would have to present himself before the king.

It might be for the best that he didn't have the time to prepare. Had he known, he might not have had the focus he needed throughout the day.

"You knew the timeline."

He had, but he thought it was a general timeline. Finn figured he'd have a chance to prepare better. Having it sprung on him like this didn't give him a chance to prepare himself at all.

They reached the gate outside of the palace. A pair of guards stood watch on either side of the gate. The Archers atop the wall were more than enough intimidation.

His gaze drifted to the Archers. They each had the stripe of the palace Archers.

They would be skilled. The kind of men he'd been warned to be careful around. The kind of men Finn had always tried to avoid. Now he headed toward a place where they would be in significant numbers.

The Archers at the gate nodded to Meyer and let him pass.

Finn felt a strange thrill at the idea that he'd be allowed

to head into the palace grounds. This was a place where he'd never expected to be permitted. His gaze looked everywhere, still looking for weakness within the grounds but not finding anything. The Archers had the grounds covered.

That had to be for the king. Without the king, Finn wondered if it would have been as well guarded. When he'd been near the grounds before, he didn't recall as many Archers around.

"Keep up," Master Meyer said.

Not only were there Archers stationed all around the walls, there were a few Archers patrolling. "Are there always so many guards?" Finn asked.

Meyer looked around. "That's what you notice?"

"I was thinking about what I'd heard about Dalton Pegg and how he'd—"

"The stories you heard about Pegg were likely fabrications."

"He didn't attempt to break into the palace grounds?"

"He did."

"Did he steal anything?"

"Not that I was able to ascertain."

"Then why was he executed?"

Meyer paused and looked over at him. "He was executed because the jurors and the magister sentenced him to that fate. It was up to me to carry out his sentencing, and I did it."

"Did he deserve it?"

"That is not my place to decide. As we've previously discussed."

Finn wanted to say something more, to object about how it was that he could simply carry out a sentencing like that, but they neared the main entrance to the palace.

They had passed through an enormous garden that made the one in the viscount's yard look tiny by comparison. Another pair of Archers stood guard on either side of the door leading into the palace.

They barred Master Meyer's entrance.

"I am Henry Meyer, first of the inquisitors, the king's Master Executioner. I present myself with Finn Jagger, condemned and saved by the Executioner's Right." The words had something of a formal feel to them, and Finn realized why.

Meyer didn't talk to the guards. He spoke to the man standing behind them.

The door had been cracked slightly. Barely enough that Finn could hardly see who looked outside, but enough that he realized someone was looking beyond.

The door opened widely. "They may pass."

This came from an older man, thin and with graying hair. He was dressed all in white, though he had maroon and black embroidered on the sleeves in the crest of the crown. The king's crest had a massive wolf head worked over crossed blades, the wolf looking as if it were snarling.

Meyer motioned for Finn to follow.

He stepped into the most ornate room he'd ever seen.

Gilded wood paneling ran from floor to ceiling, and a golden wolf's head was worked into the ceiling. Marble gleamed within the tiles, the walls, and even the massive pillars rising in front of him. Portraits twice as tall as him were hanging on the wall. Finn recognized King Porman Arcald, having seen him parading into the city during one of his visits, but there were portraits of other kings as well. Those who'd come before. Porman's father, King Ordol the Pious, and then before him was the last of the Theren line, King Yofun the Damned. Not that he would have claimed that title during his life, but he had made the mistake of warring with the Alainsith people—and failed.

Finn knew the same stories as anyone who'd grown up in Verendal. Ordol had negotiated the peace with the Alainsith, such as it was. The kingdom kept their cities, but the Alainsith prevented access—and expansion—to the forest on the western edge, and the nation of Yelind to the south prevented expansion in that direction.

"You will follow me," the older man said.

Finn's gaze settled on a magnificent vase in one corner, all finely painted and covered with gold he suspected was worth more than he'd ever seen. There were dozens of sculptures, all of them made to look like great heroes of the past, and all of them holding weapons as if anyone who came through there had to do so with their permission.

They were led to a room along the hallway.

He hadn't expected to see King Porman in person.

The king was smaller than Finn had imagined. Probably a hand shorter than Finn, and slight of build, he sat atop a gilded chair in the center of the room with distinct carvings shaped like a wolf's head in the armrest. Five men circled him, one of them the viscount wearing the maroon and black of his station. Finn recognized Bellut as well. He hadn't seen him since his sentencing.

The older man cleared his throat. "I present Master Henry Meyer, the king's executioner."

The others turned toward them, the quiet conversation they'd been having suddenly dying off. Finn felt a lump rising in his throat and began to wonder if this was a mistake.

If this went wrong, he would be sentenced to die. From the odd look the viscount gave him, that was what he wanted. Perhaps he did for having broken into his home.

A tall, regal-appearing man standing next to the king's throne nodded toward them. He had a long robe striped in maroon and black, embroidery running along each sleeve. He held a twisted staff, leaning on it as if he could no longer bear his weight otherwise. He might be much older than the king, but he looked more kingly than Porman.

"Master Meyer. The gods grace our meeting again."

The executioner bowed his head, leaning at the waist.

Finn followed his example, bowing along with Meyer, looking up as he did.

He had a sense Bellut was appraising him. More than that, he had a sense that viscount watched with irritation in his eyes. He looked away, not wanting to meet his gaze.

"I have served at the honor of the king," Meyer said. "Which is why I present myself today. I am here because—"

"You are here because you have demanded the Executioner's Right," the man standing next to the throne said. He had a hint of a smile, and his gaze drifted to the viscount, and then to Bellut, before looking back to Meyer. "Now you question whether the king will support your claim."

Meyer nodded. "Tradition allows for me to make such a claim."

"Tradition, and yet the ancient right of the executioner guild has not been made in generations. The king has questioned why this time."

Meyer glanced over to Finn. "He can still serve the gods."

"He was the criminal who broke into my—"

The older man raised his hand, silencing the viscount.

"You have chosen a criminal as your right."

"As is tradition," Master Meyer said.

"As is tradition," the man said. He studied Finn, and there was a sense of his gaze lingering upon him, some sense that left Finn feeling unsettled, almost as if he were watching him, weighing him.

Who was this man?

So far, the king had not yet spoken.

"How has he served?" the man asked.

"Briefly," Master Meyer said. "In that time, I have a sense of conflicted values within him. He questions his purpose. Yet he has a good heart. He can serve the king, and I believe he can be useful."

The other man looked over at Master Meyer, studying him. "You understand the consequences of making such a claim?"

Meyer nodded. "I understand."

"As is tradition," the man said.

Meyer took a deep breath, nodding once more. "As is tradition."

The other man turned away, looking to the king. Something must've passed between them, though Finn couldn't tell what it was. The king made a movement with his hand, and the other man turned back, looking at Master Meyer.

"The king has decided."

CHAPTER THIRTEEN

Finn walked alongside Master Meyer as they headed away from the palace. He resisted the urge to look over his shoulder toward the palace walls and the Archers stationed along it. He didn't even feel compelled to look around at the merchant buildings on either side of the street. The only thing he could think of doing was keeping his gaze focused straight ahead of him.

Meyer had been quiet since leaving the palace.

The king had granted Meyer's right, but there seemed to be something more within that request which left Meyer troubled.

"Do you really think I can do this job?"

Meyer slowed and looked over at him. "I would not have staked the claim if I did not."

"What does it mean that you have made this claim?"

"It means that I will teach. It means that you will learn. It means that..." Meyer took a deep breath, and he turned away, motioning for Finn to follow. "It's time for you to obtain clothing more suitable for your position."

"As your apprentice?"

"Would you prefer something else?"

Finn's heart still pounded within his chest after what he had just gone through.

Here he had thought he would be able to make a run for it, try to escape the city, but now that he had been approved to continue working with Meyer, perhaps he didn't have to do so quite as soon as he had intended before.

"I guess not."

"You will visit Beshear's Tailor in the morning. Master Beshear will see that you're dressed appropriately. Afterward, you will find me at Marsen's store. As you have visited both of these places with me previously, I assume that you should have no difficulty finding them."

Finn nodded. He remembered where the tailor and the general store were, though he had been left outside in the street when he had visited before. Most of the places Meyer had brought him were only visited from the street. He hadn't much experience inside the stores.

Was that the next step in his apprenticeship? Now that he had been approved by the king, Finn would be permitted to visit the shops?

That would be better than the alternative. It meant that he could run errands, clean the sword of justice, and do whatever else Meyer needed of him. Anything that didn't involve him tormenting people. Anything that didn't involve him killing people.

"You are free to go," Meyer said.

"Go where?"

"Wherever you choose. You are in my employ now, so your actions reflect upon me." Finn understood the warning. "You will receive ten fils each month. After the first year, you will be eligible for additional compensation, depending upon your performance. Once you reach journeyman level, you will be paid twice that amount each week."

Finn blinked. Ten fils wasn't all that much money, but it was consistent at least. He thought about how much he had already obtained, and how much his sister had hoarded away, and didn't think it was nearly as much as what they would need for their mother to see a physician.

"Is that not enough?"

Finn shook his head.

"Then what is it?"

"I was thinking about my mother," he said. There was no point in denying that he worried about her. He had a sense that Master Meyer read him even when he tried to keep things from him. "You had said—"

"I will see what can be done for her."

"She needs to see a physician."

"And I said I will see what can be done for her," he said.

Finn opened his mouth to say something more before clamping it shut.

He didn't want to anger Master Meyer, not when he had already committed to helping him. He followed Meyer to the river, and from there he stopped atop the bridge, looking out at the river. It served as a distinction between the city's wealthier central sections and those of the outer sections, poorer sections.

Meyer continued on, presumably heading toward his home, leaving Finn to his own devices.

He was free.

At least, he was as free as he could be under the current circumstances.

He would truly be the executioner's apprentice.

Finn sighed, looking down at the water. Moonlight reflected off the surface, and the water rippled as it ran along the shoreline.

In the outer sections, more people were out even when it was late. Voices coming toward him stirred him to move, and Finn hurried across the bridge, trying to decide what he would do for the rest of the evening.

He could return to Master Meyer's home. It was late enough that Finn could rest. Tomorrow would be different. He would go to the tailor, obtain clothing that didn't remind him of his pending execution, and then meet with Meyer at the apothecary.

Only, after having visited the palace, Finn didn't know if he would be able to rest.

At this point, the only thing he really wanted to do was to keep moving.

He could return home. His sister would need to know about his new position before she found out about it another way. Finn wasn't entirely sure that he wanted to return home just yet.

Despite Meyer telling him that his actions reflected upon him, visiting the Wenderwolf wouldn't reflect poorly upon Meyer. He wanted to see the crew. Mostly, he wanted to see Oscar and Rock, to tell them what had happened, and to let them know he was going to be all right. They both deserved that much.

Before he knew what he was doing, Finn had already started heading in that direction. Familiar buildings passed by on either side of him. By the time he reached the Wenderwolf in the familiar section of Olin, he started to slow and look all around.

Finn wasn't doing anything other than going to a tavern—though it was a tavern thieves and the King's crew were known to frequent.

Maybe this was a mistake.

A man moved past him along the street. Finn remained on the far side of the street, looking toward the tavern. When the man headed inside, the familiar scent drifted out toward him, that of food and drink and the excitement of the tavern.

He squeezed his eyes shut. That wasn't for him. Not anymore. He couldn't be here the way he'd once been. Now he had a different place in the city.

"Shuffles?"

Finn opened his eyes. "Wolf."

His face looked more grizzled in the growing darkness, and there was a faint gleam of irritation in his eyes. "What the fuck are you doing here? Heard what happened. I think the whole city heard."

Wolf crossed the street, casting a glance toward the tavern. Finn noted he was dressed in his darks, which left him wondering what Wolf had been doing. Not that Wolf didn't wear his darks when scouting—Finn knew he did— only that it was unusual for them to wear the darks any time they weren't on a job.

It was surreal coming back there. After everything that he'd been through over the last few days working with Meyer, he felt as if this was comforting.

"Listen. I probably shouldn't have come back here, but…"

It risked the crew.

That alone was a reason he shouldn't return. Were there any Archers following him, he suspected they'd use him coming here to track who else might have been working with him, and they'd probably use that against him. Meyer had warned him the Archers would keep a look out for him, so he had to wonder if this was another test.

"What is it, Shuffles?"

"I—"

"Finn?"

Oscar's voice cut through his hesitation.

Finn looked over to him. He stood across the street, ready to enter the Wenderwolf, paused with his hand on the door, studying Wolf first and then looking to Finn.

Wolf glanced over to Oscar before chuckling. "It seems as if I need to let the two of you catch up before you come in. You *are* going to come in, aren't you, Shuffles?"

Finn nodded. Now that he was there, Finn had an urge to go in, even have a mug of ale. Anything that might leave him with a sense of familiarity.

Wolf clapped him on the shoulder and shook his head.

"Thought you were going to hang, boy. Damn good to see you."

He nodded to Oscar as he crossed the street, entering the tavern and disappearing.

Finn could only imagine the comment that the King would have upon learning that Finn was out there. Possibly irritation, worried that Finn had betrayed them. Coming here put them in danger.

"What are you doing here?" Oscar whispered, crossing the street and standing in the growing darkness of the buildings leaning over them. "I saw what happened. I *heard* what happened."

"Then you know I'm free to be here."

"You aren't free."

"I don't have to be anywhere."

"Other than with your new master."

Finn shook his head. "It's not like that."

Oscar studied him. "I'm not blaming you. Gods, I'm happy you were given the opportunity to serve. Anything to keep you from hanging. I tried to do everything I could to get to you before then, but when I saw them marching you through the street, the Blood Court..."

Oscar squeezed his eyes closed. It was the most emotion that Finn had seen from him.

"I know," Finn said.

"It took me a while to understand what the hangman did with you. I thought he'd claimed you in some way, maybe that he wanted to save you for the hegen, but that wasn't it at all, was it?"

Finn shook his head. "That wasn't it."

"You have to serve."

"It seems that way."

"You considered running?"

Finn smiled. Leave it to Oscar to know that he had. "I thought about it. I spent the first few days considering whether or not I should run. I even had a plan in place. I wouldn't have been able to come back to the crew, and I couldn't leave Lena and my mother."

"I told you I would take care of them."

"I know you did. And that you would. Mother is getting worse, Oscar. Lena… Lena went to the hegen for help. If I leave now, I worry that she's going to owe them too much to ever be able to escape."

"If she's already gone to them, then she might owe them more than what she can repay now."

"This way, I'll get a regular pay."

"Is that what you want?"

"It's honorable, at least in a way." He looked over to Oscar, seeing the Hand studying him, saying nothing. "I didn't have much choice. I was the one captured, remember?"

"I know. And I think about it every day. I remember what you did for me, that you saved me. Hell, you probably saved all of us by being the one they captured. You allowed the King and Wolf to escape. They won't say it, but they know that they owe you for getting them free."

"I don't need them to owe me anything. I just want…" Did he want recognition? It wasn't as if he could return to the crew. Now that he served Master Meyer, he wasn't going to be able to return to the crew. He wasn't going to be able to return to stealing. "I don't even know what I want. I guess I just wanted to see how the crew was doing."

Oscar glanced over his shoulder, looking at the tavern. "The crew is the same as usual."

"Pulling jobs for the Client."

"Trying. Had one go wrong not too many days ago."

"The one where Rock nearly got pinched?"

"That's the one. Another crew must have been after the same thing. The Client pays well, making the King more inclined to pursue them than our usual jobs. There's more going on here, Finn. I just—"

At least Oscar saw it, too. "You were looking to try to uncover who the Client is."

Oscar flicked his gaze toward the Wenderwolf before back to Finn. "You can't say that here."

"Why?"

"Just don't come around here saying that, Finn. For that matter, it might be better if you just didn't come around here."

That stung. The crew were his friends.

If he had to serve as an executioner, at least he could have his friends. "I just wanted to see everyone."

"Why, look at what the gods brought us," a loud voice said from inside the tavern.

Finn hadn't noticed the door open and hadn't heard the chaos from inside, the music and the voices and the sound of excitement. He looked over and saw the King striding across the street.

"Damn, Shuffles. You look pretty good for a dead

man." He glanced over to Oscar. "Was the Hand trying to talk you out of coming into visit with us?"

"I was only trying to make sure that he didn't have any Archers following him," Oscar said.

"Archers? Why would the Archers follow him? What we have here is the executioner's apprentice." The King clapped Finn on the shoulder. "And here I worried about what you might have told them during your questioning. Guess that was a mistake." He pushed Finn ahead of him. "Let's have a mug of ale. You've got time for that, don't you, Shuffles?"

Finn looked over to Oscar. A pained expression twisted the corners of his eyes.

"I think I've got time for that."

The King chuckled. "Of course you do. Damn, but it's good to see you."

They reached the tavern, and the King pulled the door open, positioning himself in such a way that Finn didn't have any choice but to head inside. Once inside, the faint smoke of the tavern along with the scent of ale swirled around him. All of it was familiar. Pleasant.

The King motioned for him to sit. "Annie will be thrilled to see you again, Shuffles. Just wait here."

Finn took a seat at the booth.

Oscar sat across from him, watching him. "You shouldn't stay here. You got out."

"I didn't want to get out," he said.

Could Oscar really not want to see him?

Annie came by, a wide grin on her face, carrying a pair of mugs. She set one down in front of Oscar and slid one over to Finn while leaning forward. Her cleavage bounced with the movement, though Finn didn't have eyes for it the way he once had. He stared at the ale.

"I brought the condemned something to help him celebrate." She ran a finger along his cheek. "I don't know that I've ever met someone sentenced by the magister who returned to the world of the living. Leon tells me you got a unique sentence from them?"

"Not quite from them," Finn said.

Oscar watched him intently.

"Well? Get on with it. We all want to know what happened! Stories are one thing, but we want the truth," the King said.

Finn glanced at Oscar before shrugging. What did it matter if he shared with them what he'd been through? They were his crew. They'd likely heard rumors, anyway. He told them about the Blood Court, the march up the Raven Stone, even the rope. When he brought up the Executioner's Right, Wolf started shaking his head.

"Can't believe the old bastard would pull something like that," Wolf said.

"The hangman?" the King asked.

Wolf nodded. "Word is he didn't like the last man assigned to work with him. A bit of a prick, from those who knew him."

"The Lion," Finn whispered.

Wolf glanced at him, nodding. "That's the one. An overeager shit, from everything that I've heard. Always dug a little too deep. Not good for a crew." Wolf glanced at the King, who nodded.

"He's the one who questioned me." Finn watched them. For a moment, he wondered if they were the reason the Lion had been killed but shook the thought away. The crew weren't killers. "Anyway, when the Lion died, most thought the viscount would assign someone else. I doubt even the viscount would've expected the old bastard to circumvent him the way that he did."

"Well, it's to our benefit," the King said. He grabbed a mug from the table, and he lifted it. "To Shuffles."

Wolf grabbed his mug, and Finn took his. Oscar was the last to lift his, bringing it up slowly, watching Finn the entire time.

"To Shuffles," they all said.

They drank, and Finn sipped at the mug of ale. For some reason, he felt out of place in a way he hadn't before.

It hadn't even been all that long since he had been to the tavern and a part of the crew. In the few weeks that he'd been gone—*could it really have been such a short time?*—he felt as if so much had changed for him.

Capture, then torture and nearly dying, and now apprenticed.

All while they were free pulling jobs without him.

They were his crew. His family, in a way. Only, it didn't feel that way now.

"Now that we have Shuffles plugged into the system, we might be able to expedite some of our plans. What do you say, Shuffles?"

Finn looked down at his mug, sipping at it. "I'm not sure I can be of much use. He doesn't let me do a whole lot. Mostly errands."

"Errands for now, but in time he will pull you into more. If you're to be his apprentice, then you'll get dragged into inquisitions. Imagine the kind of things we can learn." The King glanced over to Wolf. "With enough notice, we might even get the jump on things."

Finn continued to look down at his mug. "It might be a while," Finn said. "I get the sense that he is bringing me along slowly. Chores, mostly. I did get to learn how he oils his sword." He said the last with a hint of a laugh.

Wolf leaned forward. "You saw Justice? What was it like?"

"What was it like?" the King asked. "It's a damn sword. What do you expect to be like?"

"It's not just a sword," Wolf said. "Justice has been part of Verendal for centuries. At one point, the blade supposedly was used by Harold the Just—where the sword truly got its name—when he defended the city from the attack of Alainsith. It's because of that blade the magic in the forest outside the city stops there rather than squeezing us here."

"The executioner wouldn't have a sword like that."

Wolf shrugged. "I'm just telling you the stories I've heard. Of course, a blade like that is bound to have stories told about it. Think about how many men it's killed over the years."

"And women," Annie said.

The King laughed softly. "Not too many women get the honorable death, though."

"There have been a few."

"Name one," the King said.

"Rebecca the Seamstress."

"You're making that up," Oscar said.

The longer Finn sat there, the more Oscar started to come around, but he still looked at Finn, watching him as if there was something more troubling that he feared to share.

"I'm not making it up. Rebecca the Seamstress was one of the oldest tavern owners. Do you know why they called her the Seamstress?"

"I'm sure you're going to tell us," Wolf said.

"They called her the Seamstress because she used to cut parts off of her victims and stitch them together."

Wolf frowned. "Somebody like that wouldn't be given the sword."

"They would if they were nobility." Annie got up, and she tapped the table, looking over at Finn. "I'm glad you were given a second chance, Finn."

She headed away, and Finn watched her as she disappeared to the back of the tavern and then behind the door leading into the kitchen.

The King and Wolf continued their conversation, and Finn listened, though only halfheartedly. He drank from his ale, and realized that the two of them were discussing another job.

"Think about it, Wolf. With Shuffles here, we might even get details we weren't able to before." He glanced over to Finn. "Hell, he might even know the layout of the palace."

His memory of the palace was vague, little more than a snippet of it. He didn't want to reveal to them that he'd been too nervous to pay much attention to what he'd seen in the palace. Oscar or Wolf probably would have taken details of the layout, and would have been able to determine just how many Archers were stationed around the yard, and would have known the dimensions of the garden just by walking through there.

The longer he sat there, the more he began to question if he should even be here.

Meyer would be angry.

But he'd needed the crew to know he was alive. And safe.

Finn finished his ale and got to his feet. "I had better get back to Master Meyer."

The King regarded him with a smile. "You're coming back, right? Not leaving us to worry about you for another few weeks?"

"I'll come back when I can."

The King tapped the table, turning to Wolf and chuckling as if there had never been any doubt.

When he reached the door, Oscar joined him. He leaned in closer. "You don't have to come back," he whispered.

"These are my friends."

"This was your crew," Oscar said, as if that was different. "Use this chance that you've been given. Take advantage of it. I know it's not what you wanted, but..." Oscar looked up, meeting his gaze. "It's the kind of chance your father would've wanted for you."

Finn frowned. "My father wouldn't have wanted that for me. He wanted me to find something more than he ever could do." He didn't tell Oscar that his father had wanted him to be honorable. He didn't need to.

"Trust me, Finn. Your father would want this for you."

Finn stepped out of the Wenderwolf when somebody grabbed him by the shoulder. He spun, tensing immediately.

Rock stood behind him. His normally smiling face was pinched, and his wide eyes squinted as they looked at Finn. His jacket was stained with what Finn hoped was ale and not blood, and a dark bruise shadowed one cheek.

"Why didn't you come sooner?" There was hurt in Rock's voice.

Finn glanced behind him, looking to the tavern for a moment before turning his attention back to Rock. "I didn't have a chance. I couldn't get away before tonight."

"Are you back, then?"

Finn looked to the open door of the tavern where he could see Oscar's back. It seemed to him that Oscar listened. "In the crew? Not for a while. That doesn't mean we can't talk over ale."

Rock let out a heavy sigh. "I guess that'll have to do. You'll have stories, I bet." He punched Finn in the shoulder. "I don't know what happened other than what Wolf told me. The King doesn't want to talk about it. I think it bothered him when you got pinched."

Finn wasn't so sure about that. "I'm sure what Wolf told you is true. When I got caught, I was sentenced to hang, and the executioner saved me."

"So you're with him now?"

Finn had gotten to know Rock as well as any on the

crew in the time he'd been working with them. Oscar was his oldest friend, but Rock…

Rock was Finn's friend, not just someone who felt he owed Finn's father a favor.

"I have to be. If I don't stay with him, then I end up back on the Stone."

"We could protect you. We *are* your crew, after all." Rock spread his hands to either side, and he shrugged. "I'm sure the King has ways of keeping you safe. We can figure it out as a crew."

What did it mean that Oscar wanted him to stay away, but Rock wanted him back?

Finn started to nod, but he already began thinking about what Master Meyer might say if he heard Finn talking this way. "I can't do that to the crew."

"You wouldn't be doing anything."

Finn looked to the door. "The King wouldn't want the heat me hiding out here would bring. It's better this way for now. I'll come around like I said. Besides, I still need to hear how you nearly got pinched."

Rock's face clouded. "Damn thing. For something stupid, too. Fucking Client wanted a bowl and some jewelry—"

"A bowl?" Finn asked. How many could the Client want?

Rock nodded. "I think he's a collector. They're not gold or nothing, so I can't see how he'd sell them, but the King says they're valuable to the right person. Gods if I know why. Don't care, either. The last job paid ten drebs."

"You got it, then?"

Rock nodded. "We got it. Well, Wolf did. That bastard can be sneaky, you know." He glanced behind him before turning his attention back to Finn. "I'm glad you didn't hang, Shuffles. Gods, but you're the only one on this crew I couldn't stand to lose." He released Finn's shoulder, and a smile spread across his face. "I hope you plan on coming back tomorrow."

"I hope so. I have more flexibility now. I had to prove myself first."

"Sort of like with our crew."

Finn glanced to the door. "Something like that. Although, I wonder if Master Meyer is even harder to please than the King."

Rock chuckled, and he took a step back, holding his hand on the door. "Tomorrow, then."

Finn nodded. "Tomorrow."

As he headed out into the night, leaving the crew, he felt conflicted. When Meyer had saved him, Finn quickly understood that he had to serve, but coming back to the Wenderwolf made it harder for him to know the right thing to do.

He had friends in the crew, and he didn't want to let them down.

But another emotion crept in.

Meyer had saved him. Finn didn't want to let the executioner down, either.

CHAPTER FOURTEEN

Finn didn't sleep well.

The poor sleep reminded him of how badly he'd slept while in the prison, though he didn't know why that should be. He tossed and turned, dreams drifting to him, flashes of memories of his father, mother, and sister. They were happier in all of them.

When he came awake, he looked around the small room, remembering where he was.

This would be his fate now.

Finn sighed and got dressed before heading out into the small house. It was dark, early enough that it seemed Master Meyer still slept.

His first task was to get clothes.

That was what Meyer had asked of him, though he didn't know if it was too early to visit the tailor. Most shops wouldn't be open quite this early. Instead, when

Finn reached the kitchen, he decided that he could be responsible for breakfast again. He might as well start the day off on the right foot.

Not just the day. The apprenticeship.

He sorted through the cabinets, found a pan, set it on the stove, and got a fire going and the pan hot. Scooping some lard, he let it sizzle in the pan, the smell pleasing. When it was hot enough, he cracked the first of the eggs and started frying them.

"I expected you to sleep longer," Meyer said, joining him in the kitchen, fully dressed for the day in his leathers.

Leathers. Did that mean today was an execution day?

"I couldn't sleep," Finn admitted.

"Does that have anything to do with where you went after we parted last night?"

Finn glanced toward him.

How much did Meyer know?

Probably nothing. He was intuitive. Finn had seen that in the time that he'd been working with him. It didn't take much for Meyer to guess what prisoners—and now Finn —were up to.

It was the reason he had to be careful with Meyer.

"I didn't do anything that would dishonor you."

"That wasn't the question."

"I don't know," Finn said. He flipped the first of the eggs. Something was comforting about cooking. The smells, mostly. When standing in front of the stove with a hot pan, the smells were his favorite part.

"You went back to your crew."

He didn't look back at him. "You knew?"

"I suspected you would. How did it feel?"

Finn stared at the eggs. At least with him cooking, the eggs wouldn't be burned the way they'd been when Meyer had cooked them. Finn scooped three eggs off the pan and set them on a plate, handing it to Meyer. "Off."

Taking the rest of the eggs for himself, he sat across from Meyer and ate slowly.

"When a man encounters change, he often finds those who haven't changed struggle to keep up with him."

"I haven't changed."

"No? Then perhaps I'm mistaken."

"You kept me from the rope, but how else have I changed?"

Meyer took a big bite and chewed slowly. When he finished, he set his fork down, looking at Finn. "Only you and the gods can know how you've changed."

"You said I had."

"I said it was likely."

"Why?"

Meyer sighed. "You were given a chance to leave. At any point over the preceding days, you could have attempted to run. Something inside you kept you here. Why do you think that is?"

"Because I would have been caught and hanged anyway," he said quickly. Probably too quickly.

Meyer laughed. "Maybe. The Archers were looking for you, but I imagine a thief with your background would have found a way."

Finn grunted. "I don't have the background you might think."

"You are a known associate of the Hand."

He'd mentioned that before. *How much more does Meyer know and not share?* "He's a friend. Not an associate."

"Is that right? Perhaps that makes it better. Or worse."

Finn waited for Meyer to ask him more about Oscar, or his crew, but the questions never came.

He ate in silence, and when he was done, he took both his plate and Meyer's to the basin near the stove and set them there. He imagined he'd be responsible for washing them later.

"I'm going to the tailor," he said.

Meyer nodded to him. "You can find me back here when you are done."

"Not the general store?"

"Not yet."

Heading out, Finn made his way along the streets, moving toward the Verlan section, where Beshear's was. There weren't many people out quite yet, though the sun was up, giving off just a hint of warmth, barely enough with the thin fabric he wore.

Shops on either side of the street were far nicer than the ones he'd known when he was younger. Finn stopped at the tailor, looking up at the sign, then toward the window. The clothing visible in the window looked expensive.

This was where Meyer wanted him to come?

He shrugged to himself and knocked on the door of the tailor before pushing it open. A soft bell over the door jingled when he went inside, and Finn looked up at it. The bell was shaped like the bell in Elia Tower, and he smiled at the thought of it ringing so softly.

"How can I help…" The older man who came from the back of the shop frowned when he looked at Finn. He shifted a cloth tape measure around his shoulder, his mouth pressed together in a thin line as he studied him until his expression softened. "You must be Finn Jagger. Master Meyer suggested you would be coming by. I didn't expect you so early, but…"

Finn nodded. "I'm sorry if this isn't a good time. I can return at a better time for you."

Master Beshear waved his hand. He was an older man, thin, with wispy hair, and thin lips. A cloth tape measure draped around his neck. "This is as good a time as any. Besides, I don't want to disappoint Master Meyer."

Finn smiled at that.

What reason would the tailor have in not wanting to disappoint an executioner?

"Come in. I was to measure you for two sets of clothes, along with a cloak."

"Two sets?" Finn asked, looking over to the window. He wasn't as good a judge of clothing expenses as he was with other things, but two sets would be more money than he had. Adding on a cloak would be much more than what he had. "I would be fine starting with only one."

He could wash it regularly. Finn suspected that was Meyer's concern, but with his access to the well, and the washbasin that Finn had seen in his home, he could keep the clothes as clean as he needed without spending too much.

"Nonsense. Meyer has already paid for them. Come along, Mr. Jagger."

Finn followed the tailor to the back of the shop, where he had Finn stand. He quickly made measurements of his legs, waist, hips, and chest before working the tape down Finn's arms.

"How often do you work with Master Meyer?"

Beshear shifted the tape back over his shoulders. "I've known him for quite a few years. Long before I moved to this section."

That explained why Meyer would have sent him there. It was strange to think that Meyer would choose a tailor in this section of the city, though Finn didn't really know what sort of people Meyer consorted with. He didn't really know all that much about him to begin with—other than that he took his job seriously, and he wanted Finn to do the same.

Beshear disappeared through a door for a few moments and returned with a shirt. "Let's try this. It might be a little large, though I think it will work for now."

Finn peeled the gray shirt off. There was something almost freeing about taking off the clothes he'd been sentenced to wear on his way to his hanging. Clothing that he'd grown to feel not necessarily comfortable in but at least familiar with.

When he slipped on the shirt, he sighed.

The fabric was *soft*.

"What's it made of?" he asked, running his hands along the shirt.

Meyer would want me to have something like this?

"A wool and cotton blend. It's a fine fabric. Not as soft as some that I bring in, but with the kind of work you'll be doing"—his mouth soured as he said it—"it'll keep you warm when you need and will breathe in the hotter weather. By summer, I can make a few more for you if you're satisfied with my work."

Finn shifted the shirt. It fit him well—better than any shirt he'd ever worn.

Beshear started to pinch the fabric around the sides, then along the sleeves, and then at the neck. "As I suspected. Not quite what you need, but it'll work for now. I should be able to have two of these ready for you by the end of the week." When Finn started to peel the shirt off, already feeling remorse at losing the soft fabric, Beshear waved his hand. "Keep this one for now. I think you'd probably prefer this to what you'd been wearing."

Finn looked at the gray shirt lying on the floor next to him. "It's a little nicer than what I had," he said, looking over to Master Beshear.

The tailor chuckled. "You might want to hold on to that. Working clothes, and all. Now to find you trousers. The fit will be a little bit different than with the shirt. At least with the shirt, we have less variety. You have a relatively slim build, and I wonder if I have trousers that will fit your waist."

He headed back through the door and was gone a little longer. When he was gone, Finn ran his hand along the shirt, enjoying the feel of the fabric, tracing his finger along the collar. This was to be his?

Most of the shirts he had over the years were soft because of how often they had been washed and worn, not because of the weave and the fabric.

He leaned toward it, smelling. It even smelled cleaner.

"I think these should work, at least until I can have something custom-fit for you." The tailor came out of the back and held out trousers for Finn.

He took them, noting that the fabric was the same as the shirt. Finn slipped off the gray pants and into the new trousers, marveling at how much better they fit than the gray pants had.

"These will work," Finn said.

Master Beshear knelt next to Finn, and he began to move the pants, tugging on the hem, along with the waist, before standing and clucking to himself. "They will be adequate. At least for now. Master Meyer was adamant that you have something to wear for now." He turned away before pausing. "Oh. The cloak. That should be a little bit easier. It doesn't have to be custom-fit quite the same way. Why don't you come with me? You get to choose your style."

Finn followed him, and the tailor brought him to a section of the shop where he paused, motioning to a row of different overcoats.

They came in different colors, styles, and fabrics.

Finn ran his hand along each of them, marveling at the sensation of the fabric, the way that each of them felt different from the next. He pulled out one before putting it back. He didn't care much for the pale green fabric. A dappled green one did draw his eye, and Finn looked at it, holding it up.

"An excellent choice. The fabric will shed water and should provide considerable protection from the wind. Why don't we make sure that it fits?"

Finn pulled it on, slipping his arms through and pulling the hood up. He looked down, noticing how the overcoat hung toward the ground.

It was almost as if it had been made for him.

"This will be adequate," the tailor said.

If this was adequate, Finn wondered what it would be like when something was more than adequate.

"Thank you," he said.

"I need a week. I will have two shirts ready for you, along with two pairs of trousers. If there is anything else that you need, I am more than happy to be of service. I hope that you—and Master Meyer—will continue to utilize my services."

Finn collected his other clothing and stood for a moment looking around the inside of the tailor shop.

What must it be like for people who were able to shop in a place like this frequently?

Maybe he was now able to be someone like that.

It didn't feel like it to him. The ten fils Meyer promised him for his monthly pay wasn't that much, certainly not enough to pay for clothing like this.

How much did Meyer get paid?

"Mr. Jagger? If you wouldn't mind, please send word to

Master Meyer that I require additional supplies." He flashed a smile. "He will know what I mean."

Finn looked at him, confusion filling him for a moment before nodding. "Thank you," he said again.

Back on the street, he wasn't sure what he needed to do. He carried the gray shirt and pants of the Sinner's Cloth bundled up under his arm and shifted the bundle so that it was beneath the overcoat.

Heading through the streets, back toward Meyer's home, he felt… different.

No longer quite as conspicuous as he had been, but it was more than just that. It was wearing clothes that were far nicer than anything that he had ever worn before. He felt almost honorable.

Once inside Master Meyer's home, the executioner met him at the door and regarded his new clothing while nodding. "Much better."

"Master Beshear wanted me to tell you that he needs additional supplies."

"Very well."

"What sort of supplies?"

"That is between him and me," Meyer said. "Come along. It's time to start."

"Errands?"

Meyer shook his head. "Training."

He motioned for Finn to follow, and they headed out into the garden, where Finn found seven large pumpkins set off to the side. He didn't take Meyer for the kind to decorate. The garden had a purpose, but Finn didn't feel that it was decorative.

"Wait here." Meyer went back into the house before returning with Justice and holding it out to Finn. "Take it carefully."

Finn did so. Was he to clean it? This was his training? Meyer had already shown him how to clean the sword.

"How would you hold a sword?"

Finn gripped the hilt of it. He'd seen many swords but had never held one before. "Like this?"

Meyer stopped behind him, shifting Finn's hands. When he did, the grip made more sense. "Hold here and here. It gives you a wider base. Justice is a longsword, and to wield her, you need to maintain your grip in a way that gives you the most strength."

Finn tensed. He wasn't a child, though Meyer positioned himself as if he were.

When Meyer stepped back, Finn held the sword. It *was* long. Unwieldy. And Finn couldn't shake the thought that this sword had beheaded countless people.

He almost dropped it.

"Careful. Don't think about where the sword has been. Think about the blade. The way it feels in your hand. How it must be an extension of your arm."

How had Meyer known what I'd been thinking?

"I don't know if it can be an extension of my arm."

"Not at first. No man can wield a sword without practice. Think of the Archers. They practice daily, and they don't need the same accuracy as I must have. If they miss their target, they get another strike. If I miss mine, the people are outraged."

"But your target isn't moving."

"No? Just wait until you stand before one of the condemned, holding Justice before you, your arms trembling. The man before you trembling. Do you think it's easier or harder to kill in such a manner?"

Finn would have said *easier*, but perhaps it wasn't.

"Now. You will practice."

"I'll what?"

"Practice. The pumpkins will be your first target. Your aim is to cleave them in half with a single blow. When you can do that ten times in a row, you will move on."

Finn looked down at the pumpkins. "But there are only seven here."

Meyer snorted. "If you're successful today, I will find more pumpkins."

He lifted one, and for a moment, Finn feared Meyer was going to have him slice through the pumpkin while the executioner held it, but then he set it on one of the garden boxes. It was about waist-high, not all that high, but better than trying to hack at the pumpkin while it was on the ground.

"Let's see your technique."

Finn couldn't deny the curiosity of how it would feel to swing the sword, especially after hearing some of the rumors the night before. He'd have to ask Wolf more about Justice.

Stepping back, Finn brought his arms up and twisted, swinging the sword around…

And missed.

He looked over to Meyer.

"You can't put so much force behind your movement, or you'll miss every time."

Finn swung the sword again.

This time, he caught the top of the pumpkin.

The blade barely bit into the skin.

"You have to be stronger than that. It's a balance of understanding how hard to swing and how to do so with the proper form. This is not sword fighting. This is a stationary object. There's no blocking, no forms to memorize. Not the way the Archers train."

Finn glanced over at him. By the way he said it, he had to wonder if Meyer had trained with the Archers.

"Try again."

Finn did so. Each time he tried, he found he gained a little better understanding of what he had to do. He tried to swing the sword with control, and though he hit the pumpkin, he didn't cause much damage. When he swung with more force, the sword didn't have any aim.

His arms ached.

He still had only worked on the one pumpkin.

"You will need to keep trying. I don't expect you to master this today, but you must master it."

"How long do I have?"

Meyer shook his head. "Not long enough."

He left Finn in the garden, and Finn turned to the pumpkin and kept practicing.

He'd never thought he was weak, but working with the sword in this way left his arms burning. Justice was a heavy sword, weighing enough that he felt he couldn't swing it with the control he wanted.

After practicing for the better part of an hour, he still hadn't managed to split more than a few of the pumpkins. His aim needed work. He'd cut through them, but if Meyer's goal for him was to have him cut through ten of them in a row, Finn would need more time to master it.

Meyer joined him in the garden again, noting the pumpkins. "Clean the blade and join me inside." He set the satchel with rags down near the bench.

"Am I to oil it?"

"How often did I instruct you to oil the blade?"

"Once a week."

"Then clean the blade and join me."

Finn grabbed a rag from the satchel and carefully wiped the bits of pumpkin off the sword. While he did, he admired the steel. The edge was sharp, and he imagined that Meyer honed it regularly. The metal gleamed as he wiped it clean, and swirls of gray worked along the surface. Though his father had made sure he could read well, the writing engraved on the edge of the blade was done in a language he couldn't read. Both Meyer and Wolf had mentioned the sword was hundreds of years old, so it shouldn't surprise him the language would change over time.

When Justice had been cleaned and resheathed, he carried it inside to find Meyer waiting. He took the sword from Finn without a word and placed it into the closet where he stored it.

"You'll clean up the mess when we return."

Finn glanced toward the garden before nodding. "Where are we going?"

"We have a few places we need to go this morning. Keep up."

Finn followed him.

He expected that Meyer would lead him toward the center of the city. Despite living on the border between sections, most of the shopping he'd done with Meyer had been in the merchant section. Instead of there, he headed out toward the Olin section.

Finn frowned to himself.

Was that intentional?

Meyer had already implied that he knew what Finn had done the night before. That he knew he'd gone to visit with his crew.

Is he going to Olin as a way to prove that I can't return to my old life?

The streets there were narrow and curled around, much like in every other part of the city. They created a maze, making it difficult to head directly through the city, another line of defense for the palace. Many of the buildings they passed were homes, though not all of them were. Occasional shops with doors cracked and waiting for customers interrupted the homes, though Finn suspected most shop owners lived in the nearby homes. As they neared the wall, the buildings crammed even closer together, using all the space available within the wall's protection.

"Why out here?"

"Do you know this part of the city?" Meyer asked.

"Better than some of the other places you've led me."

As Finn looked around, familiar shops greeted him.

Now that they were close to the wall, he recognized Tevel's butcher, the Ghiland bakery, the candlemaker…

Meyer stopped in front of an unassuming building. The storefront was wider than many nearby, taking up space for what would have been two buildings around it. There was no sign and nothing that really indicated it was a store.

"What is this place?"

"Come along."

Finn hurried inside. It was an apothecary.

Compared to the tailor's shop that he visited earlier that day, it was dingy and dark. Rows of shelves that seemed to lack any sort of organization. The air stank, a funky odor that felt as if it permeated not only his nose but also his new clothing.

Finn wrapped the cloak around himself protectively.

He doubted it would do much of anything, but he still felt compelled to do it, holding the cloak tightly so that the stench of the apothecary didn't fill everything around him.

Could this be the kind of place that my sister had gone to for Mother?

Finn had no idea where Lena had visited, only that the concoctions she had brought home had been of little use. Nothing that she had tried had made much difference when helping their mother recover from her illness. At this point, Finn doubted that anything would be of much use to help their mother recover. It might only be that they would be able to delay her passing, not heal her.

Meyer wandered through the apothecary, stopping in front of the counter near the back of the shop.

Finn looked all around him as he made his way toward the back, where Meyer waited. On one of the shelves, he noted what looked to be dried fingers. A clear jar of gray powder sat next to them. Many of the shelves held leaves, or oils, or other combinations of things.

The apothecary came from the back of the room and joined Meyer. "Master Meyer. What can I do for you today?"

She was an older woman, with bright eyes and gray hair tucked into a bun. A striped shawl hung over her shoulders. Her voice was sharp and robust, surprising given the way she appeared.

"Wella. I would like to introduce you to Finn Jagger."

She looked over at Finn, studying him. Though she was older, there was something in the way she regarded him that suggested she saw him clearly. She tapped on the floor with a short cane and cackled softly.

"A new apprentice? The court didn't saddle you with one of their own?"

"No," he said.

"What did the boy do to deserve this fate?"

"Does it matter?" Master Meyer asked.

"Not to me. Perhaps to him. And the gods." As she said it, she cackled again, her voice a strange and irritating sound that reminded him of Hector in Declan prison.

"I need a few items from you."

"Name them. You know the price."

Meyer nodded. "Thistledown. Reglar. Ferun oil. Jasper

berry. Fennel. Crispon leaves. Thender bark. And a dropper."

Wella cocked her head to the side, studying Meyer. "An interesting selection. What have you done to your Poor Bastards now? Based on what you're requesting, it seems as if you starved them, though that doesn't suit you, Master Meyer."

Finn only recognized a few of the items that he'd asked about. Thistledown was relatively common. Jasper berry as well. The others were not nearly as common, and he had no idea what crispon leaves or thender bark were. Probably something that came from the forest outside of the city, but who would venture out there?

"Do you have them?"

"Do I have them?" she scoffed. "You know that I do. Now, when will I be repaid?"

"You know that I've always paid my debt," he said.

She smiled at him. "Always in the past, but will you always in the future?"

"A man can't predict the future," Master Meyer said.

"Only the gods," she said, laughing again.

She leaned on her cane as she wound past the counter and began to make her way through the apothecary shop. She paused at several different shelves, taking items from them, tucking the items under her arm, before heading back to the counter.

Reaching under the counter, she set waxed paper on it and began to spoon the items together. "I could mix them for you, Henry."

"That's not necessary," Master Meyer said.

"Interesting." She looked up. "I am most curious as to what you need this concoction for."

"I'm sure you are."

She grinned, revealing only a few teeth remaining in her mouth. "Be careful with the crispon. It's still fresh, and you will need to try it out before you use it."

"I know," he said.

"Of course you do." She finished packaging the various items that Master Meyer had requested and folded the waxed paper up, stacking them. She looked over to Finn, holding his gaze for a moment. "Will you be sending him to me?"

"Not quite yet, Wella."

She sniffed. "Not yet, but eventually."

"Eventually."

She cackled again. "I will look forward to working with this one. Look at him. So young. So innocent."

"Not innocent."

"No? Ah. Then the rumors of the festival gone awry *are* true."

"It didn't go awry."

"Perhaps not for you, but for those who thought to profit off of it, it went awry." She laughed again and watched Finn, studying him. "Not that it matters. The magister has been free with his gifts these days. Hasn't he?"

Master Meyer's face darkened for a moment. "I will send the usual, I presume?"

"The usual will be adequate for now, though in the coming weeks, I might have a different requirement."

Meyer nodded, and he pressed on Finn's back. "Thank you for your help, Wella."

Finn took one last look at the inside of the shop before heading out.

Once out, Master Meyer guided him back to the streets, weaving a different way from how they had come, but it wasn't long before Finn realized where he was leading them.

Back toward Master Meyer's home.

That was the only purpose for our journey?

Once inside, Meyer began to take the items from the waxed paper out, then took a bowl from the shelf and began to pinch the combination together. When it was done, it was a slurry that he added water to liquefy it even more.

"Here," Meyer said.

"What is it?" Finn asked.

"This is for your mother."

Finn stared at it. "I'm not sure I can give her this."

"From what you've said, you have tried various other concoctions, and none of them have been effective. I suspect your sister has even gone to the hegen." Finn tried to keep his face neutral. "You don't have to tell me one way or the other. I don't know how effective this will be, but it should slow the progression. If it works, and if you begin to trust me, I might have something more that I can try for her."

Finn looked down at the concoction. He knew that Meyer often offered healing, but was he willing to try his healing?

It was free. In that way, it was far more useful to him than anything that a physician might be able to offer.

Finn took the concoction. "Thank you."

"Do what you need to do now. This evening, we will continue your training."

CHAPTER FIFTEEN

Finn sat at the edge of his mother's bed, the now-empty dropper in hand. Finn had tested it on himself before administering it to his mother. He didn't know if there was anything that he would be able to learn from it, but at least he wanted to ensure it wouldn't be poisonous to him. Other than a bitter flavor with a strange lingering taste to it, he didn't detect anything worrisome from it.

His mother hadn't moved since he'd been there. He remained at the bedside, watching her, occasionally standing and wiping the sweat from her forehead, before taking a seat and resting next to her.

Finn lost track of how long he'd been sitting there. Lena hadn't returned from her job, though she'd been working with the butcher, so he didn't necessarily know how long her shifts were. Longer than he would have expected, though. Longer than Lena deserved, especially as she would end up returning home and needing to care for their mother.

Meyer hadn't given Finn any idea of how often he was to administer the medicine. Maybe one time was enough. Neither had he given him any idea of how long it would take for the medicine to work. Finn doubted it would be immediate. Considering how long it had taken for the illness to fully take hold, he expected the recovery to be equally long.

Getting to his feet, he headed to the kitchen, cleaning up the dishes in the basin and putting them away. He might not be bringing as much coin to Lena as he had before, but that didn't mean he couldn't contribute in other ways.

When he had straightened as much as he could, including his mother's room, Lena still hadn't returned.

Where would she be?

Tucking his mother in and taking the dropper, he left the home. He'd have to check on her in the morning. She'd fed herself in the past but didn't show any interest in doing so now. She'd worsened. Lena had a technique to ensure she ate what she needed. She'd take care of it when she returned.

Night had fallen in the time that he'd been helping his mother. Finn looked up at the full moon as one of the nearby church bells tolled. The Berend bells. He listened, counting the bells, and realized that he'd been there longer than he'd expected.

He was tired.

Not that he'd done anything all that challenging

through the day, but he was still tired. The danger over the last few days had gotten to the point where he now felt the effects. Meyer would expect him back, and Finn didn't want to be gone too long. Not until he knew all that Meyer expected of him.

As he headed back toward the executioner's home, a familiar person made their way toward him.

"Sneaking out again?" Helda asked.

"I'm not sneaking," he said, give her an appraising look. "Look at you—"

A sharp frown cut him off.

She *was* dressed well for the evening, though the cut of her dress hid anything he wanted to see. She had her hair pulled back, and a small blue hat tilted on her head.

"Say, Helda. Have you seen my sister?"

Helda's face clouded. "Not as much lately. Thanks to you."

"What do you mean, thanks to me?"

"You go sneaking off, leaving her to fend for your mother." Helda stepped toward him. Were those lilacs he smelled on her? "Lena is working for the *butcher*." She lowered her voice at the end, whispering it to Finn.

"I know."

She stepped back, hands clasped behind her back. "And you *let* her?"

"You know Lena better than anyone." Helda's frown deepened. "And it's not up to me what she does with her time. Lena can work for whoever she wants."

"So long as you get to skulk around the city; is that what you mean?" Helda shook her head, meeting his gaze with an expression of irritation. "She deserves more than working at a place like that. She wanted…"

"Wanted what?"

Helda shook her head. "It doesn't matter. Just like it doesn't matter that she worried about how you were going to end up just like your father. It's already killing your mother, and Lena…"

Finn frowned. "What about Lena?"

Helda sniffed. "Even if she has to work for the butcher now, that doesn't change how Lena *would* like to find a suitable husband. How can she when she's working like she is?"

Was that what had been troubling his sister? He hadn't considered it before, but he could see how that would bother her.

"What about you? What kind of husband are you looking for?"

"One who knows how to treat a woman right."

Finn opened his mouth, thinking of what he might say were he in the Wenderwolf, before he caught himself. He liked Helda. He appreciated her loyalty to his sister, a trait not enough people had, and he enjoyed her attitude, even when she directed it at him. "If you see my sister, let her know I gave Mother a different medicine."

Helda paused as she pushed past him. Definitely lilacs. "She'll want to know what kind of medicine."

Finn shook his head. "I don't really know. It was given to me by…"

He wasn't about to tell Helda *who* had given him the medicine. That would mean that he'd have to explain what he'd been doing. That would mean that his sister would learn that he now trained to be an executioner.

"An apothecary," he finished.

"When I see her, I'll let Lena know you gave your mother something you should not have." Helda frowned at him another moment before heading off.

Finn wound toward the butcher shop where his sister worked. He needed to visit with her. If Helda were concerned about her, then Finn needed to be. He reached the Jorven's butcher shop and looked in the window, but there was no sign of Lena.

Maybe she wasn't working this evening.

Or she was in the back.

What was he thinking? He didn't need to distract her during her job and earn the ire of her employer. More than that, he needed to get back to Master Meyer. He started off, glancing over his shoulder and back toward the butcher, before turning his attention back to the road.

He caught a glimpse of a cloaked figure who reminded him of the King.

Finn followed on a whim.

The man ducked into an alley. Finn slowed, moving across the street to get a better view, and saw the figure talking to someone.

It was definitely the King.

He almost called out to him before catching himself. The King wouldn't want Finn drawing attention out here, but who was he talking to? They were on the edge of the Olin section, but near the river, as if he'd been about to cross into the better sections of the city.

The other man stepped past the King and onto the street, and Finn froze.

An Archer.

The Archer headed along the street, and even from a distance, Finn could tell from the stripes on his jacket that he wasn't just a typical city Archer.

Somebody of rank.

Knowing the King, it was probably somebody of considerable rank.

The Archer held a pouch in hand and stuck it into his pocket.

The King was paying him off. Another bribe.

Unless *he* was the Client.

Finn considered following the Archer but decided against it as the King headed away from him. Finn stayed in the shadows until the King left the alley, and he followed him again. So far, the King seemed unmindful of Finn's presence. *Oscar can't make fun of my skill this time.* When the King ducked into a general store, Finn waited.

There were too many people who could be the Client.

Finn wished that he knew who it was. The jobs were strange, even if they paid well. They'd almost gotten pinched taking the damn bowl, then he *had* gotten caught at the viscount manor. Considering what the king had said about Rock nearly getting pinched, there was a pattern that bothered Finn.

He waited, and waited longer, and when the King still didn't come out, he decided he'd been gone long enough. Finally, Finn continued back to Master Meyer's home.

It was dark when he reached it.

Not entirely, though.

A light near the back of the home caught his attention.

Finn crept slowly, quietly, and reached a cracked door. Voices drifted out, and he leaned close to listen.

Who'd be visiting Meyer at this time of the evening?

"Are you sure this will work?" a soft voice asked.

Finn looked through the cracked door. A younger woman, probably only a few years older than him, stood across from Master Meyer, holding some small item clutched in her hands. She had a drab brown dress and a gray cloak that hung over her shoulders. He couldn't really see her face from the angle near the door.

"Nothing is sure when it comes to this sort of medicinal, but I've done what I can. Twice a day. No more than that."

The woman nodded and left a stack of coins on the table near her, turning and heading out through a door in the back of the room.

When she was gone, he heard Meyer clear his throat. "You can come in, Finn."

Finn hesitated. He wasn't sure how Meyer would tolerate him listening to conversations, though Finn hadn't listened that long.

Stepping into the room, he looked around. It reminded him something of the apothecary's shop, though quite a bit more organized. Shelves had various powders and liquids, all arranged neatly, organized so that he suspected Meyer knew precisely where everything was on the shelves. A table near the back of the room held various measuring implements. Powder piled up on a plate seemed out of place compared to everything else.

"I wasn't trying to listen in," Finn said. His gaze continued to drift around the inside of the room before finally settling on the coins the woman had left stacked on the table.

Three silver drebs.

Finn stared for a moment. That was a considerable amount of money.

She had paid that much?

Seeing the girl, she didn't appear wealthy. Certainly not someone he would have targeted were he in the streets.

"I suppose you might as well begin to see how you can supplement your income. At least, when you progress in your training." Meyer picked up the plate of powder, and he carefully tapped it into another container, sweeping it completely clean before replacing the canister on the shelf near others and putting the plate away.

"You offer healing," Finn said. Finn had known that he did, but seeing it firsthand, and realizing just how much Meyer made, was a surprise to him.

He had no idea how much the city compensated Meyer for his executioner services, but if he were to make this much in additional income, what he made as an executioner wouldn't matter. He could augment his earnings considerably.

"To some."

"For a considerable compensation," Finn said. That must be the supplies Beshear had needed.

"I charge what my services are worth," Master Meyer said. "Not as much as the physicians would charge, but a bit more than your typical apothecary or surgeon. I have found that very few people mind paying." Meyer took a book off of the shelf and held it out to Finn. "I warned you that you would be busy and that you needed to begin your studies. Start with this while still working on your knots and the sword."

Instead of execution strategies or interrogation techniques, Finn found the book described the human body. He looked up, meeting Master Meyer's gaze. "What is this?"

"Part of your training."

"Why?"

"To be successful in all aspects of what you will be asked to do, you need to be prepared."

"I need to know as much as a surgeon?"

As he flipped through the pages of the book, he saw bones and blood vessels and muscles all depicted in careful detail.

"Not as much as a surgeon. More."

Finn continued flipping through the pages. How was he ever supposed to learn all of this?

"I don't know that I can do this."

"You don't have much of a choice," Meyer said.

Finn started to set the book down before shaking his head. "I didn't think the job was like this."

"What did you think that I did? Did you believe that I acted carelessly? Would the people of the city tolerate an executioner who was careless in his duties?"

Finn knew that the city wouldn't tolerate it. The magister and the jurors likely wouldn't tolerate it either. If Meyer weren't skilled, he doubted that he would have held the position that he had for as long as he had.

"You have the rest of the week to make your way through that book. I will assign others as you progress."

"Is there a rush?"

"Only to make you competent."

"Why?"

"Because the king decreed it."

Meyer took a seat at his table and moved the coins, sliding them across the table and stacking them away, before leaning back and pulling out a book of his own to read.

Finn hesitated. He had another question he'd avoided asking but wanted to know. "Did you ever learn what happened to the Lion?" Finn worried it would implicate one of his crew like the King, or worse—Oscar.

Meyer looked up at him. "Unfortunately, there have been no leads. That happens sometimes. Not all cases are solved. I suppose there's a lesson in that, frustrating as it might be."

Finn stood in place for a few moments, debating what more he might be able to ask, trying to understand if there was anything more Meyer might demand of him, before heading to the small room at the back of the home and closing the door behind him. The table with the lantern made a different sort of sense now.

Finn took a seat as he opened the book, took the length of rope to practice the knots, and began to read.

CHAPTER SIXTEEN

The whimpering turned Finn's stomach, but he made an effort to not look away. He needed to see what Meyer did if this was going to be his profession.

Meyer rubbed a thick, oily substance on the man's arm, and the whimpering eased. Finn had watched as Meyer had mixed the salve, though he hadn't known what was in it. The components of the compound were beyond him. For now.

"Easy," Meyer said softly, still rubbing the salve along the man's arm. "This will feel better in a few moments. The aloe and the honey should soothe the burn."

The man nodded.

Meyer finished applying the burn salve and wiped his hands on a towel, glancing at Finn. "You were telling me about where you were on the night Lorna Vils died."

Died. Not *murdered,* though that was what had happened. Finn didn't have all the details, but what he'd managed to pick up suggested to him that the woman had been brutally beaten and then slaughtered in her home.

This man had been found with blood all over him, and the first inquisitors to question him had tested him with fire. So far, the man hadn't given up much information.

"I don't know where I was that night. I'd been at the tavern. Having a few. That's no crime, regardless of the way the church of Heleth feels about it."

Meyer smiled at him, though there was a hint of sadness within it. "The church doesn't look down upon a man who enjoys a drink now and again," he said.

"Maybe not the gods you pray to," he said.

Meyer turned back to him. He held the jar of the ointment in hand, and the man's gaze drifted to it. Finn didn't know how bad the burns on and underneath his arms were, then neither did he know just how aggressively the inquisitors had worked with him. Meyer didn't reveal that to him.

"I'm going to ask you again where you were on that night," Meyer said.

"I told you where I was."

"Were you involved in what happened?"

"To Lorna? Gods! I liked that woman. I wouldn't have done anything to hurt her."

Finn studied him, listening to the way that he spoke.

It seemed to him that he told the truth, though the executioner's words came back to him. *Which truth did he speak?*

"Were you involved with her?"

The man's gaze lingered on the jar for a moment

before looking up at Meyer's face. He shook his head quickly. Almost too quickly. "She was a married woman. I wasn't involved with her."

That's a lie.

Finn could tell that much, which suggested that the other things he said weren't a lie.

"Her husband grieves. Her boy and girl don't have a mother. All they want is the peace that the gods can offer them. If there is anything that you might be able to say that would offer them that peace…"

The man shook his head again. "I told you I didn't have anything to do with it. I was at the tavern. Must've had too much to drink and blacked out. I don't remember anything from that night. All I remember is getting dragged down here. Damn Archers throwing me into the cell." He tried to lift his arms, but the leather straps holding him made it difficult. "My head has been throbbing. Then they burned me, torturing me as if that were going to change anything that I had told them. I wasn't lying to them," he said.

Meyer studied him for a long moment before nodding slowly. "We will see. The gods demand justice."

He set the jar of ointment on the table and motioned for Finn to join him as they departed. Meyer glanced at the nearest of the iron masters when they were out of the room and leaned toward him. "You can apply the ointment to his arms three to four times a day. Anything more than that is probably unnecessary. Don't leave any scars."

The iron master, a surly-looking man with a long, hooked nose and a scruff of graying beard, nodded quickly. "We haven't been questioning him. Warden has been."

"I will have the same conversation with the warden," he said.

Meyer guided Finn through the prison and stopped outside of a room with a heavy door. Inscriptions on the door suggested that the man inside served at the behest of the gods and the king.

He knocked but didn't wait for the door to come open. Instead, he pushed the door open and headed inside.

The warden was younger than Finn would've expected. Dark black hair. Deep brown eyes. Even a dark beard on his broad face. He looked up from a stack of papers, a long quill in hand, irritation flashing for a moment until he realized who was there.

He jumped to his feet, tipping his head in a brief nod. "Master Meyer. I knew you were visiting today, but I didn't expect to have a visit from you myself."

He glanced around nervously, and Finn smiled to himself.

What was the warden doing that would make him so nervous?

"You have been questioning Gabe Freeland?"

The warden's eyes narrowed briefly. "I have been instructed to obtain as much information from our prisoners as I can."

"Under whose authority?"

"Why, the viscount. He mentioned the king wants crime controlled in the city while he's negotiating with the Alainsith. Said he'd be in the city more often than usual and that I should—"

Meyer stiffened. "You won't question him further until I return."

Meyer turned, nodding to Finn, and Finn followed him out.

The warden tried to yell something after him, though Finn couldn't tell what it was. Meyer ignored it.

They headed out of the prison and made their way through the streets. It was early enough in the day, and quite a few people were out.

Finn looked over to Master Meyer when they were far enough away from the prison. "You don't like the warden all that much."

"It's not a matter of liking him. It's a matter of him doing more than what he is responsible for."

"He's not responsible for the prisoners?"

"The warden is responsible for the well-being of the prisoners under his care. He is not responsible for obtaining information from them."

"Why not?"

"The warden does not attend the sentencing."

He looked behind him. The prisons didn't operate at all the way Finn thought they had. "Wouldn't he be able to pass on information if he obtained it?"

"Assuming he did obtain that information," Meyer said.

"You don't think he did?"

"It is my responsibility as chief inquisitor to make sure that everything obtained in the service of the king is done so in a way that upholds the law. With what has been taking place in the city, I must be particularly cautious."

"What has been taking place in the city?"

Master Meyer looked over to Finn, and for a moment, he wondered if he would say anything more. "The warden is not wrong. The king is in the city negotiating with the Alainsith, and there have been attacks on high-level targets."

"Why would he need to negotiate with the Alainsith?"

All of this felt beyond Finn, as if it were stories he might share with the crew in the Wenderwolf. He could imagine how Oscar would laugh, Rock would probably make fun of him, and the others would add their own stories.

"The peace is tenuous and has been since those who followed King Ordol the Pious thought they could work the treaty in their favor. Too many have been tempted to break it to access the lands west of Verendal for the gold rumored to be in the Ives Mountains beyond there."

Finn hadn't known about gold, but men did foolish things for wealth. He had.

"How often does he have to meet with them?"

Meyer shook his head. "I don't worry about such things."

"But you know—"

"I might know *why* the king is here, but that doesn't mean I worry about it. King Porman will ensure the peace with the Alainsith remains."

They continued walking a little further. "What

happens if it doesn't? Will they use their magic to nearly destroy us the way they did when Yofun—"

Meyer snorted. "Those are stories, Finn. And even if they're true, they're from so long ago that it doesn't matter. We have peace. Nothing will disrupt it."

"Stories have to come from somewhere," Finn said.

"They do. And who's to say what the Alainsith could do if they attacked? If they wanted to destroy us, it might be they could, but we've given them no reason."

"You did say there have been high-level targets," Finn said.

Meyer frowned and nodded.

"Like what?"

He glanced to Finn. "Such as the viscount."

It was more than just that, and Finn knew it. There was the attempt on the palace. Maybe others. *Could it be tied to the Client?*

"Why do you think it's happening?"

"That is not for me to decide. Nor for you. Our job is to find whatever information that we can to ensure that justice is served."

"If there's something more taking place in the city with the Alainsith coming—"

"If there is, it is not our responsibility."

Finn followed Meyer, not really wanting to let it drop but getting the sense that he didn't want to say anything more. They reached a dirtier section of the city, part of the Olin section, though not near the tavern where his crew operated. Finn noticed a house in the distance with a rope around it.

"This is where the woman was killed," he said.

Meyer nodded. "It is."

"Why are you coming here?"

"I've told you my responsibility."

"I guess I understand that; it's just…"

Even though he understood that it was Meyer's responsibility, he still hadn't expected him to make a visit to the scene of the crime.

"Didn't you say he was found with her blood on him?"

"So it would appear."

"He wasn't completely honest with you when you questioned him," Finn said.

"Are you certain of that?"

Finn shrugged. "Certain enough."

"Would you stake his life on it?"

"I—"

"Would you stake *your* life on it?"

Finn shook his head. "No."

"Very good." Master Meyer turned away, heading toward the home and pausing in front of it. "Now, you might be right that he wasn't truthful with me, but lying about his affair with Mistress Vils is an entirely different matter than lying about killing her. A crime, at least in the eyes of her husband, but not the same crime that he has been accused of."

Meyer stopped at the rope that surrounded the home, marking it off. It would be difficult to miss the rope. Woven of a bright yellow and black, it served as a warning. Finn had seen rope barricades like that before, but he'd never dared step beyond them.

Most of the time, the barricades came after he had been someplace. The Archers used them during their investigations.

Meyer lifted the rope and climbed underneath it, waiting for Finn to follow him.

Finn hesitated a moment, no more than that, and climbed underneath the rope to join him.

"Now. We will see what we can uncover here. She was murdered here, at least according to the Archers who investigated her. Her husband found her yesterday morning and raised the alarm."

"What do you think you might find that Archers overlooked?"

"I don't know. That is why we are here."

Meyer began to make his way around the inside of the home, looking at shelves, picking through everything. Finn stayed out of his way. He trailed behind him. When they reached the back room, he cringed at a puddle of congealed blood.

When he motioned to it, Meyer only nodded.

"You knew that was there?"

"I knew there would be blood still here," Meyer said. "The Archers have investigated, but there has been nothing done to clean up this residence."

"Why not?"

"Because the investigation has not concluded," Meyer said. Finn looked away from the blood. Meyer chuckled. "You are going to need to tolerate the sight of blood much better than that."

"How?"

"That is for you and the gods you worship to decide. If you are going to continue in this position, you're going to need to find a way to stomach more than just the sight of blood."

Meyer moved away, reaching for something in the corner of the room.

"What is that?" Finn asked.

"I suspect that this is the weapon used to murder her," he said.

"Why would the Archers have left it?"

"They should not have," he said.

Finn studied the knife. It was a simple knife. A black handle. A serrated blade. Nothing outstanding about it that would otherwise draw attention.

"She was stabbed?"

"Many times," Meyer said.

"Here?"

Meyer nodded again.

His attention was distracted, and he looked around the inside of the room, leaving Finn to frown, studying the pool of blood, the knife, as he continued looking everywhere around him.

Something about this didn't feel quite right.

"Why would Gabe Freeland have stabbed her here?"

"I'm not convinced he did," Meyer said.

"If he didn't stab her here, then where..." Finn raised his eyebrows. "You don't think that he did it."

"Gabe Freeland may be many things. Adulterer. Thief" —he glanced toward Finn briefly, arching a brow—"but a murderer doesn't fit either the man I saw in the prison or the man that I heard about from those who have known him."

"You've already questioned people who know him?"

"A few. It's often easy to know about a man based on who they associate with. Wouldn't you say that's true?"

Finn frowned. "Not always."

"Hmm."

Finn looked around the inside of the room. "Unless he enjoys killing, it doesn't make sense that he would stab her many times."

"Why not?"

"How many times was she stabbed?"

"Over two dozen. The coroner had a difficult time counting exactly how many times it was, though it was enough that he eventually stopped keeping track."

Over two dozen. That didn't feel right either.

"Let's say Gabe Freeland did it," Finn said, and Meyer tipped his head, nodding to him. "Maybe she decided to end things with him, and he got angry with her."

"Perhaps."

"He was found with her blood on him."

"After having been at the tavern and drinking. None of the men at the tavern that night felt that anything was off with him. Most men, unless they are career-hardened criminals, don't go to a tavern after killing someone."

"What if he went to the tavern before killing her?"

"Perhaps," Meyer said.

"Who do you think was responsible?" Finn asked.

"You have already suggested the answer," Meyer said.

"I did?"

"A crime of passion, much as you claimed. Who else would be likely to have been involved in a crime of passion against someone who carried on with an adulterous affair?"

"Her husband," Finn breathed out.

"Exactly."

He looked around the room, his gaze finally settling on Meyer. "You already knew that before coming here."

"I suspected."

"Then why come here?"

"Because I didn't *know.*"

"You wanted me to know that you didn't execute innocent people."

"I try my best not to."

Meyer turned away, and he left Finn with more questions.

City Hall looked different this time from how it had the last time Finn had been there. Perhaps it was that he came as Master Meyer's assistant, or perhaps it was that he didn't fear his fate quite the same way. He understood he had to succeed and that if he didn't, he would end up hanging regardless, but he had time.

"Do you come for each sentencing?" Finn asked.

"Only those where I have been a part of the questioning."

"Such as this?"

"As we've discussed, I'm a part of the questioning in all capital cases."

Finn nodded. As they entered the jurors' chamber, a chill washed over him. It reminded him of when he had been there, making him uncomfortable. He might be dressed differently from how he had been, and he might be now apprenticed to Master Meyer, but the memory of that time was all too recent.

Gabe Freeland sat in the same chair Finn had occupied. He was dressed in drab brown clothes, at least not the gray Sinner's Cloth. He looked around the inside of the jurors' chamber with wide eyes, taking in everything, never settling his gaze.

"Poor Bastard," Finn muttered.

Meyer glanced over to him. "Don't sentence him yet."

The magister was already seated on the bench, along with several of the jurors. They looked at Finn, several of them narrowing their gaze as they did, though none said anything. All were dressed in the formal clothing of their office, the men wearing their hats, the cloaks of office, and watching while Meyer entered. The only one not present was Bellut.

The magister nodded at Meyer. "We have a majority of the jurors present, Master Meyer. What are your findings?"

"In the matter of Gabe Freeland and the death of Mrs. Lorna Vils, I have come to the conclusion that Mr. Freeland is not guilty of her murder." Gabe looked up, glancing at Master Meyer. "He is guilty of maintaining an affair with a married woman, but once we have the

Archers gather Mr. Vils, I suspect we will have our murderer."

"Her husband?" the magister asked.

"A crime of passion, unfortunately," Master Meyer said.

The magister turned to the others on the jury. "How would the jury decide?"

The jurors turned to each other, whispering softly, before the man situated next to the magister leaned close. He whispered to the magister.

The magister nodded. "In the matter of Gabe Freeland and the death of Mrs. Lorna Vils, the jurors find him innocent. In the matter of Gabe Freeland and his adultery with Mrs. Lorna Vils, the jurors find him guilty. Five lashes will do, Master Meyer."

Meyer nodded.

"Archers, remand him to Volthan Prison until such time as the sentencing can be carried out," the magister said.

Finn looked over to Gabe Freeland, but he didn't seem any more at ease than he had been before. He should be. He was going from Declan to Volthan, which meant that he wouldn't suffer nearly as much as he had in the previous prison. He probably didn't know or appreciate that.

The Archers came from the back of the room and escorted Gabe Freeland from the sentencing hall. When they were gone, Meyer nodded to Finn. They had started to turn when the door opened, and Bellut entered.

He swept into the room, wearing the maroon-and-black striped robe of office. "You have already sentenced the condemned?"

"He wasn't guilty, Master Bellut," the magister said.

As Bellut took a seat on the jury, he looked over to Meyer. "Not guilty? Surely, you understood the reports the warden has sent." Bellut pulled a folded stack of papers from inside his robe.

Finn looked to Meyer, curious how he would react. At least he knew who had been pushing the warden for information.

"I understood the reports quite well," Meyer said. "Much like I understood the investigation that revealed he had been seen in the local tavern until late; far beyond the time when Miss Vils would have been murdered. Additionally, the nature of the crime was one that suggested passion. When we find Mr. Vils, we will have the guilty party."

Bellut took a seat next to the other jurors, his mouth pressed into a tight frown.

"If there is nothing more for me, then I will take my leave," Master Meyer said.

"Thank you for your report," the magister said.

The executioner guided Finn from the chamber, and as they reached the door, Finn felt someone watching him. He looked back to see Bellut studying him, but then he nodded briefly.

Once they were out in the street, Finn followed Master Meyer. "What now?"

"Now we must find Mr. Vils. Question him, and

ensure justice has been served." He looked over to Finn. "That is how we serve the king."

"What about Bellut and the warden?"

Meyer took a deep breath as he glanced back at City Hall. "That will be addressed separately with the magister. I am master executioner in the city until either King Porman declares otherwise, or..." He shook his head. "Let's go."

There was more to it, he was sure, but Meyer wasn't saying anything.

Finn had no choice but to follow.

CHAPTER SEVENTEEN

"The whole thing was odd," Finn said, staring at the mug of ale in front of him. The Wenderwolf was quiet, not nearly as raucous as it often was. He had come looking for the rest of the crew, feeling confused and conflicted about his responsibilities, and had only found Oscar. He'd tried not to look disappointed that it had been Oscar and not Rock.

"What exactly about it was odd?"

Oscar leaned back, dressed in his darks, and remained quiet. Even like that, there was something on edge about him, the way there often was.

It might be in the way Oscar looked around him, his gaze darting from one place to another, never settling long enough for him to look at Finn for long. It might be in the way he tried to appear casual, though he doubted that Oscar was as relaxed as he appeared.

Finn leaned forward, lowering his voice.

"I don't know. It might be just that he wanted me to see how he investigates things." They hadn't found Vils, though they'd searched the city for him. Now Meyer had the Archers looking. If Vils knew what fate awaited him, Finn doubted he'd stick around the city for long.

"You think it's more than that."

"Like I said, I don't know." Finn stared at the mug of ale for another moment before tipping it back and drinking. Annie had brought it over the moment that he'd come into the tavern, smiling at him. She had disappeared to the back of the tavern afterward, and Finn hadn't seen her since then. "Something's bothering me about all of this, Oscar."

He looked up to see Oscar watching him.

"It's the timing of the attacks. Meyer mentioned how there have been high-level targets." He lowered his voice. "Now with the king's visit to the city—"

"He thinks it's related."

Finn nodded. "He doesn't say, but what if it is? The king *is* here to negotiate with the Alainsith. What if someone wants to disrupt the peace?"

Oscar smirked at Finn. "That's not the kind of thing a man on a crew thinks much about, Finn. And I don't think it's something an executioner gives much thought to, either."

Finn shook his head. "That's what Meyer says, but it bothers me thinking about the jobs we pulled. What happened. The bad luck. The strange things we were going after."

"That's all it was. Bad luck. Like the poor woman you saw murdered."

Finn wrinkled his nose and took another drink of ale. "Gods, Oscar. There was so much blood. I've never seen anything like that before."

"Because you're a thief and not a killer," Oscar said.

"For now," he said softly.

"What is that supposed to mean?"

Finn shrugged and looked over. "If I'm to continue serving Meyer, I'm going to eventually become—"

"You're not going to become anything. If you serve, then you serve. It doesn't make you a killer."

Finn could only shake his head. It was the part he struggled with the most. "Anyway, that wasn't really the point I was trying to make when I started telling you all of this." It certainly hadn't been to get into his concern about the attacks Meyer had mentioned, or about the jobs the crew had been taking, and whether they were related. Finn would have to find that on his own, he suspected.

"What point were you trying to make?"

"Only that Meyer didn't simply take the facts as they were presented to him. He asked his own questions."

"And I'm supposed to be impressed that the hangman took the time to ask questions?"

"I don't know if you're supposed to be impressed or not, but he did ask more questions than I expected."

"What does it matter if the hangman or the Archers ask questions?"

Finn didn't know how to explain it to Oscar. He wasn't

sure how to explain it to himself. It wasn't so much that questions were asked as it was more about how Meyer had made a point of showing him that he wanted to ensure he didn't carry out a sentencing on someone who wasn't guilty.

"I think he knows more about what happened with our job," Finn said, his voice quiet.

"Why would you say that?"

Finn just shook his head. "I just think that he does."

It would explain why Meyer made a point of bringing him to the home. It was almost as if Meyer had wanted Finn to know that he wasn't going to simply assume someone's guilt.

"If he knows something, then—"

"If who knows something?" The King took a seat next to them, glancing over to Finn for a moment. His deep brown eyes softened slightly, though Finn noticed the same intensity behind them that there always was. He was dressed in his darks as well.

They had been in the middle of a job. Finn had seen the King several times throughout the city. He still had no idea who the Client could be, though having seen him with a high-ranking Archer, along with one of the jurors, or even the general store owner, it could have been anyone.

Finn glanced from Oscar to the King.

"Finn was just telling me about his experience with his new master today. It seems there was a murder near the edge of town."

"Gods. A murder?" The King lifted his ale, taking a

long drink before setting it down. "He's brought you into that sort of thing already?"

"He brought me with him to look into the murder," Finn said.

The King breathed out heavily. "Maybe that's good. If everything goes as planned, we might need your help with something soon."

Finn looked over to Oscar, but he didn't meet his gaze. What strange item would the crew be sent after this time? "With what?"

"Can't talk about it just yet, Shuffles. When the time comes, we'll make certain you know what you need to do."

The King and Oscar shared a look across the table, and Finn couldn't help but wonder what else he missed. There was something more taking place there.

Oscar wouldn't tell him.

There were aspects to what they had gone through, aspects to what Finn had gone through, that had troubled him from the beginning.

Who was this Client to continue to hire the King?

"What else *have* you been doing, Shuffles?"

"Same as I told you before. He's still bringing me along slowly. I'm not entirely sure what he's going to have me doing each day, but for the most part, he still sends me on supply runs."

"I see that he's dressed you better than you were before."

Finn looked down at his clothes. He had been wearing them for the better part of the last few days and had forgotten about how they might stand out in a place like the Wenderwolf. They were nicer than the darks. A better cut, even though they weren't completely custom-fit for him yet.

"He didn't want me to wear the Sinner's Cloth."

"I suppose not. Probably better he dress you in this," the King said, reaching across to him and running his fingers along the shirt. "Look at Shuffles, Hand. He's really stepped up in the world."

Oscar turned his attention to his drink.

Finn took a deep breath. "Look. King. I'm not so sure I can help the crew just yet."

The King set his mug down, and he turned his attention on Finn. "What was that?"

Finn glanced at Oscar, but he wasn't going to get any help from him. "I don't know that I'm going to be able to help you the way you want. Not for a while. I'm still getting settled with this new apprenticeship, and I—"

"You sound like you want to keep it."

Finn shook his head. "That's not it. It's more that—"

"Listen, Shuffles. You don't want to upset me, do you?"

Finn held the King's gaze. This was his crew leader. Someone Finn had wanted nothing more than to impress. "I don't want to upset you, but you should know I can't promise anything when it comes to Meyer. He hasn't brought me all the way in yet. I don't know when he will. Or if he will."

The King leaned back, a strange smile twisting his lips. "I don't think he has much choice, Shuffles." He glanced at Oscar. "You didn't tell him?"

"I didn't have time."

"Didn't have time for what?"

"Wolf started looking into this Executioner's Right. He's the only one who'd ever heard anything about it, but there was something that troubled him. All of us, really." He leaned forward toward Finn. "We wanted to make sure it was legit, you see. Had to know our boy was safe."

He was a part of the crew. This was the King's way of reminding Finn of that.

"What did you discover?" Finn asked.

The King twisted in his seat and whistled.

Wolf had been sitting in the back of the tavern. That was strange. Stranger was that unlike the King and Oscar, he wasn't dressed in his darks.

Had he not been a part of whatever job they'd pulled? And where was Rock?

Wolf headed toward them and took a seat next to him.

"Tell Shuffles what you've discovered about his new predicament."

Wolf tipped his head at Finn in a slight nod. "You're the first in a long time."

"I know," he said. "When he claimed the right. That's when I learned."

The King took a drink from his ale, leaning back in his chair. "Not when you went to the palace?"

"We didn't have much time in the palace. We weren't there long."

"You didn't tell us what you saw when you went before the king," Wolf said.

"I guess I didn't think it mattered."

The King shrugged. "It probably doesn't, but do you

know how many people from these sections"—he swept his hands around him as if he were indicating all the sections near them—"who've been in the palace?" He arched a brow. "None. Not even the Archers can make that claim. At least, none of the city Archers. Palace Archers only."

"What did you see?" Wolf asked.

"I saw—"

The tavern door slammed open, and Nels Frenuhs—a cutpurse who worked on the crew known as Scruff—came rushing in. When he saw the King and Wolf sitting at the table, he raced toward them.

"Red got pinched! He was scoping out the next job, and the damn Archers pulled him away."

Red?

Finn knew Red but didn't know he was working with the crew.

Maybe he had since Finn was pinched.

"What?" King asked, still holding his gaze on Finn. "He shouldn't have drawn any attention while he was—" Wolf rested a hand on the King's arm and nodded toward Finn. "Sorry, Shuffles. The crew has to talk," the King said.

He was a part of the crew.

But not anymore.

Finn nodded. "I understand."

He finished his ale and got to his feet, looking around the tavern.

He found Oscar watching him. Finn flashed a smile before leaving the tavern. Out in the street, he worked his way over to the far side of the street, where he could hide in the shadows. He didn't hide nearly as well as he had when wearing the darks. Still, he should be able to hide well enough to watch.

The street was empty. The Wenderwolf was active, though. The sound from inside the tavern continued to drift beyond the walls, out into the street, giving off a festive feel.

Finn wished he felt that festiveness.

Instead, all he felt was out of place.

Could the Wenderwolf have become so unfamiliar that quickly?

The door opened. Finn sank into the shadows as much as he could, trying to hide.

The King and Wolf headed out of the tavern with Scruff leading them. He was short and thin. A few years younger than Finn, he'd wanted to join the crew, but since Oscar had vouched for Finn, he'd been given preference. It seemed Scruff got promoted with Finn's departure.

Where was Oscar?

Wolf hadn't been wearing his darks. Both Scruff and the King were.

It was easier to follow Wolf, as a result. Finn moved along the street, trying to stay in the shadows. The soft shirt and pants might be brown, but they didn't blend into the shadows along the street nearly as well as the darks did.

If only he still had his. They'd been left behind in Declan. The few times Finn had considered asking about them, he'd changed his mind. It would only raise the kind of questions he didn't need.

Following them along the street, Finn had an idea.

He could take the alley.

He generally knew the street's direction, even as it wound in a twisting sort of manner through here. Using the alleys, Finn could cut through and shave off time. By popping out of the alley, he might be able to see them pass and could figure out where they were headed.

Don't do this.

Reason suggested it was a mistake. He could go back to Meyer, rest. Get ready for more work in the morning. Gods, he probably should be studying the book Meyer had given him. It had already proven useful. Knowing the anatomy and understanding injury had been how Meyer had treated Gabe earlier in the day.

Curiosity won out.

Finn slipped along the alley.

From there, it was easy enough for him to sneak along. Few people used the alleys, and the only thing he had to worry about was stepping in piles of shit. Usually, the smell would alert him of that, so he figured he'd be safe.

Finn raced through the alley until it ended.

Then he stopped near the street. Darkened shapes moved in the distance. Two figures who were hard to see, and Wolf who moved with his dangerous stride, though much more visible.

Finn stayed in the darkness, away from the street. He waited until they passed, and only when they were gone did he creep forward.

He watched, noting how they curled around and tried to anticipate which way the street would go. From this part of the city, Finn didn't know where they might be headed. Surprisingly, they seemed to be generally heading toward the center of the city. Toward the merchant section.

Were they to be caught out late at night in the outer sections, there weren't going to be many repercussions. If they got caught in the central portion of the city, questions would be asked. Finn wouldn't be surprised if the Archers detained them and questioned them about where they were heading.

He darted across the street, reaching another alley, and slipped along it.

As he ran along the alley, he jumped over a pile of something unpleasant, not pausing long enough to consider what it was, his nose telling him it was foul. When the alley reached the next street, he paused again.

He started to question whether he had made a mistake and whether he had chosen the wrong direction. There would've been an alternative path he could've taken, and by going along that path, he might have found the three of the crew slipping a different way.

Then he saw the figures making their way along the street.

They were near the bridge leading toward the central sections of the city.

Near enough that Finn was surprised at how willing the King was to expose himself like this. The King was generally cautious. Cautious enough that he wouldn't usually dart into danger that way.

What had Red been up to?

Finn waited in the shadows, and when they came close, he tried to lean forward to listen to their conversation. He should have been doing that all along, but even in the short time that he had been working with Master Meyer, he had gotten out of practice.

"They pinched him up by the bridge," Scruff was saying. "We got to get out of here before curfew hits—"

"Quiet," Wolf growled. "The curfew don't mean shit to us. The King's got that covered."

"The King wanted to know." Scruff sounded petulant, and Finn could imagine the King getting angry with him, especially in the middle of the night and out on the street like this, having had a job go awry.

"Quiet," the King said. "And Wolf is right. Just have to pay the Archers a little extra with the curfew these days. That's all."

"I saw somethin', King. Don't know what it was. Maybe another crew," Scruff said.

"No other crew going against us," the King said.

"They did when Rock—"

Scruff cut off when the King shot him a look. Finn could easily imagine the irritation in his eyes. He'd been the target of the same look more than once.

They passed him.

Wolf glanced in his direction, his gaze lingering for a moment, almost as if he realized Finn was there. Finn backed up against the alley wall, staying as close as he could but still trying to listen.

They moved past, then he breathed out.

He wasn't going to be able to chase them down the street to the bridge.

Any farther and he would be risking exposing his presence.

He stepped forward and felt something grab him.

Finn spun, bringing his arms up, preparing to strike and run when he realized that Oscar stood near him.

"You damn fool." Oscar nodded to the retreating form of the figures in the distance. "What do you think you're doing?"

"I was curious."

"Curious enough to get yourself beat?"

"I'm not going to get myself beat," Finn said.

"You are if you go chasing off like that. The King isn't playing games with these jobs, Finn. They're dangerous. You heard you weren't the only one who's gotten pinched on them. If Red got picked up, then…"

"What have they been doing? Are you going against another crew?"

That sort of thing happened, though the King had enough standing in the city that Finn wouldn't have expected it with his crew.

Oscar shook his head. "No." When Finn opened his mouth to argue, Oscar raised a hand. "You're not going to push this issue. It's too dangerous, Finn. I don't know that you should be coming by the tavern, either."

"It's my crew, too."

"Not anymore," Oscar said.

"Thanks," Finn said.

"You know what I mean," Oscar said.

"I know exactly what you mean. Me getting caught to protect you wasn't worth anything." Oscar glared at him. "I'm just curious what the crew has been doing."

Oscar looked along the street. There was no further movement. Finally, he sighed softly. "The Client has had a few other jobs since you were picked up. Most of them have been difficult."

"Difficult like the one where we broke into the viscount's home?"

High-level targets.

What if the Client was the one coordinating the attacks in the city?

Finn should let Meyer know…

"Like that. More difficult than I like. And the King don't always tell me what we're after."

"But you're the Hand."

"And he's got Wolf. And Rock. Now Scruff. The whole crew is involved."

Finn detected Oscar's irritation. "Then don't take them."

"With what we're getting paid, that's not much of an option. But you have something else you can be a part of. It's an opportunity for more. Don't make a mistake in thinking that it's not."

"I understand exactly what it is," Finn said.

"Do you?" Oscar leaned forward, grabbing his shirt. "Look at you. You're dressed better than I will ever be. And you look comfortable in it."

"It is comfortable. The fabric is so soft—"

Oscar grunted. "That's my point. You don't belong

here with us. Not anymore. Maybe you never did. I know you were trying to do what your father did, to take care of your sister and your mother, but do it another way. Do it honorably."

"Can I do it honorably working with the executioner?"

"A man like that has a connection to the city. That's what you need to take advantage of."

Finn wasn't sure how to respond. "What were they going to tell me about Meyer? I saw you and the King sharing a look. There's something you uncovered about him. If it involves me, it matters. Come on, Oscar. You forget I'm the one who taught you how to read people. I saw the way you fidgeted when the King asked you for details about the hangman."

Oscar shot him an annoyed look. Finn didn't need his lessons to recognize it. "Listen. Ask your master what happens if you fail."

"Why? You know something, Oscar. You need to tell me what it is."

"Wolf didn't share all of it. Only that there are repercussions if you fail. I heard him and the King talking about it. Just ask him."

Finn waited for Oscar to say more, but he didn't. "Why do I get the sense that whatever job the King was talking about in the Wenderwolf will be difficult?"

"You already know the answer to that. I don't know all the details yet. Only that it's big."

"Bigger than what we attempted at the viscount's home?"

"Bigger than that."

Meyer would need to know. That was how Finn could protect the crew now. Maybe he could save them from themselves.

"I'm worried that you're a crucial part of whatever they intend to do." Oscar flicked his gaze past him. Finn followed the direction of his gaze, looking into the distance, trying to see just what was that he saw. *Was that movement?* "It's why you need to keep away from the tavern. I know the Wenderwolf is familiar. Gods know I know that. And you want to see your friends. But for now, you're going to be better off staying away."

"I can help the crew—"

Finn cut off, realizing that he had seen shadowy movement.

At first, he thought that it was the King and Wolf, but there were only two, and he heard the thudding of boots over the cobblestones, a mistake he knew Wolf especially was far too skilled to make.

Archers.

Finn glanced over to Oscar. "Go. See if you can't figure out what happened to my sister. When I went there earlier, she was gone. I'm worried that whatever she did for the hegen has gotten her into trouble."

Oscar frowned at him. "We can look for Lena together."

Finn shook his head. "I don't need to."

"You don't have to get yourself in trouble because of me again," Oscar said.

"Who said I was going to get myself into trouble? Didn't you say that I have a different life now?"

Finn pushed Oscar behind him. Oscar slipped off, heading away and down the alley. Finn could hear him for a moment, but then it disappeared.

He stepped forward, raising his hands.

The Archers approached. "What are you doing out?"

"I'm Finn Jagger, apprenticed to Master Meyer."

He wasn't sure whether that would even work, but their demeanor changed immediately at the mention of Meyer's name.

"The hangman sent you out? I didn't even know he had an apprentice," one of the men said.

It was dark, and it was difficult to see much about the man's features. He had one hand on the hilt of his sword, and his helm concealed most of his features.

"Sure. After the Lion died—" Finn started.

"Not died. Was killed. That's what we're looking for. You can tell Master Meyer that we're searching for those responsible for killing his apprentice."

Finn nodded slowly. "I will tell him."

"It's awfully late," the shorter of the two Archers said. "Why are you out?"

"Because Master Meyer sent me."

The two men shared a look.

"Listen. If you'd like to follow me back to his home to ask him yourself, you're more than welcome to. You can tell him how you've been searching for his apprentice's killer."

"Maybe we should do that. The viscount has wanted results. We got to uphold the damn curfew. We don't get paid enough for that."

"We're going to be better off by making sure." The other Archer looked over to Finn, and he shrugged. "You understand, don't you?"

"I understand. I can't help that you'll be wasting your time, but…" He smiled.

In the distance, he caught sight of movement. Darkened shapes. Three figures.

The crew.

"You can come with me or not."

They nodded, and Finn turned, heading along the street. He cast a glance down the street, looking toward the King and Wolf—able to see Wolf the best, given his clothing—before hurrying forward. The Archers kept pace.

It didn't take long for Finn to lose the crew. He didn't think the King would bother following, anyway, especially considering the Archers with him. By the time he reached the small home, he pulled the gate open, headed through the narrow garden, and opened the door.

The Archers waited on the doorstep. "You really are his apprentice?"

Finn nodded.

"We don't need to disturb Master Meyer. Good luck," the other man said.

Finn waited until they were gone before stepping inside, closing the door behind him, and leaning on it for a moment to catch his breath.

As he gathered his thoughts, he noticed a lantern light at the end of the hall, coming from the healing room.

He headed toward it quietly, and when he reached it,

he paused for a moment to listen. There were no voices from inside. No sound of anything to suggest anyone was there.

"You can come in, Finn."

Finn stepped in and found Meyer sitting at his desk, a stack of papers in front of him.

"What happens if I fail in my training?"

Meyer looked up. "What was that?"

"If I fail. What happens?"

"I will ensure you won't fail."

"There's a consequence, isn't there?"

Meyer nodded slowly. "There is."

"Why don't you want to tell me what it is? Will I be sent back to the Stone and hanged?"

"Not alone."

"What do you mean?"

Meyer leaned forward, resting his hand on the desk, covering up the papers. "By exerting the Executioner's Right, I pinned my fate to yours."

The words took a moment for them to sink in for Finn. "You mean—"

"I mean that if you fail, I will join you on the Raven Stone."

Finn stared at him for a moment. "Why would you do that?"

"My reasons are my own."

"How long do I have?"

"You don't need to worry about that."

"How long?"

"You have until the Executioner Court."

"What is that?"

"That is a gathering of others empowered by the crown to fulfill his justice."

"Other executioners."

"Yes."

"They will gather and decide my fate?"

"They will gather and decide both of our fates."

"And what do I need to do to pass?"

"That is up to the court to decide. I don't expect you to be competent to carry out all aspects of the job before you are presented to the court, but you must have a passing familiarity with them. The testing is meant to be difficult and to prove you have worked to understand all that's involved in serving as an executioner. It will be difficult, which is why it's my responsibility to ensure you are ready."

There was a moment of silence between them. "Why?"

"Why what?"

"Why did you pick me?"

Meyer held his gaze for a moment before turning his attention down to the stack of pages. "Continue your studies, Finn. Tomorrow will be another long day."

If Finn didn't pass this testing, then something was going to happen to him and Meyer. Only the gods knew what would happen to his sister and mother then. And then there was his crew and the jobs they were pulling. Finn wanted to protect them, too.

How could he do it all without disappointing someone, or worse—ending up swinging on the Raven Stone?

CHAPTER EIGHTEEN

The next few days went quickly.

Finn focused on his studies, working through everything Meyer gave him to learn as much as possible, trying to keep his mind off of what his crew might be doing. For the most part, days were spent on errands with Meyer, visiting prisons, questioning prisoners, and then studying in the evening while practicing knots. He hadn't gone back to the Wenderwolf, though partly that was because he'd been busy. Rock would be angry, but hopefully he'd understand the next time Finn made it to the tavern.

There hadn't been an execution in the time that he'd been working with Meyer. For that, Finn was thankful.

It was late, and he looked up from the book spread out on the desk in front of him. The book of anatomy was complicated, showing vessels and organs and bones that each had names, and he found himself trying to master what was depicted on the pages but struggling. He couldn't shake feeling as if he were going to anger Meyer by being inadequately prepared.

There were now three other books stacked on the desk. Each of them was a volume Meyer wanted him to work through and master, but he'd barely gotten far with the anatomy book. How was he supposed to have the time needed to get into the others?

Finn rubbed his eyes, leaning back. This wasn't at all what he thought that he'd be doing when working with Meyer. In a way, it was better. At least it was interesting.

He thought of what Oscar had said about boredom. There was no way for Finn to be bored when he was trying to learn anatomy like this. He had far too much he was expected to master.

Getting up, Finn headed out into the hall and heard voices near the back room. He paused there for a moment, listening, and heard Meyer with another customer seeking his healing. They always came late at night, never early in the day, though that made a certain sort of sense.

"How will I know it works?" a rough voice said.

"The head pain will begin to ease. The rest will be…"

Finn lost what Meyer said about the last, hearing nothing more than murmuring.

Meyer had moved closer to the door, and he seemed to position himself so that he blocked Finn from hearing anything else.

Why would Meyer want privacy with this?

He could remain there and see what more he might be able to observe, but that risked irritating him. So far,

Meyer hadn't welcomed him to any of his healing sessions. He kept Finn apart from that, though he had been willing to have Finn with him for other aspects.

Finn lingered near the door for a few moments, listening to see if there might be something that he could hear. If he was to be Meyer's assistant, he needed to better understand what Meyer did and how he helped others. His interest in staying there was more than that, though. Partly, it was because he wanted to know just what it was that Meyer did. Partly, it was because this was the part of his job that Finn actually enjoyed. He might even tell Meyer what he feared with the Client and his role in the attacks in the city.

The door shut in front of him, and Finn stood for a moment.

He turned, heading back toward the room. The lantern on the desk called to him, as did the book—along with the other books he still had yet to start.

Finn sighed.

He was tired. The days had been long, and he knew he should return to his studies or even head to sleep, but neither of them were things that he really wanted to do just yet.

He stepped out of the home, standing at the threshold for a moment before closing the door behind him. Out in the garden, the smells of the flowers that drifted to him on the faint breeze in the night reminded him of Helda. Finn breathed it in, enjoying the scents around him, and looked toward the darkened gate.

It might be late, but with his role serving Master

Meyer, he no longer had to fear being out in the city at night the way that he once did. Finn decided to search for his sister and check on his mother. He'd been checking each day, feeding her and making sure she got the concoction Meyer made for her and hadn't known how often Lena had been there.

He hurried to the streets, glancing all around him as he walked, but he didn't see anyone else out. He made his way to the Brinder section as quickly as he could.

By the time he reached it, a tension had begun to build within him. Strange that he would feel that sort of tension in the streets when he had always enjoyed being out at night before.

Of course, when he had been out at night before, there had been the thrill of fearing that he might get caught but the excitement of knowing he did something he wasn't supposed to. Finn had rarely been caught. He usually escaped, disappearing down alleys. Now, even though he didn't worry about the Archers, he still felt afraid.

Why would that be?

When he reached his home, he knocked briefly. It wouldn't do for him to scare his sister. Finn stood for a moment, waiting by the door, listening for sounds of movement inside.

There was nothing.

He knocked again.

Lights in some of the nearby homes told him that other people were up. There was enough crime in the section that the people there would fear he was doing something that he should not.

Finn tested the door.

It was unlocked.

That was strange as well.

He stepped inside and immediately noted the smell in the home that seemed worse each time he came to visit.

Closing the door behind him, he fumbled around until he found a lantern on the table in the home's front entryway. When he got the lantern lit, Finn held it up, swinging around to look whether anything had changed since he last been there.

There was no sign of Lena.

"Lena?"

There was no response.

Finn carried the lantern through the home, making his way toward his mother's room.

When he stopped in the doorway, he found her lying partially covered. It might be his imagination, but it seemed as if she didn't sweat quite as much as she had before. She moved more as well, her legs twitching.

He stepped toward her and noted how she gripped the sheet in one of her hands, squeezing it. Finn pulled the chair toward her and sat down next to her, taking her other hand. He squeezed. "I'm here, Mother."

Her head turned toward him.

Could she hear me?

In all the times that he had come to visit his mother recently, there had never been a response from her. This was new.

Had it been what he had given her, or had it been what the hegen had offered Lena?

Finn didn't have any idea, but he didn't think it was his imagination his mother had turned toward the sound of his voice.

"It's Finn. I'm here," he said.

There wasn't any further movement that would suggest she could hear him. He sat there for a few moments, just holding onto her hand, waiting for there to be some other sign that she had heard him, but there wasn't anything.

After a while, Finn got up. He looked around the inside of his mother's room. The tray next to the bed was empty, and he had to wonder if Lena had been there recently to feed her. He didn't see anything that she would have offered. Unless Lena had been and had cleaned it up.

There wasn't any medicine, either.

Finn still had the vial of medicine that Meyer had given him to use on her, and he unstoppered it before giving her a few drops of the liquid. It wasn't as much as what Meyer had wanted, or as frequent, so Finn didn't know if it would even work.

When he was done, he headed back out toward the kitchen, where he looked around. There wasn't a sign of Lena. He quickly put the dirty dishes away and then took a seat at the table. It was his home, but it didn't feel like his home anymore.

It was a strange feeling. He'd been away from here for so long that he no longer knew what to call it. His mother's home? His sister's?

Where was *Lena, anyway?*

Finn carried the lantern back toward the main part of

the house and started heading into the other room when there was a knock at the door.

He made his way toward the door carefully. "Who is it?"

"It's Helda. I saw the light and—"

Finn pulled the door open to see Helda standing in the street. A dark cloak wrapped around her shoulders. Worry lined her face.

"Finn."

He smiled, but it faltered when she didn't return it. "You look disappointed."

"Is Lena here?"

She tried looking past him.

He shook his head. "I don't know. I was looking for her."

"What do you mean, you don't know?"

"I just got here. She's not back with Mother and not in the kitchen…"

Were she there, she would have come out after having heard him and Helda talking.

"This isn't like her," Helda said. "I haven't seen her for a while. After you saw me the last time, I started to keep an eye out for her. Something hasn't been right with her. She…"

"What is it?" Finn asked.

Helda looked up at him. "She's been struggling, Finn. I think she's gone to a dark place. I've never seen Lena like that. With your mother getting weaker, and her trying to work…" She shook her head. "I tried to get her to talk with you. Work with you even. She deserves better."

Finn swallowed. "I should've been there for her."

"She knows you're trying."

Finn looked up. It was strange to have Helda trying to reassure him.

"I need to try harder," he said.

"If anything happened to her, I want to help. I can help you look tomorrow."

"You'd help me?" He didn't mean it to come off the way he knew it sounded.

Helda didn't seem to notice. "For Lena. I'm worried, Finn. The city isn't safe. Lena told me what she heard at work. There have been attacks outside the walls. The gods know Lena of all people needs to be careful."

"Why Lena, of all people?" It wasn't the question he wanted to ask, and he was tempted to argue with Helda, but this was his sister, and he owed it to her to help.

"She's a single woman in the Brinder section. Men do terrible things."

"I'm not sure what to make of that," he said.

"You can make of it what you will. What I'm getting at… I don't know what I'm getting at. I'm worried about her."

Finn was worried too. It wasn't like his sister to be gone like this. She was the responsible one. She was the one who'd taken on the job to help their mother. She was the one who had done everything she could to help their mother.

Finn looked past Helda. An Archer moved in the distance. At this point, he didn't know if his word with the Archers would even matter. He could guide them to

Meyer's home the way he had before, but doing that didn't necessarily mean they'd leave him alone. Finding him here would raise more questions. What he needed was something to prove he was who he claimed.

Meyer would likely tell him he had to keep from doing anything suspicious, and he wouldn't have to worry about the Archers. While that was true enough, there were times when he needed to come to these other sections.

"Do you want to come in?" Finn asked.

Helda blinked. "I shouldn't. I just stopped because I saw the light. I should go."

She turned away from him. Finn watched her go for a moment before closing the door and leaning on it. His heart pounded with a different feeling. It was fear, but it wasn't fear for him. This time, it was for his sister.

Where was Lena?

The morning came quickly, and there was still no sign of Lena. He had stayed at home, resting in the chair next to his mother, and administered more of Meyer's medicine after he came awake.

When he got up, he stretched. His arms and legs were stiff, and his entire body felt off. He looked at his mother a moment before returning to the main part of the house. There wasn't any sign of Lena. No sign of anyone.

She hadn't come back.

When he'd found her missing, he thought that *maybe* she would return later in the night. So, he'd stayed and promised himself that he'd find Helda in the morning to tell her that he'd found Lena. That there was still no sign of her troubled him.

Stepping out into the street, he took a deep breath. The Brinder section stank. Finn hadn't paid it much mind the night before, but now that he was there, he could smell the foulness in the air. The stench of rot and waste and an awful undercurrent of something that he couldn't place.

The sun started to come up in the distance, giving a little bit of light to the morning.

He should be back at Meyer's by now. He'd been gone long enough.

Meyer would probably ask questions about where he'd been and why he'd been gone for so long.

What would I even say?

The walk back went quickly. His mind raced the entire time, worried thoughts about his sister filling his head. *What would take her away from home this long? Had she been killed?* That wasn't a question he would ever have asked before, but having seen Mistress Vils' home, he now found himself asking questions that he wouldn't have before. Other dangerous things could have happened to her as well. Maybe the type of work that she'd started doing for the butcher had been such that she needed to stay with him because it got too late for her to return home.

It didn't feel right. Lena wouldn't leave their mother alone for that long. She wouldn't have known that Finn would be there.

By the time he'd gotten back to Meyer's house, his mind was still racing.

Meyer was in the kitchen cooking.

Finn took over for him, and Meyer took a seat.

"You were gone all night. Your crew?" Disappointment filled his voice.

Finn shook his head. "Not my crew. I went to see my mother."

"You're upset the medicine hasn't worked."

"That's not it either."

Finn didn't even know if the medicine had worked or not. It *might* have helped, if only he had managed to get it to her more consistently. He'd been by twice a day, but that wasn't nearly as often as what she needed. Finn made a point of stopping first thing in the morning to give her the medicine, and then at the end of the day when he made she sure got a second dose—along with ensuring she had as much to eat and drink as she would.

"What is it?"

"My sister. She's missing. At least, I think she's missing. It's not like her to not return to our home. Normally, she's the one who's caring for our mother, but she's not been there from what I can tell."

"How long?"

Finn shook his head. "I don't know. A few days. She's not been there when I've stopped by to check on my mother."

Then there was what Helda had told him about how Lena had gone to some dark place.

What if something had happened to his sister?

Meyer sat up and looked over at him. "What might she have been doing?"

"I don't know. She'd recently taken a job with the butcher, but she'd also gone to the hegen for help."

Meyer nodded. "I will task the Archers to look."

Archers wouldn't be able to find her. Not if the hegen had already gotten to her.

The morning went slowly for Finn. He kept thinking about how his sister had been gone. He kept thinking about his mother lying alone.

Meyer took him to several different prisons, where they questioned men, but Finn barely managed to keep his focus. They ran errands throughout the day, Meyer guiding him around the city, showing him various other apothecaries and supply shops, along with two different general stores that he preferred. Finn made a mental note of them, but none of those mattered to him.

By the time evening fell and they returned to the home, and Meyer dismissed him to carry on with his own studies, he struggled with his focus.

His mind raced.

He needed to know what happened to his sister.

There was only one way he thought he might be able to do it.

It meant he was going to have to go to the hegen himself.

He looked out in the hall, but Meyer was in his office, murmuring to someone who had come to him.

It meant Finn had time to himself and to go to his mother.

He slipped out into the night. Darkness had fallen, and it was chilly out, making him wish he had grabbed his cloak, but he ignored the chill, hurrying through the streets toward the gate. When he reached it, he half-expected that he would meet resistance, but there was none.

He didn't know what he intended to find. Maybe nothing.

When he reached the outskirts of the hegen section, he hurried forward. He tried to think about the path Meyer had taken him through this section of the city, weaving through.

Where would his sister have gone?

She would've wanted someone capable of healing their mother.

Which meant Finn had to go to Esmerelda's home.

He saw more people out in the streets than he had the last time they were here. Some of the hegen looked at him askance, but they looked away when he turned his attention to them. When he finally caught the familiar sight of the bright red door, his heart started to race.

Finn approached carefully. Slowly.

There were so many rumors about the hegen that Finn didn't even know what was real. They had magic. They stole a part of a person's soul. They killed children and drank their blood. Finn doubted any of that—other than their magic—was real.

He knocked.

He wasn't sure what to expect. When he had come with Meyer, she hadn't answered.

The door came open.

The woman who answered the door was young; Finn

would almost say pretty. She had long dark hair. Her wide eyes seemed piercing, the irises black and staring at him. Unlike the other hegen he'd seen in the street, dressed in mismatched clothing, she wore a flowing red dress cinched with a blue belt. She studied him, her gaze sweeping from head to toe, almost as if she could see through him.

"Are you Esmerelda?" he asked carefully.

She tipped her head slightly, smiling at him. Full lips curved. "And you are…"

For some reason, Finn had a feeling that she already knew.

"My name is Finn Jagger. I'm apprenticed to Henry Meyer."

Esmerelda started to chuckle. "The rumors are true, then. He claimed his right."

Finn had suspected she already knew of him. "He did. That's not why I'm here, though."

"Interesting. I wonder what makes you unique, much like I wonder what happened to your predecessor."

Her comment made him wonder what she might know. She *was* hegen. "I don't really know what makes me unique." It seemed best not to address the other comment.

"Perhaps that is what you should seek to understand. All men must come to understand their fate."

She stepped off to the side, motioning him in. When he stepped into the home, he wasn't sure what he would have expected. It was sparsely decorated. He imagined magical artifacts, but what he found was a plush carpet covering the floor. A pair of chairs sat near a table, and a large stack of cards rested on the table. He didn't see anything that would be all that strange for any other home within the city, though his old thief instincts kicked in, making him appraise everything in the room. There were a few ceramic sculptures, but nothing that could be easily moved. A small silver statue looked something like a strange dog…

She cleared her throat.

He looked up. In the pale lantern light, he realized she was even younger than he had thought. When he had first seen her, Finn had believed she was a decade or more older, but as she looked at him, he started to think she couldn't be all that much older than him.

"What brings you to my home, Finn Jagger?"

"I'm here for my sister." He said it quickly, knowing that he needed to get it out. "She came to the hegen for help, and she's gone missing."

Esmerelda regarded him for a long moment. "If she came to the people for help, then anything she has agreed to is between her and the one who offered help."

"Was it you?"

Esmerelda smiled at him. His heart hammered. "Were it me, I would have said that her arrangement was between her and myself."

"I just need to know that she is safe. Our mother is sick—"

"I imagine that's the reason she came to the people for help." Esmerelda lifted a card from the table, looking at it for a moment.

"It is. The apothecaries haven't been able to help, and

we were trying to save money for physicians, but they are too expensive. Master Meyer has offered his services, but…"

Esmerelda looked over to him. "You would like to know what I can do?"

There was something in the question that froze Finn for a moment.

Everything asked of the hegen had a cost.

This was his sister.

Wasn't he prepared to pay that price? Lena had been willing to pay the price for their mother. Meyer *had* said the hegen were calling in favors lately.

Then there was the man Finn had met in Declan when he'd been a prisoner. What had Charon been asked to do? He would need to go back to learn.

"I want to know that she is safe. I want her returned."

"There will be a cost."

She looked down at the card she held again.

Finn's heart hammered for a moment. Would Finn be one of the favors called in?

For his sister, he would.

"I understand."

Esmerelda stared at the card for a long moment before looking up. "Very well. I will see what I can find of your sister, Finn Jagger. When the time comes, I will ask of you payment."

"I can't do anything that will violate my apprenticeship."

She cocked her head to the side. "Nothing will be asked that will preclude you from serving your sentence."

Esmerelda held out her hand, the card offered to him.

Finn looked at it and finally took it.

"That is for you to keep. A marker. You will know when it's time for you to serve." She turned away. "Is that all?"

Finn stared at the card. On it, there was a figure with a noose around its neck.

He shivered.

"That's all."

She guided him to the door without saying another word and escorted him out into the street. She watched him for a moment before closing the door.

He stared after Esmerelda for a long moment before turning away. The street around him was empty, which left him unsettled. He made his way back into the city, through the gate, and to Master Meyer's home.

When he got inside, Master Meyer pulled the door open, looking at him. "You should not have gone there," he said.

Finn couldn't even argue about where he had gone. "I needed to know what happened to her."

Meyer sighed deeply. "Come along, then. We need to make preparations."

"Preparations for what?"

"For your mother—and your sister, when she's returned—to stay with us."

CHAPTER NINETEEN

The executioner had done as he'd promised, and Finn's mother had come to stay with them. He put her up in a small room near the house's healing end, though she didn't need much space. It allowed Finn to visit her more than he had even when he'd been freer, and it gave Meyer a chance to check on her—which he did, and often. There wasn't any stench like there had been coming off her before.

Finn took a break from studying, having moved on from the anatomy book, still not having mastered it but feeling as if he had taken as much from it as he could, and had begun to work on a book of medicinals. Somehow, that book was even more complicated than the last. He had to memorize what he found in the book and be able to recite it.

"Your sister did well keeping her as healthy as she did." Meyer carried a tray with another batch of the elixir he'd been giving to Finn's mother. He set the tray down and quickly drew up a small volume of the elixir before squeezing it into her mouth. "Most would have given up long before."

"Not Lena," Finn said.

They'd had no word from her, nothing that gave him any hope that she'd be found. With each passing day, Finn began to question whether she *would* be found. The hegen, and Esmerelda in particular, had made no attempt to get into contact with them, so Finn didn't think there was anything they'd be able to do to help her.

"Do you know what has made her so sick?" Finn doubted Meyer would know any more than the apothecaries they'd gone to—and there had been several. The only hope he'd had at answers had been the physician, but what physician would be willing to come to the executioner's home to heal?

"I've not seen anything like it. Whatever caused it is far enough along that it will prove difficult to slow."

Finn sighed. He'd known—or at least suspected—that much. Hearing it from Meyer made it more real, somehow.

"I need to find my sister," he said softly.

"I have tasked resources in the city to look for her. And you have tasked your own resources."

"I know I shouldn't have gone to the hegen, but I needed to know if anything had happened to her."

"I understand," Meyer said softly. "I have some experience with Esmerelda. That doesn't mean I would go there willingly were I to have other options. As I said, I've asked the city Archers to keep an eye out for her."

Finn didn't miss the irony of needing the Archers to help with something.

He tugged on the shirt, feeling the soft fabric, and closed his eyes. The studies Meyer had encouraged of him were to research some of the symptoms his mother displayed. Sweating. Rapid heart rate. The clammy skin. All were signs of something systemic.

Not that he knew what to do with that knowledge. A base of knowledge did nothing to help.

"She's resting comfortably, and we have somewhere we need to be."

Meyer left the room, and Finn squeezed his mother's hand, thinking that maybe she squeezed back. That had to be more his imagination, though.

"This late?"

"This late. Unfortunately."

He unfolded a scrap of paper and handed it to Finn.

Finn took it and read.

Thief. Break-in at antiquities shop. Declan.

"What's this?"

"When someone is captured and ready for questioning, the warden sends word. At least, that's how it's supposed to work. Lately, it hasn't been as seamless as it should be."

"Because of the high-level attacks?" He really *should* say something about the Client.

"Possibly."

"You have to question a thief at this time of night?"

"I don't have to, but I fear if I don't, then others will get there before me. Besides, it's time for you to begin this other aspect of your training."

Meyer waited as Finn gathered his cloak and met him at the door. Once they were out in the street, a cool air whipped through, and a few swirls of snow danced within it. Meyer moved quickly and confidently through the street. It seemed strange to Finn to be out like this in the evening without fearing any repercussions.

As they neared Declan Prison, Finn thought he saw someone, but there wasn't anyone there when he turned to look. Maybe an Archer, but if that were the case, why didn't he see them?

"What is it?" Meyer asked.

Finn shook his head. "Probably nothing," he muttered.

Nothing for him to be concerned by, at least. They reached the prison entrance, and Meyer pulled the keys from his pocket, unlocking it and stepping inside. A single iron master stood watch at the door, though he seemed bored when they entered and barely looked up at Meyer before nodding to him and waving him on.

Finn followed Meyer.

They reached a familiar stair leading into the depths of the prison. Finn's cell had been down there.

He paused.

"You'll have to get over it sooner or later," Meyer said.

"It's not so much getting over it," he said.

"Then what?"

Finn shook his head. "Memories."

"You weren't here long enough for memories."

"It felt like an eternity." And he'd only been in Declan

for a week. Maybe a little longer. What must it feel like for his father, who had been imprisoned for much longer?

Finn had no idea where his father was imprisoned, but he couldn't imagine any prison being any better for a longer time. Given that Oscar hadn't been able to track his father through the prisons—even with his connections—he suspected he had been taken out of the city to a different prison.

He took a deep breath, steadying himself.

Meyer was right. He was going to have to get over it sooner or later.

Eventually, new memories would form, and Finn would be able to look past the others, but for now, all he remembered was how the Lion had come for him, bringing him to the chapel, tormenting him for information that Finn was unwilling to provide.

They headed down the stairs.

When they reached the second lower level, the iron master nodded to Meyer. It wasn't one Finn recognized. "Didn't expect to see you tonight."

"I have a new apprentice, and he needs experience."

The iron master grunted. "Hopefully, he's not such a pain in the ass as the Lion."

"Time will tell."

The iron master glanced over at Finn. "What do we call him?"

"Nothing for now."

"No? He's not going to be the new Lion? Maybe the Cub?"

Meyer glared at the iron master. "Where is he?"

"Down here. I'll take you to him."

Finn followed the two of them down the hall.

This had been his cell.

When he reached the cell where he'd been held, he paused. He looked over at it for a moment before turning and looking across the hall.

Hector lay curled up in the back of his cell. He was quiet, and he breathed slowly enough that Finn thought he slept. Hector was thin, dressed in dirty and tattered clothing of the prisons, his lanky hair spread out around him.

At least, he hoped he slept.

At the end of the hall, the iron master and Meyer stopped in front of another cell.

The iron master opened the door and dragged a large man out.

Rock?

The shock of seeing Rock struck Finn.

This wasn't just someone he knew. This was a friend.

His heart hammered, and it seemed the moisture left his mouth.

Rock looked at Finn, locking eyes. There was a moment where something passed between them—hope? —but then it was gone.

They guided Rock along the hall.

When they reached the end of the hall, Finn stepped off to the side. Rock stared straight ahead, seemingly ignoring Finn and Meyer. He marched along, his gaze fixed straight ahead of him.

Something grabbed Finn, and he spun.

Hector pressed his face up against the bars, grinning. "The gods have answered all your prayers. No more tears and no more sorrow. Time to march toward their demands. Preparing for the war 'morrow!"

Hector cackled, reaching out toward Finn.

"Shut up!" The voice came from the end of the hall.

It was Charon.

Finn had planned on asking him if the hegen had demanded something of him, but coming with Meyer to question Rock stole those thoughts from him.

As Finn jerked away, Hector leaned toward him, trying to squeeze his face through the bars of the cell. "It's your right, it's his right, it's all right!"

Finn shook his head, leaving Hector.

When he caught up to Meyer, he glanced over to Finn, who shook his head.

"Hector," he whispered.

Meyer nodded. "He's been here a while. When he gets close to his sentencing, the guards get aggressive with him. He's not as crazed as it seems."

Finn glanced over to Hector. *Why prolong everything?* "He did that with me, too."

Meyer nodded and turned back toward the hallway. When they reached the chapel, the iron master brought Rock inside and strapped him into the chair, binding the leathers around his wrists and ankles. He stepped off to the side when Meyer cleared his throat.

"We will question him ourselves," Meyer said.

The iron master shrugged. "Be my guest. I'll be outside."

Finn looked over to Rock. His head was down, and he stared at the floor.

What would Rock say about me? Better yet, what would Rock say to me?

He debated how much to share with Meyer, but given what he knew of the executioner, it was likely that Meyer already knew that Finn had a connection to him.

"I know him," he whispered. "We were on the same crew. We're friends." He felt he had to add the last, otherwise Meyer would learn it eventually.

Meyer frowned. "Unusual."

"What is?"

"A single crew to get into enough trouble to draw the attention of the Archers so frequently."

"It's probably—"

Finn didn't have a chance to say that it was probably tied to the Client. With Rock here now, he felt as if he *had* to say something.

Rock began to jerk, shaking the chair, but it was anchored to the stone. He was strapped in tightly, and thankfully the straps held. He looked up, leveling his gaze on Meyer. "I get the hangman." He turned his head, looking toward Finn. "And Shuffles."

Finn couldn't tell if Rock was angry or disappointed.

Probably both.

They hadn't even had the chance to share a drink of ale like Finn had promised him.

Meyer stood across from Rock, seemingly unperturbed by the aggression within him. "You are Luca Grobbe."

Finn had never known Rock's real name. He'd always been Rock. Solid. Strong.

His friend.

"Since you're asking, it seems as if you already know," he said.

"Tell me about where you were captured."

"I was captured minding my own business. There's no crime in being out at night."

"No crime other than violating the curfew."

"The curfew," Rock scoffed. "A damn joke, if you ask me. A man can't go to a tavern and wander the streets on his way home?"

"The curfew is set late enough that a man can visit the tavern as long as he wants without violating it. It's only when he's out beyond the curfew that trouble ensues." Finn doubted Meyer wasn't about to remind Rock the reason for the curfew was the king's visit. Or visits. He didn't know how often he was in the city, only that he'd come to negotiate peace with the Alainsith. "Why don't you tell me where you were?"

"Why don't you have Shuffles tell you where I was?"

"The question wasn't for him. The question was for you."

Meyer stood across from Rock, watching him.

Rock glared at him. "I wasn't doing anything."

Meyer smiled slightly. "The Archers who found you in the shop in the Theden section would claim otherwise."

Theden was one of the sections near the palace. No wonder Rock had gotten pinched.

"They only say that to get a bonus."

"The Archers are not paid any commission for bringing in additional criminals."

"I'm a criminal now?"

"That remains to be seen. It also remains to be seen how much you will choose to share with me."

"I already told you—"

"Yes. You were minding your own business."

"That's right. Minding my own business until your Archers decided to harass me. They can't even let a man make his way home."

"Where do you live?"

"What does that have to do with the price of piss?"

Finn wanted to warn Rock not to push Meyer. It wasn't like he was in a position to argue with him. Depending upon what Meyer reported, Rock could find his sentencing going poorly for him.

"Where do you live? Which section. You can begin with that."

"Olin. Why?"

Finn shook his head. *Rock, you fool.*

He wanted to intervene and help Rock, but what could he even say?

"You live in Olin, yet you were found in Theden late at night. I find that strange."

"I got lost."

"I am sure of that." Meyer studied Rock. Finn had seen that look on his face before and recognized the way Meyer regarded him. "I'm going to ask you a few questions. Depending upon how you answer them, you will either escalate the kind of questioning or deescalate it. Do you understand me?"

"I told you all you need to know. You don't need to hold me."

Meyer turned and headed toward the table with interrogation tools.

Finn used the opportunity to slip forward. He risked upsetting Meyer, but he needed to say something to Rock. This was his friend. "Tell him what he needs to know, Rock. He's going to find out anyway."

"Don't worry about me, Shuffles."

"I... I don't want you to go through what I went through here."

He looked at Rock, trying to plead at him with his eyes.

Rock turned away. "I'm not telling your *master* shit."

Meyer approached carrying two pieces of iron over to Rock. "This is a terrible device, and I'm truly sorry it is necessary to use it, but I can tell you're not forthcoming with me. Perhaps with a little pressure, you might find it within you to answer my questions." He knelt in front of Rock, who tried to kick, but his legs were bound by the leather straps. "Now, these will fit on either side of your leg. As I twist, pressure will be applied. At first, it is tolerable. The more I squeeze, the less tolerable it becomes."

In the time that he'd been working with Meyer, Finn had seen the questioning side, he'd seen the soothing side when he'd applied the healing salve to Gabe, he'd seen the defiant side with the way that he'd stood up to the jurors and the magister. Even though his first experience with

Meyer had been when he'd slipped the noose around his neck, he still hadn't seen this part of him.

Until now.

When Meyer had the boot fashioned around Rock's leg, he began to twist. Finn could scarcely look at Rock. He cried out softly.

Meyer went to the table and grabbed the other boot, and applied it much like the last.

Finn had experienced the boots himself, so he knew how painful they could be. When the Lion had applied them to his legs, Finn didn't have the same sense of remorse from the Lion as he did from Meyer.

Still, he did it.

Because it was his job.

Meyer stood in front of Rock. "Where were you heading in the Theden section?"

"I told you," Rock started, his teeth gritted. "I was heading home. I got lost."

"You got lost. And found your way into a shop. Would you care to tell me why that shop?"

Finn shared in the curiosity. The Client must have wanted something from it. *But why would* Rock *have been the one to head there?*

Rock wasn't the skilled thief. That was Oscar. Even Wolf.

The jobs had been going south lately. Something had gone wrong with each one.

Finn. Almost Oscar—twice. Red. Now Rock.

"I got lost. I'm telling you the truth!"

Meyer leaned down and twisted the boots tighter.

Rock cried out. It was a horrible sound that carried through the inside of the chapel. Finn wanted to cover his ears, but he didn't think Meyer would appreciate it if he were to do that.

"I am ready for the truth. All I ask is for honesty. What were you after in that shop?"

Rock started to thrash, trying to jerk his way free. The leather around his arms started to creak. Finn had a moment of panic, but Meyer didn't.

He'd been through this before. Likely, he'd been through it with men who were more terrifying than Rock. There wouldn't be many who were stronger, but that didn't matter.

"We can keep at this as long as you would like. Perhaps if I leave a little pressure for a while…"

Meyer headed back to the small table of torture tools.

Finn stood in front of Rock. It was almost as horrible being on this side of the chair. "Just tell him what he needs to know," he whispered. "All he wants to know is what you were after. That's it. He doesn't care about the crew."

At least, Finn didn't think Meyer was after the crew. The Lion had been curious about it, but Meyer seemed different from that. He wanted to know what, then why, and Finn didn't know if he viewed it as his responsibility to find out who.

"I don't want you to go through this."

Rock looked at him, and the expression in his eyes shifted. "Fuck. Him. Shuffles."

This was his friend.

It had been hard on them after Meyer had claimed

Finn, but there had been a part of Finn that thought he'd be able to keep his friendships, especially with Rock.

After this, Finn doubted it would be possible.

Finn swallowed before backing away from the chair. Rock cried out again.

Finn looked over to Meyer. If he left Rock alone, Meyer was going to continue applying pressure. Rock was going to continue to suffer.

Ignoring the soft cries Rock made, Finn moved closer to him. He crouched down, getting in front of Rock's face. "All we need is to know what you were doing there. You don't gain anything holding out. All you do is make this worse."

Rock looked up at him.

"You have to have a reason. Just let me know what it is. I can help you." Finn glanced over to Meyer. "He's only going to make this worse. Trust me when I tell you that it can get worse."

"How can I trust you? Look at you. You're not even a part of the crew anymore. You've become one of them."

It stung even more when Rock said it than it had coming from Oscar.

This was his friend.

How much had he lost when Meyer had saved him from dying?

"Maybe not, but I'm still your friend." Doubt crept across Rock's face. "All we need to know is what you were doing. Why you are doing it. There has to be a reason. Something you can tell me."

Rock stared at him for a moment before his gaze turned to a hardened glare.

"I'm not betraying the crew. I'm not betraying the King."

Finn glanced over. He didn't know how much Meyer knew about the crew. It was possible he didn't know anything about the crew and, by mentioning the King, Rock revealed more than what he had already been able to uncover.

As he looked at Meyer, Finn couldn't tell.

Meyer carried a long, pointed rod over toward Rock.

"I can't do this," Finn said, shaking his head.

Meyer studied him for a moment. "Stand back there," he said.

Finn backed away.

Meyer crouched down, and he tightened the boots around Rock's legs again.

He didn't cry out any more than he already had.

For that, Finn thought he should be thankful. Still, Rock groaned, a pained sound.

"We will remain here as long as necessary to find why you went into that shop. When you provide me with a satisfactory answer, I will remove the boots." Meyer smiled sadly. "I'm afraid I won't be able to remove them until then."

Meyer leaned down and tightened them again.

Finn realized he had gotten off easy. Had Meyer been the one questioning him, he would have told him anything that he wanted to know.

"What were you after?"

"I was on my way home," Rock said.

Meyer leaned down and tightened the boots again.

This time, Rock cried out.

It was a shriek, a piercing sound that ripped through Finn's ears, into the back of his head. He covered his ears.

Meyer stood in front of Rock. "What were you after?"

Rock thrashed. He trembled, trying to work his arms and his legs free. Rock was a big man, strong, but the leather straps bound him in place, and he wasn't able to get free of the bindings.

Meyer just watched.

Finally, Rock stopped thrashing.

"There was a necklace," he said. His voice was a whisper.

"A necklace. In an antiquities shop?"

Rock looked up. He leaned back, and Meyer dropped down.

The spittle he had targeted at Meyer missed.

Meyer twisted another turn.

Rock screamed.

Meyer stood, facing Rock. "If it was only a necklace, describe it to me."

"I didn't get it," he said, his voice rising at the end. "I went for it, but your damn Archers got to me before I could grab it. Is that what you wanted to hear? Dammit, Shuffles, tell him that's all I was doing. Tell him to stop hurting me."

Finn swallowed.

Meyer tipped his head as he regarded Rock for another moment.

Then he crouched down and twisted the boots one more time.

Rock screamed.

"I told you what you wanted!"

"What else?"

"A necklace. That's all!"

Meyer shook his head. "Unfortunately, you're still holding out on me. I think that I will leave these boots on you for a little while longer."

"You can't do that!"

Meyer nodded to Finn, and they headed through the door. Rock's screams followed them, and even when they were out in the hall, Finn could still hear the muted cries coming from the large man through the door. The sound tore at his heart, and he wanted nothing more than to go in and release Rock from his torment.

The iron master looked over to Meyer, chuckling softly. "That one didn't want to talk, did he? Seems as if he would rather sing."

"You may go," Meyer said.

"Afraid I can't do that. Warden wants me to make sure that I'm here while you question."

"Is that right?" Meyer asked.

The iron master shrugged. "Not that I really want to be here. Don't care for it when the condemned sing like that."

Meyer started pacing the hall, and Finn looked back at the door to the chapel.

"How do you know he's keeping something from you?"

"Because he gave up the necklace too quickly."

"What if it was just a necklace?"

"Maybe," Meyer said.

"You don't think so."

Meyer shook his head. "As I've said before, I have decades of experience questioning men like him. He doesn't want to talk. He feels as if he will be betraying his crew. Does that remind you of someone?"

Finn flushed. "He thinks I talked."

"I imagine they all do," Meyer said.

Finn thought that his going to the gallows, having the noose around his neck, and nearly hanging would have been proof enough that he hadn't shared anything.

"You knew," Finn said.

"It's a logical step," Meyer said. "Not my intent. Far from it. But when you return to your crew, they will naturally be suspicious."

Finn looked over to Meyer. "Let me have a chance to talk with him."

"Talk?"

They had been friends ever since Finn had worked with the crew. Rock had been a part of everything he'd done. He had to have this chance. "I don't know that I can do what you did, but I can talk with him."

"For you to maintain your position, you're going to have to use these questioning techniques."

"Maybe, but not this time." Not on Rock.

Meyer glanced at the door before nodding.

Then Finn headed over to the door, resting his hand on it for a moment, and he took a deep breath before stepping inside.

Rock had fallen silent, his head lolled forward.

Finn made his way over to him.

He crouched down, and he twisted the boots, reducing some of the pressure. Meyer couldn't fault him for that.

"They're not coming for you. They can't. Not in this place."

"Go away, Shuffles."

"When I was here, no one came for me. The only time I saw anyone was during my sentencing. I'm the only one here, Rock. Let me help you."

Rock looked up briefly before his head slumped down again.

"Give him something. It has to be more than a necklace. Whatever you give him will buy you some time. Maybe you need proof the crew isn't coming for you. I know when I was here, I thought they'd somehow find a way in for me." Finn flicked his gaze to the boots. "I was questioned much like you. Boots and water."

The memory of it made him shudder.

"Water?"

"They filled a pitcher of water and poured it into my throat. It felt like I was drowning. It was a horrible thing. A terrible feeling. At that point, I wanted nothing more than for it to end." Rock's breathing continued quickening. Finn reduced more of the pressure on the boot, and Rock looked up at him. "Just give them what you were after. They don't care anything about the crew."

"I told him. It was—"

"More than a necklace. I know it was. There has to be some reason the Client wanted you to go after this necklace." And it had to be the Client. That was the one person the King worked for these days, though Finn had no idea why he continued to work only for him. "What did the King ask you to get?"

"Nothing."

"I know you didn't take a job outside the crew. I know you, Rock."

Rock held his gaze. There was a moment where Finn saw a sign of his old friend, but then it faded. "It don't matter what we were after."

"It does."

"No. It don't. The Client wants something we can't get. That's why I was there."

"What does the Client want?"

"I told you what he wanted. I'm not keeping that from you, Shuffles. Just a necklace. Silver with a strange little charm of something that looks like a dog."

That reminded Finn of something he'd seen somewhere, though he couldn't quite place it. Could it be on another job? He squeezed his eyes shut a moment.

Not a job.

Hegen.

There had been a strange silver figurine in Esmerelda's house.

"Why that?"

"I can't tell you." When Finn started to say something, Rock shook his head. "Because I don't know. All I know is we do that, and we don't take another job."

Finn frowned, his mind working. "What other job?"

Rock said nothing.

"Dammit, Rock. Just tell me!" Finn hissed.

"You're not in the crew no more."

"Not by choice, and we both know it." Rock didn't say anything. "I'll go ask the Hand. You think he'll keep it from me?"

Finn didn't know if he would or not. It *was* Oscar, and they were friends, or so Finn thought. So was Rock.

But Finn wasn't in the crew.

"A job in the palace," Rock whispered. "None of us want to do it, so we took an alternative. That's what the King told us. Do this, then we're off the hook."

"Why would you be *on* the hook?"

Rock shook his head. "Don't ask me questions I can't answer."

"So, you were in that shop to avoid another job?"

"We can't very well break into the palace. You know what happened to the last bastard who tried that."

Finn glanced to the door.

What had the King gotten the crew into?

He had to protect them. Somehow. Whether they knew it or not, they *were* his crew.

How much of this did he need to share with Meyer?

"What happens if you don't finish that job?"

"I don't know. The King don't know. I get the sense the Client isn't the kind of man you disappoint. You heard what happened to Pegg's crew."

"I did."

"That was the Client. The King has made it clear that we have to finish this. No choice but to do so."

Finn started to shake his head. That wasn't the way the crew took jobs.

"And if we don't do this job, and if we don't succeed, that's what's going to happen to us." Rock grunted. "Do what you need to. Tighten these damn boots as much as you need to. I've said all I can."

Finn stared at Rock. He believed him.

Which meant that he believed him about the danger the crew was in.

They were his crew.

He wanted to protect them the same as he had when he'd been sitting in Rock's position.

Much like then, he didn't know how.

The door opened, and Meyer came in.

Finn turned to him. "He told me all we need to know." Meyer looked at him. "You can stop hurting him now. He's told enough."

Rock lifted his head, holding Finn's gaze, glaring at him, but a question lingered in it.

CHAPTER TWENTY

Finn lingered outside of the Wenderwolf, dressed in the grays from the day of his hanging, preferring to be a little less noticeable than he would be in the finer clothes Meyer had purchased on his behalf. At least the Sinner's Cloth blended into the shadows along the street a little better. Not perfectly, and they made him wish for his darks, but better than what he'd worn when he'd been there before.

In the growing darkness, the Wenderwolf glowed with a soft light. Welcoming, in a way. Muted music came from inside, a jaunty sort of sound. A few people had entered, but none that he wanted. The buildings neighboring the tavern were all quiet for the night. A butcher a few doors down had a sign featuring a pig with a red streak across it. A little too on the nose for Finn. The smokehouse next to the butcher had a soft trail of smoke drifting from the chimney that carried the scent of meats. Up close, it was almost overwhelming, filling the street with the aroma.

He'd been waiting for the better part of an hour. Finn started to question whether he should even remain there, or whether he should move along, but he couldn't get past thinking about Rock, even though there was much he still had to study. The books Meyer gave him continued to pile up. There was only so much time in the day to study what Meyer asked of him. Though he'd now worked through three of the books, all of them on anatomy or various healing compounds, he still had much more studying to go. None of them had gone into torture techniques, anything that he thought he should be learning about were he to be useful as Meyer's assistant.

After seeing Meyer torment Rock, Finn wasn't sure he could do that anyway.

There had been no sign of the King. Wolf. Oscar. Even of Scruff. None of them had been by the Wenderwolf in the time that he'd been watching. What were they doing, then?

Finn wanted to warn Oscar away from taking the job that would endanger him to the Client. *Will he listen?*

When it came to Oscar, Finn didn't know. He could be stubborn.

Finn didn't know how long he could stand there and wait.

He needed rest. More than that, he wanted to know what more Meyer had uncovered from Rock, if anything. Finn hadn't heard anything more from him, though Rock probably wouldn't share anything more with him.

It was time to head back.

Voices drifted toward him.

Wolf.

Finn retreated to rest against the nearby building. A broker. There were many of them in Olin. The title of broker sounded fancier than it was—nothing more than a place to trade personal items for money. Too many thought they could borrow from the broker, but the fees were so exorbitant that most just ended up deeper in debt than they were before. Brokers were buildings Finn never minded breaking into, if only to steal coin from the owners.

"Still haven't been able to get to him." Wolf's voice drifted down the street, soft enough Finn could tell he tried to keep it from carrying, though it was loud enough that he wasn't able to do so.

"See what the Hand can do. He's got the connection. And find the last one. Then we can get the rest of this over with."

"I've got a lead. It shouldn't be long now."

Wolf and another—the King—came into view. Neither wore their darks, though it was late enough that Finn would have been surprised if they were simply out for the night. *What were they doing dressed the way they were?* Wolf had a dark, dappled cloak that didn't necessarily hide in the shadows, and the King looked dressed for a party. The hat on his head was tilted askew, and his boots had a gleam to them that reflected the moonlight. Neither of which would blend in the way they needed were they wanting to sneak.

"Not sure this is something the Hand will want a part of. Might have to pinch him a little bit more. He's got a soft spot, you know. Especially with how he feels…" Wolf paused, looking around the street.

He nodded toward Finn.

They'd spotted him.

Should have found my darks.

Meyer would have to have them. Knowing that Finn still came to Olin and still came to visit with the crew, he wondered if Meyer would even have allowed him to have them again.

Finn stepped toward them. It was better they thought he'd been waiting for them rather than trying to spy on them.

"Shuffles?" the King asked.

Finn forced a smile. "I've been waiting for you. Took you long enough to make your way to the tavern."

The King and Wolf shared a look. Finn wished he recognized what passed between them.

"Annie would have welcomed you had you wanted a drink. Gods, I'm sure she's got some girls she could have sent to you." The King smiled, though there was an edge of darkness in the back of his eyes.

Finn shook his head. "That's not why I've come."

He took a step closer. Wolf tensed.

What was he concerned about? Could it be me?

"What is it, Shuffles?"

They'd know something happened to Rock. Finn counted on that.

"I needed to tell you about Rock."

The King glanced briefly to Wolf, tipping his head to the side.

That was an expression Finn recognized. It was almost as if the King told Wolf, *You see?*

"What about Rock?"

"He's in Declan."

"Declan?" Wolf asked. The deep frown suggested that though he might have known that Rock had been taken, he hadn't known where he'd been imprisoned. "What would he be doing in Declan?"

"Same as me, I suppose," Finn said. "Though Rock has more priors than I did."

The King glanced around him before flicking his gaze to the Wenderwolf. "Why don't we have a seat inside and talk about this?"

"You sure about that?" Wolf asked.

The King nodded to Finn. "Shuffles probably needs a drink. I know I do. And we can talk about what happened to Rock and what we intend to do to get him out."

The King led them toward the tavern. Wolf watched Finn, who kept his gaze locked straight ahead of him. He wasn't entirely sure what he was doing there, other than wanting to warn the King of the heat coming his way. He didn't want any of them to get into more trouble than they could handle.

Inside, Finn realized the musician was a singer with a mandolin. She picked the instrument with a fast pace, strumming every so often, her voice rising above the rest of the din of the tavern.

Annie noticed them come in right away and headed in their direction.

The King guided him to a seat at the usual table, and he and Wolf sat across from Finn. It felt like they were prepared to question him. In that way, it made him think of his sentencing.

When Annie brought mugs of ale over, she took a seat next to Finn.

"Not tonight, Annie," the King said.

She looked across the table. "You got problems, Leon?"

"I don't know yet."

She glanced over to Finn and patted him on the arm. "Gods be with you."

When she got up, she disappeared to the back of the tavern, though Finn had the sense that she watched them. Annie always seemed to watch.

The King didn't touch his ale. Neither did Wolf.

They were on edge, but given the kind of job he knew they were involved in, he understood *why* they'd be on edge. They worried about what happened to Pegg's crew happening to them. They'd worry about failing.

"What do you know, Shuffles?"

"Just what I told you. Rock is in Declan. Saw him myself last night."

"And you waited until now to tell us?" Wolf asked.

The King turned to him. "Shuffles came as soon as he could, I'm sure." He glanced to Finn. "Isn't that right, Shuffles?"

Finn nodded. "I wouldn't have been able to come last evening after we questioned him."

"*You* questioned him?" Wolf asked.

"I was there when Meyer questioned him." He licked his lips, swallowing. "I tried to help him. Damn, but Rock is my friend." He swallowed again, looking from Wolf to the King. "He didn't say anything about the crew, if that's what you're concerned about."

"It's not the crew that I'm worried about," Wolf said.

The King shot him a look.

Wolf shook his head. "We need to get this resolved," he said. "If Rock said something—"

"He didn't say anything," the King said.

"That's what Shuffles was telling us, but how sure are you that we can trust him?"

The King turned and looked at Finn. He regarded him for a long moment, and the darkness that he'd seen in his eyes lingered for that moment before fading. "We can trust Shuffles," he said.

"And if we can't?"

"If we can't, then the gods had better favor him," the King said.

The coldness in his voice surprised Finn.

"I wouldn't have come if you couldn't trust me," Finn said. "I don't want anything to happen to the crew."

"You're here because of the crew?" Wolf asked.

"I'm here to warn you. Whatever job you're doing is too dangerous. You need to back off."

The King leaned back, lifting his ale, and he took a long sip of it. "I don't think you understand, Shuffles. I know you didn't have much time in the crew, but you should have known that once we've taken on a job, we need to complete the job. The consequences can be severe."

Finn understood what the King alluded to, only he also knew the King was mostly concerned about the financial repercussions, not the physical, and not about what could happen to them.

"Rock was concerned about not finishing the job," Finn said.

Would the King tell Finn anything about the job at the palace?

"Rock is always more concerned than he needs to be." The King shrugged. "If he were less concerned, he might not have gotten himself pinched."

"That's not why he got pinched," Finn said.

"No? And why did he get himself pinched?" The King leaned forward.

Finn struggled with the answer. If he shared too much now, he would potentially reveal details that he wasn't supposed to.

He also didn't know if there were details that he wasn't supposed to reveal.

Nothing that had happened to Rock had been secretive. He had been picked up in the Theden section, breaking into an antiquities shop. That much would be common knowledge, at least among the Archers, and considering how the King had contact within the Archers, he doubted that there was anything that the King didn't know when it came to Rock's role.

"You know why he got pinched as well as I do," Finn

said. "He was in that antiquities shop and got himself the wrong kind of attention. The Archers snagged him."

The King sneered at Wolf. "The damn Archers."

"Probably tipped off. Too much of that lately," Wolf said, his eyes narrowing.

"They weren't even supposed to have been there. So much for paying them," the King said.

Wolf glanced at Finn. "Are you sure you want to be having these conversations?"

The King glanced at Finn. "Shuffles isn't going to say anything."

"Are you sure?"

The King leaned forward. "Can we trust you, Shuffles?"

It was a loaded question and the kind of question that Finn wished he could answer honestly. The problem was that he didn't know the honest answer. *Could* they trust him?

He'd come to the King to share what he could about Rock, wanting to warn him, if nothing else. At the same time, Finn couldn't deny that he had a growing loyalty to Meyer.

How could I not when Meyer had brought his mother in?

Meyer had saved Finn from the noose.

But it was more than about his family.

This was for his crew.

"You can trust me," he said.

The King nodded. "That's what I thought, because we're going to need your help. Seeing as how Rock got himself pinched, we're going to need a lookout. Can't hit the store again now that they'd have it under surveillance. Means we've got no choice."

"Are you—" Wolf started.

The King glanced over to Wolf, shaking his head. "I'm sure. If we do this, we're going to need to do this well, and we won't have much time to reassemble a new crew. With Rock out of the picture, we're down two men until we can count on Scruff. I don't like going into anything like this shorthanded, and certainly not something this critical. The others can pull Archers away, but they aren't ready for this kind of job."

"What's happening with Scruff?" Finn asked.

The King shook his head. "He might not be working out."

Finn waited for more of an explanation, but that was all he left him with.

"I can't do anything that would jeopardize my place," he said.

"You enjoy your time with the hangman that much?" the King asked.

Finn shook his head quickly. "I don't enjoy it." At least, there were significant portions of the job that he didn't enjoy. "You wanted to make sure I could be useful to the crew. I'm not going to be of much use if I get pinched doing a job this soon. Think about it, King. If I stay working with the hangman, I'm far more valuable to the crew."

The King regarded Finn for a long moment, his smile starting to spread into something almost menacing. "See?"

he said to Wolf. "Shuffles wants to make sure he helps the crew. And you were worried about his loyalty."

Wolf said nothing.

Finn took a cautious drink of his ale. He had to be careful here.

The King wanted to pull a job that would endanger the crew.

Finn needed to keep him from doing it.

"I still don't think this job is the right one for the crew," Finn said. "If what Rock told me was true, then it's the kind of job that will get everyone killed. Think about what happened to Pegg."

"Pegg didn't have the same advantage that we have," the King said.

"What advantage is that?" Finn asked.

He already thought he knew, just like he knew what the job entailed.

"We have someone who's already been there."

"I've been there, but I wasn't paying attention like I would have were I scoping it out."

"I'm sure you'll manage," the King said. "You wouldn't want anything to happen to the crew because you didn't give us the right information, would you?"

"You know I don't want anything to happen to the crew."

"Good," the King said, as if it were settled. He leaned back in the chair, looking over to Wolf. "Wolf will ask you a few questions, and by the time he's done, I think we ought to have a solid idea about what we need to do."

"Why this job? It's dangerous." Finn needed the King to

reveal something about the Client. Maybe Finn could use that to stop this from happening.

"We've taken other dangerous jobs before," the King said.

"Not like this," Finn said. The attack on the viscount's house had been dangerous, but there were only hired guards stationed there, not an entire squadron of Archers. Palace Archers, at that.

"You let me worry about the reasons," the King said. "You just focus on remembering everything you can about the layout of the palace. It's going to be up to you to make sure we get through there safely, Shuffles. For what this will pay, I promise you it'll be worth it."

Finn wandered back toward Meyer's home, making his way slowly. It was late enough, and he wasn't dressed the same as he had been over the last week or more, wearing the gray Sinner's Cloth. They felt fitting for some reason tonight.

There was a lump in his throat after sharing everything that he remembered of the palace layout with Wolf. He had asked about specific doors leading off of the main hall. Finn had only a passing memory of it, and though he didn't know if he should keep the details to himself, he realized that there would have to be others who had spent time in the palace as well. It wasn't as if Finn were the only person to have gone there.

Wolf had taken everything Finn had said, making

notes on a piece of paper and asking ever more probing questions. When Finn had failed to answer them adequately, he got a look of irritation from the King, and Finn had done his best to search his memory to come up with other answers as to what else he could remember.

The trouble was that he had a good memory when it came to things like that. It was why he had been so successful when trying to navigate the alleys. Finn had only to go through them a single time, and he could recall the layout fairly easily, creating it in his mind.

It had been the same way with the palace.

At one point, while making his way toward Meyer's home, Finn thought he heard footsteps coming along the street.

It was late enough that any footsteps would have a nefarious purpose behind them.

He quickened his gait, hurrying through the streets, making his way as quickly as he could, not wanting to get caught out in the night by one of the Archers.

It would force Finn to answer questions.

He didn't have answers to those questions, and even if he did, he wasn't sure that he wanted to provide them. He would have to explain why he was wearing the grays of his sentencing rather than the clothing that Meyer had bought for him.

He would have to explain why he was out in this section of the city at this time of night. Neither of those were answers he wanted to give.

Finn glanced behind him.

He didn't see any sign of Archers.

Archers would make their presence known. At least, the Archers Finn had experienced in the city. Still, he couldn't shake the feeling someone trailed after him.

He ducked into an alley, slipping through the narrow passageway, stepping as quickly as he could. The stench of the alley filled his nostrils, and Finn tried to ignore it, but when the alley opened up into another street, he hurried along it, taking a different path back to Meyer's home.

He was in the Brinder section. His home section.

At least he knew the streets like the back of his hands.

Finn raced along the street, and he still had the sensation that someone followed him. He didn't know if it was imagined.

At one point, he looked toward his home street, debating whether he should revisit his home. Maybe Lena had gone there and found it empty. She wouldn't have known where to find Finn, but Finn had made a point of leaving a note behind, a way for Lena to follow. With that note, she would have been able to reach Master Meyer's home. She would've found their mother safe.

Which meant that Lena still hadn't returned.

Maybe she was off on whatever the hegen had asked of her, but Finn couldn't shake what Helda had told him.

Finn turned away.

He paused at another alley, looking behind him.

There was still the sense of someone following him, though he didn't hear it any longer. There was no sign of Archers. No sign of anything. Only the instinct Finn had.

He hurried along the alley. He could take this, and he

could weave through the alley to make his way back toward Master Meyer's home.

Something moved along the alley.

Finn hesitated.

It was dark enough that he had a hard time seeing what was there. He turned, heading back the way he had come. When he reached the street, Finn hurried along it. It felt as if he were forced farther and farther away from Meyer's home.

Eventually, he was going to have to take a gamble.

He thought about what he knew of the alleys.

There was one possibility that he could take.

A narrow alley in this section weaved in a twisting manner, barely more than wide enough for him to pass. It would be dangerous if someone actually were following him.

The feeling that someone chased him lingered.

That decided it for him.

Finn turned down the alley. He raced along it, following the weaving path, and gradually the sensation of someone following him began to fade. When he reached a side street, he paused for a moment before heading across it and toward another intersecting alley. Finn went alley to alley, heading toward Meyer's home. When he started to hear the sound of the river rushing by, he knew he was getting close.

Then he reached the street.

Stepping out into it, movement from a pair of figures caught his attention.

Archers.

They turned toward him.

Finn didn't really want to deal with Archers. He jogged toward Meyer's home, reaching the gate. When he did, he cast a glance behind him, toward the Archers. He found them marching in his direction. A shadowed form moved behind the Archers.

He hadn't imagined the pursuit, then.

Finn stared at it for a moment before darting into the closed garden, closing it behind him, and hurrying toward the door. Once inside, he leaned on the door for a moment.

Light glowed from the end of the hall as it often did. The sound of Meyer's voice caught his attention. Finn headed toward him. It would be better to admit to Meyer where he'd been and what he'd been doing, especially as the Archers would likely follow him to the door.

When he reached Meyer's office door, he listened.

A soft voice drifted out. Female. Hushed, almost concerned.

Meyer's steady, comforting murmuring came from the other side. Finn leaned forward and could see his back. He leaned toward whoever had come for his help, likely offering a healing treatment.

A knock came at the door behind him.

The Archers.

Finn cleared his throat.

Meyer turned toward him. His eyes took in the grays Finn wore, then flicked past him.

"I was just—"

"Excuse me," Meyer said to the person sitting in the

chair opposite his desk. He headed toward Finn, grabbing his arm. "Come with me."

Finn turned with him reluctantly.

At the door, Meyer greeted the Archers with a nod. "How may I help you this evening?"

"Master Meyer," the first of the Archers said, his voice gruff. "I hate to disturb you at this time of night, but we followed a ruffian through your garden."

Meyer grunted and shook his head. "Not a ruffian. My apprentice. He was out later than he should have been." Meyer pulled Finn forward and into the view of the Archers. "I apologize for the confusion. I will make certain he returns before curfew unless on official business."

The Archer regarded Finn for a moment before nodding. "Good evening, then, Master Meyer."

The Archers departed, and Meyer closed the door, resting his hand on it for a moment.

"You should not have been gone."

"I didn't realize you had any assignments for me this evening."

He frowned. "No assignments, but…" He sighed. "You returned to your crew."

"I did." There was no use denying it.

"To warn them?"

"I wanted them to stop whatever they had planned. I was worried they'd end up killed."

"You were worried they'd end up caught." Meyer looked at him. "I fear your connection to your old crew is going to lead you into danger. And, by extension, lead *me* into danger." He shook his head slightly. "There's nothing that can be done about it now." He motioned for Finn to follow to the end of the hall. "Go on."

Finn hesitated. Did Meyer want him to study healing together?

Meyer nodded as Finn reached the door.

"What do you need me to do?" Finn whispered.

"I need you to go in," Meyer said.

"Am I supposed to perform the healing?"

Meyer grunted. "Do you think yourself capable of it?"

Finn frowned. "No."

"Neither do I," he said. "That is not to say that you won't develop that ability in time."

"Thanks," Finn said.

"Don't find offense when none was implied," he said. "Go on. You are needed."

Finn looked over at Meyer, confusion on his face.

He turned his attention back to the room, heading inside.

As he neared, the woman turned toward him.

Finn's breath caught.

"Lena?"

They sat in the small kitchen. Lena on one side of the table and Finn on the other. She sipped the mug of tea Meyer had made for her before stepping out of the kitchen, leaving the two of them to catch up.

"Where have you been?" he asked.

She barely looked up at him. Her eyes looked haunted

and dark. The gray dress she had on looked a little dirtier than what Lena normally would wear.

"Lena?"

"You don't want to know."

He breathed in the steam coming off the tea Meyer had made. "What did the hegen have you do?"

They'd been calling in favors. Dangerous ones, from what Finn had learned.

"I didn't even want to go to them. She was getting sicker."

"I know."

She stared at her mug. "I thought about letting her go."

She looked up at Finn, her eyes red and welling with tears.

Finn held her gaze. Helda had said Lena had gone to some dark place. That wasn't what he would've expected from his sister.

"It was going to happen anyway. I knew it. We've been watching her get weaker over time. I… I just couldn't do it anymore." She looked down again. "Then I thought of what Father would say if he knew how I was thinking."

"That's why you went to them."

She nodded. "I had to do something. I couldn't do it like that anymore, and I didn't know what else I could do. I wanted to tell you, but I didn't think you'd understand."

Finn hadn't been there every day like Lena had been. He couldn't know how hard it had been for her. "What did they ask of you?"

She looked down again. "I didn't know what to expect. I'd paid for the medicine, but then they'd asked me to gather some supplies." She shook her head. "I had to visit apothecaries throughout the city and then organize the supplies when I brought them to the hegen."

"That's it?"

That wasn't anything like he would have expected from the hegen.

"That's it. They were... kind to me. Then I was sent away."

He breathed out a sigh. Lena had suffered more than he had known. Her darkness, as Helda had said.

Now she was here. Safe.

"What happened to you?" Lena asked. "He said Mother is here."

Finn nodded and got to his feet, motioning for her to follow.

Finn showed Lena to the room where their mother rested. She'd not come around since Meyer had brought their mother to stay, but her color had improved, and her breathing seemed more regular. Boney hands gripped the tan blanket covering her. Between both Meyer and Finn, they'd made certain she ate.

Lena stood in the doorway, and tears streamed down her face again.

"What is it?" Finn asked.

She swallowed, looking over to him as she wiped the tears away. "I just never imagined she'd get help like this. When we were struggling, trying to find *any* help, I just never could have imagined."

"I wish I would've helped sooner," Finn said.

"But you helped now." She looked over to him and frowned. "What happened? Why are you here?"

He had debated how much to tell her. When he'd asked Oscar to protect his family, he'd wanted to keep as much as he could from Lena and his mother. Now that Lena was here, Finn didn't think he could.

"It's complicated."

She waited, and he knew that he owed her the truth.

He motioned for her to follow him back out to the kitchen. From there, they took a seat at the table, and Finn took a long sip of the tea before looking up at his sister. "I was pinched."

As he started sharing with her what happened, the words spilled out. He half expected that Lena would react negatively, perhaps chastise him for getting caught or lecture him about what he'd done, or even refuse to accept Finn's fate, but she watched him without interrupting.

When he was done, she held his gaze. "You're staying here now?"

Finn nodded. "I'm working with Master Meyer."

"What about—"

She didn't get the chance to finish.

"I think it's time for you to get some rest," Meyer said, poking his head through the kitchen door.

Lena glanced to Finn before looking over to Meyer. "I'm not sure it's safe to return home."

"You will stay here."

Lena's eyes widened slightly. "Here?"

"I promised Finn I would make sure that your mother

was cared for. Now that you have returned, I offer you the same protection."

"What do I have to do for it?" Lena asked, her voice soft.

"Pick up after yourself. Other than that, you can continue your work at Jorven's butcher, or you may find alternative employment."

"What kind of employment?"

Meyer regarded her for a moment. "Whatever you choose."

Lena turned to Finn, looking to him for confirmation, and he nodded.

She squeezed her hands together in her lap before forcing a smile. "I can stay with Mother."

"The room is too small." Meyer motioned for her to follow, and he guided Lena to a room on the upper level.

Finn knew Meyer's room was upstairs but had never ventured up there himself.

The room he offered to Lena was enormous, at least compared to the one Finn occupied. A massive bed took up most of the room. A stuffed bear rested on the bed, and Meyer hurried across the floor and grabbed the bear before turning to Lena. "You may stay here."

Lena's eyes widened even more. "Whose room am I taking?"

Meyer hesitated before shaking his head. "No one's."

Lena approached the bed, sinking down on it. She smiled at Finn.

Meyer guided Finn out of the room, closing the door behind her.

"Thank you," Finn said.

"I told you that we would find her," he said.

He left unsaid that Finn still owed the hegen some debt. Eventually, he would have to pay it.

"Get some rest. Tomorrow will be another long day. We don't have much time."

"Why not?"

"You will be asked to prove your worthiness soon."

"How soon?"

Meyer shook his head. "Soon."

"Why so quickly? I thought we had more time than this."

"I did, as well. Unfortunately, it seems as if matters have taken a turn. When the Executioner Court arrives, you will begin your testing."

Finn headed down the stairs, his mind spinning. How was he supposed to handle what Meyer asked of him? He didn't feel as if he knew anything about what was involved in serving as Meyer's apprentice.

When he reached the small room at the front of the house, he stepped inside. The lantern remained glowing softly with the light that he'd left on. The stack of books remained near the edge of the desk.

Finn glanced at it for a moment.

Something in the center of the desk caught his attention.

A card.

He lifted it and looked at it.

A *hegen* card.

It was blank, but there was no doubt in Finn's mind that it was a hegen card.

It was a message, a reminder that he owed a debt.

What would they ask of me?

They'd been calling in favors lately. The timing couldn't be a coincidence.

What choice would he be forced to make?

CHAPTER TWENTY-ONE

The morning sunlight crept over the rooftops in the central sections of the city and reflected off the river in sweeping streaks of orange and red. It would be lovely, were it not for Finn's mood.

He hadn't slept much the night before. How could he when all he thought about was the card the hegen had left for him? With his sister's return, he now owed them a debt he knew they would ensure he paid.

Finn hadn't known whether to share with Meyer that a card had been left for him. *What would the executioner do about it, anyway? What* could *he do about it?* He had been the one to bring Finn to the hegen in the first place, so he might not even be concerned.

That didn't mean Finn wasn't concerned.

Meyer looked over at him. "You've been quiet."

Finn shrugged. "Just tired, I guess."

"You shouldn't have been out visiting your crew, then."

"It wasn't the crew…" It was better to take the criticism than argue about what it had or had not been. The reason Finn was as tired as he was had nothing to do with the crew and everything to do with the return of his sister.

That wasn't entirely true.

He was worried about Rock. He wanted to go to Declan to check on him but couldn't.

Even if he did, Finn doubted Rock wanted to see him. The look in his eyes when Finn had been there had been painful to see. That had been his friend.

Now they were something else.

Finn had gotten up early and practiced with Justice. Since showing him the technique, Meyer had made certain there were always enough pumpkins in the yard for him to practice with. Finn had gotten through five at one time but never more than that. Something always went awry. If the testing involved getting through ten in a row, he worried that he wouldn't have a steady enough hand for it.

That wasn't the only concern he had, though. There were other aspects of the responsibility that he had that made it difficult for him to know if he would master everything needed before his testing—whenever it would be. He still hadn't learned anything about the gallows or any of the more arcane techniques Meyer had shared with him that were involved in the kind of punishments the city could hand down. Not only had he not experienced any of them, Meyer hadn't required Finn to read about them.

At least he thought he would be better prepared when it came to knowing about torture. He'd gone through one torture himself and had been a part of the one with Rock, not counting how he'd seen Gabe after his torture. That had to matter.

"It's good to see you dressed better again," Meyer said.

Finn looked down at his clothing. "The grays aren't all that bad."

"They're fine for your practicing. That would be it."

Finn had worn them while working with the pumpkin. It was either that or end up with pumpkin guts all over his finer shirts.

"Why do you dress so well during executions?" Finn asked as they headed over the bridge. Meyer hadn't told him where they were headed this morning, and Finn had learned that when Meyer remained silent about such things, it was better not to ask.

"Because there's an expectation of decorum during the proceeding. The people of the city demand we appear a certain way."

"Much like they demand the condemned wear the gray?"

"That's tradition. A man—or woman—is given fresh clothing before they're brought to their death. It's a symbol of rebirth. A way of asking the gods to welcome you anew."

Finn grunted. "What happens to the men who refuse to welcome the gods?"

"They are greeted no differently than anyone else. It's up to the gods to decide how to address them."

Finn smiled at the thought of the gods choosing to accept murderers to them. He thought of Mistress Vils and the brutal way her husband had killed her. *Would the gods accept a man like that back, even if he repented—assuming they ever found him in the city?* The priests certainly believed they would. When Finn had been the condemned, the priest marching him to his doom had believed.

In that moment, Finn had reverted to his childhood. He had prayed, speaking the words of Heleth along with the priest, though he had spoken the modified version he'd learned from his mother.

"What if the gods choose to send them back?"

Meyer glanced over. "The gods will make their choices. It's up to men to decide what to make of it."

They continued through the streets of the merchant section. Not a prison, then. Finn had been to several prisons with Meyer and didn't know of any in this section.

Could he be leading me to some sort of testing? Meyer had mentioned the Executioner Court would be coming soon. *Had he meant* this *soon?*

Finn wasn't ready.

Meyer would have to have known that. Finn would have expected Meyer to prepare him better than he had, only so far, Meyer had barely mentioned it, nothing more than in passing.

"We have previously talked about the techniques used in a hanging. There are different purposes for each one, though the end result is the same. Depending upon the severity of the crime, the punishment is meant to either lead to the suffering of the condemned or a demonstration for those who gather. Often, the goal is both. It has long been my preference to make the death quick. With enough force, the condemned's neck snaps, killing them instantly. Not enough force and they slowly suffocate. While the jurors and the magister occasionally want the condemned to suffer, most of the time, I am given the freedom to exact the punishment as I see fit."

"The type of knot you use."

"Mostly."

"Mostly?" Finn asked.

They turned a corner. Finn was glad there weren't others out. He could only imagine what they might think hearing the executioner casually describing ways the condemned were hanged.

"Now, too much force is also unwelcome. The head can come free, which is not only a bloody mess but distressing for those observing. Finding the balance is key, which is why I have learned to calculate the height needed based on the weight of the condemned. Unfortunately, it's not an exact science, but it's one you will learn to employ with experience."

Finn only half-listened, the way he often did when Meyer gave information like this. It was one thing to know about sentencing, but hearing Meyer describe it was something entirely different.

"Now, the other key when hanging the condemned is

to ensure the proper placement of the noose. We have talked about the proper technique in tying the noose. You have been practicing?"

Meyer glanced over to Finn, who nodded.

He probably hadn't spent as much time as Meyer wanted him to. He thought that creating the proper noose and applying it to the condemned's neck would be easier than mastering the sword. That was what Finn had spent his time on.

"Very well. Different knots can take additional forms. You will begin to understand the implications of making each knot the longer that you work with them. I have tried to share with you the key to making the basic knots, but the more that you learn about some of the more complicated knots, the greater your skill will become."

Finn still didn't know where they were heading. He looked everywhere around him, trying to get a sense of where Meyer might be leading him, but couldn't tell.

It wasn't until they turned another corner that he began to understand.

The Theden section.

This was all about trying to understand what Rock had been up to.

That didn't surprise Finn. Meyer liked to know more about the reason behind the crimes.

They stopped at a nondescript shop. A sign hanging out front didn't indicate to Finn what the shop sold, but the yellow-and-black rope barricading it told him everything that he needed to know. This was where Rock had broken into.

"Do you think he took anything more than what he admitted to?" Finn asked.

Meyer frowned, studying the building before turning his attention to the street. "I think he wants us to know that all he took was a necklace."

"Why?"

"The better question would be why this shop?" Meyer continued to frown, and he stared along the street. "This is an unusual place for a break-in."

"If it is an antiquities shop, there would have to be valuable items within it."

"Valuable to who?"

Finn frowned. He was right.

Anything in the shop like this would be difficult for Rock to sell. It would be difficult for anyone to sell.

Other than to an antiquities dealer.

Rock had made it sound like he had broken in there to find a necklace and a bracelet, but Finn wondered if there were more to the case. Anything inside a store like this would have to have value to Rock but also value to the Client.

It reminded Finn of the strange item he and Oscar had taken when Pegg had been executed. That strange bowl had not had any obvious value. Considering where it was, Finn could easily imagine it being sold, not needing to be stolen.

The same thing could be said about this.

"Why wouldn't he have just come in and bought it?" Finn asked.

"What was that?"

Finn shook his head. "The necklace. If this is an antiq-uities shop, then why wouldn't the Client have come in here and bought it himself?" he said it mostly to himself, but Meyer watched him.

"What makes you think this is an antiquities shop?" Meyer asked.

"Isn't it?"

Meyer nodded to the sign. "No."

"What is it, then?"

"Something different."

Meyer stepped over the rope without answering any more of the question and tested the handle on the door, opening it.

Finn lingered before following him.

Once inside the entrance, he realized what Meyer had been getting at.

This wasn't a shop.

This was a home.

An eclectic one, and stuffed with more decorations than Finn could imagine owning, but a home nonetheless.

Rock had misled him.

Or had he?

Meyer swept around the inside of the home, shifting things around, his gaze darting everywhere. Finn had heard about the antiquities shop break-in from Meyer, not from Rock.

It had been a test.

He chuckled.

Meyer glanced over to him. "What is it?"

"I just realized what you did by sending me in to question Rock. You knew that I knew him."

"Your known associates were no secret, Finn," he said.

"You wanted me to find out whether he was telling the truth."

"I figured he might share something with you that he wouldn't share with me. I didn't realize that he would be so obstinate about it."

"We're not as close since… Well, not since *you*."

Meyer frowned. "Yet he shared with you details that he would not share with me."

"He didn't share with me anything about the fact that he'd broken into a home."

"No. It makes you wonder."

"About what?"

"About what else he hadn't shared with you."

Meyer regarded Finn a moment, making Finn wonder what else Meyer knew, before he continued to look around the inside of the room, then headed to a back room, where he disappeared.

Finn turned, not even sure where to start.

If this was another aspect of Meyer's job, it was one Finn didn't know if he could participate in. He certainly wasn't an investigator the way Meyer seemed to be. He wasn't even sure the right questions to ask.

He stepped into the doorway leading to the back room. It was a kitchen, though much larger than the kitchen in his childhood home or even the one in Meyer's home. And Meyer had a magnificent home.

"What are you looking for?"

"I'm looking for anything that seems out of place," Meyer said.

"How do you know?"

"You learn to watch for what is where it should be and what is where it should not be."

Within the kitchen, Finn thought that it would be easy enough to see what was where it should be, but everywhere else in the home was difficult. There was just so much clutter in the outer room that Finn would have a hard time determining whether or not anything was where it belonged.

"You could ask to investigate with the homeowner," Finn said.

"I could," Meyer said. "Only, there are times when they are less than reliable."

"Why? Wouldn't they want to have what was taken returned to them?"

"If it is something they were permitted to have."

Meyer stepped past him, back into the main part of the home, and began to sweep his gaze around again. Every so often, he paused, resting his hand on a shelf, or a sculpture, or even crouching down at one time and running his hand along the carpet. His mouth pressed into a thin line as he looked.

"Can I help with anything?"

"I'm sure that you could," Meyer said. "See what feels wrong."

Finn started to chuckle. "That's it?"

"It's little more than that. You must search for what

feels off to you. When you uncover it, then you can begin to question why." He glanced up from where he crouched on the ground, studying a strange wooden sculpture of a man with a long nose painted blue. The sculpture had a small metal staff in one hand and pointed it at the ground. Meyer stared at it for a long time. "It's not so different than what you do when talking to someone and you're feeling whether they are telling you the truth or not."

Finn started to look. He didn't see anything that drew his attention the same way that Meyer did. There was no reason for him to get down on his hands and knees, and as he looked around, he didn't find anything unusual.

Meyer continued crawling around, getting to his feet, studying shelves, a painting on one wall of an older woman sitting in front of a fire, and even what looked to be a jar of feathers. After a while, Meyer headed out of the room and made his way to the back, where he disappeared again.

Finn followed him and realized that the organization was far better in every other part of the house than it was in the entryway. Strange that would be the most chaotic place.

Finn headed back out, and he looked around that area on his own.

He didn't see anything unusual—at least, nothing more unusual than what he already saw there. He wondered how Rock would have even been able to find what he needed. With as much of a mess as was there, Rock would have had to have searched a while.

"He came for the necklace but never got it." There had

been bowls taken on other jobs. Could there have been one here? Rock would have said something. No bowl was worth torture. "But he was caught here?"

"He was."

"So, he was guilty of breaking in but didn't steal what they were after." And the King hadn't mentioned anything, though Finn didn't know if he could trust what the King told him. "And if they did take it, then the others got away."

"Is it so different than what you were accused of doing?" Meyer asked.

"I wasn't accused of doing anything. I was found."

Meyer smiled at him. In the dim light of the home, little more than a faint sunlight drifting through the open door providing the light by which to see, it was difficult to see the expression on his face. "You were found in the viscount's home. Yet by all reports, you had not taken anything."

"I *didn't* take anything."

"What about the one you helped escape?"

Finn stiffened. "I didn't—"

"I investigated the viscount's home myself. You know what I found?"

"No," Finn said.

"I found the room where you were apprehended. I found an open window. And I found a damaged shrub outside of said window, blood staining the branches. Who did you help escape?"

"Does it matter?"

"Your allegiances matter."

"I haven't betrayed you. I haven't done anything that would make you regret exerting your right for me."

Only, Finn had begun to. If he did what the King asked of him, and if he participated in their job, and whatever form that would take, he would most definitely have betrayed Meyer. It would bring him into the crew. There would be no way that the King could exclude him from the crew if he did that, but it would also put him at odds with Meyer.

Meyer had been the one to protect him. To save him.

He needed to tell him about the Client.

"You have not," Meyer said.

Finn let out a small sigh. "I helped a friend. I didn't want him to get captured. He had more prior convictions than I did."

"So, you risked yourself for a friend."

"Yes."

"Even knowing you were at the viscount's home and the repercussions would be much greater than any other job you had taken."

"I didn't think I would be sentenced to die."

"Perhaps not." Meyer stepped into the room, and he looked up to the ceiling. "What of the others who were there?"

Finn shook his head. "They escaped."

"Unharmed, I presume?"

Finn nodded. "I don't know what happened to… my friend." He almost said *Oscar*, which would have been as bad as admitting that he was there with the Hand. As he looked at Meyer, Finn suspected he already knew who he had helped escape. "I found him in the room. He was injured. The others had run."

"Did they take anything?"

"I don't know, but I'd heard they were after a bowl."

Meyer studied him for a long moment. "Thank you for your honesty."

Finn could only nod.

Meyer had known. All along, Meyer had known.

What was I thinking, that I could keep anything from him?

He had decades of experience interrogating people. What was his time working with Finn but a prolonged interrogation?

Finn followed him back out in the street. Meyer closed the door and pulled the rope free, bundling it up and stuffing it into his pocket.

"You don't need to investigate anymore?" Finn asked.

"It's doubtful we will find anything else. I requested the Archers who apprehended Luca to leave the ropes in place so that I might have an opportunity to take a look myself. I didn't think I would find anything. I thought it would be beneficial for you to accompany me, as well."

"I didn't find anything either."

"I'm not so sure about that."

Meyer nodded for him to follow, and Finn trailed after him. They made their way deeper into the city, toward the palace. Bells tolled in the distance, ringing ten times. It was still early in the morning.

Lena might be up by now. He imagined her checking on their mother. *But what else would she be doing?*

They turned a corner, and in the distance, Finn saw City Hall.

"Another sentencing?"

Meyer nodded. "Another, though this might go differently than the last one."

When they reached City Hall, Meyer headed straight inside and to the sentencing room. Most of the jurors were there already, along with the magister. The only one Finn didn't see seated was Bellut.

The magister nodded at Meyer as he appeared. "This sentencing should not take long."

"I present myself for the requirements of the jury," Meyer said.

The magister looked behind Meyer, and two Archers stepped into the room, leading Rock. Rock glanced to Finn, as if hoping for help. He walked more comfortably than Finn had when he had come for his own sentencing. Rock must not have experienced the boots quite as long as Finn had.

"Luca Grobbe," the magister said. "You have been brought before the jury of Verendal accused of stealing. What say you?"

Rock glared at the magister before turning his irritation on the other jurors.

What was he thinking, doing that?

He seemed annoyed more than anything else.

It was a dangerous gamble and one that was bound to end poorly for him. The jurors didn't look kindly upon thieves, and Finn could tell from the way they watched him that they didn't care much for Rock.

Only one of them seemed to give him the benefit of the doubt. It was the heavyset older man he'd seen talking with the King, and he regarded Rock with a look of concern in his eyes.

"I've already told your hangman that I didn't do anything."

"You were observed breaking into the home of Bellut Indar."

Finn blinked.

That had been Bellut's home?

Had that been intentional, or had that just been bad luck? If the Client were another juror, then maybe they were trying to implicate Bellut.

What other reason would there be?

"I don't know what you're talking about."

"Two Archers have reported finding you within his home. You were apprehended there and brought to Declan Prison, where you were questioned." The magister turned to Meyer.

Meyer stepped forward. "He admits to having been in the home and admits that he was after a necklace but did not take anything."

"And your recommendation?"

"He has multiple prior sentences, and unfortunately, they have been ineffective in deterring his current behavior. Given his known associates, he is at great danger of repeating this pattern."

"Understood," the magister said. "Do you have

anything more to say?" He looked at Rock, who glared at him, saying nothing.

This was the time when Rock needed to say something. Multiple prior sentences and imprisonment at Declan suggested that the jury would convict him harshly.

Finn tried to get Rock's attention.

Rock didn't look in his direction.

Stubborn man. Look over at me!

Even if he did, Finn didn't know if there would be anything that he could do to convince Rock to say anything else.

"Very well," the magister said. "As you have multiple prior convictions, and Master Meyer fears a repeat offense, I will make the suggestion to the jury that we exile Luca Grobbe from Verendal for his crimes. What say the jury?"

The magister turned to the jury, and Finn let out a relieved sigh.

Exile was far better of an outcome than what he had expected.

It was a far better outcome than what Finn had been offered.

Knowing Rock, he likely wouldn't abide by the exile. Which meant that eventually, Rock would end up back before the magister and the jury, and he would end up sentenced even more severely.

The door at the back of the chamber opened, and Finn glanced over to see Bellut come striding in, dressed in the same clothing he'd seen him wearing each time the jury met. Rage twisted his face, and he glared at Finn for a moment before glancing at Meyer and hurrying past Rock to take his position on the jury bench. Finn understood his anger. If his home had been broken into, he'd be angry, as well.

"I apologize for my delay. It seems the Archers had cordoned off my home, making it difficult for me to prepare myself for the day."

"The cordoning-off of the crime scene is tradition," Meyer said.

"Indeed it is," the magister said. "I imagine that as Master Meyer has presented himself and the facts before the jury, he has removed such barricades?"

Meyer nodded. "There is no further need for the barricade," he said.

"Very well. As you have just arrived, we have made a motion to vote on the exile of Luca Grobbe."

"No exile," Bellut said.

"He has prior convictions," the magister said. "Master Meyer remains concerned that he will be a repeat offender."

"No exile. He deserves a greater punishment than simply exile." Bellut swept his gaze at the other jurors before looking to the magister. "The viscount is most adamant about this. You understand the stance he has taken on crime in the city on the king's behalf."

"I am well aware of the viscount's position."

"It is a position that was affirmed by the king himself during his last visit. If you have questions about it, you can ask him when he returns. He will be here in a few days to complete the treaty."

"That will not be necessary," the magister said. "It's time to vote."

"The viscount, along with the king, has been adamant that crime such as this poses a danger to the kingdom. A man such as Luca Grobbe, who would dare attack a servant of the crown such as myself, has little regard for the rule of law. I move that we proceed with capital punishment."

Finn jerked his head around and looked at Bellut.

He could tell from the expression of the others on the jury that they knew they had little choice in the matter.

"The magister called for the vote," Bellut said.

"It is far past time that an example must be set." He glanced briefly to Finn before turning his attention to the other jurors. "I suggest execution by the hanging."

"Hanging for stealing?" This came from the heavyset man. "I understand it was your home, but that *is* a bit much."

"If the viscount and the king feel that capital punishment for repeat offenders is appropriate, then perhaps the rope is an adequate deterrence," one of the other women said.

"We serve the king," the fat juror Finn thought could be the Client added.

Others murmured their approval.

Bellut turned toward the magister.

The magister seemed to consider for a moment and then turned his attention to Rock. "In the matter of Luca Grobbe, the jury has made a recommendation of execution by hanging. All in favor?"

All hands went up on the jury, though the heavyset man raised his hand more slowly.

"The sentence has been voted and approved. May the gods carry you to the afterlife, Luca Grobbe."

A pair of Archers came into the room, and they grabbed Rock. As he started past, Rock grabbed Finn by the arm and leaned close.

"Rock, I'm—"

He didn't let Finn finish.

"You tell the King to get the money to who he promised. You understand me, Shuffles?" The Archers dragged him away, but Rock kept staring at Finn. "You tell him!" Rock shouted.

Finn turned slowly and found Meyer watching him.

The jury stood, stretching, and the magister looked in Finn's direction. "You won't be able to exert your right on this one, Master Meyer," he said.

Meyer said nothing.

"As the jury has no further sentences to enact, I call for dismissal," the magister said.

Meyer nodded to Finn. "Come. We go."

Finn followed him out of the chamber, out of City Hall, but couldn't help feel as if he had one of the juror's gaze on his back the entire time.

"Can't you do anything?" Finn said.

"What would you have me do?"

"I don't know. I have the sense you disagreed with the sentencing."

Meyer glanced over. "I am not a juror. It is my responsibility to carry out the sentencing, not to question it."

"You did with me."

Meyer was silent for a few steps as they continued to put distance between them and City Hall. "Yes. I did with you."

Finn couldn't tell if Meyer thought that had been a mistake or not.

CHAPTER TWENTY-TWO

Finn waited outside of the Wenderwolf, though he didn't know if he should even be there. The tavern looked different in the daylight, though the light faded, leaving a trail of sunlight streaking across the ground. He hadn't bothered to change out of his more formal clothing this time. There wasn't a point in it. He didn't intend to hide.

He would have to go into the tavern.

The day had gone slowly. Meyer continually pressed him about various things that Finn had been studying in the anatomy book, almost as if he were concerned that Finn hadn't been studying the way he wanted him to. When Finn managed to answer some of the questions the right way, he had received a bit of praise from Meyer, something rare with the executioner.

There hadn't been any further lessons about executions. Finn should be thankful for that. He didn't want to think about what they'd have to do to Rock. It would be a *they*, too. Now that he was an apprentice, he was going to be a part of it.

And this was Rock.

His friend.

Oscar had been his oldest friend, but Rock had been his closest friend in the crew.

He couldn't kill a friend. He knew that much.

Can I risk helping him?

He didn't know if he dared.

After all the time he'd worked with Rock, there was still more to him than Finn had known. He needed to get to the King to find out who Rock wanted to get money to but didn't know how to bridge the subject.

There had been no real movement in or out of the tavern. It was still early enough in the day that he didn't know if he'd even see anyone heading in or out of the building, but he continued watching and waiting. Nervous energy filled him so that Finn danced from place to place, staying on his toes, worried about what he'd say to them.

This time, it didn't matter to him who he found. It could be Wolf or the King, though Finn wanted to find Oscar. That would be the best for everyone in the crew, mostly because Finn didn't intend to actually help the King with the next job. With his family now settled with Meyer, he couldn't.

It had started to get late, and Finn had started to debate returning to Meyer's to continue his studies when he saw the Hand's distinctive gait.

Oscar had a stealthy way of moving, but there was

something about the dangerous grace he carried himself with that made it so that Finn identified him easily.

Finn separated from the growing shadows and headed over to Oscar.

It didn't take long for Oscar to notice him.

Oscar spun, his body tense as if to either strike or run, before relaxing. "Finn. What are you doing out here?"

"Waiting for you. I don't have much time"—at least, he shouldn't take much time, whether or not he had it—"but I wanted the crew to know what happened with Rock. He got sentenced."

Oscar cocked his head to the side. "Already? That seems soon."

"I don't know whether the timing is sooner than usual, but he's to be executed. Hanging."

Oscar regarded him a moment. "Do you know when this is supposed to happen?"

Finn shook his head. "I tried getting Meyer to give me more information, but he's focused on my training. He's concerned about the testing I'm supposed to be getting ready for."

"What kind of testing?"

Finn shrugged. "I don't really know, to be honest. Some sort of Executioner Court. He didn't really tell me much more than that." Finn had an idea of what it would entail but didn't know with any certainty. Questions about what he'd been studying. Probably a sentencing. The gods only knew what else.

Oscar glanced toward the tavern before looking back

at Finn. "If you're supposed to be preparing for testing, then you should prepare. Don't let this keep you from your responsibilities."

"It's not. I just want to—"

Oscar squeezed his shoulder. "I know what you want to do, Finn. It's what you've wanted to do for as long as your father's been gone. Don't let this opportunity slip away from you. Use it to make things better for yourself."

"I can't sit by while the crew puts themselves into danger." And while Rock prepared for his sentencing. Finn had to help him somehow. "Just let the King know what I told you. And let him know that Rock wanted to make sure that he got the money to the person he promised."

Oscar frowned. "He said that?"

Finn nodded. "Who is it?"

Oscar sighed. "His niece. Poor bastard. She lost her father years ago."

"How did she lose him?"

Oscar mimed a rope and hanging. "His sister got caught up with a man running a crew. Had a little girl. Her man got pinched and sentenced to hang."

"Who was it?"

"Rog Lether."

Finn groaned. Lether. The same man the iron masters had mocked. At least Finn knew why he'd been crying going to his sentencing. "I didn't know."

"Ever since then, Rock has been providing for them. Tries to keep some distance, though, which is why he asked the King to get money, I suppose. Rock never liked to talk about it."

"I didn't know." Rock hadn't shared, though that wasn't uncommon in the crew.

"I only knew because I snooped around. I like to know as much as I can about the people I'm working with."

"Like you know about Wolf and the King?"

"They're a little harder," Oscar said. "And what really matters with the King is the jobs."

Finn frowned at Oscar. He knew there was more to it than that, and that Oscar was keeping something from him, but didn't push.

"You need to stay away from here, Finn. I don't want you to get caught up in this job they're trying to pull. That's not what you need to be a part of."

"I can help."

"You can. That's why you need to stay away. You do this, you get involved the way you're thinking, and you're going to lose whatever connection you have with the hangman. I don't know him at all, but I know his reputation. He's a good man, isn't he?"

Finn nodded slowly. "He's a good man. He helped me find my sister, and I think he's trying to help my mother." And if Finn did a good job for him, he had to think there might be something Meyer would be able to tell him about what happened to his father. He wanted a chance to know more about that, to see if there was anything he might know about where his father ended up and what Finn could do to help him, if anything.

"Then it's even more imperative that you go back. Stay away from this job. It's dangerous enough as it is. You've got your crew now. Don't lose it. Maybe he can even help you figure out what happened to your father."

Finn looked at Oscar for a moment. Finn had considered asking Meyer about his father, but there had never been a good time. If he could figure out what happened to him, maybe he could get word.

The Hand's eyes darted all around him, and with the darks he wore—Finn hadn't even paid attention to the fact that he had his darks on tonight—he blended into the shadows around the street.

"I don't want what happened to him to happen to you."

Oscar smiled sadly. "It's too late for me, I'm afraid. It doesn't have to be too late for you. I can make sure you stay safe. Which is what I'm going to do. That's the promise I made to your father."

Finn smiled at Oscar as he did when he mentioned his father. "You did him proud. You don't have to keep me safe any more. I'm old enough to keep myself safe."

"I know, but I owe him that much."

The door to the Wenderwolf opened, and Finn glanced toward it. There was a movement from the tavern, though not so much that he could see anyone coming out yet.

"Get back to your studies."

Oscar squeezed his shoulder again before heading into the tavern, leaving Finn on the street alone. He waited there a moment, wondering if Oscar would send the King or Wolf out, but no one came. After a while, he turned and headed through the streets. It wasn't that late, but he should be studying. His path led him past the Brinder section, his old home, and finally away and back toward Meyer's home. Other than a light in his office in the back of the home, it was quiet. Finn hadn't seen any lights in the windows overhead, so he suspected his sister had already gone to bed. Their mother had gradually improved, though it was slight. Not enough that she was up and able to care for herself yet, but she had started to come around in ways that she hadn't in the last few months. Meyer really did have ways of healing.

Finn didn't bother Meyer. If he was healing someone, he would leave him alone. Most of the people who came to Meyer for healing did so wanting a level of anonymity. They wouldn't be able to get that with him rushing into the office and disrupting everything that he did.

Instead, he went to the small room at the front of the house and took a seat at the desk and began reading. He couldn't get his mind off of what would happen to Rock, but he could focus on what he needed to do for his studies.

A knock came on his door, and Finn pulled open to see Lena standing there. She had on a yellow nightgown, her hair pulled back with a loop of ribbon.

"I couldn't sleep."

"I'm sorry," he said.

"It's just..." She looked past him, toward the desk. "What are you doing?"

"Reading. I have some studying to do."

"I don't need to bother you, then," she said.

Finn shook his head, motioning to the bed. "No bother. You can come in."

Lena took a seat on the bed, clasping her hands together and looking down at them. "I could help you."

"You could help me?"

"I could. If you need to study, I could help."

He glanced over to the table in the stack of books. He and Lena had never been close, but they had always wanted the same thing. They had always wanted their mother to get well.

"I would like that."

Finn came around, still sitting at the desk. At one point, he'd rested his head and had fallen fast asleep. That hadn't been his intention, but sleep had come quickly for him, and now that he was awake, he rubbed his head.

Finn's neck ached from how he'd been sleeping. He'd rested with his head forward, pressing up against the table. The book in front of him had been mostly unread, though he'd needed to see what more he could learn from it. It was another healing book. Meyer had wanted him to read mostly books on anatomy and healing, which he found strange, but if nothing else, they *were* interesting.

When he awoke, he got to his feet. He didn't need to get dressed. He was still dressed from the night before, so there wasn't the need to change. He headed out of the room to discover the smell of bacon and eggs.

Not Meyer…

He didn't want to eat the executioner's cooking. More than that, he didn't want Meyer to be angry that Finn had overslept. He didn't have much in the way of formal expectations, but he had come to expect that Finn would cook for him in the mornings.

It wasn't Meyer.

Finn found Lena in the kitchen cooking. She hummed softly as she did, and when he entered, she smiled at him. A real smile, not one of the halfhearted smiles she'd been so fond of lately.

Finn joined his sister at the stove, but she waved him away.

"Sit. Let me do this. I didn't really understand all of the plants he has you studying. Then you had that book on anatomy, as well."

He took a seat. It had been a while since he'd had the pleasure of eating his sister's cooking, and he did enjoy it. She was a skilled cook and had been the one who taught him.

"Does he have you here learning to be an apothecary?" Lena asked, glancing over her shoulder.

Finn shook his head. "Not really. It's all part of what he does. I keep waiting for the *other* lessons, but they haven't really come." Not the way he expected. There were the discussions about hanging, and about the techniques involved, but nothing more than that.

Lena turned back to her work at the stove. "It's nice to have you focusing on your studies like this, Finn. Father always thought you had potential. He wouldn't have wanted you to have wasted it."

"He always knew you had potential, too," Finn said softly.

She stiffened slightly before returning to her cooking. Lena carried a pan over to him, sliding two eggs and three pieces of bacon onto his plate. "Seems as if we both wasted it, didn't we?"

Finn took a bite, savoring the flavor of the eggs. The bacon had the right crispness to it as well. He imagined her cooking for him regularly again but wondered if that was what she wanted. She had seemed content working, even if it had been the butcher. Who was he to take that from her?

"Mother looks better," she said.

"I think so too."

"I haven't thanked you."

"For what?"

"For this," Lena said. "All of this."

Finn sighed and looked up from his plate, ignoring it for now. "I haven't told you how I ended up working with Meyer."

She brought the pan over to the basin and set it there, keeping her back to him. "You told me enough."

Finn had wanted to shield his family from what he'd done. He hadn't wanted to admit to his sister what he'd done and how far he'd been willing to go. Maybe Lena needed to know. Honesty, for a change.

"You said that Mother needed to see a physician. But when I found out how much one cost, I took on a job I shouldn't have. I was caught. Brought before the magisters and the jurors and—"

She turned sharply to look at him. "Why would they have brought you before the entire jury?"

"Because they sentenced me to hang."

The words lingered in the air.

It felt strangely good to admit to his sister what had happened. He'd tried to keep it from her, as if he could protect her from the truth, but perhaps that was the problem. He couldn't even protect himself from the truth. How was he supposed to protect anyone else from it?

"When will it happen?"

Finn shook his head. "It won't. At least, it won't so long as I work with Meyer. He claimed something called the Executioner's Right. We had to go before the king and everything. So long as I continue my studies with him, I'll be permitted to be his apprentice."

"And if you fail?"

"Then I hang."

She held his gaze. "Which means we would have to find someplace else."

The practicality of what she said hurt, but it was true. Were he to hang, he couldn't imagine Meyer letting her stay. Though were he to fail, it meant Meyer would face punishment as well.

"I suppose it would."

Lena seemed to consider for a moment. "Then you can't fail. Do what you need to remain his apprentice. Mother needs that from you."

Finn could only nod. There was a time when he would have said their mother needed her more than him, and perhaps she still did, but now she needed him as well. Finn had to do whatever he could to give her the chance to survive.

Lena returned to her work, and Finn stood quietly in the kitchen before retaking his seat and sitting to eat. When he finished eating, he left Lena alone. She hadn't said anything more.

Returning to his room, he considered sitting and studying for a bit more but decided to practice with pumpkins. It would help take his mind off of everything else.

Finn had been chopping at pumpkins, slicing through seven in a row, when Meyer returned to the yard. He watched Finn for a little while saying nothing. After a bit, he nodded.

"Time for us to go."

Finn wiped the blade clean, resheathed it, and carried it inside. Lena glanced at him, her gaze slipping to the massive sword Justice, before she headed up the stairs and to her room.

When Finn returned to the small garden, Meyer still waited for him. "What do we need to do this morning?"

"We will talk as we go along."

He led Finn from the garden and out into the street.

They headed away from the river, toward the outer sections of the city. At first, Finn thought they were traveling to one of the prisons, but they veered down a different street than they would have needed to reach the debtor's prison or Declan.

The gate loomed into view, and Finn glanced over to Meyer.

"What's outside the gate for us today?"

"What can you remember from the first book you borrowed?"

Finn looked over at him, frowning. "The first book was on anatomy."

"It was. What do you remember?"

Finn shrugged. "The body is more complicated than I had known. There are more muscles and bones and—"

"What do you remember?"

"What am I supposed to remember?"

Meyer looked over to him as they reached the gate. A pair of Archers manning the gate nodded to Meyer. "You've had several weeks with that book. What do you remember?"

"What in particular are you asking me about?" Finn felt frustration rising up within him, though he knew he needed to be careful. It wasn't Meyer's fault that he had struggled with the anatomy book. The only way that he'd been able to learn anything from that book had been trying to tie it to what he'd seen before.

"Maybe it was too much to ask," Meyer whispered.

There was activity outside of the gate today. Some of it came from near the hegen, where he saw quite a bit of scurrying in and out of their section of the city, though not all. In the distance, the Raven Stone rose like a taunt, reminding him of Rock's sentence and the role he would have to play in enacting it. The gallows loomed above the stone, something stark and powerful.

How would I be able to help kill a man I call a friend?

Meyer veered them away from the hegen and the Stone.

Finn stayed close to him. They headed farther from the city than he'd expected, taking the road leading toward the city of Vur and away from the forest.

"Are we going to be gone from the city long?"

"Not long. The testing isn't far from here."

Testing.

It was *that* time.

"Should I have brought more with me than I did?"

Meyer looked over at him. "You've brought all you will need. The Executioner Court consists of master executioners. It meets periodically, and I had not known they would be meeting so soon this year, but given the king's movements, and his concern about the Alainsith…" Meyer shook his head. "The court is responsible for determining who serves in the kingdom. You must convince them of your readiness. When you do, then you can truly be my apprentice."

They made their way past a few neighboring farms. Several of them had livestock, one with a pen containing what had to be a hundred pigs. The stench of it was worse than even the worst of the sections of the city. Some of the farms were small, little more than patches where farmers could grow corn or potatoes or other vegetables, while others were much larger. Some of the larger farms already had people working in the fields. Land granted by the king, the farmers were usually wealthy merchants who lived in the city and rarely came outside its walls.

Finn glanced back toward the city. From what he could see, the palace rose high over the city walls, resting on the hillside. Several of the bell towers for the churches scattered throughout the city were visible. A few taller buildings could be seen as well, though not much more than that. A wagon caravan appeared in the distance along the side of the road. It didn't look to be moving.

"Should we veer around the wagons?"

"That's our destination," Meyer said.

A man appeared near one of the wagons around the road. Thin and with a bald head, he nodded toward Meyer with something of a familiarity. The dark leathers he wore reminded Finn of what Meyer wore for the Gallows Festival.

Others stood in the circle of the wagons behind him, though Finn couldn't see them well from where he stood. Meyer blocked part of his way, but this man blocked more of it. A wooden structure rose up within the center of the wagons.

"Henry Meyer," the man said, raising one hand briefly before touching it to his chest. "You have answered the call."

Meyer nodded solemnly. "I present myself before the court."

Finn could see a gallows in the middle of the wagons. The Executioner Court.

"So you have."

He stepped to the side, and Meyer started forward, guiding Finn with him. He followed slowly, glancing everywhere around him as he did. The wagons created a natural barricade along the road. They were far enough from the city that they wouldn't encounter many people, and they were near enough that they wouldn't come across any brigands. Not the way they would farther from the city.

When they entered the center of the wagon caravan, the gallows kept his eye. It reminded him of the one atop the Stone, but this was made more simply. A few timber crossbeams supporting it. A rope dangling, the end of it barely moving in the soft breeze.

Was that for me?

The Executioner Court was his testing. Which meant he had to pass or he would face the remainder of his punishment.

Hanging.

Finn's gaze lingered on the gallows.

At least it wouldn't be a public spectacle. That had been worse. This was almost private.

"I didn't expect the court to convene so soon," Meyer said.

Finn tore his gaze away from the gallows. If he were to be tested, he had to steady his mind. It was no different from any of the jobs he'd taken when working with the King. He couldn't do those jobs worried about what would happen. He had to remain focused, prepared.

"And we would not have, were it not for King Porman's travels."

Meyer nodded as if that answered everything.

"The timing is unfortunate."

"I am sorry, Henry," the man who'd greeted them at the

wagon entrance said, lowering his voice to a near whisper. "Truly I am. I delayed as long as I could."

"It is appreciated."

The man turned to Finn, regarding him. "This is your apprentice?"

"Finn Jagger." Meyer met Finn's gaze for a moment. "Apprenticed to me according to the ancient right. I hereby present him for testing to the court."

"As is required," the man said, his voice rising.

"As is required," others around him said, their voices a chant.

Finn hadn't realized how they had gathered, but now saw that they were arranged behind the first man. First executioner, probably.

"Have you trained him according to custom?"

"I have begun his training according to custom," Meyer asked.

Finn hadn't fully trained. He'd been working with Meyer, trying to learn what he could, but Finn had thought he would have more time than this. Now their fates were tied together.

"Then let us test him according to custom. If he succeeds, he may continue his path toward serving the kingdom as a royal executioner. If he fails, Verendal will seek a new executioner."

Meyer nodded.

The lead man turned to Finn. "Present yourself, Finn Jagger."

He looked to Meyer for guidance but didn't see anything from him. He watched Finn, his eyes intense, and Finn didn't know what else he needed to do or say. There hadn't been preparation for this.

What was I supposed to do to present myself?

Finn looked all around him. The other executioners—and he suspected they were all executioners—waited for him to say something.

"I present myself to the Executioner Court for testing."

"Very well."

They guided Finn to the center of the wagons, close to the gallows. Finn couldn't help but glance toward it, curious whether there was anything they would demand of him with it. Meyer had taught him about the noose, ways of tying it, and he'd explained the various parts of a hanging, but would that be all that they wanted him to know?

Three executioners stood in front of him. Finn was surprised to realize one of them was a woman. Heavyset and nearly as tall as him, she regarded him with a suspicious glare.

"Describe the proper technique for setting a humerus fracture," the woman asked.

It took Finn a few moments to realize what she asked of him. *Fracture* meant *bone,* and he'd seen something in the anatomy book. What was the humerus?

When he didn't answer quickly enough, the man next to her frowned. "Well?"

Finn searched his mind for what to do. The answer was there. He had seen it just last night while studying with his sister.

Humerus. Arm bone.

"It seems that he's—"

Finn cut the woman off. "Splint the fracture. Binding to the body to support the bone while it heals. It's a painful break but should heal in a few weeks with appropriate binding."

He had seen something like that in one of the other books, but even that wasn't quite where he remembered it. It came from remembering what they'd done to Hector when his arm had been broken.

"How would you treat a partial thickness burn?" one of the others asked.

Finn didn't know what they meant by *partial thickness*, but he had some idea of how to heal a burn.

"Aloe and honey mixed into a salve," Finn said.

He wanted to look to Meyer for support, but he felt that he wasn't supposed to do so.

"What would you place on an infected wound?"

Unlike the others, Finn hadn't seen an infected wound with Meyer. He'd read about them, though. This time, the answer came to him from what he'd read, the memory of it sliding into his mind.

"A mixture of buttleworm and filst can help. A compound of spilen ash and leven leaf. Or a—"

"That suffices," the woman said. "Describe how you would concoct a sedative."

Finn had seen Meyer using something like that—and providing it to someone who'd come to him for it.

When he answered, he found another question. Then another. He answered them all as well as he could, though he started to feel as if they exceeded what he knew.

None of that mattered. All that mattered was that he find the answers that he could. That he pass the test.

Some of the questions he didn't know the answer to. When he told them that, they continued with another question.

After a while, these three moved off to the side. Another three joined. They looked harder than the others. Two of them were older, of a similar age to Meyer, though one reminded him of the Lion. All were dressed in similar gray leathers. The older men both had beards, while the younger of the three kept his face clean-shaven.

"Describe the questioning technique known as the ungar."

The first three had been to find out what he knew about healing. It surprised him that they would care whether he was able to heal, though he'd seen there was a concern about ensuring the prisoners weren't defiled in any way. They had to be pretty for the gods, after all.

This was different.

Now came the real test, he suspected.

Ungar?

Where had he read about that?

The questioners started to stir.

"The ungar involves narrow rods slid under the finger-nails," Finn began, describing what he'd read. "The rods are slender and separate the—"

"Describe the use of water in enhanced interrogations," the younger of the three asked.

Finn had to gather himself. The change was disconcerting, though he suspected that was part of the intention. They didn't want him comfortable with the questioning. At least he had first-hand experience with this. "Water is poured into the person's mouth until they cannot breathe. They are given a chance to answer—"

"Share the use of the lagur."

Finn closed his eyes, thinking back. Had he seen or heard of anything called a lagur?

A flicker of a memory came to him.

"The lagur is a device strapped to a person's head—"

"How would you apply the berinth?" the first man asked.

It was another device or technique that Finn didn't know.

He hadn't been around Meyer enough during torture to know all of these techniques.

"Where would you use fire when questioning?"

Finn licked his lips. "I don't know. Under the arms?" That had been where Gabe had been burned, though Finn didn't know if that was the proper location.

They asked a few more questions about devices and techniques, but with each one, Finn realized that he didn't know enough.

How could he? Meyer hadn't taught him about this. There hadn't been time.

The three moved off to the side. The first man, the one who had greeted them when they came to the court, stepped forward.

He watched Finn. "Describe the types of knots involved in creating a noose, along with their uses."

"There are several I know. The traditional knot is

known as the hangman's knot. It's often used for the gallows tree, and the force to close is easier to adjust than the gallows knot, which is a simpler knot and less likely to break the neck, resulting in a suffocation. There are a few other simpler—"

"How do you clean the sword of justice?"

That was his next question? After everything that he'd been through, Finn thought the simple question almost too easy, but he was thankful for it. He wanted an easier question to answer. "Justice must be oiled weekly, and the scabbard monthly. The blade must be maintained at a sharpened edge to cleave the neck cleanly. There are—"

"How would you apply the wheel?"

Finn frowned. This time, he did look to Meyer. The master executioner watched him but didn't say anything. "Tying him to it?" Finn started, shaking his head. "I'm sorry, I don't have that experience," Finn said.

"How would you bind a man sentenced to be quartered?"

He resisted the urge to shudder and started shaking his head. "I don't... I suppose one of the traditional nooses wouldn't suffice. A different knot"—as he searched his memory, he didn't know what kind—"to tie to a man's arms and legs. I'd want to give him mercy beforehand so that he didn't die screaming and suffer."

The lead executioner watched Finn, saying nothing.

Finally, he stepped away and returned with a long-bladed sword.

"Demonstrate your skill."

He held out the blade and motioned to one side of the wagon Finn hadn't seen before.

A large pig lay motionless.

He looked to Meyer but didn't get any response from him.

Finn carried the sword over to stand in front of the pig. The legs were bound, and he could see that it had bled out already. This was a test of technique only.

"Do I do this here, or do I have it elevated?"

As an answer, two of his testers hoisted the pig, holding it in the middle.

Finn swallowed.

He'd practiced on pumpkins, but this was something different.

He could feel Meyer's eyes on him as he took his position next to the pig. The others of the court stood silent as they watched.

Finn took a deep breath, raised the sword, and swung.

The blade came down faster than Justice did. Justice was heavier and more substantial. As the blade whistled down, he had a moment where he thought it would miss.

The blade cleaved cleanly, but it only cleaved through half of the pig's neck.

Finn lowered the blade, breathing out slowly.

He'd failed.

He couldn't even look at Meyer.

The others lowered the pig and gathered together, speaking softly for a long while. Every so often, Finn heard a more animated voice and worried that he wasn't going to pass the test. Which meant that Meyer wouldn't survive the testing.

The lead executioner turned back to him. "There is one more test, Master Meyer."

Meyer came to stand next to Finn.

Even though Finn suspected what was coming, it didn't make it any easier.

"He must carry out a sentencing."

CHAPTER TWENTY-THREE

Neither of them spoke on the walk back to the city. Finn wondered what Meyer must be thinking, though suspected it had something to do with putting his fate in Finn's hands. He hadn't done well with the testing and worried that he would be the reason Meyer died.

The court wanted to observe Finn carrying out the sentencing. He knew what it meant. It was something he'd suspected as a part of the testing but hadn't been sure.

Now he would be the one responsible for Rock.

And it was something Finn didn't know if he had the stomach for.

That made it an effective test. He understood that all too well.

He would fail. Given his performance so far, he might already have failed.

Finn would hang.

Meyer would hang.

Then his sister and mother...

Would be no worse off than they had been before.

That was what Finn had to keep in mind. They had already been miserable. Lena had worked at the butcher, her job terrible and taking her away for long hours, but hopefully she could return to it. Their mother hadn't improved that much from the time with Meyer, so even she wouldn't have a vastly different fate.

When the gate came into view, Finn looked over to the Raven Stone. "When would they need to observe an execution?" he asked, finally breaking the silence between them.

Meyer looked over. "The court only convenes for a few days. The timing is unusual this year."

"Which means you will have me execute Rock."

Meyer turned to him. "Luca Grobbe. You must refer to the condemned by their gods-given name. Only in doing so will you be able to do what you must."

"I don't know that I can. You made a mistake. You shouldn't have taken me in. I don't know why you did, but it was a mistake."

Meyer watched him. "Would you rather have ended up there?" He motioned to the gallows. "Would you prefer the crows have picked the flesh from your bones? The hegen harvesting your hands and feet? Your body dumped beneath the gallows to rot like so much refuse?"

Finn shook his head. "I could have run."

"You could have. You didn't."

"I didn't know you would suffer for my mistake."

"If you ran, then it would be my mistake. I *should* be the one to suffer."

"Why?"

Meyer didn't answer.

They reached the gate, and Meyer glanced over to him.

"Find me this evening, and we will make your preparations."

He started to head off when Finn hurried after him. "What would have happened if there wasn't a prisoner for me to carry out the sentencing?"

"I don't know."

"How don't you know? You're the master executioner!"

Meyer regarded him a long moment. "There hasn't been an executioner who has exerted their right in many years. Which means that I don't know."

"What about the testing?"

"What about it?"

"I didn't know… well, a lot of what they asked me."

Meyer regarded him for a long moment. "You did not. Take the rest of the day to prepare. There is no failing the next test."

Meyer left him.

Finn sighed. *What would I do now?*

There was still quite a bit of the day remaining, enough that he didn't know what he should do. He found himself walking, wandering through the streets, his path heading along familiar streets in the outer sections. At one point, when passing through the Brinder section, he thought he saw Helda. He wanted to tell her that his sister had returned and that she was unharmed and chased after her before deciding it had to be someone else. He'd have to send word to her to let her know about Lena.

Finn neared Meyer's home...

And nearly ran into Wolf.

"Shuffles. What are you doing out here so early in the day?" he asked.

"I'm on an errand for Master Meyer," he said, looking over to Meyer's home. Had Wolf followed him?

More likely, he knew where to find him. There wouldn't be the need to follow him.

He didn't want to deal with Wolf. There would be enough to deal with when they learned he had to be the one to place the noose around Rock's neck and carry out the sentencing. There wouldn't be any way he'd be able to return to the crew.

How could he protect the crew and pass the court's test?

"What's the hangman have you doing?"

Finn tried to come up with a good answer, but nothing came to mind. "He has me running to the prisons to see if there are new prisoners he needs to question."

That would be believable, though Finn could tell from the hint of the smile on Wolf's face that he wasn't completely convinced. "Is that right?"

"There's something at the debtor's prison I needed to check on. He wanted me to—"

Wolf slipped his arm around Finn's shoulders and guided him along the street. He squeezed with a bit more force than was necessary. "Since you're out on your errands, maybe you'd like to come by the Wenderwolf. We don't have much time left. When we pull this job, we're going to need your help."

"I don't know that I can be of much help." He looked back toward Meyer's home, but Wolf had already started to guide him around the corner and away. Olin section wasn't that far from here. "I told the King that."

Wolf snorted. "You told the King you'd be happy to help. For the crew, I think you said. Scruff is coming along, but he's going to need help with keeping watch. Figured you have enough experience with that you could help."

"If I do that, then you risk losing me if something were to happen," Finn said.

"I think you can manage. Besides, I saw you talking with the Archers one night. Didn't have any trouble then, did you? That's the kind of help we're going to need."

Wolf had seen him when he'd followed.

"I was able to get them to bring me back to Meyer's home. Not much more than that."

"How long you been his apprentice? A few weeks? Long enough that you got some connections, Shuffles. Long enough they start to recognize you. That's all we're going to need. You use those connections so that if anything happens, we have a way to get past it."

It might work.

Maybe he *could* protect the crew that way.

They neared the Wenderwolf.

"You can get back to your master's errands when all of this is done. Job isn't happening now, anyway. Just a few more questions for the planning."

They stepped into the tavern. In the daytime, there wasn't the same energy as was present at night. Finn had been there in the daytime before, but it had been in preparation for jobs they were taking when he had.

Wolf shoved him toward the booth and slid in next to him. "You told us about the layout before, at least what you said you remembered of it. Now I need to know what more you might be able to remember. There has to be more that you can recall."

Finn shook his head. "When I went there, I worried about what would happen to me. I wasn't thinking clearly, Wolf."

"Sometimes, things stick in our heads that we don't remember at first. I'd like for you to hold on to what you can and see if there's anything that sparks a memory." He leaned toward Finn. "You know it could mean the difference between success and failure with the job. You don't want anything to happen to the crew."

The door to the tavern opened, and Oscar came in. He glanced at Finn briefly before turning his attention to Wolf. "What's going on?"

"Just found Shuffles in the street and thought he might be able to provide a bit more detail about what he saw when he went to the palace."

"He's not going to be involved with this."

"That's not your call to make."

"It is this time. I let the two of you drag him in the last time, and it nearly ended up with him dead. I'm not going to let you do it to him again."

"Why would he end up dead?" Wolf asked.

"You know the penalty as well as I do. If he gets pinched with us or goes off with someone he's not supposed to be with, he's going to end up hanging like he would have the other time. None of us want that for him." Oscar leveled his hard-eyed gaze on Wolf. "Get up, Finn."

"You're going to push it like that?" Wolf asked, not moving from his seat.

"I'm going to push it the way it needs to be pushed." There was a look in Oscar's eyes that Finn hadn't seen before.

"Better talk to *him*," Wolf said. He nodded toward the back of the tavern.

Finn noticed the King sitting alone in the darkness of a corner. He hadn't paid attention to the rest of the tavern when he'd first been dragged in.

The King got to his feet and came toward him, moving slowly. "Have a seat, Hand."

"I'm not having Finn a part of this."

"I'm afraid we're past that. Wolf is right. He can be useful. With him being able to wave off the Archers, we could use him." The King looked to Wolf. "He's coming. The crew needs him. After this job is done, things settle back down. Then he can return to his new master."

"You're going to make it like that, are you?" Oscar asked.

The King approached. "I don't think you understand what we've got going on here." Oscar twisted his hands the way he did when irritated, and Finn didn't think he did understand. "He don't do this, and you're done, Hand. And don't forget about what *else* I promised." The words lingered in the air a moment, and the King grinned at Oscar. "I see I have your attention. You don't want that now, do you? Don't want to be unprotected in a city like this. A man needs a crew."

Oscar glanced at Finn. "We don't need the kid. You saw what happened the last time he got involved in a job."

"I seem to remember that the last time he got involved in a job, you were nearly pinched. The kid saved your ass."

This was one of the few times when Finn didn't want to argue about what he'd done. He didn't need the recognition, and he thought it might even be better if he didn't get noticed for his contributions.

The King took a seat at the table, looking across it to Finn. "Wolf is right. You're going to be with us. And it's happening soon."

"We aren't prepared for it to happen soon," Oscar said.

"Maybe you aren't, but we are," the King said. "Wolf got the last of the supplies we need. Since the Client gave us a deadline, I'll be damned if we aren't going to meet it."

"We'll be damned if we try to do it without proper preparation," Oscar said, taking a seat next to the King. Finn recognized the look of defeat in his eyes. It was an expression he never thought he'd see from Oscar. "I've been telling you we can't do this without the right kind of preparation. We know what happened to Dalton—"

"You've got to stop bringing Pegg into this," Wolf said. "The man fucked up. We won't. We've got it planned. With Shuffles here, we've got the right person to lead us." Wolf glanced to Finn. "Don't we?"

How could Finn refuse?

There had to be a way to do this and not get caught.

He could keep from disappointing Meyer while helping the crew.

The solution was obvious: He had to tell Meyer.

It would be hard. The crew might suffer, but they'd suffer less than were they caught pulling an impossible job. This was how he could protect them best.

"Is it worth risking your access to the executioner?" Oscar asked.

He needed them to move on so he could get back to Meyer.

"How much will it pay?" Finn asked.

"We do this, and each of us can take home nearly five crowns," the King said.

His heart skipped.

That was more than he'd expected. Far more.

That was enough for Finn to leave Verendal. There was enough for him to provide for his sister and his mother. Even a single crown was enough to hire a physician and not fear the cost. It was more than he would earn working with Master Meyer for years. How could the Client afford to pay that?

Finn had to stop thinking like that. It wasn't just about the money. Or the crew.

If he did this, Meyer would suffer.

"What happens if the Client doesn't deliver? What happens if you can't move what is taken?" If he knew who the Client was, maybe it wouldn't be an issue, but Finn still had no idea. Oscar didn't either. "What happens if the

Client is the one to betray us—or hires another crew to compete?"

The words had the desired effect and hung for a moment.

The King grunted. "No other crew is taking this job. We've seen to that. And the Client has always delivered."

"If he doesn't?" Finn glanced from the King to Wolf. "Do you have an alternative plan in mind?"

The King flicked his gaze to Wolf before he smiled at Finn. "I've always got an alternative plan. Just be ready tonight."

"That's not enough time," Oscar said. "We still need to coordinate more. We need to be prepared. We need to—"

"It's going to have to be tonight. The Client has decided." King turned to Wolf, flashing a bright smile. "It'll be good to have the crew all working together."

"Other than Rock," Finn said.

"Sure," the King said. He tapped the table and slid out of the booth, leaving Finn with Oscar.

Wolf stared at Finn for a moment. "You'd better show."

"I'm going to need a new set of darks," Finn said. "You know the size."

Wolf frowned at him. "Do I look like your servant?"

"You look like the kind of man who can get something for me," Finn said. "And considering that I'm now apprenticed to the executioner, I'm not exactly able to go wandering the city for darks."

Wolf glared at him. "Be here at dusk."

When he was gone, it left Finn sitting across from Oscar.

Oscar shook his head. "What are you doing? I tried to protect you from this."

"I know you have. And now I have to protect you. All of you." Finn glanced over at the King. "He has to do the job," Finn whispered. "What I can't figure is why."

The strangeness of the items they'd gone after kept tugging on Finn, as did the memory of what he'd heard Meyer say. What if these were hegen jobs?

Finn should have asked Esmerelda… and maybe he still could.

Oscar sighed. "He owes a debt. I'm not really sure who it is, but the more I keep digging into the Client, the more I start to suspect the King's debt is the reason he's taking his jobs."

"You know what it *could* be," Finn said, keeping his voice low.

"It's not."

"You don't even know what I was thinking."

Oscar grunted. "I know what you've been thinking from the moment you sat down. He don't owe *them*. This is different."

Finn sat back, mind working. Going to Esmerelda wouldn't help him, then. "Does he owe the Client?"

Oscar shrugged. "I don't know if it's the Client or someone else. And at this point, it don't matter either way."

Finn got to his feet. "I'll figure this out. We aren't going to hang for the King's debt."

Finn headed out of the tavern.

He headed back toward Meyer's home. When he got

there, a stack of fresh pumpkins waited for him. Working with Justice had brought him a sense of peace in the past. He fetched the sword from inside the home, carried it out, and set the scabbard down before beginning to hack at the pumpkins.

He cut through eight of them in a row, slicing them cleanly. As he started to lift the ninth one, he set it on the bench, his mind still working through how he'd talk to Meyer. That was what he had to do.

Finn slashed through the pumpkin, carving it cleanly. He grabbed another, staring at it for a moment, trying to think about what he would do, but not having the answer. He sliced at the pumpkin, carving through it again.

"That is ten," Meyer said.

Finn blinked, looking over. "What was that?"

"Ten. You cut through ten pumpkins. Perhaps it's time for you to move on to something else."

Finn glanced down at the pumpkins.

Had I actually cut through ten of them?

"If you're worried about carrying out your friend's sentence, you can relax. You have a reprieve, such as it is," Meyer said.

"What sort of reprieve?"

"The sentencing."

Finn frowned. "I thought we had to carry out the sentencing for the court."

"And you will need to," he said.

"Then why the reprieve?"

"Because Luca escaped."

Finn's heart seemed to stop.

Meyer headed past him, into the house, and Finn followed when he could get himself moving again, now his heart hammering.

He had planned on talking to Meyer.

They would work through the details, figure out some way to keep the crew from risking themselves for the Client. He would protect the crew the way he had always wanted to. Then Finn would have to figure out some way to save Rock.

Now…

"How did he escape?"

"I'm not certain. Declan is secure, though he was moved to one of the upper levels. We allow the condemned to have a window in their final days, and it places them closer to the kitchen for their final meal." Meyer glanced back at Finn for a moment. "I suspect he had help. I am not concerned. He will be captured. His sentence will be carried out."

"Help?" *Why Rock and not me?* "What happens if he's not captured?"

"We had both better hope he's recaptured," Meyer said.

"Why is there such a time limit on this?"

"Because that is tradition," Meyer said.

"And if we don't do it in the timeframe that they have established?"

"Don't ask questions you know the answer to, Finn. Look for answers to questions you don't know the answer to."

Meyer wouldn't be able to help Finn now.

There might be only one option for him, and only one way to really help the crew.

He'd have to actually do the job.

He headed to his room. The lantern glowed with a soft light.

He didn't think he'd left it glowing, though maybe Lena had been there and turned the light on. He took a seat at the table, pulling the stack of books over to him. Maybe it didn't matter if he studied, but the habit had begun to become ingrained for him.

As he stared at the books, he realized there was something else on the desk.

A card.

The hegen *were* involved in these jobs. The card proved it.

Finn lifted the card, turning it in his hands for a moment, and stared at it.

As he did, his heart started to hammer.

There was a single image on the card. An illustration. The target was clear to Finn, though not the meaning.

Depicted on the card was a hand painted in red, as if in blood.

CHAPTER TWENTY-FOUR

The fading sunlight drifted across the plains outside of the city. He studied the card. It signified Oscar in some way, though what was it? The blood Hand. That had to matter. Did the hegen want him to betray Oscar somehow?

Finn had come out to the gate to see if he might come up with an answer, but there wasn't an answer for him there. Standing there left him no closer to knowing what he needed to do than he'd been when he'd been in Meyer's home.

What am I thinking?

Darkness would fall soon. When it did, Finn would have to meet with the crew.

When he'd left before, he'd thought Meyer could help.

Now Finn didn't see how he could.

The only way he could get through this was working with the crew.

Music drifted from the hegen section. It had a bouncy rhythm, and he felt drawn by it. Magic rhythm, most likely. Were he to go down there, he'd be compelled to do something else on behalf of the hegen.

Finn slipped the card into his pocket and turned back to the city.

It was time.

Dread filled him as he made his way through the city. Help the crew, and he betrayed Meyer. It felt harder than he would have expected. But it might be the only way Finn could ensure his friends didn't fail.

What truth would he follow tonight?

It didn't take long before he reached Olin.

The section of the city felt dark and unwelcome. The sounds around him more threatening than they should be. Finn neared the Wenderwolf, looking at shadows swirling everywhere. A cold wind gusted, leaving him wishing for his warmer cloak, though he'd left that behind. There was no point in bringing the cloak with him if he would only have to lose it.

Finn paused at the door to the tavern before taking a deep breath and heading inside. There was nothing for him to do but keep moving.

Music drifted out. It wasn't as haunting as the music from the hegen, but there was something about it that wasn't quite as exciting as it had been before. He stood in the doorway for a moment before seeing the rest of the crew sitting in the booth.

They were all there. The King. Wolf. Oscar. Scruff. Even Rock.

Finn's heart skipped a beat seeing Rock.

Finn wouldn't have been able to hang Rock anyway. He would have failed the testing and ended up hanging for it. Meyer, too.

Why should two men die?

Finn didn't want anything to happen to Meyer—he'd been good to him, after all—but perhaps this was the only way forward for him. Meyer had made his choice with Finn. Now Finn had to make his. There was nothing to do but get it over with.

"There he is," the King said. "Told you he'd come."

Oscar looked at him, shaking his head slightly. Finn ignored it, much as he tried to ignore thinking of the card in his pocket and what it meant. He didn't want to think about why the hegen wanted to target Oscar.

Rock watched at him. "You sure about this, Shuffles?"

"Don't you worry about Shuffles," the King said. "He's doing what he knows must be done."

Finn took a seat, and Wolf handed him a bundle. When he took it, he looked down to see it was a set of darks. Nicer than the ones that he'd had before.

"Get ready," the King said, looking to Finn.

Finn looked to the others surrounding the table. "Are you going to tell us what the Client wants?"

The King cocked his head to the side. "I've got part of it covered, and he's going to let us know the rest when we're there."

Oscar jerked his head around and stared at the King. "The Client is coming?"

"We're meeting him along the way."

"You sure that's a good—"

Wolf cut him off. "The Client is coming. That's the condition of the job."

"Was it the condition of the job Pegg took?" Finn asked.

The others fell silent, though he didn't care about the others. The only one he wanted to get a reaction from was the King. He needed to know how much of this he had planned, if any. If the Client were coming along, nothing about this had a plan.

It worried Finn.

The King had always been a skilled planner. He ran one of the better crews in the city, so he had to be. Nothing of this smacked of skill.

For that matter, nothing lately had the feel of skill. There had been too much coin involved. Greed had made the crew careless. Finn had gotten pulled into it the same as others.

"Pegg made a mistake we aren't going to make," the King said. He looked to Finn. "Get ready."

Finn carried the clothes to the side of the tavern and started changing. First the pants. They weren't as soft as the fabric he'd gotten from Master Beshear and not even as comfortable as the Sinner's Cloth on the day he'd been condemned. They were rough and scratchy, and Finn didn't care for the way the fabric rubbed against his legs. When he pulled on the shirt, anxiety began to work through him.

He wouldn't be able to back away from this.

Wearing the clothes from Meyer gave him a chance to

go to the Archers; to at least be believable in telling them that he served him. Wearing darks made him a criminal

It was strange that he felt more honorable as an executioner's apprentice than he did wearing the darks.

Oscar headed over to him, looking down at the pile of clothes on the ground before looking up at Finn. "Don't do this."

Finn thought about the card in his pocket. He had moved the hegen card from the pocket of his more formal clothing and into the pocket of his darks. It weighed heavily there, almost as if he could feel the power of the hegen trying to pull on him, trying to drag him toward serving them.

Finn looked over to Oscar. "For me to continue serving, I was going to have to prove my ability as an apprentice."

"You're a bright man, Finn. I have little doubt you'd be able to prove your ability," he said.

"I was tested. At least, the test started. There was an aspect of it that I haven't carried out. That was going to be the next step. The final step before I was going to be allowed to remain as an apprentice."

Oscar glanced over to Rock. "I see."

"Do you?"

"That is a brutal punishment."

"For both of us," Finn said.

"That's why you came," Oscar said.

"I think I was going to come regardless," Finn said.

The others got up from the table, and King looked over to Finn.

"Leave your clothes here."

He gathered them, folding neatly, running his hands along the fabric one time. It might be the last he was given the opportunity to touch that fabric, feel the softness of it, and feel as if he were able to be a part of something different.

Once he went out into the night wearing his darks, he became something he'd left behind. He rejoined the crew. Finn didn't know if it was anything that he could come back from.

He felt as if he were squeezed regardless of what he chose.

If he were caught now, he would hang.

If he stayed with Meyer, he would hang.

At least this way, he might be able to help his crew.

They left the tavern.

Night had fallen in full, and there was a gusting wind that continued to pick up, kicking around them. As the wind whipped around, Finn wrapped his arms around himself. He wished for a cloak, something warmer than what he wore.

None of the others seemed bothered by it. They hurried off, heading into the darkness, making their way toward the center of the city.

Rock came over to him, and he looked over at Finn. "What did you tell the executioner?"

"Nothing."

"And them?" he asked, nodding to the King.

"I told them you did what the King always tells us to do. You protected the crew."

Rock clasped him on the shoulder. "I'm sorry I doubted you, Shuffles. It's good you're back. They tried to tell me… I suppose it don't matter no more."

Finn just nodded. He wasn't about to tell Rock what would have happened had Rock not escaped. That would have been the real betrayal of their friendship.

In the distance, a bell tolled, ringing softly into the night.

Finn counted, trying to determine which church the bell rang from. Maybe if it came from one of the churches celebrating the gods that would favor them, Finn wouldn't have to be nearly as concerned about what they were doing and where they were going.

It seemed to come from Heleth. He didn't know whether or not that meant they were favored by the Blessed Mother. Most likely not.

When they reached the bridge leading over the river, Finn looked along the water. From there, it wouldn't be that far for him to make his way toward Meyer's home. His sister was there, as was his mother.

Neither of them had any idea about what he was doing. What he had planned.

Finn didn't even know what he had planned. Whatever he did would have to ensure that his family survived. Finn was determined to make sure that they were able to get through this.

On the far side of the river, he paused, looking back.

The others kept moving, and only Oscar lingered, slowing long enough to watch Finn. Finn flashed him a forced smile and continued to run after him.

As the night continued to fall around them, there were fewer people out. Part of that came from how they moved closer to the center of the city. From here, Finn would need to move more carefully.

They couldn't simply approach the palace directly. They would have to find a way to come at it indirectly. The Archers would be standing guard, watching.

The King signaled for them to slow.

Finn paused behind Oscar, listening.

"The Client is going to meet us near here," the King said.

"And if he doesn't?" Oscar asked.

"He will," he said.

Finn sensed the irritation from within Oscar. He tried to conceal it, though Finn thought he recognized the frustration. It was in the way he kept his shoulders tensed and the way he flicked his gaze from the King to Wolf.

"Can you believe it?" Scruff asked, leaning close to Finn. "We do this, and we get five silver drebs."

Finn looked over to him. How much had he promised to the others?

The King either was telling the others whatever they wanted to hear, or he'd promised Finn a windfall that he wasn't going to be able to deliver upon.

Could the King betray them?

Finn wouldn't have thought him willing to do so, but the jobs *had* been going sideways.

"That's right. Five whole drebs for this job," Finn said as he looked toward the end of the street where a dark figure moved.

At first, Finn worried that it was one of the Archers, but the way they moved was wrong for the Archers. They stayed in the shadows, away from the center street. Darkness seemed to swirl around them, almost as if it swallowed them.

"Here he comes," the King.

"Who is it?" Scruff asked.

"We don't talk about that," Wolf said.

"He's got to have a name. What am I supposed to call him?"

"You're supposed to call him the Client," the King said.

The man stopped, and he waited until the King approached him.

They spoke softly, but then the man turned, heading away.

The King turned to the others and motioned for them to follow.

Oscar tapped Finn on the arm. "Now is the time you could refuse this. You don't need to have anything to do with this job."

Finn looked at the Client. His darks seemed to somehow prevent the streetlight from getting too close to him. It was almost as if they shielded him.

An idea started to form.

There *might* be a way for him to protect the crew—and satisfy the testing.

If it worked, *he* wouldn't have to hang. Maybe Rock could be saved, too.

Finn didn't have any particular allegiance to the Client.

If he could figure out who it was, it might even erase the King's debt.

How could he get to the Client, though?

"What do you know about the hegen?"

Oscar tensed and didn't look over. "I know the same as anyone, I suppose. Magic users. Kept outside of the city. The king tolerates them."

"I told you that Lena got involved with them."

"You did. But you also got her back."

Finn took a deep breath, letting it out slowly. "I did, but I… well, I went to the hegen, looking for help getting her back."

Oscar grabbed his arm. "You did *what?*"

"I knew that she was caught up in something that she wasn't going to be able to escape them on her own. I went to the hegen to see if there was anything that I might be able to do to get her back."

"What did you promise them?"

"I didn't promise them anything."

"That's not how it works, Finn."

Finn reached into his pocket, fingering the card. Even in his pocket, he could imagine the outline of a hand on it, and he looked over to Oscar. Did the bloody hand mean that he was going to somehow have to betray Oscar?

Finn couldn't betray Oscar. Not even to pay the price the hegen would ask of him.

"We'll have to talk about this later," Finn said. Oscar reached for his arm, but Finn shook him away. "Right now, we need to keep up with the others."

When they reached the end of the street, Finn could

see the palace in the distance. The King and the Client spoke softly, with the Client motioning down one of the side streets.

What if he called out to the Archers?

It would betray the crew, and though Finn *might* be able to capture the Client, they didn't have the necessary proof needed. Meyer would need proof.

And the King would stop him. Wolf. Maybe even Rock.

There would have to be a different way.

The King came over to them and leaned close. "We're going to split up. Wolf, Scruff, and the Hand are going that way," he said, motioning along the street. "Make sure it's clear." He looked to Wolf, and something passed between them. "You know the plan. I'm taking Rock and Shuffles with me."

"What about the Client?" Oscar said.

"He's going to keep watch," the King said.

"I thought he was coming with us."

"He's coming with us, but he's not coming all the way with us. That's why we were hired."

Oscar glowered at the Client. "You're going to trust the Client to keep watch?"

"He knows the signals. That's the hardest part of it."

It wasn't all there was to it, and the King knew it.

Finn looked over at the Client, studying him.

He couldn't see anything about him. With his hood up, his face was concealed, even his eyes difficult to see. He was too thin to be the fat juror. Maybe the Archer Finn had seen the King talking to?

Calling the Archers wouldn't help if that were the case.

"What are we going in after?" Finn turned his attention to the Client.

The man barely turned toward him. "Is this how all of your jobs go?"

There was something about the Client's voice that seemed familiar to Finn.

"This one is special, but don't worry. We're going to do the job," the King said. "Come on."

He motioned to Rock, and he started off down the street, moving closer to the wall, getting beneath the shadows of it.

There weren't any Archers on this section of the wall. That seemed strange.

The King tapped Finn on the arm, signaling for him to keep moving as well. The Client backed up along the street, retreating into the darkness until Finn could barely see him.

"Where do you want us to cross?" Rock asked.

Finn turned his attention back to the King, who guided them along the wall's inner aspect. He didn't see any of the Archers atop the wall from where they stood, which gave him hope that they wouldn't be able to see them, either.

"Keep moving, and I'll show you," the King said.

Another bell rang out. The sound was sudden, a gentle pealing of the bell. Finn still looked up, feeling startled by it.

"You're jumpy," the King said.

"I can't help it."

"There's nothing you need to be concerned about."

"Other than risking ourselves breaking into the palace?" he whispered.

The King chuckled. "Other than that. We're not going to get caught."

"How do you know?" Finn looked over to Rock. "He's already got the notice of the Archers."

"And a sentence. So, doing this don't matter. Not to you, either."

Finn frowned at him. "What's that supposed to mean?"

"You don't do this, you go back to your new master. Considering how you've already failed what they asked of you, you're not going to find the reception you want. You'll end up back on the gallows."

Finn stared at the King. He knew.

That shouldn't surprise him, but for some reason, it still did.

"Did you tell him?" the King asked, keeping his voice low.

"Tell him what?" Rock said.

The King smiled tightly. "Ask Shuffles why he's here."

Finn's stomach sank.

The King nodded to him. "No going back now, Shuffles."

Rock watched Finn, but he didn't say anything.

"What about the Archers?" Finn finally asked, needing to break the tension.

"You let Wolf and the Hand worry about that while they take care of their assignment."

Finn looked behind him. That was where they'd gone. They were going to distract the Archers, but what else?

"Who's getting betrayed on this job?" Finn asked. The King didn't answer. "It's been Rock and me. Who gets to suffer this time, King?"

A whistle split the night, and the King looked up. "Time to move."

He pushed them toward the wall and pulled a rope and hook from under his cloak. He tossed it, catching the hook atop the wall, and nodded to Rock.

"You first, Rock. Clean up the other side."

Rock grabbed the rope before starting up it.

When he reached the top of the wall, he crouched a moment before jumping down to the other side.

"Now you, Shuffles."

Finn glanced along the street before taking the rope.

He started to climb.

When he was partway up the wall, he paused and looked around him.

It was too late to back out.

Finishing the climb, he reached the top of the wall and crouched down, looking around him. From there, he scanned the top of the wall, looking for Archers. There would have to have been some up there. When he'd come close before, he'd seen Archers patrolling regularly. There weren't any.

Down in the garden on the other side of the yard, he didn't find any, either.

Finn held onto the wall, then dropped.

Rock was there and grabbed him.

Finn jerked back.

"What was the King talking about?" Rock asked.

Finn looked up. The King hadn't reached the top of the wall. When he looked back to Rock, Finn knew he had to tell him. This was his friend. "Meyer wanted me to be the one to hang you. I couldn't do it."

Rock watched him. "Because I got out. What would you have done had I not?"

"I couldn't do it," Finn said.

Rock opened his mouth to say something more, but the King reached the top of the wall and then jumped back down.

Finn had wondered if he were even going to join them. There was some part of him that had been concerned that the King would have stayed on the other side of the wall, leaving him and Rock to get pinched.

When the King came toward them, he motioned to follow. "Now we move quickly."

They hurried through the garden. The garden looked different at night from how it had during the day. In the daylight, there was the path they'd taken that led straight toward the main entrance of the palace. At night, they weaved through the plantings, around trees that created more shadows, and used them to shield them from anyone seeing their approach. Through it all, the massive palace loomed in front of them.

The King led their approach. Any concern Finn might have had about the King avoiding the risk in the job was mitigated by how willing he was to guide them. Were they to be caught, the King would face the same fate. Though he'd done the same at the viscount's home.

The King raised his hand, motioning them to stop.

"We need to wait," he whispered.

Rock nodded, and Finn used the pause as a chance to look around him.

There hadn't been any sign of the Archers in the garden. None on the wall. They weren't there. The King wouldn't have been able to manipulate things so well as to prevent the Archers from coming for them.

He turned his attention back to the King. Another soft whistle split the night.

The King held his hand up, motioning for them to wait.

Rock looked over at Finn, a question in his eyes.

The King motioned for them to follow.

They stayed along a row of shrubs, and as they went, the palace grew increasingly closer, looming overhead. Almost as if it pressed upon him. Finn slowed before realizing what he was doing. He hurried forward until they were right in front of it. Enormous windows lined the front of the palace, spaced evenly along the length of it. He couldn't even see the top of it up close, but he felt the dampness coming from the stone. The scent of earth and stone there was almost too much.

The King paused, considering the windows, and it seemed as if he were counting them. He moved off to the left, reaching one of the windows and grabbing at it. It came open without a sound.

The King pointed to Rock. "Get moving."

"Where do we go when we're inside?"

"I'll show you."

Rock nodded, and he climbed into the window, disappearing.

The King turned to Finn. "Your turn, Shuffles."

Finn held the King's gaze a moment, then he climbed into the window.

He looked around. Faint light filled the room from two lanterns on either wall. They were dim but bright enough in the darkness for Finn to see where he was. He quickly looked for anyone else in the room, but other than Rock, it was empty.

It was a massive room. A thick, plush carpet covered the floor. An enormous hearth occupied one wall. Luxurious high-backed leather chairs angled near it, with a finely made wooden table resting between them. Shelves lined one wall, books filling the shelves. A few sculptures took up space on the shelves as well.

The King climbed into the window after them.

"Let's get moving," the King said.

"What are you taking from here?"

"Not from here," the King said.

"Then where?"

"The second level."

"Why?" Finn asked, worry creeping into his voice.

"Because that's where we're going."

The King guided them through the room, to the heavy oak door, and pushed it open just a little bit. There was a movement in the hallway, and the King lingered there for a moment, the door barely cracked but enough that Finn was able to make out the sound of boots across the slick tile.

Archers.

"We're not going to be able to get past them," Finn whispered, leaning close to him.

"Just wait," the King said.

The boots continued to thunder across the tile, the sound loud in the silence of the palace.

Finally, they began to fade, growing ever more distant.

The King nodded to them.

"Get moving," he whispered to Rock. "You know your task."

The large man studied the King for a moment before stepping out into the hall.

Shouts rang out.

The King stepped back, moving away from the wall.

"You sent him out there to be captured?"

"I didn't send him out there to be anything," the King said.

Finn studied his reaction. There was something *off* about it. He wasn't telling the truth. The King had anticipated this. Gods, he'd probably used Rock this way on purpose.

The same way he'd use Finn.

That was all he was. Maybe that was all he'd *ever* been.

The sound outside of the hall died down, and the King turned to the door, pushing it open a crack. He lingered there for a moment, looking out, and when he was satisfied, he slipped out of the door, and Finn had no choice but to follow.

The hallway was as he remembered it. Gleaming white marble stretched out in front of him. A row of doors lined the hall, but the King didn't lead him to any of the doors. Instead, he hurried along the hall until they reached the stair leading up.

The King glanced back at him before heading up.

At the top of the stair, Finn paused.

There was movement, though he couldn't see it clearly. He could hear it. Voices.

One voice came distantly but close enough that Finn could hear it clearly. "Let Porman know we've got it controlled."

A cold sweat worked across his skin as he started to suspect the reason the job had to be done tonight.

King Porman was inside the palace.

CHAPTER TWENTY-FIVE

Finn grabbed for the King's arm, pulling him back toward the stairs.

The King glared at him a moment before pulling free and leaning forward. If he had leaned out any farther, he would have been seen.

"What are you doing?" Finn hissed. "Didn't you hear what they said?"

"I heard. It doesn't matter. We'll complete the job and—"

The sound of boots along the tile came to him, louder than they had been before. They were close. Archers. Not just any Archers, either. These would be palace Archers.

"We do this, and we end up caught. You know what will happen then," Finn said.

The King frowned at him, glowering for a moment. "You know the price."

Finn started to turn. He might still be able to slip out

of the palace, back through the window, and escape before the Archers caught up to them. If he moved quickly, he had to think he could get back into the yard and find another way out. This wasn't how he was going to fail.

"You leave, and I'll make sure your sister and mother suffer."

The King hadn't spoken loudly, but the words cut through the quiet.

Finn turned to him. In the time that he'd been working with the King, there had been subtle threats made to others, but never to anyone on the crew. Never anything overt like this.

The King stared at him. The darkness in his eyes told Finn everything that he needed to know. The short time he'd spent with Meyer had shown him men like this. He'd seen the lies and the truths.

This was a truth.

The King *would* do exactly as he promised. If Finn didn't help him, his family would suffer, regardless of whether they were safely at Meyer's home.

But then, they wouldn't be safely at Meyer's home if he didn't get back out of there and finish his testing. Were he to fail, Meyer would find the end of the sword—he'd get an honorable death, unlike Finn and the others. Which meant that Finn's family would be left behind.

He had thought he could somehow work this to his advantage by capturing the Client, but he might have to find another way.

Buy time.

"Before I do anything, you need to tell me exactly what we're after. What's so valuable to the Client?"

The King breathed out heavily. "It's a carved wooden staff."

Not a bowl this time? A staff was just as ridiculous, though.

"We're in King Porman's palace. Some of the crown jewels are stored here. And we're after a staff?"

"Why do you think I haven't told you before?"

"Because it's ridiculous." He looked around, realizing that he'd raised his voice more than what he had intended. There wasn't anyone near him, but that didn't mean there wouldn't be someone coming. *How long did we have before someone appeared?* There were Archers near them. The boots on the tile sounded far too close to be anything else. "A staff isn't worth what you've claimed he's paying. Unless he's not paying that."

"Oh, he is," the King said.

"Are you sure?"

"We've been paid for every job before this."

"How much did he offer?"

"I told you—"

"How much?" Finn stood in the middle of the stairs, realizing how exposed he was. He should get moving, but until he knew what the King intended, he didn't intend to do so.

"A hundred crowns."

Finn squeezed his eyes shut for a moment. "A *hundred* crowns?" And here the King had offered him five. That was still an enormous amount. Five crowns was more than he would make working with Meyer for years.

"That's why we're doing this, Shuffles."

"There's no way he's paying that much."

Voices started to get closer. They weren't going to be able to stay there much longer. Finn worried about what would happen were he to linger beyond what he already had.

"I've told you what he's willing to pay."

A carved staff.

What the Client had hired them to collect was incredibly strange. They weren't the kinds of jobs the crew normally did, but any job that paid what the Client had been willing to pay was worthwhile.

Was it worthwhile for *him*?

Finn already knew the answer. He'd been willing to break into the viscount's manor to steal enough for his family. To protect them.

He needed time to figure out how he would continue to protect them.

The only way to do it was to keep going.

"Fine. Let's get moving. Where would this staff be found?"

"That's the only other thing the Client told me. It's in the library. That's where we need to head."

Finn frowned. *Why would a staff be found in the library?*

There was just so much that was strange about the entire job that he didn't think questioning it anymore made sense.

"And the library is on the second level."

"This one is," the King said.

The second level, where King Porman was in residence. Archers would be guarding him. Death would follow if they were caught.

Finn sighed. They might as well get moving.

The King lingered for a moment, watching him. It seemed as if he weren't sure what Finn would do.

For that matter, Finn wasn't sure what he was going to do.

When the King started up the stairs, pausing at the landing, Finn followed him, staying close behind him. The sound of voices was more distant.

Could that mean that the Archers had gone somewhere else?

Rock had drawn some of the Archers away.

What had Oscar and Wolf done?

They would have been a part of it as well.

Finn had to think that Oscar would have been far more skilled at sneaking through the palace. This was the kind of thing the Hand was made for.

Why wouldn't they have involved him in this aspect of the job?

The King motioned for Finn to follow.

He stepped forward, his heart seeming to stop.

Moving forward like this put them out in the open, and Finn worried that he was far too exposed. There was no one else out in the hallway. No movement. No Archers.

The King guided him along the hall, and he seemed to be counting the doors before pausing in front of a set of double doors. He rested his hand on the handle for a moment.

Voices behind them caught Finn's attention, and he pushed on the King's back.

The King threw the door open and hurried into the other room. Finn followed him, stepping inside the room quickly, and the King closed the door behind him.

Once inside, Finn looked around. It was a library, much like the King had claimed they would find.

It was not quite like what he had expected. When Finn thought of libraries, he thought of vast, massive structures filled with dusty books and faded tables such as those found within many churches. This wasn't anything like that.

It was a single story. Shelves lined the walls. Books filled all of the shelves. A single table and a leather chair that could have been the twin of the two that he'd seen in the room they'd entered occupied the center of the room.

Finn turned in place, looking all around the shelves. He didn't see any sign of a carved wooden staff.

"There isn't anything here," Finn said.

"This was where we were told to find it," the King said.

A hint of irritation entered his voice.

Was the King now saying the Client couldn't be trusted?

He leaned up against the door, cracking it slightly.

Voices along the hallway caught his attention, though he couldn't hear what they were saying. They were muted, but he had a sense of something from within them.

Irritation. Agitation.

They were looking for something.

Gods, they had to be looking for *them*.

Maybe Rock had been captured and had revealed that there were others within the palace.

The King continued to look around the inside of the room, searching the shelves.

Finn wanted to tell him that there was nothing to find but had a sense the King was agitated because they were not going to find anything.

All of this for a carved wooden staff that wasn't even going to be there?

He leaned on the door for a moment. "We're going to have to find a way out of here," Finn said.

"Not until I find the item."

"The item isn't here," Finn said. "The Client sent you here for nothing."

The King turned to him, anger flashing in his eyes. "It's something, and we're going to find it, so you had better start helping me look, Shuffles."

There was a different edge to his voice.

Not just anger, but could there be worry?

The King had debt. Just how much? Enough to take an impossible job. Enough to bring others in on it. Enough to betray the crew.

"Where do you expect me to help you find it?"

"I expect—"

Voices came from the other side of the door.

Someone was near.

Finn held his hand on the door, pushing it closed.

He motioned to the King, silencing him.

The King joined him at the door. They both took up places on either side of the double doors. If nothing else, were the doors to open, they might be able to hide behind them if Archers came in.

The doors opened.

Finn couldn't see anything.

He held his breath, waiting.

The doors remained open for a moment. Then another. Then another.

Nothing moved.

He remained motionless, waiting.

Finally, the doors pulled closed again.

He let his breath out, and the King moved to stand in front of the doors. He pulled one open slightly, little more than a crack, and he peered out.

Finn wanted to pull him back, but there was no point in it. The King was going to do what he wanted.

Finn took the opportunity to search the inside of the library.

A carved wooden staff.

He didn't see anything on shelves other than books.

He paused at the chair, looking it over, but it was a leather-bound, high-backed chair. Nothing more than that. He checked the table and didn't see anything there, either.

Finally, he turned to look overhead.

Not that Finn expected to see anything overhead.

Beams crossed the ceiling, though there *was* something else there.

"What's that?" Finn whispered.

The King turned, frowning. "What?"

Finn pointed overhead. "That?"

The King looked up. A hint of a smile began to curl his lips.

He hurried to the chair, standing on it. "Hold it so that it doesn't tip over," the King said.

Finn leaned on the seat of the chair. The King climbed up to the top of the high back, and he reached up. A length of wood crossed over the beams, as if joining them in some way.

The King pulled it down, a sharp *crack* echoing in the small room, before climbing back down from the top of the chair and standing next to Finn.

"This has to be it," King said.

Finn looked down at the length of wood. There were carvings on it. Symbols that looked to be some sort of writing that he couldn't read. The wood itself was a strange color and texture. It was as long as one of Finn's legs and about as thick as his forearm. It seemed to twist, spiraling around, though Finn couldn't tell if that was the wood's shape or some aspect of the carving. It could be either.

"This is worth one hundred crowns?" Finn asked, tracing his hand along the surface before looking up, another question lingering in his eyes as he looked at the King.

"We'd better hope so," the King said.

He scanned the ceiling, and Finn followed the direction of his gaze. There was nothing else within the room.

That *had* to be the staff. It certainly was carved and made of wood, but he still couldn't believe that it would be as valuable as what the Client offered to pay for it.

Now that they had the staff, the key was going to be getting out of there.

Finn left the King with the staff and pulled on the door.

Voices and footsteps were in the hall. Which meant Archers were in the hall.

Finn looked over to the King. "We aren't going to get out of here without a distraction."

The King watched him. "I know."

He intended it to be him.

Of course he did. That had been why Rock had come too.

"Getting in was only a part of the challenge," the King said.

"You used the crew as a diversion. You've *always* used the crew as a diversion."

"You aren't in the crew. Not since he claimed you."

"What about Rock? That's why you sprung him from Declan?" He was curious about how the King had managed to do that. It shouldn't have been possible for him to get out of Declan so easily. The prison was well guarded, though Oscar *had* come in and visited Finn.

"Rock knew his purpose."

Finn grunted. "That's why you were so adamant I come all the way up here with you. You needed someone to distract the Archers."

"Assuming we found it, yes. That was Pegg's mistake. He wanted to protect his crew. He didn't want them to risk themselves." The King shrugged. "Now it's your turn to prove what you can do for the crew. No more games. Can your new connections keep you safe?"

Finn doubted the Archers would let him out of this one.

He shook his head. "This was never about just the crew."

"You get this done, and you've got my protection."

"I don't care about your protection. I want a cut."

"I told you I'd pay—"

Finn shook his head. "This kind of a job is worth more than five crowns. Much more. I do this, *and* I escape"— which he knew was unlikely, but he wanted to be prepared for the possibility that he might—"and I get an even cut."

Finn didn't know if that would leave enough to settle whatever debt the King owed, but suspected it wasn't the money so much as the job the Client needed done.

The King studied him a moment. "Fine. We get through this, then you get an even cut."

If they got through it. Finn knew that was the hardest part at this point.

He leaned on the door. He would have to serve as the distraction.

Get into the hall. Draw the Archers off. Make a run.

Then what?

Were he to get out, he'd have to find a way to get off the grounds. He wouldn't have the King's rope. No way for him to scale the wall. There might not be a way for him to escape the grounds without it.

"Time to get moving, Shuffles."

Finn grunted. "We get through this, and I get a better name," he muttered.

"What kind of name do you want?"

Finn shook his head. "I don't know. Anything is better than Shuffles."

The sounds along the hall had grown more distant. Muted, even.

He pulled open the door and headed into the hall.

Finn remained there a moment and raced toward the stairs.

A shout rang out behind him.

He didn't wait.

He was the distraction.

He ran.

Racing down the stairs, he reached the main level and looked the way they'd come, only to find several Archers coming toward him. The other way was free.

That didn't give him a choice. He turned and headed that way.

It led toward the main entrance of the palace.

That would be a mistake.

When he reached the next door along the hall, he pushed it open and stepped inside.

A sitting room. Several chairs. A leather bench. A few lanterns. Paintings hung on the walls. A bowl in the middle of the floor. And a window.

Finn reached the window.

A bowl.

Why would it be there?

He paused, spinning back, and grabbed the bowl, stuffing it into his pocket.

Something still wasn't right.

Racing to the window, sweat slicked his palms. His heart pounded. Finn struggled to open it.

It reminded him of the job at the viscount's home. He shouldn't even have been in the home that time, and his getting caught was because he'd gone after Oscar. This time, he didn't know if Oscar was even in the palace. That might have been more distracting.

The door started to open.

Finn pulled on the window.

It came free with a soft scream.

Finn pulled it all the way open and started to climb through.

An Archer raced toward, reaching for him. Finn jerked free of the Archer's grip and dove through the window. He rolled forward in the grass, tumbling away from the palace.

Then he sprang to his feet and ran.

Archers chased him out of the open window.

He had to stay ahead of them. He could hear the sound of their boots on the hard ground, along with their heavy breathing as they chased.

Finn ran. When he neared the familiar section of the garden where they'd come in, he glanced in either direction but decided to move straight ahead. He had to reach the wall. Then he could work on climbing it.

Archers in the distance caught his attention. They

were coming toward him from both directions along the road.

Finn wasn't going to be able to outrun them.

A whistle came.

It was soft. Once. Twice.

A warning.

Finn turned toward it. Probably not the King, but maybe it was Wolf or Oscar. Gods, it could even be Rock, if he'd managed to escape himself. He would take any of them at this point.

The wall loomed into view as a shadowed form stretching fifteen feet overhead. Far too high for him to easily climb.

When he reached the wall, he raced along the inside of it. The sense of movement came from all around him, Archers following him, but he ignored that and continued on as quickly as he could.

Where would he try to climb?

He didn't see a place.

Maybe he'd find one of the crew and could get help, but the whistling didn't come again. Finn was certain that he'd heard it, so there had to be others of the crew out there, only where had they gone?

There wasn't a sign of anyone else.

There had to be some place for him to cross, though there wouldn't be another gate.

Finn continued racing forward, keeping his gaze searching all around him, trying to uncover how he might be able to get out of there. The Archers were near him. He could feel the sense of them nearby, close enough that he recognized the sound of their boots, and every so often, Finn heard a shout come from behind him. As long as he stayed ahead of them, he might be able to escape.

He started to circle around the entirety of the palace garden.

If he were to do that, then he would end up right back where he had started, and Finn worried that doing so would only end up with his capture.

He reached a place behind the palace. From there, Finn noticed a grove of trees.

He hadn't circled around behind the palace before, though there had been no reason for him to do so. The palace was situated in the center of the city, and the wall surrounding it made it so that he wouldn't have been able to see anything on the inside of the palace grounds anyway.

He reached one of the trees.

The sound of the Archers chasing him persisted. He had managed to stay ahead of them so far, though Finn doubted he would be able to keep ahead of them for much longer.

Eventually, the Archers would catch him.

He was getting tired.

Finn ran through the trees, and as he did, he caught sight of one with a branch looming close to the ground. He jumped for it.

Finn scrambled, trying to get a little higher. An Archer reached the tree. Another one came into view below him as well.

Finn climbed.

He moved as quickly as he could, getting higher into the tree, high enough that he thought that he might be able to get up and over the wall, but it would involve jumping, risking himself.

Finn scrambled higher into the tree.

One of the Archers started to climb after him.

Finn got a little bit higher… and then he saw his way out. He knew what he had to do.

He scrambled out onto the branch and worked his way as far and as fast as he could. When he reached the end of the branch, the top of the wall loomed into view.

This was his chance.

Finn glanced behind him. The Archers were coming toward him. He didn't hesitate any longer. He dropped.

It was a far drop from where he was, but he landed on top of the wall, and he almost slipped back into the yard.

Finn caught himself, scrambling back to the top of the wall. When he was up to the top of it, he glanced back to see the Archers trying to work their way along the branch.

They only had to jump, and they would be able to reach him.

Finn had to move quickly. Archers were heading toward him along the wall as well. He was going to get pinned in.

Moving forward, he hung from the wall, dangling for a moment, then dropped. He rolled his ankle but ignored the pain shooting through it.

The Archers shouted after him, but he ignored them as well.

Finn ran as quickly as he could, getting farther into the

surrounding streets and then into the shadows where his darks would hide him. If only they would conceal him completely. Finn didn't know if they would mask him as well as he needed them to.

He ducked along one of the streets and then slipped into an alley.

It wasn't an alley he was familiar with, though he thought he knew where it would lead. He moved along the alley as quickly as he could, following the twisting and turning, before it paused at another street outlet.

From there, he waited.

Four Archers marched along the street. They came from the palace.

Staying in the shadows of the alley, Finn managed to avoid detection. He could see them disappearing into the darkness. He breathed out a sigh of relief.

He'd escaped. *What of the others in the crew?*

He waited in the alley for a little while longer before making his way along the street. From there, Finn needed to find where the rest of the crew had gone. He didn't know if they would meet up anywhere, though he suspected the King had something in mind.

Finn moved as cautiously as he could along the street. He caught sight of a couple more Archers, though they were in the distance, moving away from him.

There was no one else out in the night.

He followed the alleys and the streets until he reached the section of the city where they had entered. Once there, Finn waited.

He was willing to wait as long as it would take to see

whether the others had made it out safely. His distraction hopefully had been enough for the King, but what about Wolf? What of Oscar? Even Rock?

While he was waiting, a shadowed figure moved along the street. At first, Finn thought it was an Archer, but something about it was off.

As he watched the figure making his way toward him, Finn didn't think it was one of the Archers.

He didn't know *who* came toward him.

Another figure appeared, carrying a long cane.

Not a cane. A staff.

The staff.

The King.

He headed straight toward the shadowed figure.

The Client. It had to be.

From the other end of the street, Finn noticed another person coming toward them. They were moving quickly, staying near the shadows, and only when they got close could he tell it was Wolf.

Where was Oscar?

Finn thought about moving forward, but he didn't want to reveal himself yet.

"Did you do it?" The soft voice of the Client barely carried in the darkness.

"Got it. Wolf took care of placing the rest. And I did what you told me. It took a bit of work. Can't say anything happened."

"It takes time," the Client said.

"We didn't have time."

"You didn't need it. You knew it would require sacrifice on your part. The reward is worth the risk. With these items you've placed, and now with this," he said, taking the staff, "the plan will come to fruition. And *they* will be blamed."

"I didn't care about any of that."

"Of course you did," the Client said. "Had you not, you know what would happen."

"I know what you plan," the King said. "And I don't care. Let the fucking Alainsith attack for all I care. I just want to make sure my debt is erased." The King held out his hand. "Oh, and the payment."

"As we agreed." The Client reached into his pocket and pulled a pouch out, holding it out for the King.

They swapped quickly.

The Client studied the staff, tracing his fingers along the surface. It practically seemed to glow in the moonlight.

The King nodded to Wolf, and they turned, heading down the street.

Finn waited where he was for a moment. Had he not, he would have missed what happened next. The Client stopped near the shadows, practically disappearing, and whistled softly.

Three Archers appeared out of the darkness.

They went straight toward the King and Wolf.

The Client intended to betray them.

Finn wanted to see what happened next. Not that there was any question about it.

He turned and raced through the alley. He might be able to get ahead of them.

When he reached the end of the alley, opening up onto the opposite street, he paused and looked out. The King and Wolf slipped along the street—but so did the Archers, creeping behind them.

Finn could wait. They would reach him, and he could lead them through the alley and to safety. Another figure stepped forward.

It took Finn a moment before he recognized it.

Oscar.

He started toward the King and Wolf. Toward the Archers.

He would get caught.

The card.

What if the hegen card had not wanted him to betray Oscar but was a warning?

Finn darted forward across the street. The King looked toward him, but Finn ignored him. Instead, he reached Oscar.

"You've got to get away," Finn said.

Oscar looked at him. "Did he get it?"

Finn frowned. "He got it. I'm not sure what he wanted with the staff."

"Not just the staff," Oscar said. "Wolf was placing the bowls we'd stolen. There were seven of them. I managed to grab five, but two were missing."

"You got them *after* Wolf placed them?"

Oscar shrugged.

"Damn," he whispered. "You really *are* the Hand." Finn pulled the other bowl from his pocket. It was slick and warm and had small symbols engraved on its surface. "I took this on my way out. I don't know what happened to the last one."

Oscar swiped it and stuffed the bowl into his cloak. "You did good, Shuffles."

There was more going on here than Finn knew.

But there would be time to figure that out. Later.

First they had to escape.

Footsteps thundered toward them. The sound of the Archers coming.

"Go!" Finn said.

"Finn—"

They didn't have time to argue.

Finn pulled the hegen card from his pocket and shoved it toward Oscar. "This is going to be you if you don't go!"

Oscar took the card, his gaze flicking from it to Finn's face.

"You shouldn't do this."

"Dammit, Oscar! I'm not doing anything. Just go!"

Oscar spun and darted off, quickly disappearing into the darkness.

The Archers reached the King and Wolf. Both of them fought, but the Archers were stronger and armed with swords. The fight did not last long.

One of the Archers noticed Finn and started toward him.

He took a deep breath. Though he might be dressed in darks, he could be the executioner's apprentice. That would get him out of this.

The Archer reached him. "You are out past—"

Finn nodded curtly, cutting him off before he had a

chance to get settled. "Good evening. I'm Finn Jagger, apprenticed to Henry Meyer, executioner in service to King Porman."

The Archer regarded him.

"I'm on the official business of Master Meyer."

"Is that so."

He glanced behind Finn. *Had he seen Oscar?* It didn't matter. All that mattered was that Finn keep his attention.

"It's regarding the escaped prisoner Luca Grobbe. Master Meyer wanted me to check known locations for him, as he hasn't been seen since his escape from Declan Prison."

Finn hoped it was enough to convince him. And that they didn't fully serve the Client since he still didn't know who it was, only that he had connections. *This* was how he needed to use his connection to Meyer.

One of the other Archers approached. Two others remained standing guard with a sword stretched toward the King and Wolf, who watched Finn.

"Says he serves the hangman."

The other Archer studied him. "Hangman *does* have a new apprentice."

"That's what I heard. Look how he's dressed, though. Like them." He motioned toward Wolf and the King.

"I'm working on a job for Master Meyer and under-cover," Finn said hurriedly. It might work to explain his clothing.

"Claims he's looking for Luca Grobbe."

"Also known as Rock," Finn added.

The new Archer grunted. "Seems as if he's telling the truth."

"You don't think we should bring him in?"

"And do what? Let them know we've caught the hangman's help?" He shook his head. "These two will be enough." He nodded to Finn. "Tell the hangman he's been recaptured. And his associates."

Finn nodded and turned. He glanced toward the King and Wolf. He might be able to say something to free them, but the King had been willing to sacrifice him. And he *had* sacrificed Rock.

"Looks like we'll be busy tomorrow," Finn said to the Archers.

As he headed along the street, the King called after him. "Don't you leave us, Shuffles! You know what happens if you do!"

Finn ignored him, disappearing into the night.

CHAPTER TWENTY-SIX

Finn spent the night wandering the city.

The King and Wolf were captured by Archers. Rock, too. Finn had no idea what had happened to Scruff, though considering he hadn't come with Wolf—and neither had Oscar—Finn suspected what had happened. The only ones who'd gotten away from the Archers had been Oscar and Finn.

And the Client.

The Client had never intended the crew to succeed. Maybe he never had. Pull a job, do whatever he intended with those bowls, claim what was stolen, and have someone to accuse. It would make for a tidy crime.

Whoever it was had some pull with the Archers, enough to send them after the crew. Finn doubted the Client was the reason he'd been caught in the first place— that had been his own mistake—but the Client had to have been the reason Pegg's crew had failed.

It was also tied to the Alainsith, though all of that was beyond Finn's ability to understand. Meyer would likely tell him that it wasn't his responsibility to understand.

His responsibility was justice.

And how could I serve justice if the Client were still out there?

By the time dawn had started to work through the city, Finn still didn't know what to make of what had happened. He headed back toward Meyer's home. It was time to return.

The garden greeted him with the scent of the flowers and the sight of a stack of fresh pumpkins. Finn passed through the garden, exhaustion working through him, and headed inside. The home was quiet, and he moved as silently as he could into his small room, where he rested his head, lying down for what seemed a moment.

A hand on his shoulder awoke him.

When he came awake, he looked over to see Meyer standing over him. Dressed in his gray leathers, a dark, almost angry expression crossed his eyes. "Explain."

Finn took a moment to get his mind working. How long had he been sleeping? Not long enough for him to feel rested. Not nearly enough.

"Explain what?"

As he sat up, he realized he'd lain down in the darks.

Which meant one set of his clothing was still at the Wenderwolf.

He should have gone back for it, but with the entire crew getting pinched, he hadn't wanted to return there, regardless of how much he might like Annie.

"Explain. It had better be believable."

Finn looked up at Meyer. He wouldn't be able to deceive him. Meyer would be able to tell if he tried. "My crew was in danger."

"Which meant you had to take a job?"

Finn got to his feet, rubbing his eyes. He didn't like sitting, having Meyer staring down at him. It felt too much like he was being questioned. At least on his feet, he could feel as if he were on equal footing as Meyer.

"That wasn't why I had to take a job."

"Then why?"

Finn looked up. "Because I failed you. I was going to die anyway. I thought I could help them."

Meyer cocked his head to the side. "You failed me how?"

Finn waved his hand. "With the testing. With what you expect of me. With all of it."

"Why would you think you failed me?"

"Because I was at the Executioner Court. I couldn't answer most of those questions. I got some of them right, but the longer they questioned me, the less I knew. I failed you. Then Rock got away, and there was nothing I could do about it."

"Failure isn't a reason to run."

"I didn't run."

"You took a job."

"To protect my crew. My family." Finn met his eyes, trying to be as defiant as he could but not certain he did a good job. "You risked yourself for me. I understand that." Finn closed his eyes. He wasn't going to tell Meyer about the hegen. He might know already, but this was something he *would* keep from him. "But you wouldn't have been able to protect my family if we were both dead."

Meyer said nothing for a few moments. Finally, he frowned at Finn. "Your sister and mother have already been provided for. And we would have found an alternative test. The court is not so rigid. You had to do nothing."

"What does that mean?"

"It means I ensured that they would be provided for. Were you to have failed, they would have been taken care of."

Meyer said *were he to have failed.*

"I didn't fail?"

Meyer shook his head. "The testing was not meant to be passed so easily. You were questioned by seven master executioners. You would not know as much as they have learned through decades of experience. And the court understands we have not had as much time to work as we should have. The jurors might think they can influence the court, but the court serves the king."

"And Rock's execution?"

"You must demonstrate that you can carry out an execution. That would have been the next step in your training."

Finn turned away.

"What did you do?" Meyer's voice wasn't as hard as it had been. The disappointment was plain, though.

"The job was to get into the palace for something."

"The jewels?"

Finn shook his head. "Not the jewels. A staff of some

sort." He turned to Meyer. "The other items that were stolen were brought to the palace. They were bowls. Alainsith, I think. I don't really understand it, but that was what he'd been after all this time. Now this staff. The gods only know what reason he had for it. I don't know who the Client is, and I don't know the purpose of these items, but they were for him to instigate something with the Alainsith."

Meyer watched him. Studying him. Trying to determine if Finn lied to him.

"Did you succeed?"

"In taking the staff?" Meyer said nothing. "We got to it. I don't really know why it was worth a hundred crowns to the Client, but we got it. When we got out, the Client sent Archers after the crew."

"Is that right?"

Finn nodded.

"You escaped."

"I… I told them I was with you."

Meyer cocked his head to the side. "Get dressed. Then come with me."

Finn hurriedly changed his clothes, getting out of the darks and back into the new clothing Meyer had supplied for him, even drawing on the cloak. Out in the hall, his sister looked toward his room from the kitchen, a question in her eyes.

Finn forced a reassuring smile, but she turned away.

Meyer waited for him by the door leading to the garden, and Finn followed him out.

It was later in the morning than he'd expected. He

must have slept for longer than he'd realized. Long enough that the morning had started to slip by, and now it was nearly midday.

Meyer didn't say anything.

Finn had been this way enough times now that he recognized where Meyer guided him. They headed toward Declan Prison.

The iron master at the door waved them in.

Finn followed Meyer through the prison, down to one of the lower levels. The iron masters on this level followed him, heading with them as they made their way through the narrow halls to stop in front of a cell.

It was the same cell he'd been in.

Meyer nodded toward the iron master. "Bring him up."

Finn looked into the cell. The King was inside.

When he saw Finn, he grinned. "Look at Shuffles," he said. "Come to question me?"

Meyer nodded to the iron master, who fumbled with his keys a moment before getting them sorted and unlocking the door. He grabbed for the King and shoved him forward along the hallway. The King glanced behind him, sneering at Finn.

When they reached the stairs, another voice called out along the hallway.

"The gods watch over us all, then they smile when we fall! 'Seek salvation,' the priests sing, while the people shout, 'All hail the King!'" Hector sang.

This time, Finn almost smiled.

They headed up the stairs, and the King was guided into the chapel, where the iron master strapped him to the chair. Meyer focused on the King, darkness glittering his eyes.

"You are Leon Konig, also known as the King."

The King looked past Meyer, holding Finn's gaze.

Finn didn't look away.

"You coordinated a break-in of the palace last evening."

The King turned his attention to Meyer. "Is that what Shuffles tells you?" There was a snide sort of mocking to his voice.

"That is what both Felix Wolf and Luca Grobbe have told me."

The King's mouth twitched, but only a little.

Finn looked over to Meyer.

He already knew what happened the night before.

Finn let out an amused grunt. Meyer had been interrogating him, only he had done so in his own way. A very Meyer-like manner. Testing him.

Finn wondered what would've happened were he to have lied to Meyer. Meyer probably would've handled things differently. Instead, he had brought him to Declan.

Since Meyer had already questioned Rock and Wolf, he had to wonder if they would hang. Finn didn't care if Wolf swung. He probably deserved it. Rock had been sentenced already. Hanging the King would be hard. If he had to do the same to Rock… that would be impossible.

"I coordinated nothing," the King said.

"You would have me believe that your known associates would both mislead me?"

"Yes," the King said. "I'm a business owner. Nothing more than that."

"And Finn Jagger?"

The King turned to Finn, his eyes hardening. "What has Shuffles told you?" he sneered.

Finn glanced over to Meyer. He squeezed his eyes shut, thinking about everything that he had done for the King, everything that he had attempted to protect him and the crew. All to be betrayed.

The King had had the ability to rescue him from prison. Finn had thought he couldn't reach him at the time, but he had gotten to Rock. It was more that the King had not wanted to help Finn. Which meant that Finn had been sentenced to death and would have been executed were it not for Meyer saving him.

Why would I ever have thought the King could be his crew?

He could not.

Meyer had saved him. Meyer had protected his mother, attempted to heal her. Meyer had helped his sister when she had returned.

Meyer was his crew.

"Leon Konig, also known as the King, coordinated an attack on the palace on behalf of a man known only as the Client," Finn started. "He stole a wooden staff from an upper-level library within the palace. He has been responsible for the theft of other items throughout the city, artifacts designed to instigate trouble with the Alainsith. The staff was a part of it."

Meyer looked over to Finn, holding his gaze for a moment. There was something unreadable in the expression. Finally, he turned to the King. "What do you have to say about this?"

"You would trust him?"

"Yes," Meyer said.

"This is laughable. I'm a business owner in Verendal. Anything with the Alainsith is beyond me." The King nodded to the tools on the table behind Meyer. "Do what you need to question me. You will find that I am telling you the truth."

Meyer stopped in front of the King. "There is no need to question you any further."

"There's not?"

Meyer shook his head slowly. "No. I brought you here to allow you to confess. Seeing as how you have no interest in confession, there is no need for me to proceed any further. You'll be brought before the jurors and the magister for sentencing later today."

The King glared at him. "You can't—"

Meyer turned away, ignoring the King.

He motioned for Finn to follow, and they stepped out into the hall. The King shouted after them.

"You aren't going to escape your fate, Shuffles! You were in on this! When they learn what this was about—"

The door closed behind them, and the King's shouts were muted.

He stared at the door, wishing *he* knew what that had been about.

"You already knew what happened," Finn said.

"I knew," Meyer said.

He looked to the closed door. "I've wondered whether he had anything to do with the Lion's death." There was a time when he wouldn't have believed that possible. Now he no longer knew. If the King were willing to sacrifice Finn and Rock, what else might he do?

"I followed that lead before, Finn. There was nothing to it."

Which left Finn without an answer. He didn't know why, but he thought he should understand who had killed the Lion. His death had given Finn an opportunity.

Maybe that was reason to leave it alone. Meyer *had* said that some crimes went unsolved.

He looked back to Meyer. "What now?"

"That depends upon you."

"How?"

"You have one more aspect of your testing."

When the magister arrived at the prison, Finn wasn't expecting it. Dressed in the hat of his office, his jacket bearing the colors of the crown, the magister glanced over to Meyer, a frown on his round face. A priest of Heleth followed the magister, dressed in his formal robes of office, clutching the Book of Heleth in his arms.

"Ugly business, this," he said.

"It's always ugly business," Meyer said.

"Indeed. In this case, it's even uglier. King Porman would like to have this dealt with as expediently as possible. Given that the attack took place within his palace, I think he would prefer to ensure that it is resolved before departing again. He has dealt with enough trouble recently, especially with the item discovered in the palace. I presume you learned it was Alainsith?"

Finn straightened. That had to have been the seventh bowl Oscar had mentioned.

As he looked over to Master Meyer, he saw him nodding but not saying anything. Finn had wanted to understand, but Meyer's lack of reaction might be all he needed to know.

It wasn't his responsibility to understand.

As Master Meyer had said, it was neither of theirs. They served as the arm of justice. He still didn't know the Client's identity, but when he did, justice could be served.

"That is what I was told."

"It seems someone wanted the treaty to fail. It would be a shame, of course. We've known peace with the Alainsith for generations. Losing that now..." The magister looked at the door, shaking his head slowly.

"When will King Porman be departing?" Meyer asked.

"He only planned on remaining within the city for a few days. From what I understand, now that this is over, he plans on meeting with Alainsith again."

Meyer nodded as if he had expected that.

"I suppose he has not confessed?"

Meyer shook his head. "I doubt he will. We have corroborating testimony from others who confirmed that Leon Konig, also known as the King, is responsible for coordinating the attack. In fact, he is responsible for coordinating other attacks as well."

"That is unfortunate," the magister said.

He nodded to the iron master, who pushed the door open, and the magister entered.

"Do we need to go in there with him?" Finn asked Meyer.

"No. The sentencing is going to be straightforward."

"The jury doesn't need to be present?"

"Not in this case," Meyer said. "Given that the attack was on the palace itself, the king wanted to ensure that he had the right man, but he has dictated the terms of the sentencing."

"Death," Finn said.

Meyer looked over to him, holding his gaze before nodding for a moment.

Finn took a deep breath. "What about me?"

"Given your role in the testimony and your ties to me, King Porman granted you clemency. Now it is up to you to take advantage of it."

Finn nodded. "How will Leon's sentence be done?"

"He took pity on him. He offered him the rope."

"What about the others? Wolf and Rock?"

"Use their names, Finn," Meyer chastised. "And as Luca Grobbe offered testimony, he has been given leniency by the king himself. Exile from Verendal, though probably less than he deserves."

Finn shook his head, relief sweeping through him. Finn didn't think it less than Rock deserved, but at least he wouldn't die. "And Wolf?"

"That is to be determined. You will be a part of the questioning—and the sentencing."

It might have been easier were Meyer to keep him from it, at least when it came to Rock.

The magister pulled the door open again and stepped back out into the hallway. "You may begin," he said, nodding to the priest.

He entered the chapel, leaving Finn and Meyer with the magister.

"An odd thing," the magister said.

"Indeed," Meyer said.

"We have no idea why he would have taken the staff rather than other valuable targets in the palace?"

"Not yet. The Archers who interrogated him have been unable to ascertain the reason. I suspect he's telling the truth about that much."

"He doesn't know," the magister said.

"If we find the one known as the Client, we may be able to understand what he intended, but until then, we will not have any answers about who is ultimately responsible."

The magister nodded slowly. "Dangerous times, it seems. Even if we find this person, who is to say this Client will provide us with any answers?"

"He hired Mr. Konig for other similar jobs."

"Indeed?"

"There have been several, including the one that involved the theft at Bellut's home."

The magister pressed his lips together in a tight frown. "It's unfortunate this has taken place in such a sensitive time for the kingdom. The king has instructed us to be particularly firm on crime during these times. He didn't want anything to interfere with the meeting."

"The timing is certainly suspect."

"I imagine you have shared that with his Archers?"

"I have."

The magister offered a curt nod. "Preparations have already begun. I imagine there won't be quite the festival as there is most times, but perhaps that isn't necessarily a bad thing."

He left them, and Finn glanced over to Meyer. "You know this is not over. The Client—"

"That isn't for us to determine," Meyer said.

"I thought the magister suggested—"

Meyer raised his hand. "It isn't my responsibility. Nor is it yours. Others offer that protection for the kingdom. The threat has been revealed. That is enough. And we merely serve as the arm of the throne empowered to carry out his sentencing."

The priest pulled the door open and stepped back out into the hallway. He glanced at Meyer. "Master Meyer. Unfortunately, the condemned does not wish to seek the blessing of Heleth."

"That is unfortunate."

"I will continue to pray with him as we venture to the gallows. As you know, I wish to offer a prayer before the sentencing is carried out."

Meyer glanced to Finn. "Mr. Jagger will be carrying out the sentencing."

"Your apprentice? On such a significant criminal?"

"Each of us must start somewhere," Meyer said.

The priest regarded Finn before nodding and heading back into the chapel.

"Can you do it?" Meyer asked.

Finn looked toward the closed door leading into the chapel.

When it had been Rock, he hadn't been sure that he would be able to do it. Even now, he wasn't entirely sure that he would be capable of carrying out the sentencing. It involved killing another man.

It involved exacting punishment. Revenge.

Even if it wasn't truly revenge, it felt that way.

The other option was his own death.

"I can do it."

"Good."

Meyer nodded as if there had never been a doubt. They headed out of Declan Prison, making their way out into the street. Some of the vendors had already begun to get established, setting up their places, and a sense of activity and festivity filled the streets. Finn looked over to Meyer, who had a solemn expression on his face.

Finn mirrored it.

It wasn't long before the door to the prison opened, and the priest guided the King out. He was dressed in the clothing of the condemned, the dark gray of the Sinner's Cloth that Finn had worn for so many days. The King glared at everyone, looking all around, forced forward by the Archers, but making a point of showing how reluctant he was to follow. When he reached Finn and Meyer, he spat at them.

"You will suffer for this, Shuffles."

The Archers shoved him forward.

Behind him, the priest read from the Book of Heleth. His words rose and fell, crying out against the crowd, a prayer for the condemned. The last time Finn remembered hearing those words had been when he had been led to the gallows. At that time, he had spoken them himself.

Surprisingly, he found himself repeating the prayer, speaking the words of Heleth along with the priest. Meyer glanced at him but showed no look of surprise.

A crowd followed them. He was far more aware of the crowd this time than he had been during his own execution. He was far more aware of the crowd than he had been when he had followed Dalton Pegg during his sentencing. The throng of people pressed up against them, a crowd all surrounding them from all sections within the city. Only during the Gallows Festival did all of the sections of the city come together.

They passed through the gate. The gallows loomed into view, along with the Raven Stone. The priest continued to pray, and for the first time, Finn noticed a hint of fear from the King. His hands trembled, though he tried to make it seem as if they did not. He squeezed his hands into fists, balling them up, but when he straightened them, the ends of his fingers twitched. His gaze darted from side to side, looking all around them. When it settled on Finn, he glared at him.

They reached the base of the Stone.

Finn recognized several of the men standing there. Executioners, all of them. There was one woman, the same woman who had been present at his testing.

"The Executioner Court is here?"

Meyer nodded. "This is the final stage in your test."

Regardless of what the King had put him through, this was still someone he knew. His crew. Someone who'd helped him all the years he'd been with the crew.

Who I thought *helped me.*

Someone who had been willing to let Finn hang.

Still, complex emotions rolled through him.

He *knew* the King.

A stranger would have been an easier test. Which made this the right test. He understood that. Do this, and he could prove himself to the court. To Meyer.

He would have his crew.

Not just Oscar, but Lena and his mother. Meyer.

Finn's real crew.

"I won't fail you."

Meyer smiled tightly. "I know."

In addition to the Executioner Court, the jurors and the magister were all there, standing in a row in front of the Raven Stone. All were dressed in their markers of office, a formal air to them.

Bellut glanced at Finn, and he glanced over to the Executioner Court, his brow furrowing even more. The jurors had wanted him to die. They'd wanted him to suffer. Meyer had saved him. And now Finn would complete his own salvation. It meant that he would become an executioner in full, but Finn was ready for that.

He had no choice but to be ready for it.

The priest continued his prayer, and Meyer nodded to Finn.

They took up a position on either side of the King, leading him up the Raven Stone.

"I still don't understand why anyone would attempt to break into the palace," one of the jurors said.

Their voice was loud enough for Finn to hear above the din of the crowd.

He reached the top step of the Raven Stone, guiding the King with him.

"I can't imagine the reward was worth the risk."

Finn glanced back, realizing that it was Bellut who had spoken.

He stumbled, suddenly remembering where he had heard that phrase the night before.

The Client.

It had been Bellut?

His heart pounded a moment, and he resisted the urge to look back at him. *Could it be?*

Breaking into his own home would draw attention away from him.

He would have to tell Meyer. He might know what to do with the information.

Not now, though.

After.

Complete the sentencing. Finish the test.

Then deal with Bellut and the other juror the King had bribed.

Finn gathered himself, and he finished the climb up the stairs and guided Meyer to the gallows. He and Meyer turned the King so that he faced out toward the crowd and the jurors. The priest continued to pray to him while Meyer handed Finn the rope.

Finn held it in his hand.

He had practiced tying knots. Meyer had wanted him to work through the technique for how best to hang a man.

"What kind of knot was he sentenced to?" he whispered to Meyer, stretching the rope out and debating how to tie it.

"The king took pity on him. For a crime such as he committed, it is often the case that he would be subjected to much more severe punishment. You may decide how to tie the rope."

Finn looked down at the rope. There were two options. Suffering or a quick death.

He carried it over to the King. He ran the rope around the King's neck, determining the length.

"This should have been you, Shuffles."

"This was me," Finn said. "Because of you. You could have saved me."

"There is no saving someone like us."

Finn glanced over to Meyer. "I'm not like you."

He stepped back and quickly tied the rope, looping it up over the gallows and securing it. He nodded to Meyer, who helped guide him up the stairs, where Finn slipped the rope over the King's neck.

His heart hammered.

He hadn't known how he would feel doing this. His hands were steadier than he would have expected. Maybe his anger with the King—*Leon*, he corrected himself—made it easier. Still, his mouth was dry, and nausea threatened to overwhelm him.

Finn had to take a moment and steady his breath. He could feel Meyer watching him.

He wouldn't disappoint him.

"Do you have anything else to say?" Finn asked.

"The gods might have protected the Hand, but they won't watch over you."

"What's that supposed to mean?" Finn asked, but he already suspected he knew.

The King had been responsible for Oscar almost getting caught at the viscount's manor. Because of him, Finn had been sentenced—and was now there.

The irony was almost enough to elicit a smile but now was not the time.

"This is bigger than you know. Beware of who you trust."

Finn hesitated, but when he saw the cold look in the King's eyes, he knew what had to be done. There was no remorse.

"Goodbye, Leon."

Finn stepped down, and he nodded to Meyer.

Taking a deep breath, he removed the steps, and the King dropped.

It happened quickly. He fell. The rope pulled tight, the length accurate. His neck snapped.

Finn took a long breath, watching the King as he hung dead.

Finally, Meyer nodded to him. "A good death. Quick."

"Probably more than he deserved," Finn whispered.

Meyer regarded him a moment. "I chose well." He guided Finn forward, and they made their way down the stairs. They stopped in front of the Executioner Court. "My apprentice, Finn Jagger, has completed his first execution. He has passed the testing of the Executioner Court. I hereby claim that my right has been fulfilled."

The bald executioner stepped forward. "Your right has been fulfilled." With that, he clapped Finn on the shoulders. "You will bring him to the court to celebrate later."

Meyer nodded.

The others of the Executioner Court turned and slipped off into the crowd.

"We can depart. Our role here is done. The priests will pray for a little while longer, and then the hegen will come and claim their prizes."

"I have fulfilled everything I need?"

"For now. King Porman agreed to the terms the jurors placed upon me exerting my right. You had to be accepted by the court."

"They didn't think they would accept me?"

"I suspect the jurors knew the court would be convening sooner than was typical." His gaze lingered a moment on Bellut. *Did Meyer already know?* Finn wouldn't put it past him. "You did well."

"And now I stay as your apprentice."

"Yes."

"And my sentencing?"

"Has been commuted, as has the danger to me."

Finn smiled tightly. "Just a moment."

He made his way over to Bellut, who nodded to him and said, "It seems you have been approved by the court."

"I have," Finn said.

"Very well."

He had started to turn when Finn reached for him, catching his arm.

Bellut turned back toward Finn, a flicker of darkness in his eyes that quickly passed.

"I know what you did," Finn said, pitching his voice low.

"And what is that?"

Finn flicked his gaze toward the King. "I hope the reward was worth the risk."

With that, he turned away, following Meyer away from the Raven Stone, back through the gate, and into the city. He would find the evidence to convict Bellut later. This time, he'd include Meyer in all of it.

He was an executioner's apprentice. For the first time, that title felt as if it fit him.

When Finn returned to the small room in Meyer's home, he found a blank card waiting for him. The hegen.

He stared at it for a moment before daring to lift it and look at it. There wasn't anything to the card. Just a marker—reminding him of the marker he'd been given when he'd met with Esmerelda.

The hegen had been there.

He looked around the room. The books stacked on the desk looked no different from how they had before. There wasn't any sort of organization to them. A few sheets of paper he'd borrowed from Meyer to make his notes were there as well, along with the bottle of ink and the pen.

The bed looked untouched, the same mess of the sheets as when he'd been startled awake by Meyer.

Finn took the card. After making it through the job,

then finishing the testing, and learning the Client had been Bellut, he had wanted to rest. With the hegen leaving this, he didn't think he could.

He had to deal with it. Now.

Out in the hall, he paused for a moment. Meyer had disappeared back to his office, and the sound of voices drifted from the back of the room. He was meeting with someone. Offering healing. Eventually, Finn would need to join in those sessions, if only so that he could master that aspect of the job.

Not today, though.

He headed toward the door.

"Where are you going?"

Finn turned to Lena. "There's something I need to take care of."

"Like last night?"

He shook his head slightly. "Last night was different."

"He was worried about you."

"Meyer?" Finn asked, and Lena nodded. "I thought… I suppose it doesn't matter what I thought. It's been taken care of."

"What has?"

"Meyer says that you and Mother will be taken care of."

Lena pushed a strand of brown hair back behind her ears, frowning at him. He hadn't realized how thin she had become. How tired she had looked. He had been so focused on himself, and everything that he had gone through that he hadn't paid nearly as much attention to his sister as she deserved. "Why does that sound as if you're leaving us?"

"I'm not. Just for tonight."

"Why?"

Finn considered keeping the truth from her, but with everything she'd done to help their mother, he figured she deserved to know some of the truth. He held the hegen card out, and her eyes widened, obviously recognizing it.

"What do you owe?"

Finn shook his head. "I don't know. I didn't do what they wanted, so…"

"What did they want?"

He took a deep breath and pulled the other card out of his pocket. He had kept it with him. When he handed it over to her, she frowned.

"I don't understand."

"I think the Hand is Oscar Richter."

"Father's friend?"

Finn took the card back and placed it into his pocket. "Yes."

"You were supposed to take his hand?"

"That's his nickname. I think he was supposed to be captured, too. I prevented it, protecting him."

Lena inhaled deeply before letting out a slow breath. "Be careful, Finn."

"I'm trying to be."

She started to turn before hesitating, wrapping him in a hug. "Thank you for what you've done."

"I don't know that I've done anything."

"You have. And he's helped. Mother seems to be getting better. It's slow, but she's getting better. I don't even know that we need to meet with a physician at this point. I think Master Meyer will be enough."

"That's good," Finn said.

She released him, and he headed out into the street, moving quickly toward the gate, nodding to the Archers, before slipping out into the night. In the distance, the gallows loomed. The hegen would have already gone and claimed their prizes, taking hands and feet and whatever other parts of the King needed for their magic.

He gave the gallows a wide berth. Not because he feared it, though it did unsettle him, especially at night, but because he didn't want to encounter the hegen before he was ready.

A sliver of moonlight shone overhead. It was barely enough to illuminate his way, though Finn didn't need much light for him to know how to reach the hegen section of the city.

When he reached the outskirts, he paused, though only a moment. A faint drumming came from deeper in this section, and firelight danced, giving an erratic light to the road leading through the hegen section.

Finn made his way, moving as carefully as he could, heading toward Esmerelda's home, though he wondered if perhaps she would be gone. It was a night following the festival, after all. For all he knew, she was out by the gallows now.

Regardless of what he'd thought at the moment, the

bloody hand could only be one thing. Maybe Oscar had left a similar debt unpaid. Maybe some old lover carried a grudge. Whatever the case, Finn hadn't done what was asked of him.

When he reached the home, it seemed as if shadows moved around him. Distant voices drifted along the street, doing nothing to settle his nerves. Finn knocked.

He waited a moment before the door came open.

Esmerelda looked out into the street before turning her attention to him. "You came by yourself. That's unexpected."

Finn handed her the card. "I take it this was yours?" He pulled the other one from his pocket, offering it to her. "And this?"

She took both of them, looking down at them. "Why don't you come in?"

She stepped aside, and Finn entered her home.

As before, something was unsettling about going into one of the hegen's homes. Perhaps not Esmerelda herself, but the home had something strange about it. An energy, though Finn thought that only his imagination. Faint lantern light glowed softly in the room, lighting up the shelves, and the strange collection of items scattered all around. Oddly, it reminded him of Bellut's home.

"I'm sorry I didn't do what you wanted with Oscar. I couldn't let him be captured."

She paused at a stove, pouring liquid from a kettle into a cup before carrying it over to him. "What do you presume I wanted with Oscar?"

"You wanted him captured. Or dead. Either way, I didn't do it."

She poured a cup for herself and set the pot down, turning to Finn. "Why do you presume that?"

"The bloody hand."

"Interesting. I would've taken that for something else."

"What exactly should I have taken it as?"

She smiled at him, taking a drink. "A warning."

"I don't understand."

She took another drink before meeting his gaze. "Had you not acted the way that you did, Oscar Richter would have been captured by the Archers."

A wave of cold washed through him. "You knew?"

She nodded slightly. "I know many things, Finn Jagger."

"If you didn't want Oscar harmed, then what did you want for him?"

"That is between Oscar and me. Much like your arrangement is between you and me. As is the arrangement between Henry Meyer and me." She took the card signifying Oscar and held it between her fingers before holding it to one of the candles where it burned in a flash to little more than ash. "There. You no longer have to worry about Oscar Richter."

"He's my friend."

"Oh. I know."

"I don't want anything to happen to him."

"Must something happen to him?"

"If he owes you something, I…"

Finn bit back what he was about to say. *What was I going to do?*

If Oscar owed the hegen something, it was between him and the hegen. There wasn't going to be anything he would be able to do.

She smiled at him. "You have served well, Finn Jagger. I suspect you will continue to serve well."

"If you had wanted me to help Oscar, I've already served."

She twisted her fingers, and another card appeared. On it was a face, one that looked far too similar to his sister's face. She twisted the card, and then it seemed to be his mother. She twisted it again, and the card was blank.

"You might find another request comes," she said.

"And if I don't comply?"

"You are now the apprentice." She took another sip of her drink, smiling at him slightly as if the answer told him anything. "Is that all?"

Finn looked around, his gaze lingering on the jars that seemed to contain fingers. He resisted the urge to shudder. "I suppose it is."

"Very well."

He turned toward the door, and an item on a table caught his attention. A bowl.

He looked up from the table, the bowl atop it, and fixed Esmerelda with a frown. "That's an interesting bowl," Finn said.

She smiled at him. "It is."

"I've seen something like it recently." He said it casually, knowing he wouldn't get straight answers from her.

"You don't have to play coy, Finn Jagger."

"You?"

She strode forward, lifting the bowl and tracing a finger around the inside of the bowl. "An item of power. Alainsith power."

His mouth had gone dry. He felt like he'd escaped from the threat of his impending sentence only to come upon something as deadly. "You used the Client."

"I can see how you would think that," she said, her voice soft.

"You didn't want to destabilize the treaty with the Alainsith?"

Esmerelda continued tracing her finger around the bowl. "This would do more than destabilize, I'm afraid."

"What would it do?" Finn asked.

"With the right activation, these could lead to great destruction."

"So you *were* responsible for the bowls."

"They are called *swial'onthel*. Old. Powerful. There were seven claimed during the war many years ago and secured around Verendal." The word sounded strangely fluid when she said it. "Until recently they were responsible for securing peace with the Alainsith, along with the *varethar*."

"The staff, I'm guessing."

She nodded. "Very good."

"Why did you have the Client take them?"

"With the right connection, I'm afraid these would destroy the palace and all within it."

He stared at the bowl. "I don't understand."

Only, he did.

Oscar.

"You used Oscar."

She held his gaze. "He had a price to pay."

His card made even more sense.

Oscar had gone after the bowls.

Finn had been there to protect Oscar.

"Why?" It was the only question he could think of. "You didn't want to see the treaty fail?"

"This was about more than the treaty failing. Had the *swial'onthel* been used, the king would have perished. More than Verendal would have suffered then. The result could only have been war."

And he would have been a part of it. A dishonorable thief who had helped start a war.

But the executioner's apprentice helped to stop it.

That had to mean something, even if the hegen had directed it.

"And the favors the hegen have called in?"

"Only those necessary to ensure your Client failed. Unfortunately, he nearly succeeded. There is more at work here than we realized."

The King's final words came back to Finn.

What would they have learned from him had he not been executed?

Probably nothing. Leon hadn't known anything. Like the crew, he had been used.

Esmerelda traced her finger around the inside of the bowl. "Thankfully, they have all been reclaimed before they could be used against the kingdom. They will be placed where they cannot be retaken."

"And the staff? The Client has it."

"Does he?"

Finn frowned. "Are you saying he doesn't?"

Esmerelda set the bowl back down. "A warning might have been sent."

Finn grunted. "We didn't even take it. Not the real one. Did we?" The comment he'd overheard the King say to the Client made more sense. She met his gaze. "You wanted to learn the Client's identity."

"Didn't you?"

Finn nodded. "I suppose I did, though I don't have any way of proving what I learned."

"You are the apprentice, now."

Which meant that it would be his task.

Find a way to prove Bellut responsible.

She tipped her head to him. "You did well." She smiled. "Now I think it's time you have a good night, Finn Jagger."

She guided him toward the door, and he stepped outside into the cool dark night. When the door closed, Finn frowned to himself.

As he made his way back toward the city gate, winding around the Raven Stone, he noticed movement. Hegen claiming their prizes.

Meyer might claim all of this was beyond them and that they were to serve the arm of justice only, but how could he do nothing if there was some greater plan against the kingdom?

More than that, how could I prove Bellut responsible?

He had to find proof, even figure out why Bellut had hired the crew to target his home—unless it had been nothing more than a distraction. Afterward, he would have to convince Meyer. And if he could not…

Maybe it really wasn't his responsibility.

As he made his way back toward Meyer's home, he was troubled. There were no answers, only more questions. Now that he served Meyer as his apprentice in full, perhaps Finn would have the opportunity to answer those questions.

He stuffed his hands into his pockets and realized that Esmerelda had left him with another card. He didn't remember her giving it to him; she had kept the two that he had brought with him. He pulled the card out as he reached the door leading into Meyer's home; he stared at it for a moment, trying to understand the meaning behind it.

Finn had no answer, much like he had no answer when he had been left the card with the bloody hand. No bloody image was depicted on the card this time. It was made neatly, with what appeared to be a golden ink. The image was unmistakable, but the meaning was unclear to him.

On the card was a crown.

Get the next book in The Executioner's Song series: The Executioner's Apprentice.

Executioners search for justice, not vengeance. Finn questions why it can't be both.

As apprentice to the master executioner, Finn struggles to understand his place in the city as he searches for truth in those sentenced. The job is more complicated than he ever imagined. He's proven his understanding of the basics, but for him to serve as an executioner—if that's what he wants—he needs mastery.

Distracted by his search for a way to heal his still ailing mother despite the hegen magic, he finds himself at odds with the master executioner.

When assigned his first solo case, he knows he needs to impress Meyer. An investigation into a fire that burned through an entire section of the city leads Finn to learn of a greater threat to Verendal—and the entire kingdom.

When only Finn believes there's more to the fire, can he save the city or will his quest for vengeance finally lead to his downfall?

Sign up to my newsletter to get the free novella, The Fading Lion, set in the world of The Executioner Song!

The Teralin Sword

The Lost Prophecy

The Volatar Saga Series

The Volatar Saga

The Book of Maladies Series

The Book of Maladies

The Lost Garden Series

The Lost Garden